# PRAISE FOR THE AUTHOR

"Walsh has penned another endearing novel set in Loves Park, Colo. The emotions are occasionally raw, but always truly real. Readers will root for the characters to discover their potential and realize that love is right in front of them. It takes a little long to get to the point, but the journey is enjoyable."

—RT Reviews, ****

"Walsh (*A Sweethaven Summer*) pens a quaint, smalltown love story, complete with an overbearing mother, an unscrupulous business partner, and a group of busybodies whose hearts are in the right place even if their actions are questionable. While certain elements are predictable, Walsh develops enough plot twists to make this enjoyable to the end."

—*Publishers Weekly*

"Heartwarming! *Paper Hearts* is as much a treat as the delicious coffee the heroine serves in her bookshop. Courtney Walsh's warm author's voice tells a story of a doctor and a bookstore owner, both living in a town centered on romance, yet both disillusioned by love. Like the matchmakers that surrounded the couple in the novel, I couldn't help cheering them on. A poignant, wry, sweet, and utterly charming read!"

—Becky Wade, award-winning author of *Meant to Be Mine*

"Delightfully romantic with a lovable cast of quirky characters, *Paper Hearts* will have readers smiling from ear to ear! Courtney Walsh has penned a winner!"

—Katie Ganshert, award-winning author of
*A Broken Kind of Beautiful*

"Walsh's touching debut will have readers longing for a visit to the idyllic vista of Sweethaven, Michigan. The touch of mystery, significant friendships and a charming setting create a real treasure."

—*Romantic Times*, ****

"This book captivated me from the first paragraphs. Bittersweet memories, long-kept secrets, the timeless friendships of women— and a touch of sweet romance. Beautifully written and peopled with characters who became my friends, this debut novel is one for my keeper shelf—and, I hope, the first of many to come from Courtney Walsh's pen."

—Deborah Raney, award-winning author of the Chicory Inn series and *A Vow to Cherish*

"Courtney Walsh puts the sweet in Sweethaven. If you're looking for an uplifting, hope-filled story filled with characters you'll feel like you know, *A Sweethaven Homecoming* has it!"

—Marybeth Whalen, author of *The Mailbox* and *The Things We Wish Were True*

# THINGS LEFT UNSAID

## ALSO BY COURTNEY WALSH

*Hometown Girl*

*Just Look Up*

*Paper Hearts*

*Change of Heart*

*A Sweethaven Summer*

*A Sweethaven Homecoming*

*A Sweethaven Christmas*

*A Sweethaven Romance*

# THINGS LEFT UNSAID

## COURTNEY WALSH

**Waterfall**
PRESS

Text copyright © 2018 by Courtney Walsh
All rights reserved.

Published by Waterfall Press, Grand Haven, MI

www.brilliancepublishing.com

Amazon, the Amazon logo, and Waterfall Press are trademarks of Amazon.com, Inc., or its affiliates.

ISBN-13: 9781503901476
ISBN-10: 1503901475

Cover design by Eileen Carey

Printed in the United States of America

*For my boys, Ethan & Sam, you make me so happy to be alive.*

Pastor Timothy & Nora Preston
request the honor of your presence
at the wedding of their son
Travis James Preston
to
Elle Porter
Saturday, the twenty-second of June
two thousand nineteen
at 2 o'clock in the afternoon
Sweethaven Chapel
Sweethaven, Michigan

**Lyndie,** Elle texted, **we're finally doing it. We're getting married!**

Congratulations, Elle! That's so great—took you guys long enough!

Can you call me later? There's something I want to ask you!

Oooh. I'm in a session all day today. Tomorrow?

Oh, I know it's not proper etiquette to ask in a text, but I can't wait till tomorrow! Will you be my maid of honor? You're my oldest friend—it has to be you.

. . .

Lyndie?

Sure, Elle. Of course I'll be your maid of honor.

:) THANK YOU! You won't have to plan anything! I just can't wait to see you again! It's been too long.

It has. It'll be so good to catch up.

# Chapter One

*This is it, Lyndie. Don't blow it.*

Lyndie St. James stood in the hallway of Judson Music Studios, willing herself to open the door. A door that, in the past few months, had come to mean so much, thanks to constant reminders that this was a *once-in-a-lifetime opportunity*. And *do you know how many songwriters would kill for a chance to pitch to these people?*

She knew. She'd been in the industry long enough to know.

But if she thought about that for too long, she'd buckle under her fear.

"You going in, St. James?" Dylan Markert. The guy behind this *once-in-a-lifetime opportunity*. "Or are you going to stand out here all day?"

Lyndie forced a smile. "Just gathering my courage."

"You've got me in your corner—what do you need courage for?" Dylan put his hand on the knob of the reclaimed-barnwood door. The studio was tucked inside a renovated warehouse in Nashville. It seemed everything old was new again, at least at Judson Music.

Lyndie took a step back on wobbly legs. Dylan must've sensed her trepidation, because he faced her then. "Look, Lyndie, you're a rising star. You're one of the most promising young songwriters in the business today. You know this, right?"

She gave him another feeble smile. How else was she supposed to answer that question?

"You've already written three huge hits. The fact that Jalaire Grant wants to hear your new stuff proves I was right about you all along. Everyone sees it but you."

"I just don't want to mess it up."

"Then don't." He grinned. "Now, let's go. Jalaire is waiting."

Lyndie had a matter of minutes to impress Jalaire Grant and her people. Jalaire Grant! Should she pinch herself?

*Don't mess this up.*

She followed Dylan through the door, and he motioned for her to take a seat on a stool at the center of the space. She did, then perused the room of men in suits sitting in a semicircle on either side of one very important woman—Jalaire Grant.

How had Lyndie gotten here?

*Oh, Cassie, if you could see me now.*

She could almost imagine her friend was sitting beside her, that she wasn't a solo act, that they'd actually made it.

Almost.

Slowly, Lyndie dared a glance at Jalaire. The woman was tiny— really tiny—and while usually decked out in layers of makeup, wild hair and the kind of costumes that would make her mother blush, today Jalaire looked very . . . normal. Plain, even.

Her paper-thin white button-down was partly tucked into jeans paired with wedge heels. Honey-blond hair hung in loose waves down her back. Without the costumes and makeup and colored wigs, Jalaire Grant was just another woman.

But if that was true, then why did she make Lyndie so nervous?

Lyndie had heard the stories—the woman was a diva—but today she almost didn't believe those rumors. Today, Jalaire Grant looked like someone Lyndie would have coffee with.

Regardless, it didn't matter. Jalaire was a huge star, and she wanted to hear Lyndie's new songs.

Surely this was all a dream, right?

Lyndie's eyes found Dylan's. Her manager was older, wiser, savvier. Lyndie wasn't thirty yet. She knew she didn't have the life experience many songwriters did, but apparently she had a "new sound." And apparently that was important.

Dylan had spent a good five minutes pumping her up with his *she's-coming-to-you* speech in his office at Judson Music when Lyndie had first arrived that morning. He wanted her to feel like she had the upper hand, but as soon as she'd walked into the room and seen Jalaire, any delusion of that disappeared.

Jalaire Grant hadn't said a word, but she was in control here.

Lyndie admired it. It terrified her, but she still admired it. One day, maybe she'd be the one calling the shots.

"What do you have for us, Ms. St. James?" one of the men asked.

His words pulled her from her thoughts. Now was not the time to lose focus.

Not the time to think about the wedding. Or Elle and Travis. Or Cassie. *Or Tucker.* Not the time to think about the fact that in just three days she was expected in Michigan, and the only thing waiting for her there was heartache.

"Lyndie?"

She found Dylan's watchful eye. He knew she was prone to daydreaming, though he probably assumed she filled those daydreams with song lyrics and not unwanted memories. She'd been doing so well with the latter, as if she'd found a box, placed everything she wanted to forget inside and buried it in a place no one would ever find.

But every now and then, the box cracked open—just enough to leak something noxious—and it infected her like a virus.

*Why can't I just let it all go?*

Dylan stared at her, eyebrows raised, expecting something amazing. Did she have something amazing to give? Ever since she'd agreed to be in Elle's wedding—one that could've easily been held in Chicago, where Elle and Travis lived and which would've been much more manageable— she'd been off her game. Apparently when the box cracked open, it made composing difficult.

And this wasn't a good time for writer's block. She hoped what she'd come up with would be enough to spark Jalaire's interest, but Lyndie's stomach roiled, her breathing unsteady.

Hooking her heels on the rung of the stool, she set the guitar in position on her knee. She situated herself and, for the first time, made eye contact with Jalaire.

The woman had been in the music industry for years now, and according to Dylan, she was looking to reinvent herself.

"What does that mean?" Lyndie'd asked him—because *reinvention* could mean a million different things.

He'd shrugged. "I guess we'll find out. But whatever you do, don't gush over her. Celebrities hate that. You're a professional. Be professional."

Lyndie felt like anything but.

"I have three songs for you today," she said now to Jalaire, feeling removed from her own body, like her voice wasn't her own.

*Don't gush. Be professional.*

"Thank you for giving me a chance to play for you." She started strumming the familiar chords of a song she'd been working on for several weeks. It still wasn't perfect, but it was different, and if Jalaire was looking to reinvent herself, maybe this was one way she could go?

Lyndie sang through all her new songs, and as she played the final chord, she kept her eyes on the ground, almost too afraid to look up and discover her future in the eyes of strangers.

After a long beat, she finally raised her eyes. The men all seemed to be waiting, as if none of them could speak without first getting Jalaire's thoughts. Lyndie's eyes shifted to the singer and found Jalaire staring. At her. Lyndie didn't dare look away, but Jalaire's gaze unsettled something inside her. Was this music icon reading every private thought Lyndie had?

"Gentlemen, can we have the room?"

Lyndie's eyes darted to Dylan, whose surprised expression told her this wasn't normal. The other men did as Jalaire said, filing out of the room in silence. Dylan, however, sat—unmoving—in the chair at the end of the semicircle.

"Mr. Markert?" Jalaire faced him.

"Lyndie's my client, Jalaire. I'm not going anywhere."

She met his gaze. "We're just going to have a conversation. She's not signing anything, and we're not negotiating. But the conversation is private."

Tension hovered for several seconds until finally Dylan stood. He looked at Lyndie.

"It's fine, Dylan," she said, though it didn't feel fine at all.

Once he'd gone, Jalaire stood and shook out her arms, as if loosening her muscles. "These things are always so formal." She walked across the room and picked up a bottle of water. "Dylan played me your demo."

Heat rushed to Lyndie's face.

"There's something missing."

She braced herself for hard truth. "What's missing?"

Jalaire took a drink of water, recapped the bottle and faced her. "You."

Lyndie stood. "I don't understand."

"Your songs are beautiful. Melodies that are unique but catchy—I'll be humming them for weeks. But your words are . . ." Jalaire drew in a breath. "Empty."

So, she'd blown it. That was that. "Well, thank you for the opportunity." Lyndie opened her guitar case and set the instrument inside.

"Hold on. Are you really giving up that quickly?"

Lyndie stilled. "You just said the songs are empty."

"The *words* are empty. But the songs are fabulous. I'd suggest you work with a lyricist, but I think that's wrong here. I think you're supposed to write these songs."

"But I've already written them."

"But they aren't finished."

Lyndie's mind spun. She didn't know how to do what Jalaire wanted.

"Look, Lyndie, I made it to the top singing bubblegum music for tween girls, but that's not who I am anymore. I've lived more life. I don't want to sing about anything I don't personally feel connected to—but in order for me to feel that, you've got to give me songs *you're* personally connected to. I know there's more depth to you than this. You're holding back."

Lyndie met the other woman's eyes. She'd mastered the art of looking strong and confident, but inside, Lyndie felt like a phony. Inside, she wanted to cry.

"You bring me something authentic," Jalaire said. "I know I'm going to love it."

Jalaire strolled over to where she'd been sitting and picked up her oversize bag off the floor. That bag probably cost more than a month of Lyndie's rent.

"What are you saying?" Lyndie asked.

"Get back to work. And call me when you have a new song." She reached inside the bag and pulled out a small white card, then walked over and held it out to Lyndie. "Something real. I don't want to put anything else out there that doesn't actually say something."

"So, you're giving me another shot?" She took the card, which was completely blank except for a phone number. Jalaire Grant was giving Lyndie her phone number?

Jalaire smiled, and for the briefest moment, she seemed like an older sister. "You're talented, Lyndie. You're just detached. Tell me how it feels to have your heart broken or to lose someone you love. Tell me about a time you lost something important or screwed up so royally it still keeps you up at night. Put it on the page. You're going to have to revisit your own heartache to come up with anything that means anything. That's what artists do. We bleed."

Lyndie's throat went dry. She wasn't about to do that.

Could she fake it—better than she'd faked it this time?

"Let's meet up again in a couple of weeks and see where you are." Jalaire slung the bag over her shoulder. "I'm expecting great things."

But Lyndie knew better. Some pain might be worth reliving in order to bring about great art, but Lyndie's was not.

And she wasn't about to try.

# Chapter Two

The apartment was warm. Stuffy. With the royalties from her last song, Lyndie had been able to move into a place of her own six months ago, but she had yet to make it homey. There were no photos on the walls, no cute pillows or curtains or quotes. All in all, it was perfectly functional, but nothing about it would make anyone feel cozy.

When would she stop living like a nomad? She was putting down roots here. She'd be smart to actually unpack. After all, she should be thrilled to be out of the three apartments she'd lived in since graduation. They hadn't been much of an upgrade from campus housing, and she'd always had at least two roommates.

It was June, and even she had to admit it might be time to turn on the AC. She went through her home-from-work ritual: Hang up keys. Take off shoes. Change into something comfortable (shorts and a tank top). Fill up water bottle with ice water. Water plants. Go through mail.

Stop.

A crisp white envelope fell from the stack of junk mail. The black cursive on the return address read *Jacobs*.

The wedding was all she could handle. It was more than she could handle. She'd agreed because she felt obligated. Because she knew Elle didn't have anyone else. It had taken Lyndie months to reconcile the fact that she'd agreed to return to Sweethaven at all, and often when she thought about it, it still didn't seem real.

*I'm flying to Michigan in three days.*

It was real.

And now this?

*A crack in the box.*

*No.* She wouldn't relive it. She couldn't. She'd worked too hard to bury it.

But the white envelope taunted her from the counter. She picked it up, tore it open and read the words on the card inside.

*You're invited*
*to a Celebration of Life*
*memorial service & gathering*
*in honor of our dear daughter*
*Cassandra Joy Jacobs*
*Join us in Sweethaven*
*as we commemorate*
*the tenth anniversary of her passing*
*and celebrate the bright light*
*she was in our lives.*

*With love,*
*Karen & Davis Jacobs*

Instinctively, Lyndie flipped the card over and found a handwritten note from Cassie's mom.

*Dearest Lyndie,*
*    I'm sure you're coming into town for Elle and Travis's*
*big day, and we know you'll be busy, but we'd love to see*
*you, and we'd love it even more if you stayed with us*

*while you're here. It would mean so much to me to have Cassie's two best friends here on the anniversary of her death. I can't believe it's already been ten years. I pray you're doing well, and look forward to catching up.*

*Love,*

*Mama J.*

*P.S. We can make s'mores in the backyard, just like old times. If I remember right, you like yours with Reese's Peanut Butter Cups?*

Lyndie set the card down and left the kitchen, trying to erase the image of Cassie's face from her mind. Her dark-haired, dark-eyed friend had been so full of life. Which made her death that much more difficult.

S'mores had been such a summertime ritual. The older the girls had gotten, the more Cassie would pretend to be annoyed that her mom insisted on making the treats in the backyard to kick off every summer. But the truth was, they all secretly loved it. They loved the way Cassie's mom made such a big deal about having them all together again.

"It's not summer until *all* my kids are under one roof," she'd say with a glance at Lyndie and Elle. Lyndie had a perfectly fine family, but having a "bonus family" in the Jacobs—it had made her feel like she'd hit the jackpot. The bonfires were just the kickoff to a full summer of practically living with Cassie and her family. They'd stay up too late and still get up early, pull on their swimsuits and disappear down to the lake for the whole day.

Mama J. would bring them a cooler stocked with sandwiches, lemonade and chips every day around noon. She'd call out reminders, like "make sure you put sunscreen on all the places you can't see, not just the obvious spots. Tops of your ears, back of your neck . . ."

Cassie would inevitably cut her off with a long, drawn-out, two-syllabled "Mo-om," and Karen Jacobs would wink at Lyndie and head back up the dune with a wave.

Those summers had sustained Lyndie through so many cold Illinois winters. Her quaint Chicago suburb was perfectly lovely, but it didn't hold a candle to Sweethaven. From the moment she left Michigan in mid-August, she'd count down the days until she returned in late May. Thinking of it now, even she could see what a shame it was that she'd cut that part of her life out completely. Thrown the good out with the bad, like functional but stained Tupperware that didn't seem worth washing.

Normally, reminders of Cassie brought conflicting feelings, a battle between deep grief—still so strong after all these years—and the sweet memory that, once upon a time, she'd had a friend she could say anything to, someone who knew her secrets and loved her anyway.

But then, not even Cassie had known everything, had she?

The past, dredged up like a mess of seaweed from the floor of the ocean, had wrapped itself around Lyndie's ankles and was doing its best to bring her to her knees.

But she wouldn't bend. She couldn't relive this again.

Robotically, Lyndie sat down on the couch. The phone rang, caller ID: *Mom*. History told her that if she didn't answer, this particular caller would call back as many times as it took for her to get through.

"Hey, Mom."

"Oh, you answered this time. I thought maybe you were avoiding my calls."

Classic Mom.

Susan St. James was what modern-day psychologists would call a helicopter parent. The trouble was, her only child was grown and gone.

Lyndie was twenty-eight years old, but she was still waiting for her mother to treat her like an adult. Only two months ago, Susan had sent a "strongly worded letter" to a music critic who'd said Lyndie's lyrics were "trite." Lyndie still hadn't lived that one down, especially since the critic was someone she'd actually met face-to-face. Seeing him again would've been embarrassing enough after his less-than-glowing review, but now it would be downright humiliating.

"What's up?" Lyndie tried to keep her tone light, as if that could push away the anxious feeling in the pit of her stomach.

"Karen Jacobs called me tonight."

*Of course she did.*

"I hadn't put together that the wedding was so close to the anniversary."

Funny, it was the first thing Lyndie had thought of when Elle's wedding invitation arrived three months ago.

"Elle and Travis must not have realized how hard it would be on Karen."

*Or on me.*

Her mother would talk about this for hours if Lyndie let her—and Lyndie couldn't let her. She had her own problems to sort out. Like, how could she write an emotionally charged song for a superstar when she'd worked hard to clear away every ounce of emotion from inside herself?

"How've you been, Mom?"

"Oh, we're good. You're going to Cassie's ceremony, right?"

She was obviously set on discussing this tonight. Lyndie paused for a moment to put a mental wall in place—one with a sign on it that said "No Feelings Allowed Here."

Thinking about Cassie meant thinking about the night she'd died. And that was the night everything had gone sideways.

*Wall up. Nothing getting in. Nothing getting out.*

"I wouldn't call it a ceremony," Lyndie said.

"Well, you know we can't make it with our trip to Jamaica scheduled, but you're going, right? I mean, you'll already be there. It wouldn't make sense for you to miss it. And maybe it'll be good for you."

Lyndie didn't respond. She was engrossed in the fringe on the afghan hanging over the arm of the sofa.

"Lyndie?"

"What?"

"Did you hear me?"

"I heard you, Mom. You want me to go. You think it would be good for me."

"Are you okay?"

Even though Lyndie was very much an adult, something about her mother asking that question twisted her insides like when she was a teenager. She wanted to scream, *No! I am not okay! I haven't been okay for a very long time!*

But such an outburst would require an explanation—and that, she wasn't willing to give. Not to Susan. Not tonight.

"I'm fine, Mom." A lie if she'd ever told one.

"I know this is a lot for you to handle right now."

Lyndie held the phone away from her ear. She couldn't take it. She couldn't listen to encouraging words from a woman who had only fragments of truth, slivers of a story that didn't need unpacking.

When Lyndie put the phone back to her ear, her mother was still going on about how worried she was.

"You've cut off all your old friends—it's no wonder Elle had to ask me for your contact information."

Lyndie pulled the phone away again and leaned her head back, wishing she could teleport or, at the very least, hang up the phone without repercussions.

She dared another listen.

"Why do I feel like you're not paying attention? Am I talking to the air?"

"I'm listening, Mom," Lyndie said absently. "Where's Dad?"

"Always wanting to talk to your father instead of me," she said. "He's out in his garden. You know how he gets about those plants."

She did and she didn't. It wasn't like Lyndie had been back to Illinois lately. She'd left for Belmont University in Nashville at eighteen, and she hadn't looked back. How could she? Home reminded her of everything she was supposed to be—which was everything she wasn't.

"Listen, I know you don't like to think about Cassie," her mom said.

Sorrow poked the surface of Lyndie's heart. She'd put this behind her, hadn't she? Why couldn't she think about Cassie—at least remember all the good times—without feeling like she might crack in two? Ten years should've given her the time and space to be okay, but she wasn't. Why did the past still have such a grip on her? This was why she kept it locked away. This was why she'd never write a suitable song for Jalaire.

". . . it will be good for you." Her mom's tone signaled finality, and Lyndie realized she'd zoned out and missed most of what her mother had said. She could fill in the blanks, though. Good old Susan wasn't that original.

"I'll try to make it, Mom," Lyndie said, wishing she could crawl in bed, slip under the covers and go to sleep. Though sometimes the memories even seeped into her dreams.

Nowhere was safe.

"Karen said she invited you to stay with them, and we both agreed that if you get there on Friday, you'll have a day or two to spend with the Jacobs family before all the wedding craziness begins, which Karen would really appreciate. Staying with them makes the most sense, of course, since we don't have our cottage anymore. Some days I really miss that place, don't you?"

Lyndie mumbled an indecipherable response.

"It'll be good for you to get away. Change of scenery. Maybe you'll feel inspired. After all, you wrote a lot of songs sitting on the beach in Sweethaven."

She remembered. It was where she'd fallen in love with music, mostly thanks to Cassie. Cassie was the performer, whereas Lyndie preferred to be in the background. But her friend had a contagious excitement for melodies and chords and finding the perfect lyric. Cassie dreamed the two of them would make it big someday—she'd been so sure they had that "it factor."

But for Cassie, someday never came.

And for Lyndie, well, making it big on her own felt impossible.

"I should go, Mom." Lyndie knew it was abrupt, but she needed air. She murmured a quick goodbye and hung up, willing oxygen to her lungs.

The image of Cassie's room popped into her head.

Did her full-sized bed still have that same old quilt on it? The one her grandma made her when Cassie was just a baby? Soft and worn, that blanket had been right there with them through so many of their giggly teenage sleepovers. How many times had the three of them crammed into that bed and fallen asleep talking about boys, dreaming of the future? That, or they'd trudge down to the sleeping porch, where the sound of crickets singing lulled them to sleep in the warm summer nights.

How could she go back there? Back to that room, as if time hadn't marched on, as if she hadn't changed?

And yet, how could she not? She was going to be in Sweethaven. She would have to see Karen and Davis Jacobs. She would have to show up at Cassie's memorial.

It wasn't an ideal situation, but Lyndie had learned how to keep her unwanted memories locked up tight. Maybe it was time to revisit her old haunts, to face it all head-on.

And to walk away with that ever-so-elusive closure everyone talked about.

# Chapter Three

Karen Jacobs looked over her legal pad with the smallest bit of satisfaction.

"What is it?" Davis asked, peering at her from over the top of his newspaper.

"Just putting the finishing touches on Cassie's party." She looked at Davis, who held her gaze for only a split second, then disappeared behind the paper. "Did you get a chance to look over the guest list?" she asked, hoping, as always, for some clue as to what her husband was thinking.

"Looks great, hon."

"Have you heard from Tucker?"

Davis stilled at the mention of their son's name.

"I called him yesterday, but he didn't answer, as usual," she said. "Got ahold of Jade, at least. She seemed to think he was planning to come out next Friday for the wedding. Isn't that just like Tucker? Fly in the day before and fly out the day after?"

Davis folded the paper in half and set it on the table. "You can't push him, Karen."

She looked away. "I'm not pushing him."

"You're always pushing," he said, his soft tone contradicting his words.

She shot him a look.

"You know what I mean."

Karen stood. "I don't, actually."

"Never mind."

Of course. *Never mind* was his favorite phrase, wasn't it? He'd been saying that for years instead of anything that truly mattered.

What she really wanted here was an ally, not an enemy, but it seemed she and Davis were always at odds. It had been that way since Cassie died. And Tucker—she didn't even know what to do about her son. She knew from the town rumor mill that this wedding was a weeklong event. She'd found that out when she went down to the newspaper office to take out a small ad inviting the town to the memorial service.

Ruby Mae, who worked behind the counter at the *Sweethaven Gazette*, had taken one look at the ad Karen had created on her computer and frowned.

"I know it's not anything fancy." Karen wasn't tech savvy, and she didn't know a thing about designing an ad.

"No, it's not that, Karen," Ruby Mae said. "It's just that you've planned this for the Thursday before the Preston wedding."

Karen frowned. "I planned it for the anniversary of my daughter's death." Saying the words aloud set something off inside her.

Ruby Mae's face fell. "Of course. Forget I said anything."

"Well, I can't forget it now," Karen said. "What's going on the Thursday before the wedding?"

"I would've thought Tucker would've told you, given that he's the best man and all." Ruby Mae tucked a strand of dark hair behind her ear. "But Nora Preston has turned the wedding into a weeklong affair. They've got something scheduled every single day and most nights, and you know Nora—most of the town is invited."

Karen had been annoyed when she'd found out the date of Elle and Travis's wedding, but she'd set aside those feelings because, one, she loved Elle and Travis, and two, she had no claim on any weekend in

June. Never mind that it was insensitive of them. Never mind that Nora should've known better. Never mind that she'd been trying to compete with that woman since they were kids.

And especially never mind that Karen had never, ever won.

In the end, she'd told Ruby Mae to run the ad as it was and made a mental note to send Nora a sugary-sweet invitation to the celebration of life. She shouldn't have to run anything by that woman, especially not a gathering to celebrate the life of a daughter who should be there with them now.

But she would. Because Karen was a peacekeeper. And that's what peacekeepers did.

Peacekeepers also held their tongues when their passive husbands refused to engage in any kind of conversation with their wives.

Her sigh was audible. Davis seemed not to notice.

The cottage had always been a place of peaceful relaxation. They'd struggled to get back there after the accident but finally tore off the Band-Aid a few years ago. Standing in the entryway, surrounded by suitcases, they'd stared at each other for a long moment. Karen had fought back tears.

*The last place we saw Cassie alive.*

*The last place we were all together as a family.*

*The last place love and not heartache seemed to rule our days.*

She'd eventually developed a sort of numbness to her surroundings. She didn't let herself dwell on every little memory that popped into her mind. She spent the days swatting them away like fruit flies, but they always came back.

Cassie's laugh when she and Elle and Lyndie were upstairs talking about who knows what. Cassie's door slam when she was mad she had to clean her room before going to the beach. Cassie and Lyndie harmonizing on the sleeping porch while Elle looked on in quiet admiration.

The cottage had buzzed with the heartbeat of life once upon a time. It had brimmed with laughter and celebration far more often than

19

sadness and disappointment. Davis had filled his days with work, golf and gardening, but his nights were just for her.

They'd talked back then. Really talked. About dreams and hopes and prayers—not just for their kids, but for them. They were going to go to Italy after Cassie graduated, just the two of them. The honeymoon Davis said he'd always wanted to give Karen. They had plans. They were friends.

She couldn't have imagined it any other way.

But now the divide between them was so great, she didn't know how she'd ever find him again. Now, she spent her days mourning for her dying marriage and feeling like a hypocrite for giving her clients advice that hadn't worked in her own life.

*You need to reconnect. Get away together, out of your daily routine. It'll be good for you.*

How many times had she said those words? But in most cases, her patients weren't returning to the place of their grief—and surely that, and not something else, was the cause of the distance between her and Davis.

And she couldn't fathom that trip to Italy now. It would be silent and awkward and just another reminder that somewhere along the way, things had gone horribly wrong.

She glanced at Davis, who had returned to his newspaper. She wished she could take all that empty advice back now, but of course she couldn't. What would people say? She'd endured years of pitying expressions and soft whispers behind her back, and of course, an endless chorus of *Are you okay?*

And sometimes when she walked through the grocery store, she marveled at how "okay" she seemed. Other times, she broke down in tears in the produce section.

And every day she wondered if the people getting on about their business—people like Davis, who seemed to navigate life and loss with flying colors—knew how broken she was. She'd make eye contact with a perfect stranger and wonder, *Can she see that I'm barely holding it together right now?*

But she always forced a smile and moved along. A picture of strength in the midst of loss. How many times had other women come to her and told her she was an inspiration?

"I got through my husband's affair because of you, Karen," Marnie Richardson had told her last year. "It was awful, and it ripped my heart out, but I found myself thinking of you and all you've been through, and I thought, 'Well, if Karen can do it, then I can do it too.' And I instantly felt stronger."

How would Marnie feel now if she knew the truth? That inside, Karen was falling apart.

"Do you think it's okay that I'm having this party just a couple of days before the wedding?" Karen heard the worry in her own voice, and she knew what Davis would say. Sometimes she annoyed herself asking questions that didn't need to be asked so he could give answers that didn't need to be given.

"I think it's fine," Davis said.

Ah, yes. *Fine.* Her husband's other favorite word.

"What are you making for dinner?" he asked, eyes still on his paper.

"I thought we'd grill tonight. I picked up chicken breasts from Scooter's, and I saw you had a little vegetable harvest."

Even his vegetables didn't excite him. Not today. Not anymore. He simply nodded and went along with her plan. What if she'd told him they were having shellfish and ice cream—two things he was terribly allergic to—would he have argued with her then?

Or would he simply nod and fetch himself something else to eat?

Or worse, force down the toxic food because it was easier than telling her he didn't want it?

She wished Tucker would call. He never called. She knew his assistant better than she knew him. In fact, if it wasn't for Jade, Karen wouldn't know a thing about her son's life. Although maybe that would've been better. She'd never been comfortable with his thrill-seeking. Snowboarding, skiing, parasailing, rock climbing, bungee jumping, cliff diving—Tucker did it all. Gave her something else to worry about. Something else to keep her up at night.

The phone rang. Rotary and on the wall, the old thing was more of a prop than anything else, but theirs was one of the few cottages that still had a landline.

She glanced at Davis. She supposed she should be thankful the bell had saved her. One more moment of silence might finally be the thing to suffocate her to death.

# Chapter Four

The coolness of the ocean water lapped over Tucker Jacobs as he paddled the surfboard a little bit farther—deeper—than last time. He needed to catch one more good wave before he could call it a day. There was something about hauling his gear back to shore on a win.

He reached his stopping point and waited—waited—until it was time to start paddling. With all his might, he pushed his arms through the water until the wave caught up to him, its force lifting him as he pulled himself up on his board.

A shout tore through him, like something spiritual needing release. He balanced himself on the board, wrapping his mind around the way it made him feel. Inhaling the smell of the saltwater, feeling the rise of the wave, relishing the morning sun that promised another new day.

Another do-over.

Another chance.

Even for those who didn't deserve it.

He rode the wave in toward the shore, wiping out after several glorious seconds of pure adrenaline. If it wasn't almost eight, he would've gone again.

All day long.

He pulled himself out of the Pacific and unzipped his wet suit, tugging the top half down around his waist. The sun felt good on his back, and he fought the urge to lie down in the sand and stay awhile.

But as much as he hated to admit it, he did have adult responsibilities—though most days running an adventure-tour business felt a lot more like play.

Tucker dropped his board on the beach and toweled off, then pulled a worn gray T-shirt over his head. As he peeled the wet suit off, he spotted Jade walking toward him, wearing black dress pants with a frilly white shirt and carrying a pair of high heels in one hand.

Probably thought he forgot his meeting. He supposed that's why he paid her—to keep him on task—but sometimes it annoyed him that she was so thorough. He hadn't finished his morning ritual, and Lord knew if he didn't get a good start, the whole day would take a quick nosedive.

"I didn't forget," he said.

She looked at her watch. "Cutting it kind of close, aren't you?"

He brushed a hand through his hair, a lame attempt to get the sand out. "They'll appreciate that I'm not just some stuffy suit trying to sell them an adventure tour. I'm living it."

He picked up his surfboard and positioned it under his arm with Jade on his other side. They walked toward the parking lot where his black Jeep Wrangler was parked, but he could tell his assistant had something to say. Something he wasn't going to like.

"Just tell me," Tucker said.

"Your mom left another message."

He ignored her.

"Tucker?" Jade stopped walking.

"I heard you," he said, still walking.

"You really should call her back."

He stopped. "Got it."

"Well, you should probably know that your parents are staying at their cottage in Michigan right now," Jade said.

"What? How do you know that?"

"Because when you don't respond to her messages, your mom calls *me*."

Tucker groaned. "I'll deal with it."

"Tucker, if your big plan was to swoop in there and not deal with your parents, you'll have to rethink that."

"You already changed my flight, Jade. What's next? Are you planning to manage my lodging too?"

When his assistant first told him about the wedding festivities lasting a full week, he'd shaken his head. He owned a business. He had to work. He'd fly in Friday and fly out Sunday. That was all he could handle of Sweethaven in June.

"Too late," she'd told him. "Mrs. Preston's assistant said it was vital you be there for the whole week, and your mom asked that you arrive a little earlier so you can have some family time first." Jade had cleared his schedule accordingly.

*Family time. Great.* Tucker had tried not to groan. "I didn't agree to this."

"Well, you are the best man," she'd said. "You kinda did."

That was what he got for allowing someone else to handle all of his affairs. He looked at her now and instantly knew there was more.

"What?"

Jade grimaced. "I canceled the hotel."

He stared at her. "Tell me you're kidding."

"I thought I was helping. Your mom said you probably didn't know the cottage was open and they were staying there, and it would be easier on everyone if you just stayed with them. They have an open room and everything. It sounded important to her, Tucker."

*Easier on everyone?*

"I didn't hire you to manage my personal life, Jade. Some things aren't your business." He started off toward the Jeep, knowing the words had been too harsh. And it wasn't the first time he'd snapped at her. This stupid wedding—this week of all weeks. It had him in knots.

Still, he didn't apologize.

He loaded up his gear, shook out his wet suit and did his best to dry his trunks. They'd be dry by the time he pulled into the meeting—a huge tech firm wanting to put together a staff retreat. It would mean big business for Adventure Seekers, the business he'd started a few years ago.

Might as well turn his passion into profit, right? Turned out there were lots of people out there who craved the adrenaline rush as much as he did.

It was like an addiction.

"I guess I'll see you back at the office," Jade said, her eyes still wounded from his harsh words. She took a few steps in the opposite direction, heading toward her car.

"Jade?"

She turned.

He threw her his wallet. "Go buy something for yourself."

She caught the wallet, then stared at it for several seconds. "I don't need anything."

He shrugged. "Doesn't matter. There must be something you want. It's on me."

She held it up with a slight wave. "Thanks."

But even Tucker knew buying her off didn't replace the words he should've said.

Then again, his life seemed to be made up of those words, didn't it?

# Chapter Five

Elle Porter stood on a platform in the center of the bridal shop, staring at her reflection in the three-way mirror. Her wedding dress was anything but traditional—an organza and tulle gown with floral appliqués, capped sleeves and a design that revealed the lace shorts and bralette she wore underneath.

"It's quite modern, isn't it?" Her soon-to-be mother-in-law, Nora Preston, circled her, scrutinizing every detail.

"It's the latest trend," Elle said.

"It hardly flares at all," Nora said. "How are you supposed to feel like a princess without a tulle skirt on your wedding dress?"

"It feels more elegant than that," Elle said. "And it has a train."

"I think it's stunning." Robin, the sales associate, winked at Elle. God bless Robin.

"It looks a little snug." Nora met Elle's eyes. "Are you bloated?"

Elle ran her hands over her stomach. "I don't think so."

"Celia, can we let it out a little right here?" Nora waved a finger toward Elle's midsection. Elle glanced at herself in the mirror. All she saw was a dress that lay perfectly flat on her torso.

Celia, the short, stout woman Nora had hired as their personal seamstress, frowned. "Here?" She pinched the organza.

"Yes, just a little bit. Give her some room to breathe."

*I can breathe just fine.*

"I can try, but we don't want it too loose," Celia said, sticking a pin in the dress. "It'll lose its shape."

"But we don't want to accent her love handles either, do we?" Nora flashed a smile highlighted by her perfectly applied lipstick.

Celia didn't respond. Instead, she gave a tug on Elle's dress, drawing her attention, then squeezed her arm.

"You get changed, Elle. We've got so much to do today to get ready for the big week." Nora waved and disappeared, followed by Robin.

Celia stood. "What do you think, Miss Porter?"

Elle turned sideways, studying herself in the mirror. "I guess it's a little tight, maybe?"

Celia followed her gaze to the reflection, the two of them standing side by side, Elle a couple of feet taller up on the bridal platform.

"Maybe I could lose a few pounds before the wedding," Elle said. "That would be less work for you."

"Don't worry about me," Celia said. "I can handle the work. That's what I'm getting paid for. The real question is, What do you want for your big day?"

Elle picked up the skirt of her dress and stepped down onto the floor, still a head taller than the seamstress. Nobody had asked her that, in all the months of planning. In fact, it had gotten to the point where Elle stopped allowing herself to have opinions because they didn't seem to matter. As usual, Nora steered this ship.

The dress was one of the few things about this wedding that was Elle's, and she'd gotten away with it only because she'd bought it the day after Travis proposed. She'd been eyeing it for weeks on her walk home from work. It had looked so beautiful in the window of the bridal boutique that it pulled her attention every single day until, finally, she went in and tried it on. The employees weren't happy when they learned she wasn't actually engaged, but their sideways glances did nothing to dull the feeling she had when she stepped in front of the three-way mirror wearing that dress.

It was as if it was made for her.

A few weeks later, she came back, this time with a ring on her finger and a credit card in her purse. And the dress was hers. Even after months had gone by, she still loved it.

She met Celia's eyes. "I guess we should do what Nora says. She knows more about these things than I do."

Celia frowned. "She doesn't know more about what you want for your wedding day."

"But she knows about fashion," Elle said. "Let's take the dress out."

"Of course, Miss Porter." Celia's eyes dipped low as she nodded in agreement.

Elle swept across the small staging area and pulled the door closed on one of the fitting rooms, letting out a heavy sigh. She just needed to get through this wedding—that was all—and then her life could begin.

Travis's mom wouldn't be nearly as involved once they were married and living their own life. She simply wanted to ensure they had the perfect wedding, and Elle should be thankful. After all, her own mother wouldn't provide that kind of moral support. It was good to have someone who cared, at least.

Elle quickly changed back into the sundress Nora had bought her on their last shopping trip.

"If you're going to be a Preston, you need to start dressing the part," Nora had said, handing the cashier her credit card. "You need to always be prepared for one of our parishioners to pop in on you, or to bump into someone from church while you're out running errands. They can't see you looking a mess, now can they?" Nora went on about Elle's generation going out in yoga pants or workout clothes—completely unacceptable.

Elle made a note: *Yoga pants for in-home viewing only.* She wasn't sure they were okay even then. Suddenly the thought of being "on" all the time exhausted her.

But Travis was worth it. Of course he was.

She'd loved him for years, though she'd kept that little nugget to herself. Cassie's crush on Travis was well-documented; so much of their conversation had been dedicated to it. How could Elle admit she, too, had feelings for the cute boy with the bright-hazel eyes and honey-colored hair? Cassie would never have forgiven her, which meant Lyndie wouldn't have either—and Elle couldn't risk losing both of them. She didn't have anyone else.

But after the accident, everything changed. Lyndie left Sweethaven almost immediately, sullen and forlorn, and Elle had to pick up the pieces by herself. On the really sad days, she'd head down to the beach, remembering how it felt when the three of them would sit on the dock for hours without a care in the world.

One day, Travis showed up. He must've sensed her sadness, because he seemed intent on cheering her up. Their dockside conversation turned into ice cream at Sweet's and a kind hug good night, which led to another day spent together and then another.

She hadn't intended to date him, but she couldn't deny that she wanted to. Lyndie would be mad when she found out, but what was Elle supposed to do? Put her life on hold? Cassie was gone. Travis and Elle were both still here.

Things between her and Lyndie hadn't been the same after that. It turned out Cassie was the great equalizer in their friendship, and without her, the other two weren't all that comfortable together.

Despite that, Elle still considered Lyndie her best friend. How sad was that? They hardly even spoke anymore. And while Lyndie didn't know everything about Elle, she knew more than anyone else, and she'd never made her feel like anything but a part of the family.

In spite of Elle's mother. In spite of her upbringing and social status. If only the Prestons had been so receptive.

Travis and Elle spent nearly every waking moment of the rest of that summer together, and after he went back home to Chicago, they committed to making it work, even long-distance. But months went by, and Travis hadn't told his parents about the two of them.

"They're just not cool about girls," he'd told her. What he should've said was "They're just not cool about certain kinds of girls." Or even, "They just won't be cool about you."

When Nora eventually did find out the following summer, she forbade Travis to continue dating Elle.

Travis didn't tell her what his mother said, but Elle filled in the blanks over the years. Nora didn't think Elle was good enough, smart enough, pretty enough, refined enough or Christian enough for her son.

And back then, Travis hadn't been strong enough to stand up for himself. So, they'd gone their separate ways. Now, after a chance meeting in a Chicago coffee shop over eight years later, here they were— engaged to be married whether Nora Preston liked it or not.

Nobody had said so, but Elle imagined Nora absolutely did not like it.

Travis had given his parents the news by himself, probably protecting Elle from what was likely an unkind reaction. Surely his parents thought he was making a mistake. He and Elle had reconnected only a few months prior, and they'd chosen a wedding date just three months away.

But Travis had insisted. *When you know, you know.* That's what he'd told Elle. Then he'd kissed her and said, "And I absolutely know."

The way he'd looked at her made her stomach somersault the way it had the very first time he'd kissed her. Nobody else had ever had that kind of effect on her.

*When you know, you know.*

Would Nora ever accept Elle as a daughter? Would Elle ever feel like a part of a family again?

She ran a hand through her long auburn hair, then sat to buckle her sandals around her ankles. Sometimes when she spent time with Nora, she felt like the woman had begrudgingly made an agreement to give Elle a chance. Maybe Nora's husband, the good and dutiful Pastor Timothy Preston, had pointed out that Nora wasn't going to change Travis's mind, so she might as well accept it.

Maybe she'd agreed through gritted teeth and with a fake smile, knowing in the back of her mind that she could never see Elle Porter as family. Or maybe she'd decided that if she couldn't change Travis's mind, she could try to do the next best thing: change his fiancée.

It was working, too, wasn't it? So far, Elle had let Nora have her way on almost every point. She'd relinquished control of her own wedding because, truth be told, she didn't care that much. She didn't care if the wedding cake had pink or teal flowers on it. She didn't even care which guests sat at what table. She just wanted to marry Travis and start her life.

It felt as if she'd been sleepwalking until the day Travis walked back into her life, and it was finally time to wake up.

Elle reapplied her lip gloss, then pulled open the door. She handed Celia her gown.

"I'll be in Sweethaven for your final fitting a few days before the wedding," Celia said. "But I'm not worried—it already looks so beautiful on you."

"Yes, but an extra half an inch will make all the difference," Nora said, entering the staging area. "Are you ready, Elle? We're meeting the boys for lunch."

"The boys" was what Nora called Travis and his father.

Elle suddenly felt giddy that it was almost time to see Travis. He could calm her uneasiness just by looking at her.

They settled into a small bistro after a quiet drive from the bridal boutique. Seconds after they arrived, Elle spotted Travis and his father near the front door. She waited until Travis's eyes found hers, then smiled and waved him over.

His hazel eyes could still melt her heart. They'd always had such power over her, immediately catching her attention that day in the coffee shop. Over eight years had passed since they'd broken up, but she'd known his eyes in an instant. And after their first awkward exchange, it was like no time had passed between them at all.

They'd both pretended they were on their way to nowhere (even though she was going to be late for work), sat down at a table, and caught up on life. He'd been away for a few years, working as a youth pastor in a small church in Ohio that paid him almost nothing, and he'd only just returned to Chicago to take a job at his father's church, which everyone always knew he would do.

"Interesting it's my first week back and I run into you," he'd said.

"Yeah, how about that?" She'd smiled and listened as he told her about his job in Ohio. He spoke about it with such excitement and maybe a bit of sadness.

"Do you miss it out there?" she asked.

He shrugged. "It was hard to make a living. And I guess I always knew eventually I'd come back here. They're grooming me to take over for my dad one day."

Elle widened her gaze. "That's a tall order."

He nodded.

"And a big spotlight."

He shrugged again, not seeming to care about that. Being a famous preacher had never been his dream. Travis had always said he just wanted to help people.

Elle was almost embarrassed when he asked her what she'd been up to. She was working as an office manager for a pediatrician just outside the city. It sounded so basic, so small. But at least she'd gotten out of Sweethaven. She comforted herself with that, whenever it felt like it wasn't enough.

"Sounds like a good job," Travis said.

"It is." It was a good job. If she wanted a placeholder. Something to pass the time until life could actually begin.

*Tick-tick-tick.*

"Who do you spend most of your time with?" he asked, finishing the last of his coffee.

Her cheeks flushed. How did she tell him she spent most of her time alone? How did she explain that her only real friendships had ended nine years before and she'd been struggling to find a foothold ever since? She had no one to confide in, no one who really knew her—it all sounded so mortifyingly pathetic.

"What I really want to know is if you're dating anyone." Travis wore that same boyish smile he'd always worn.

She relaxed then, thankful she didn't have to confess how lonely she was. "No," she said. "I'm not dating anyone."

He found her eyes. "Good."

The rest had been a whirlwind of phone calls and text messages and dinners and the overwhelming feeling that they'd wasted the better part of the last decade. They could've been together all along.

Instead, she'd been floundering this whole time, trying to figure out if this was everything life had for her.

Now, standing in this expensive bistro in downtown Chicago on a Thursday afternoon, Elle wanted to pinch herself. And that man—that beautiful hazel-eyed man—was looking right at her.

Right through her.

And he wasn't running the other way. Not this time.

He flashed a smile, then made his way to her.

"For goodness' sake, Travis," Nora said. "You could've shaved."

He ran a hand over his scruff. "Trying something new, Mom." He leaned down and kissed Elle on the cheek.

"I like it," she whispered.

"That's all I care about." He smiled at her, and for the briefest few seconds, they seemed to be the only two in the room.

"Pastor Preston?" A woman stopped beside their table just as they'd all taken their seats. "I wanted to stop and say hello. We've been attending your church for two years now, and we're so blessed by it every week."

Travis's father stood and took the woman's hand in both of his. "I'm so glad to hear it, Ms. . . . ?"

"Taryn Hadley." The brunette flashed a bright-white smile, still holding on to Pastor Preston's hand.

"Mrs. Hadley," he said.

"It's actually Miss Hadley," she corrected. "I don't want to interrupt your lunch. I just wanted to thank you for all you do for the people of your church."

She smiled, then moved across the room to a table near the back of the bistro.

"Well, that was nice," the pastor said.

"Two years in the church and none of us knew her name," Travis said.

Nora lasered her focus on her son. "Please, Travis, you know it's impossible for your father and I to know everyone who attends our church."

It was a fair point. The church did have over twenty thousand people attending each weekend. They *were* just two people.

"I know," Travis said. "I just think we need to make an effort to get to know everyone a little better. Isn't ministry supposed to be about the people?"

"You go right ahead and do that," Nora said. "We'll see how long you last."

Elle's hand found Travis's underneath the table. She knew his views differed in many ways from those of his much more traditional father, who'd turned his ministry into an empire over the years. Travis could appreciate that, and they'd all certainly benefited financially, but sometimes Elle wondered if he'd prefer a small congregation with fewer but more meaningful relationships, like the one he'd left back in Ohio.

That wouldn't happen, though—he was heir to the so-called throne, which was why, Elle supposed, Nora felt it important to groom Elle for the role she would eventually take on.

First Lady of Morning Star Church.

Just the thought of that made her nervous. As if by simply marrying a pastor, she now had a call to ministry. But what if that particular call had passed her over? Did that mean she and Travis were not a good match?

Unlike the first time they'd started dating, Travis had brought her around his parents immediately. He'd told her he'd always regretted keeping their relationship a secret, and this time, he wanted nothing but radical honesty between them.

Elle had nearly collapsed at the idea. She didn't believe in radical honesty with anyone—certain things about her needed to stay secret. She hated the way those secrets kept Travis from ever really knowing her, but it was the only way.

After all, if he knew everything about her, he never would've slipped that ring on her finger.

Part of keeping their relationship out in the open was going to church together, and Elle was determined to play her part well. In all this time, though, she'd never once felt like a woman who could lead anyone.

Could she keep up this charade forever? It had already begun to exhaust her.

The thoughts would consume her if she let them. And she often let them. But not today. Not when she'd just come from a fitting for a dress that was above and beyond anything she'd ever hoped for. Not when there was a wonderful man sitting beside her who wanted her to be his wife. Not when her wedding was just around the corner, and finally—finally—her lonely days would be in the past.

Elle shook the thoughts aside as a waiter took their orders. The food arrived after some polite conversation, and Nora cleared her throat, her way of informing them all she wanted the floor.

"There's something we should discuss," Nora said. "As you all know, we have an entire week of wedding festivities planned in Sweethaven leading up to your big day."

Travis squeezed Elle's hand.

"We'll do a small mocktail party on Sunday evening to welcome our guests, followed by dinner and a few other fun activities. Oh, I have all kinds of things planned—a picnic, a trip to the winery, a fish fry on the beach, a girls-only spa day, and a sunset cruise following the rehearsal dinner."

"A mocktail party?" Elle asked.

"Faux cocktails," the pastor said. "Nora's idea."

Nora straightened. "We can hardly serve alcohol, now can we?"

"No, we can't." Elle didn't say so, but she was actually thankful. There had been way too much alcohol at every low point of her life. A mocktail party sounded perfect to her.

"Sounds like you've got the whole week planned," Travis said.

"Of course I do," Nora said. "There's just one problem." She reached inside her handbag and pulled out a white card. "I received this in the mail today." She set it on the table. "Have you gotten yours yet?"

Elle picked it up and opened it, eyes scanning words that brought back a whirlwind of memories. Carefree summers that made her forget who she was. Friends who linked arms with her as they walked down the street toward the beach. Bonfires and beach parties and Sunday school and feeling like a part of a family for the first time in her life.

"They're having a celebration of life for Cassie," Elle said, the words nearly choking her. She'd originally planned their wedding for the middle of May, but Nora had said a three-month engagement was ridiculous to begin with, and did they want everyone assuming Elle was pregnant?

Nora couldn't possibly understand that Elle and Travis had already wasted so much time apart—they both wanted to just be married already. She'd insisted the couple push it back enough so she could book the chapel, photographer and florist. But the week they'd pushed it to . . .

It was the tenth anniversary of Cassie's death.

"I'll be calling Karen Jacobs as soon as I get back to the house," Nora said.

"What? Why?" Elle hated the lump that had formed at the back of her throat, hated even more the guilt that accompanied it. She should've insisted on a May wedding.

Nora's eyes widened at Elle's outburst. "Because this is unacceptable. Surely she knows when the wedding is."

"Mom," Travis said. "It's one night. Thursday. Not the wedding day."

"It's the day of the vineyard tour," Nora said.

"Which is during the day," Travis replied.

"But followed by a big fish fry on the beach that night. A lot of thought went into this, and it's all been planned for weeks."

Elle stilled. The Jacobs family had lost their daughter—didn't that mean anything to Nora?

"So we move the fish fry. I don't mind changing the schedule to make room for this," Travis said as the waitress returned with their food. "We can shift things around, Mom."

"I agree," Pastor Preston said. He accepted his plate from the waitress with a quick wink, then turned to Nora, whose puckered face revealed her annoyance. "We can spare one night."

"But it's already been planned," Nora said.

"Then we'll change some things around," Pastor Preston said.

"It's unacceptable and thoughtless." Nora sipped her water with lemon. "And I intend to let Karen and Davis know."

"Please don't," Elle said, the words escaping before she could stop them.

Nora shot her a look that silenced her. "I'll be kind about it. But sometimes a gentle reminder is in order."

"They've already been through so much," Travis said. "We can spare an evening. Plans can be changed, Mother." He held Nora's gaze for several pregnant seconds, then took a bite of his pasta.

"Fine," Nora said. "But I won't be attending, and I don't see how the two of you can either, so close to your wedding day."

No matter how hard it was, no matter how guilty she felt, Elle owed it to Cassie to be there.

She glanced at Travis. How many times had she, Cassie and Lyndie discussed his chiseled features and striking eyes? How many times had Cassie admitted she sometimes wanted to reach over and run a hand through his messy hair?

Sometimes when Elle was alone with Travis, it would hit her all over again, and she'd feel like they were still sneaking around so nobody would find out. She couldn't shake the feeling that Travis was off-limits to her. He belonged to Cassie.

But Cassie was gone. She'd been gone for a long time. And Elle wasn't doing anything wrong.

So why did she still feel like she was stabbing Cassie in the back?

As far as Elle was concerned, that day was Cassie's day. And if it meant canceling one of Elle's wedding events, fine. Maybe saying a proper goodbye would take away the guilt. Maybe she'd stop feeling like the worst person in the world.

*If anyone ever finds out the truth . . .*

"I'm staying at the Jacobs' cottage," Elle said. "I'm not sure I can get out of it."

"And Tucker's one of my best friends," Travis said. "I'm not going to miss it."

Nora frowned. "Tucker probably won't even show up. I had to get on the phone with his assistant to explain why he couldn't just zip in here next Friday."

"He owns a business, so I wouldn't blame him if he couldn't come till Friday," Travis said. "Some people can't take a whole week off for a wedding."

"Then you should've asked your cousin Russell to be your best man."

Travis's deep breath told Elle he was mentally censoring himself. He didn't see any point in arguing with his parents, though Elle was anxiously awaiting the day he told Nora off once and for all.

"He's my best friend, Mom," Travis said.

"He's trouble."

"He's not a kid anymore. And neither am I." Travis set his fork down on the plate.

Nora held his gaze for several awkward seconds, glanced at Elle, then looked back at Travis. "Well, I just hope he shows up. And I hope he's sober."

"He doesn't drink anymore, Mom." Travis was starting to sound exasperated. "Aren't we supposed to give people the benefit of the doubt?"

"He got you into so much trouble, Travis," Nora said. "I never worried about you unless you were out with Tucker Jacobs."

"And still I seem to have turned out fine, despite that terrible influence."

Nora stopped midchew. "I don't like your tone, young man."

Elle wished she was bold like Cassie. She wished she could say exactly what she was thinking: *He's not a child. You're not his boss. You can't control everyone else's lives!*

Instead she remained, as she always did, silent.

"Tucker will be fine, Nora," the pastor said. "The wedding will go off without a hitch, and you two can head straight off on your honeymoon." He took a swig of water.

In the Preston family, Travis's father was the peacemaker. Or perhaps the pushover, depending on how you looked at it. Nora was in the driver's seat, and she and Travis routinely butted heads, though it hadn't always been that way. Elle was still figuring out her place in this dynamic. So far, she'd mostly been a sounding board for Travis, but she was learning he was a lot of talk and no action.

"We're taking a few months before our honeymoon," Travis said.

Nora seemed not to have heard him. "What about your family, Elle? We haven't received any RSVP's from them," she said, moving the conversation to a place Elle did not want to go.

She thought about the small stack of wedding invitations she'd addressed, then stuck inside the desk in her shoebox-sized apartment.

"Elle?" Nora raised her brow.

What could she say? Certainly not the truth. "They're not very good at RSVP'ing for things. I can call them and find out how many are coming."

"I've already asked the caterer to wait on his final count twice," Nora said. "I don't think he'll appreciate it if I ask him to wait any longer."

"I understand." Elle's eyes fell to the plate of half-eaten food in front of her, her appetite suddenly gone.

"Maybe you should count on them," Travis said. "And then if they don't make it, we just have extra."

Nora glowered. "We're already spending a fortune on this wedding, Travis. We don't want to pay for food that won't be eaten."

An uncomfortable silence hung over their table as guilt niggled its way to the back of Elle's mind. Her family had nothing to contribute to this wedding, not even their attendance. The truth was, she barely knew most of them. An uncle. Two aunts. Three cousins. They were all strangers, all names on envelopes written in haste in an effort to add bodies to the seats at her own wedding.

*You're trying to be someone you're not, Elle Porter. And everyone knows it.*

Her thoughts spun back two decades. An eight-year-old Elle sat on the front step outside the trailer, wearing blue footie pajamas and waiting for her mom to come home. She'd had a bad dream, but when she woke up, no one was there to comfort her but a tattered teddy bear. Her eyes were heavy and she had school the next day, but where was her mom? Why wasn't she home?

Hours later, a car rumbled up toward the trailer, its headlights rousing her from fitful sleep. Elle had dozed off, right out there on the porch, but it didn't matter now—her mom was home.

The car came to a stop and the engine shut off, but Elle quickly saw that her mother wasn't alone. Elle stood, the tattered teddy bear hanging from her hand, as a man—tall, lanky, tattooed—emerged from the driver's side.

Her mother got out of the passenger side, stepped over to the man and slid her arm around his waist as the pair started toward the trailer. Their laughter was loud—too loud for the quiet of the middle of the night—and neither one of them walked a straight line.

When they reached the bottom of the steps, they finally saw Elle.

"Who's this?" The man held a cigarette between his fingers, and he took a long drag as he studied Elle, then flicked it off into the yard.

"What are you doing out here?" her mother spat.

Elle's stomach turned. She didn't like it when her mom was like this. "I had a bad dream."

"Nobody wants to hear it, little girl, you understand me?" She looked around the trailer park. "Do you know how much trouble you could've gotten me into if anyone had seen you out here?" She gave Elle a push back inside the trailer.

"I'm sorry, Mama."

"Just get over there and go back to sleep."

She wanted to tell her mom about the bad dream. She wanted to tell her that moms were supposed to help their kids go back to sleep, to stroke their hair and tell them everything was going to be okay. She wanted to remind her that kids were scared of the dark and parents were supposed to make that fear go away.

But she didn't. She couldn't. Instead, Elle scurried off to the opposite end of the trailer, into the closet her mom called her room. She peeked through the crack of the door and saw her mom press herself up against the man. Moments later, she heard sounds—terrible sounds—sounds she didn't want to hear, but she stopped looking. She covered her ears and hummed quietly to herself.

And she promised herself that one day she'd get out of Sweethaven. And once she did, she'd never come back.

But things hadn't exactly worked out the way she'd planned. That's what happened when you got yourself out of a place that everyone else considered an escape.

Sweethaven had never been that for her.

The Preston family was a pillar of society, wealthy and influential, and their future daughter-in-law was trailer park trash with a shady past and a trunk full of baggage.

She didn't belong with any of them, and she knew it.

"I'll eat the leftovers." Travis took Elle's hand. "If there are any, that is."

She glanced at him and gave a halfhearted smile. She didn't belong, but she wanted to. She wanted it more than anything.

And even Nora Preston wasn't going to stand in her way.

Not this time.

# Chapter Six

*The night is so dark, black like tar seeping into the crevices of a newly paved highway, with no moon and the lights of land too far away.*

*The boat rocks in the lake, back and forth, as the waves move across the water.*

*The dock sways underneath her feet as she tries to make out the outline of Elle and Cassie in the boat. She should be out there with them. She shouldn't be here, on the dock. It's not right—not for her. His hand finds the small of her back.*

*"Lyndie?"*

*But she can't pull her eyes from the darkness in front of her.*

*Now, the boat is in motion, picking up speed as it drives by. She waves, but they don't see her. She waves again, this time more furiously, the dread, the knowing of what is coming, overtaking her. She shouts for them to stop, to come in to the shore. She calls out her name.*

Cassie! Cassie! Cassie!

*The boat disappears beyond the horizon, and her eyes fall to the lake in front of her, where she sees the bluish image of Cassie's face under the water, surrounded by tendrils of her wavy dark hair moving in slow motion around her.*

Cassie! *She falls to her knees and reaches into the water, but as she does, Cassie's eyes close and her translucent face disappears into the depths.*

◆   ◆   ◆

Lyndie awoke with a start, her pajamas damp with sweat, her breathing short and labored.

She hadn't had the nightmare in years. She'd thought she'd pushed it away with sheer will. She'd thought wanting to be free of it had been enough. Clearly, it wasn't.

She stood and padded her way to the kitchen in the darkness. She pulled a glass from the cupboard, filled it with water, and drank, but it didn't calm her down.

For years, her dreams had betrayed her, forcing her to piece together remnants of a night that had grown hazy in her own mind. There were still so many questions—so many missing pieces of the puzzle.

*I'm so sorry I wasn't there with you, Cassie.*

She groaned as she refilled her water glass. This was exactly why she shouldn't have agreed to be in Elle's wedding. Exactly why she didn't want to go to this celebration of life. Couldn't she mourn her friend in the peace and quiet of her own apartment?

How could she go back to that place and keep her world intact? How long could she pretend that she didn't think about that night every single day?

She took another drink. Was this how it would be the whole next week? Would she have to face the sting of regret every moment she was back in Sweethaven? And most importantly, when she returned home, how long would it take to bury it all again?

She'd written the story of Cassie's death a dozen different ways, but she still wasn't clear on what had actually happened that night. An accident, they'd said. She'd gone overboard, knocked her head on the boat and disappeared.

Elle had confirmed it—right before she'd told Lyndie she should've been there. "If you were there, none of this would've happened." Elle's voice had cracked. "Where *were* you, Lyndie?"

Lyndie couldn't think about that. Not right now.

She walked into the living room and picked up her guitar. Jalaire's words raced through her mind, and the pressure of writing one perfect, meaningful song came right along with it.

She strummed a chord. Then another. She hummed a tune. It was catchy, hooky—maybe she was finally onto something. Another chord. More humming.

And then she realized she wasn't singing something new.

This song was as old as her pain: "Cassie's Song." And just like that, she was eighteen again. She was sitting in the deepest sorrow of her life, and she was sinking. She'd tried praying her way out of her grief, but God had been so quiet in those days after Cassie's death.

But then, Lyndie knew why. She didn't deserve His comfort and she knew it. Not after the choices she'd made.

How could she have been so stupid? She was Good Girl Lyndie. The level-headed, intelligent, Most-Likely-to-Succeed valedictorian of her graduating class. She was on a very straight, very narrow path.

But in one night, that all became the memory of the girl she used to be. The song had been a paltry attempt at an apology—for not being there, for failing her friend so miserably—but even it had failed. As the days passed, the gap grew between Good Girl Lyndie and the girl she'd become, and suddenly she knew she was too far gone.

Redemption wasn't something she deserved.

That's when these familiar chords, this haunting melody and the words that were meant to accompany it, all went into the box.

*That stupid box!* It taunted her. It threatened to show the world the ugly truth. She didn't care what Jalaire said, she wasn't opening it.

Not for Jalaire or anyone else.

Lyndie set the guitar down and made a pot of coffee. Then she flipped the television on to drown out the deafening quiet of never-ending silence, but didn't stick around to watch it. Instead, she moved toward the window.

She was going back to Sweethaven. She was going to say goodbye to Cassie—for real this time. She was going to come face-to-face with the past.

Lyndie steeled her jaw as she stared out over the street below.

She needed to properly prepare herself for this. She was no stranger to putting on a happy face, able to fake it with the best of them. She'd go, do her maid-of-honor duties, give a charming and witty speech. She'd even figure out a way to be cordial to Tucker. Cassie's mom would love having them there. Lyndie would be the picture of a perfect guest.

She'd be the good girl everyone assumed she was.

And she would purposely deny every feeling that contradicted her charade.

Maybe somehow she'd even squeak out a song in the process. Maybe if she put herself in someone else's shoes, felt their fear or tapped into their inner darkness, she'd emerge with a melody and lyrics that scraped the soul yet still kept her at a safe distance.

Jalaire wouldn't know the difference.

After she showered and changed, Lyndie pulled her suitcase out from under her bed. Thanks to her mother's guilt trip, she was going early—a decision she still wasn't comfortable with. Her flight was tomorrow. She should pack.

She should also call Karen to make sure the details of her visit were understood, but something stopped her every time she almost dialed the number. Fear, maybe?

How could she face Cassie's parents?

Around lunchtime, Foster showed up at her apartment. She wasn't sure why she hadn't broken things off with him yet. She'd known he wasn't right for her on their second date.

They'd been introduced by his friend Brandon, a singer Lyndie sort of knew. Foster had come to an open mic night to support Brandon and left with Lyndie's phone number in his suit-coat pocket.

He was a lawyer, and he was nice enough. But she was sure they weren't a good fit for so many reasons.

She pulled open the door and found him standing in the hallway. "Hey, baby."

*Reason Number One why I should break up with Foster: He calls me "baby."*

She forced a smile.

"I was just on my way back to the office. Lunch?" He held up a brown paper bag. "It's Chinese from that place down the block."

"I'm not really hungry, Foster." She was making excuses, but she knew he wouldn't see through her. He didn't pay close enough attention.

"Well, you can watch me eat and tell me about your meeting with Jalaire Grant."

She opened the door wider so he could enter her apartment. It was sweet of him to check on her meeting, she supposed. The kind of thing a real boyfriend would do.

For three months now, she'd been thinking of Foster as her sort-of boyfriend. She knew it wasn't fair to him, but somewhere in the back of his mind, he had to know they weren't exactly connecting.

He pulled a plate out of her cupboard and opened the bag of food. "So, what was she like?"

"Jalaire?"

"Who else?" He grinned at her.

*Ah.* So that's why he was asking. Lyndie vaguely remembered a conversation between Foster and Brandon about how hot Jalaire was.

"She was nice," Lyndie said. She walked back into her bedroom and pulled a stack of T-shirts from a drawer. Foster followed her.

"That's it? That's all you're going to tell me?" He held his plate and fork in front of him.

She shrugged. "What do you want me to say?"

"Did she like your songs? Is she going to record them? Can I meet her?"

Lyndie rolled her eyes as she pushed past him into the bathroom.

"What?" He set his plate down on her dresser and followed her into her bathroom. His following her around was beginning to suffocate her. "Did the meeting not go well?"

She met his eyes. "It went fine."

His arms wrapped around her waist. "Then why do you seem upset?"

"I'm fine, just busy."

He smiled at her. He was a perfectly acceptable sort-of boyfriend. He was smart and successful. He was decent-looking. And he was safe. No chance of this one ever breaking her heart. But if Foster told her tomorrow (or right at that moment, for that matter) that he thought they should call it quits, she'd have a hard time not dancing a jig.

And Lyndie wasn't a jig dancer.

But Foster was kind. And that was something.

He kissed her. It was, as all his kisses were, a little sloppy.

*Reason Number Two I should break up with Foster: He is a sloppy kisser. Like, discreetly-wipe-your-chin-with-the-sleeve-of-your-shirt-when-the-kiss-ends kind of sloppy.*

She pulled away and forced a smile, hiding her chin wipe. She really did need to break up with him.

"Hey, can I crash here over the next week? My place is being fumigated." Foster picked his plate back up and leaned against the bathroom's doorjamb.

"Here?" She spun around and opened the medicine cabinet, pulling out random bottles that were probably three years old, and stuffing them into a bag. He absolutely could not stay at her apartment.

She scanned her mind for an excuse—anything—to keep this from happening.

"Don't you think that would be a little cramped?" she asked with a shrug.

"It's small, but we can cuddle and stuff."

It was the "and stuff" she was worried about. She'd made up her mind on date number one that she was not sleeping with Foster. Ever.

Why he'd hung on to her for three months was beyond her—usually guys got the hint and stopped coming around. Not this guy.

She knew she'd have to be straight with him. He required a clear explanation. Or maybe she could just move away and not tell him? That might be easier.

"I don't know, Foster," Lyndie said, still searching for that excuse.

"It'll be fun," he said. "Like a big slumber party that lasts a whole week."

*You'll make a huge mess. You'll walk in on me when I'm in the shower. You'll do gross man things, and don't even pretend you're not going to try to sleep with me before I leave.*

"I'm actually going to be out of town," she heard herself saying, though she originally hadn't planned on cluing Foster in to her plans. She couldn't risk him asking to come along. She pushed past him and back into her bedroom.

"Where are you going?" He scooped a bit of fried rice into his mouth and washed it down with a can of Mountain Dew he must've fished out of her refrigerator.

*Reason Number Three I should break up with Foster: I won't have to stock my fridge with Mountain Dew anymore.*

"I'm in a wedding." She walked away. "In Michigan. And there's this celebration-of-life party for a friend of mine."

His eyebrows drew downward into a tight line. "Your friend died?"

"Years ago," she said. "It's the tenth anniversary." Why did it sound so commonplace when she talked about it now? As if it had happened to someone else? As if she were so far removed from it, she didn't carry it with her in her back pocket as a reminder of all she hadn't quite forgiven herself for?

"Sounds like a rockin' party," he scoffed, like it was the dumbest idea in the world. But it wasn't dumb. It was a good way to keep Cassie alive.

She'd almost forgotten what Cassie's laugh sounded like. Sometimes Lyndie pulled out the stupid videos they'd made, searching for any trace of her. She used to, anyway—it had been a long time since she'd gone looking for a memory of Cassie.

The thought shamed her.

"And there's a wedding?"

Lyndie pulled her bathing suit out of her top dresser drawer.

"Wait a minute, why do you need that?"

"It's at the lake, Foster, where I grew up." She didn't mean to sound condescending, but she absolutely did—she heard it in her own voice.

"So it really is a party?"

Lyndie shoved the suit in her suitcase and shook her head. "It's a week of events—some of them at the lake."

"So you'll be gone a whole week?"

"Yep." She stuck her hair dryer in the pouch on the inside flap of her suitcase.

"Man, you should've told me. I could've come along so you could show off your hot boyfriend to all your old friends."

Looking at Foster now, she could see something earnest behind his eyes, and while she couldn't think of a worse idea than him coming to Sweethaven with her, she didn't want to hurt him.

"I can try to get off work?"

"No, don't." She smiled up at him. "It's really not a big deal. Lots of old stories and inside jokes. You'd hate it."

"Will there be beer?" He grinned. "Because if there's beer, I wouldn't hate it that much."

*Reason Number Four I need to break up with Foster: Beer. I hate beer, and I hate the way he smells when he drinks it.*

"It's better if I go alone." Lyndie did her best not to sound desperate, but she *was* absolutely desperate for him to *not* come to Sweethaven with her.

Foster nodded for a few seconds. "So, if you're going to be out of town, can I just stay here?"

"Without me?"

"Yeah, you won't even know I was here. Promise." He held up three fingers as if he could pass for a former boy scout.

She stuttered something unintelligible and turned away.

"Lyn?"

*Reason Number Five (and maybe the last straw): He calls me "Lyn."*

She faced him, fully prepared to tell him she was very sorry, but she didn't think it was a good idea, and, *Oh, by the way, this isn't really working out.* She'd let him down gently. Kindly. Try to keep things amicable.

But when she opened her mouth, she heard herself say, "Fine, Foster."

"Yeah?"

*That's it. I've lost my mind.*

She nodded.

"It's a party! I'm moving in." He grinned like a frat boy who'd just tapped a new keg. "You're the best, Lyn."

"Yeah, I know."

He glanced at his watch. "Whoa. I gotta go." He set his Chinese takeout container on the dresser next to his soda can.

She tried to busy herself to avoid his sloppy goodbye kiss, but as usual, Foster did not take the hint.

"Baby," he said, holding his arms open in front of him. "Get over here. I know you want some of this."

*Mind. Blank. No. Words.*

He wrapped a beefy arm around her waist, pulled her closer and leaned down, lips fumbling like a rookie quarterback in his first big game. Finally, just as she predicted, his lips left their wet and messy mark squarely on her mouth.

When he pulled away, he kept his eyes closed for too many seconds, but it gave her time to readjust the expression on her face, which was surely more *Seriously?* than *Wow, that was awesome.*

"You sure you don't want me to come to that wedding with you?"

"I'm sure. But thanks."

"All right. But if you change your mind . . ." He opened the door. "Just leave me a key under the mat outside before you go."

Once he'd gone, Lyndie brushed her teeth, trying to remove every trace of him from her face. It sort of worked. She plopped down face-first on the couch and buried her head in the pillows, where she could finally let out one muffled scream followed by another. One more for good measure, and she thought she'd gotten most of it out.

She flipped over and stared at the ceiling. "What am I doing?" She spoke the words aloud, but there was no one to hear them. No one to respond. No one to point her in the right direction.

She was an adult now. Time to get on with life and start acting like one.

That was it. She'd break up with Foster as soon as she got back from Sweethaven.

Maybe.

# Chapter Seven

Early Friday, Tucker pulled into the garage of his sprawling ranch house and parked next to his Lexus. He got out of the Jeep, still dripping from his morning swim in the ocean.

He dreaded what the day held.

He'd messed up so many times in his life, but the mistakes he'd made in Sweethaven still haunted him today. In spite of all he'd done to get his life on track.

It took only a split-second to remember how it felt to bottom out (twice) before finally cleaning up his act. He didn't want to revisit rock bottom. It would take every shred of willpower to get through the next week.

Jade didn't understand that, though. She hadn't known him then, thank God. Those days of too much alcohol and too many women were long gone, but he could trace their beginning straight back to Sweethaven. His old demons would be waiting for him as soon as he crossed the town line.

How was he supposed to survive without his morning ritual? Without the ocean? Without the time to clear his head? How would he think straight in a place that would surely send his mind tumbling? Who would keep him accountable when Pastor Kyle was thousands of miles across the country?

"It'll be so good for you to get away," Jade had told him. "I've been working for you for three years, and you've never once taken a vacation. Have you ever heard of one of those?"

He'd ignored her. When you worked in his industry, every day could feel like a vacation, especially now that his business had grown large enough to hire out all the things he'd hated doing when he first started out. Accounting, scheduling, billing, taxes, answering phones, hunting down leads, marketing, building his brand. Employees handled it all, which left Tucker wonderfully free to live the life he'd dreamed of.

*Should feel a little better than it does,* he thought.

He hadn't expected his business to take off like it did, not so quickly. But with a few key clients and repeat customers, he'd found word of mouth was his best friend.

It didn't escape him that the growth hadn't started until his second year, which was (not-so-coincidentally) around the same time he'd gotten clean.

He was doing well. He'd made a real life for himself, one that any man would be proud of.

And yet, memories still sometimes tormented him, most of which he'd be forced to face in a few short hours.

How would he deal with any of it?

He walked into the house through the garage and stripped off his wet clothes in the mudroom, inhaling that new-house smell. This room had been his most brilliant change to the original house plans— the mudroom had wall-to-wall tile and a shower that kept him from tracking sand and dirt through the house, no matter how messy the adventure.

He rinsed the sand from his body in the shower, then wrapped a towel around his waist and tossed his trunks in the laundry room next door, hanging the wet suit on the hooks beside the back door.

"You're all packed!" Jade's voice echoed through the house.

"Great."

She knew after one too many uncomfortable run-ins not to come back to the mudroom till he had time to pull on a pair of sweatpants. It embarrassed her more than him, and her boyfriend didn't much appreciate it.

Tucker traded the towel for the sweats he'd left on top of the dryer before going out that morning. All part of his routine.

A routine he'd grown to love. He clung to it. It kept him sane. And clean.

The dread returned. More than a week without routine—was he ready? Or was he walking into a minefield?

"Your plane ticket is printed here, but I also sent it to your phone. I checked you in already. Do you have your license?"

"Somewhere." He found her in the chef's kitchen, standing at the marble counter, rummaging through the man purse he'd finally given in and purchased. Business owners had too much stuff to lug around not to have some kind of bag, and Jade promised him it didn't call his masculinity into question.

He wasn't so sure.

"Not funny, Jacobs," Jade said. "Your wallet is right here." She held it up. "I'm putting it in the outside pocket."

"I should make you come with me." Tucker grabbed a bottle of water from the stainless-steel refrigerator. "See for yourself what you got me into."

Jade shrugged, obviously not concerned. She reached into her bag and pulled out the mail. "You didn't read your mail at all this week."

She slid a stack of envelopes—probably all bills—across the counter.

"I'll look at it on the plane," Tucker said.

"No, you should look at it now." Jade turned and opened the refrigerator, helping herself to some water too. Or was she avoiding his eyes?

He glanced down at the stack and saw a letter addressed to him in familiar penmanship.

He'd know his mother's cursive anywhere.

He picked it up and turned it over. Jade had already opened it, same way she opened every piece of mail that came to his office.

"You never told me you had a sister," she said, turning back around.

Tucker bristled at her words. He hadn't told her because he didn't want to talk about it. His eyes scanned the card. A memorial service would never be a memorial service with Karen Jacobs in charge. Instead, she'd called it a "celebration of life."

For Cassie.

"It's Thursday," Jade said quietly. "I set up an alert in your phone." She watched him, as if waiting for some sign of sadness. People often reacted this way when they found out his sister had died.

"You don't have to get all morbid," Tucker said, blowing it off. "It's not like she died yesterday."

"Tucker . . ."

"Sorry," he said. "It's just that she's been gone a long time. I don't know why my mom has to bring it all back up now."

"Maybe it'll be good for you?" Jade opened her bottle of water and took a drink.

"I'm fine," he said, knowing he was definitely not fine.

Cassie's death was ten years ago, but it still had a hold on him, didn't it? Sure, to everyone else, it seemed like he'd gotten his act together, but there were things that had happened, things no one knew about. Would he ever be able to let any of it go?

"Your mom was really nice, Tucker. You should call her more."

He tossed his head back and drank half his bottle of water before meeting her gaze. "She's cast a spell on you, I can see it."

"Funny." She frowned. "You need to go. I don't know why you're acting like you've got all the time in the world. Your flight is in less than two hours."

"The airport is twenty minutes away." He finished off the bottle of water. "Plenty of time."

Jade rolled her eyes. "Just hurry up, will you?"

*No. I can't rush to go back there when it's the last place in the world I want to be.*

"Go get dressed, Tucker, come on."

He glanced at Jade, who was squinting at something on her phone. "Hey," he said, "I'm sorry I snapped at you the other day."

"I already forgot about it." Jade had a way of letting his little tantrums roll off her back, but that didn't mean it was okay.

"Did you buy yourself something?"

"I bought you a new wallet," she said. "Yours was falling apart."

He eyed her for a few seconds.

"And I bought myself a pair of shoes."

Tucker grinned. "Good."

"Go." She pointed toward the door.

"Calm down, bossy." Tucker reluctantly left the kitchen. He made his way down the hallway toward his bedroom, his bare feet slapping on the hardwood floor. He'd installed those floors himself. He'd done a lot of the work renovating this house himself. Anything he could do without sacrificing excellence—and even then, he'd watched the carpenters, asked questions and tried to learn what he could so if he ever decided to build a house from the ground up, he could do it on his own.

The floor had turned out especially nice. Dark stain on hand-scraped wood throughout the entire space. Jade had found some interior designer to pull the place together. She knew Tucker so well by now that they'd barely consulted him—and still managed to nail the aesthetic he was going for perfectly.

Last month, *San Diego Magazine* had done a feature on him, his business and his new home. They called him one of the city's savviest businessmen bachelors, making it sound like winning him would be some woman's dream come true.

He was hardly a prize any sane person would want to take home.

They didn't know the person he'd been, and they never would. He'd perfected the fine art of telling the truth without revealing a single thing about himself.

He didn't talk about Cassie. Not to anyone. Not even to Pastor Kyle, and that man had single-handedly pulled Tucker out of a pit. Some things were better left in the past, no matter how much confessing and explaining he'd had to do to get himself clean and sober.

Cassie was the one area of his life that remained neatly tucked away.

Maybe he hadn't really dealt with it. Maybe it had been the root of a lot of his problems. But he'd found a way to move on in spite of it. That had to count for something.

He stood at the sink in his large en suite bathroom and shaved quickly, willing away the sense of dread that had settled in the pit of his stomach. How long had it been since he'd spent any time with his parents? Years. Almost as long as it had been since he'd gone back to Sweethaven. He'd also perfected the fine art of blowing his parents off.

Even at Christmas. And Thanksgiving.

He always had another trip planned, a business to build, a life to live. Didn't they understand he couldn't hang around in the past like a deflated balloon hovering lifelessly overhead while time marched on?

He splashed water on his face, rinsing off the shaving cream in the sink before turning on the water in the shower—almost too hot to stand, just the way he liked it.

So maybe he wasn't as well-adjusted as he'd made himself believe.

Steam filled the tiled shower, clouding the glass doors. He stepped in and washed his hair, willing away the train of thought. He leaned against the wall as the hot water ran down his face. Why had he agreed to this? When he'd found out where the wedding was being held—and when—he should've told Travis he couldn't do it.

He'd had breakfast with Kyle just yesterday, and when the subject of his trip came up, Tucker had tried to play it off like it was no big deal. But then his mind had wandered back to the day Cassie had saved his life. He'd gone rock climbing with some buddies, but like an idiot, he hadn't worn a helmet. The fall was swift, and it knocked the wind out of him. It wasn't till hours later he realized he also had a huge knot on the back of his head.

Cassie recognized immediately that something was wrong. Apparently, he'd been mixing up his words. If she hadn't forced him into her car and driven him to the hospital, he could've died.

She'd always been so in tune with everyone around her—the best kind of person. And he'd always been the exact opposite, consumed only with himself, with instant gratification.

And when she'd needed saving, where was he?

He didn't want to think about where he'd been. Making another colossal mistake.

Eventually, he'd told Kyle that Sweethaven was where a lot of his problems started.

Kyle had eyed him from across the table. "Do you have a plan in place for that?"

Tucker had shrugged, thinking in that moment how strange it was that he'd become such good friends with a pastor after so many years of avoiding church like a child avoids homework. They'd met on the beach one day at dawn, both early morning surfers. Kyle struck up a conversation about surfboards, and Tucker showed him his prized Pyzel, which led to an intense conversation about where and when to catch the best waves.

They'd started meeting early to surf, which led to big breakfasts afterward, which ultimately led to the discovery that Kyle, the cool dude from the beach, was actually Pastor Kyle Granger. Before he knew it, Tucker was spilling (most of) his guts to Kyle, telling him about his business plans and trying to pinpoint what was going wrong.

In true pastoral form, Kyle suggested praying about it. Tucker did his best not to roll his eyes.

"Look, you've got nothing to lose," Kyle told him. "You can keep struggling and trying to do this your own way, or you can actually lay it down and let God do whatever He wants with it."

Tucker argued that God couldn't care less about him or his business, but Kyle shut that one down with a handful of scriptures and a follow-up text: Just give it a try.

Ultimately, and maybe out of desperation, Tucker decided to give it a shot. Thirty days doing things God's way. No booze. No women. And praying every day.

"But I'm not coming to church," he'd told Kyle.

"Wouldn't expect you to."

Those thirty days were a game changer. Maybe it was a coincidence that Tucker reeled in his first celebrity client, which led to more celebrity clients. Maybe it was luck that he met Jade, who swooped in and streamlined his entire scheduling system. Maybe it was just good fortune that he cleared more that month than he had in the previous six months combined.

On day thirty-one, Tucker expected Kyle to meet him with self-satisfied smugness, but the pastor couldn't have been more gracious. Never once did he say, "I told you so." Never once did he order Tucker to get to church. And never once did he bring up the fact that Tucker was still a hot mess who needed more grace and forgiveness than he knew how to ask for.

Instead, he listened as Tucker shared what had happened the past thirty days, and then he nodded and took off for the ocean. "Don't get all sappy on me, Jacobs," he hollered as he ran for the surf.

Later, Kyle explained that what Tucker had experienced was awesome, but it wasn't going to be the norm. Sometimes bad things happened. After that, Tucker did get himself to Pastor Kyle's church. It wasn't stuffy or traditional, and he found himself wanting to go back. Eventually, he even joined the worship team. If anyone from Sweethaven knew that, they'd think it was a practical joke.

But it wasn't. It meant something to him. And that worship team had been a touchstone in his life.

"The key is having a plan in place for when those things do happen," Kyle said. "You've gotta know how you're going to handle disaster before it strikes."

Tucker had nodded, of course, and then spent the next three years riding this wave of business success, keeping his romantic entanglements to a bare minimum and maybe getting a little overly confident that he'd be just fine with the tides turned.

Now, as the tides were turning again, he realized how naïve he'd been.

He should call Kyle. Come up with a plan. But then how weak would he seem? All those breakfasts after surfing, and Tucker had yet to come clean about what had happened the night Cassie died.

It would be like walking straight into the fire, going back there. He couldn't expect to emerge without burns.

More than a week in Sweethaven, haunted by a past he'd spent years trying to forget. How many people had he hurt? How many apologies should he give? How could he face anyone with any amount of dignity? They would all still see him as the boy he'd been, not as the man he'd become.

But then, maybe the man he'd become was just an act, a hopeless attempt to pretend he wasn't still floundering.

Toweling off after his shower, he threw the last of his toiletries in the bag Jade had already packed, dreading the days ahead. Days spent with his parents, his demons and a pile of regrets.

Suddenly the man he'd become felt like a distant memory, and the man he'd been like a familiar old friend.

# Chapter Eight

The flight from Nashville to Chicago took just under two hours. Lyndie rented a car at O'Hare and would have to drive another couple of hours to Sweethaven.

She'd lost count of how many times she'd driven this route growing up. It was the start of every summer. Her parents had sworn one day they'd pass the cottage on to Lyndie and the quiver of children they'd been sure she'd have by now.

But after nine years of begging her to come back to Sweethaven, and a paltry retirement fund, they'd sold their cottage, severing their tie with the small lakeside town for good.

At least she'd thought it was severed. She hadn't counted on weddings or memorial services.

If only they'd given her another few years away from this place—surely that would've made all the difference. Wouldn't it?

As she drove, her mind wandered back to the day her parents had introduced her to Cassie and Tucker.

Church picnic. Summer she turned nine.

"We have a daughter the same age." Her mother was talking to a tall, thin woman with dark hair. The other woman looked professional—more so than Lyndie's own mother. She'd later find out Karen Jacobs was a therapist. She learned that when her father cracked a joke about Karen shrinking heads, and for two straight years, Lyndie thought Cassie's mom had actually discovered a way to take big-headed people and make them normal-headed people, and that Andy Thompson, a boy in her fifth grade class, could greatly benefit from her services.

Lyndie had always been painfully shy, so when the tall woman's daughter—a big-eyed, dark-headed girl with skin turned golden by the summer sun—grinned at her, Lyndie barely responded.

"Oh, Lyndie, be nice," her mother said, always taking her shyness for unkindness.

"I'm Cassie," the dark-headed girl said. "I'm going to be a singer when I grow up."

"Lyndie loves music, don't you, sweetheart?" Her mom stared at her, wide-eyed and expectant, waiting for her daughter to overcome her quiet and actually speak. She'd always seemed so embarrassed by Lyndie's difficulty talking to new people.

Some days Lyndie still felt like that shy girl, disconnected from a world that seemed to move a hair too fast for her to keep up.

Cassie had grabbed her hand and pulled her away from their parents and said that now that they'd found each other, they could be "friends forever." She'd meant it too. Cassie had shown up on Lyndie's doorstep the very next day and asked if she wanted to go to the beach with her.

"My brother and his dumb friends will be there, but we can ignore them," she'd said, her eyes sparkling.

They'd been nearly inseparable that whole summer and every summer after that. All because Cassie had been the kind of kid who made everyone feel welcome.

Over the years, they'd traded letters, and Cassie's almost always came with some sort of gift, like handmade friendship bracelets. "I know they're kind of babyish, but if we both wear the same one, that would be cool, right?" Or a key chain she'd had custom-made with Lyndie's name on it, "because I know it's impossible to find anything that says 'Lyndie.'" Or a journal for song lyrics, "because I know you're writing them. And if you're not, you should be."

Lyndie and Cassie had been instant friends. How would she ever step foot in Sweethaven without her?

More to the point, how were Cassie's parents in Sweethaven without her? How did they still go there, knowing it was the place where Cassie had taken her last breath?

But then again, how could they not?

Now, for the first time since her parents had accepted the offer on the Sweethaven property, Lyndie wished they hadn't sold it. It might've been uncomfortable, but it still would've been ten times better than where she was headed. How was she going to face Mr. and Mrs. Jacobs? How was she going to sleep on that porch with Elle as if they were still kids? How was she going to pretend there wasn't a gaping hole in the fabric of her life, and there had been ever since Cassie's death?

And worse, how was she going to make it through the next week without thinking about the night Cassie died, every single day?

Everything had started in Sweethaven. It was the last place in the world Lyndie wanted to be.

The cracks in the road clicked underneath the tires in an even-paced staccato. She flipped on the satellite radio and found the eighties station. Mama J. had always played eighties music when cooking dinner or baking cookies.

It had turned out that as professional as Karen Jacobs was, her first job was being a mother. And she was one of the best. A fact that only made Lyndie's guilt that much harder to bear.

She pulled off the interstate, following signs to a little coffee shop that was most definitely not Starbucks. She ordered the closest thing she could find to a white-chocolate mocha and got back in the car. She had only another half hour before she arrived in Sweethaven.

Was she stalling?

A text from Dylan came in: Know you're going to be busy this week with that wedding, but get some writing time in. Your career depends on it.

Lyndie groaned and stuck the phone in the cup holder. She didn't want to think about emotionally connecting with a song right now. She turned the car back on, stared out the window and drank her coffee. "Take On Me" came on the radio.

In a flash, she was thirteen again. Technically in ninth grade, though school didn't start for a couple more months. It was the night of the Stargazers' Ball, a Sweethaven tradition they all looked forward to all summer long.

Sure, a teen dance might seem silly to a lot of people, but it was the first year Lyndie was old enough to go. And she *so* wanted to go.

When Tanner Doyle invited her, Cassie jumped in with a quick yes on Lyndie's behalf and then made plans for them all to go together. Lyndie and Tanner. Cassie and a boy named Charlie, whom she'd known since elementary school.

Lyndie was nervous. She'd gotten a new dress and went to Cassie's house so they could get ready together. Her own parents, who were part of the decorating committee, were waiting for Lyndie at the dance, where she expected they'd embarrass her with their photo taking and fawning over her.

Lyndie would let them take three photos, but that was it. Then they had to leave her alone. She wasn't a kid anymore, after all.

Around six o'clock, Lyndie and Cassie stood side by side before the full-length mirror in Cassie's room.

"You're gorgeous, Lyndie," Cassie said. "Your hair is so pretty up."

"Thanks for doing it for me. And for letting me use your makeup."

Cassie grinned. "That's what friends are for. Duh." She pushed her shoulder into Lyndie's and giggled as the doorbell rang. "They're here!"

But when Karen opened the door, only one boy stood on the porch, and it wasn't Tanner Doyle.

Charlie's cheeks were pink as he handed over a corsage.

"Where's Tanner?" Cassie asked.

Charlie shrugged. "Maybe he's running late?"

But they waited a full half an hour, and Tanner never showed.

"You guys get to the restaurant," Lyndie said. "I'll wait here. I'm sure he'll be here any minute, and we'll meet up with you."

Cassie's expression turned skeptical, but she reluctantly agreed after her own mother promised to bring Lyndie to the dance the second Tanner showed up.

An hour later, Lyndie was still sitting on the front stoop. Alone.

Mama J. had probably been staring at her back for the full sixty minutes, trying to decide if she should join her on the steps. She wouldn't want to embarrass her, Lyndie knew, but she also wouldn't want to leave her alone.

About the time Lyndie had decided to give up and walk home to her family's cottage on the other side of town, the front door opened and Cassie's mom walked out. She sat down on the steps next to Lyndie and handed over a large bowl of ice cream.

"Peppermint stick?" Lyndie asked, wiping a humiliating tear from her cheek.

"Only the best for my girl."

Lyndie gave her a halfhearted smile.

"That boy doesn't know what he's missing."

It was something mothers said at times like this, to make heartbroken girls feel better, and Lyndie supposed it worked. A little, anyway.

They'd eaten their ice cream in silence, and just sitting there beside Karen had somehow made everything better.

Mama J. had always had a way. Lyndie imagined she was a pretty great therapist, now that she understood what a "headshrinker" actually did. But she supposed it was easy to fix things like a ninth grader's wounded ego. The broken places inside her nowadays went so much deeper than that. Those—nobody could fix.

And that was exactly why she'd dreaded this trip. She didn't think these things in her normal day-to-day life. She thought about chord progressions and guitar strings. She thought about her manager and song play and iTunes and sometimes Foster, but not very often.

She never thought about the night Cassie died.

And she never, ever thought about what had happened next.

But now, how could she avoid it? The thoughts pelted her like hail on a windshield. They came hard and fast, disguised as pleasant memories.

"In Your Eyes" came on the radio, and Lyndie turned it off.

These songs would only make the memories feel more real. She forced herself to think about something—anything—else.

Jalaire. She'd think about Jalaire. Jalaire Grant needed a song. A reinvention song. A song that proved she wasn't a bubblegum pop star. A song that gave her depth.

Lyndie started humming.

Music had always filled her soul. Cassie said it flowed out of Lyndie like water from a spigot.

If only that were true now. Lately, Lyndie had to fight for every chorus, every line. She kept humming, letting the melody go where it wanted to go.

But the new song became familiar—that melody she carried around with her, a faithful companion to her sadness. She stopped humming as soon as the hook of "Cassie's Song" entered her mind. The song was unfinished—she'd never be able to find the words. And digging around for them would cost her too much. So it, like so many days-gone-by memories, stayed locked away.

Things had been so much easier before Elle's text. If only they were getting married in Chicago, none of this would be happening right now.

Lyndie flipped the radio back on and found a talk program. No memories. Just constant babble she wasn't invested in and didn't care about.

The detachment was refreshing.

And detachment, she feared, was the only way she would survive a week in Sweethaven.

One hundred percent detachment.

She detached when she spotted the town's name on a road sign, indicating she needed to take the next exit.

She detached when she took the exit and then saw the much-too-cheerful sign that read "Welcome to Sweethaven."

And she certainly detached when she saw the sign for Sweethaven Beach—knowing that just beyond it was Silver Beach. Their beach.

Hers. Cassie's. Elle's. Travis's.

And *Tucker's*.

Her heart stuttered at the very thought of him. She'd mostly trained herself not to think of Tucker when she was fully conscious. But sometimes her mind betrayed her and he'd show up in her dreams.

Cassie's older brother had been the one guy Lyndie'd sworn to never fall in love with. Never mind that she'd made that promise when she was twelve with absolutely no idea how beautiful Tucker would become.

And Tucker had been to Lyndie what his best friend, Travis, had been to Cassie. The kind of first love a girl never forgets.

By the time she'd finished her freshman year of high school, Lyndie realized her silly little crush on Tucker had turned into something more. Two years older, Tucker was flirtatious and dangerous, the kind of guy who could (and did) date any girl he wanted.

He was confident. Fearless. And far too good-looking.

When Lyndie, Elle and Cassie came home after a night out, they'd always find Karen sitting in her recliner or on the back deck, waiting with that anxious expression on her face. Somehow even then, Lyndie knew the expression had nothing to do with the girls and everything to do with the fact that Tucker still had an hour until his curfew.

And Karen would stay up waiting to be sure he got in safe.

What would Karen say if she knew where her son had been the night Cassie died?

What would Karen think if she knew who he was with?

All those years of worrying he and Travis and Dewey and the rest of the boys were going to get into trouble, and when it came down to it, it hadn't been any of them who'd influenced her son. At least not that night.

Lyndie had never breathed a word about her feelings for Tucker—she'd never told a single soul. Some of the popular girls had pretended to be friends with Cassie to get to him, and Lyndie had promised she'd never do that.

But that was years ago now. She was a different person. More resilient. She'd learned how to keep herself from thinking about people like Tucker. It would be easy to put him out of her mind, even if she had to see him face-to-face.

And in a matter of days, maybe even hours, she *would* have to see him face-to-face.

Ten years had gone by.

Ten years, and she still wasn't ready to see him.

*Detach. Detach. Detach.*

She drove down Main Street, the brick pavers kerplunking underneath her tires. While Sweethaven had seen some updates, so much of the town seemed frozen in time. The gazebo. The old-fashioned streetlamps. The old wooden carousel down by the lake. The striped awnings over the shops.

Familiarity—a sense of belonging—seeped into her bones, maneuvering its way under her skin, and though she'd been gone a decade and had done her best to empty every notion of this place from her memory, it took only a moment for it all to come rushing back.

And it was dangerous. She needed to get that wall up—higher, taller, sturdier than usual.

"You're going to have a hard time here, Lyndie," she said aloud. "You're going to have to prepare yourself."

She drew in a deep breath and asked a God she hardly ever talked to anymore for strength, something she seemed especially low on. She followed the signs to Sweethaven Beach, though she didn't need them to get her there. She moved as if by muscle memory to the exact location where she'd grown up.

She bypassed downtown, choosing instead to take a parallel street— much quieter and not nearly as much a risk of setting her mind racing again.

She passed the public beach and kept going, about a mile down the road.

There wasn't even a sign for Silver Beach—it was a hidden gem only the locals knew about. Lyndie parked the car at the top of the dune and finished off her mocha.

Midday. June. What if this beach had been discovered by tourists? What if it was crawling with children and families and teenage boys?

She groaned at the thought, which almost made her turn back.

But she had to see the water. It had been so long . . .

While the public beach had an entry point—a long set of wooden planks that created a stairway down to the water—Silver Beach had a dune, thick with sand that baked in the summer sun. Stepping out of the car, Lyndie took her shoes off then stared out across the water, the view stealing her breath.

One scan of the beach told her it was still secret, as if it were reserved for summer residents and locals. People who, in her mind, had claim to the white-capped waves that reminded her of the ocean.

She started down the side of the dune, her feet struggling to find firm footing as the ground shifted beneath her weight. She grabbed on to branches, roots, trees—anything that gave her a bit of leverage— until, finally, she slid to the bottom.

She took a moment to catch her breath, and only then did she wonder how she'd manage to climb back up the dune. It had been much easier when she was a child. No wonder this beach was so empty.

*So here we are again,* she thought. *You and me.*

It had been ten years since she'd seen that water, the backdrop of her childhood, but within seconds, she was tumbling in the chaos of remembering.

She'd loved this lake. She'd loved this beach. Even as a child, she'd been enamored with it, the way it stretched on as far as she could see. With every summer that passed, her love for it only grew. It was familiar. Comfortable. Home.

Until that night.

So far, she really sucked at this whole detachment thing.

Lyndie started for the water, the sand scorching in the sun's heat. She threw her sandals down and pushed her feet into them; a layer of sand clung to her feet, chafing her skin as she walked. In the distance, she saw sailboats. Water lapped onto the shore, covering her feet, then her ankles, with coolness.

The lake stretched in front of her like a giant screen, replaying all the memories of a life that seemed so far away now.

*Cassie, I know you're out there somewhere. I'm so sorry.*

Off to her right, three young girls walked arm in arm down the shoreline. They wore bathing suits and ponytails and tossed their heads back when they laughed.

Once upon a time, that had been her and Cassie and Elle.

It was only yesterday.

It was a lifetime ago.

The seagulls called out to each other overhead, turning Lyndie back toward the water. In the distance, she could see the boardwalk, the marina, the carousel. She'd grown up here. She'd eaten cotton candy and corn on the cob and walking tacos. She'd convinced her dad to give her money for Skee-Ball, and she'd ridden the carousel more times than she could count. They'd all docked at the marina and played hide-and-seek on the boats.

It all felt so foreign to her now. Her life had faded into vague recollections, like photos in an old scrapbook.

A warm breeze pulled strands of her hair from the loose braid at the side of her head. She watched the waves, unmoving, feeling like an outsider observing an unfamiliar scene.

"First time back?"

The voice came from behind her, and while she couldn't see the man who'd asked the question, she recognized the voice.

Ten years later, and it could still stop her heart.

*Tucker.*

He didn't wait for her to turn, but came up to the water, next to her. His shoulder brushed against hers.

She was instantly eighteen again, unable to stop the onslaught of nerves.

She dared a glance. He stared down the shoreline in the opposite direction, giving her time to study him unnoticed. He wore a faded gray T-shirt and navy-blue board shorts. He still had that same sandy-colored hair, though he wore it longer now, and his face was a little fuller than back in those days, looking less like a boy and more like a man. His skin was bronze, the way Cassie's always was in the summer. He practically glowed. Somehow the years had only made him more attractive.

Unfair.

He glanced back at her, probably wondering why she hadn't responded.

The eyes—steel blue with flecks of gray. No wonder she hadn't said a word. How could she?

"Hey." He was tall, sturdy, strong. Lyndie wondered what it was like to be any of those things. Her strength had always been a front.

Anyone could see right through it if she let them get close enough to her. She never did.

"I didn't think I'd ever see you again." She stared in front of her, eyes locked on a small boat in the distance.

*I didn't think you ever wanted to see me again.*

"Wanna swim?" he asked.

She shook her head. "My suit's in the car under a whole lot of junk."

Besides, swimming felt so . . . carefree. She didn't.

"You're missing out." He pulled off his T-shirt, and Lyndie did her best not to stare. She failed.

"Where'd you get all those?" She pointed to his stomach.

"All what?"

"All those . . . abs." Lyndie felt a blush rise to her cheeks as she realized what she'd said. What did she think, there was an ab store out there where you could go in and pick up a six-pack?

He grinned. "Last chance."

She gave her head a slight shake. "Another time."

He kicked off his flip-flops and ran a hand through his hair, its unruly natural state suiting him well.

And as he jogged into the water, he took her resolve right along with her.

Suddenly, detaching felt like a pipe dream.

# Chapter Nine

Karen stood on the front stoop of her cottage and shook out the rug from the entryway. They'd painted the porch a light gray last summer, and she was pleased to see it had held up nicely. The last week had been spent cleaning and making plans for the celebration. She'd rented out the entire park next to Sweethaven Chapel, including two shelters and the little church. There weren't many people coming, but enough to make the party too big for their backyard.

Less than one week from today, it would be ten years since she'd lost Cassie.

Ten years.

She'd be twenty-eight now. Maybe she would've fallen in love. Surely, she would've had her heart broken, probably a few times. She might be the one planning a wedding or traveling the world, working her way up the corporate ladder, singing in a stadium.

But Karen would never know.

The celebration of life had been her idea—a way to bring closure to an event that had left them all undone. Their entire family had splintered the day Cassie died, and they'd never been able to put the pieces back together.

Was she hoping for too much?

Davis seemed to think she should adjust her expectations. But then, Davis never seemed to expect much of anything these days.

While she'd initially bristled at the date of the wedding (and all of Nora Preston's planned activities), she'd eventually decided to embrace it. Not only because it was what a good mother would do, but because it gave them all a happier reason to reunite, which could unravel the knot Karen had been carrying around inside herself for the past ten years.

One thing was for sure: time didn't heal all wounds. Some were still every bit as fresh as the day they were inflicted.

How was she supposed to *just move on*, after all, without her daughter? It wasn't like Cassie was distant or out of touch. She was gone.

Karen dropped the rug. When she went to pick it back up, she spotted Davis down the road in his golf cart. He spent a lot of time out on the course—alone. She'd joined him a few times, another sad attempt to force conversation, but mostly she felt like she was in the way, interrupting some sort of sacred ritual he'd created for himself.

Whatever he thought about while logging hours smacking that ball around, she'd never know. Cassie's death seemed to have severed the connection between Davis and Karen. Some days she wondered why they were still married at all.

They were like strangers. Sometimes when he smiled or laughed or told a buddy a joke or funny story, she found herself resenting his normalcy. How could he move on as if everything was fine? Some days she wondered if Davis missed Cassie at all.

Did he remember the way her buoyant laugh could fill the whole house?

The oven timer went off behind Karen. She left the rug in the entryway and raced into the kitchen. She didn't want to overbake the oatmeal butterscotch cookies. Tucker's favorite.

Tucker was coming home.

According to Jade, his flight was today. Karen had a whole meal planned—pork chops on the grill, mashed potatoes, watermelon and corn on the cob. All her son's favorite things. The cookies were a last-minute bonus.

It felt good to be mothering again. How long had it been since she'd had anyone but Davis to take care of? And half the time, he took care of himself, something most wives would appreciate, but Karen found it made her feel useless.

She didn't know who she was without people to take care of.

As she pulled the cookies from the oven, she inhaled their cinnamon aroma and realized her willpower might take a hit in the next week. It'd be easy to convince herself she deserved to indulge in food she rarely let herself eat—especially on a week like this.

A knock on the door drew her attention away from the cookies and onto the porch. Davis was outside and could've intercepted any visitors, but he must've stopped along the way to talk to one of the neighbors. That man could go on for hours about lawn care and garbage pickup and the weasel that had made its home in their backyard.

But some topics had the opposite effect on him. Off-limits topics, like how it felt to pretend they weren't falling apart.

Through the screen door, she saw a young woman with wavy blond hair and a slender, almost boyish build.

*Lyndie.*

Karen hadn't seen her in years, but she recognized her immediately. How would it feel to have her here without Cassie? Karen prayed this wasn't a mistake. She had to be strong—who knew how the kids were holding up?

She rushed to the door and enveloped her daughter's best friend in a hug that undoubtedly revealed her loneliness.

Lyndie stiffened a little at her touch, but Karen held on anyway. After several seconds, the younger woman softened in Karen's arms. How long had it been since someone hugged Lyndie like this? Karen knew from talking to Susan that her daughter didn't get home very often.

When she pulled away, she looked at Lyndie through clouded eyes.

Karen sniffed, blinking back the tears that always seemed ready to fall. "I think I'll be doing a lot of that this weekend."

"It's been too long," Lyndie said. Her eyes had lost their sparkle, and Karen suddenly realized the years had gone by in a blink. She should've been better about staying in touch. Lyndie and Elle had both meant so much to her, but after Cassie died, it was like Karen had lost the right to be in their lives. Surely they didn't want their best friend's mother checking in on them—or maybe that's a lie she'd believed to let herself off the hook.

It was hard to feel so displaced.

Looking at Lyndie now, Karen regretted letting her slip away. She should've insisted those girls stay in her family—with or without Cassie.

"You're all grown up," Karen said, opening the door wider and motioning for Lyndie to come inside. "I'm so glad you're here."

"I hope I'm not imposing. I saw Tucker down on the beach, and I'm sure you guys will all want to spend time together as a family. Elle and I can make ourselves scarce." Lyndie dropped her bag on the floor of the entryway next to the heap of rug Karen had abandoned earlier.

Karen stilled at the mention of her son's name. "You saw Tucker?"

"I stopped at the beach before I came here." Lyndie's face changed as she searched Karen's eyes.

It was too late to pretend she'd already seen Tucker, that of course her son had come here first, that she knew he was at the beach.

"I think he was going for a swim," Lyndie added, her voice quiet.

Karen looked away. Why hadn't he come by the house when he'd gotten into town? Why had he gone straight for the beach?

"I'm sorry," Lyndie said.

Karen lifted her chin. "No, don't be. You know Tucker—he's always got to be doing something, usually something dangerous." As much as she hated it. "Did you know he has his own business now?"

Lyndie shook her head. "We haven't stayed in touch."

"He's got a whole website and everything. It's called Adventure Seekers. I suppose you'd have no reason to look that up, though, would you?" Karen was proud that Tucker was doing well, making a good living, living a clean life—but the way he did it still unnerved her.

"Anyway," she said, "this gives us girls a chance to catch up and get you settled. And no more talk of making yourselves scarce. You know you and Elle *are* family." Her eyes fell to Lyndie's suitcase. "You must be tired from the drive."

"I'm okay."

Karen picked up the luggage and motioned for Lyndie to follow her. "Let's take this stuff upstairs and let you rest a bit before dinner."

"Are you sure I'm not putting you out?"

*No. It will be nice to have someone else to talk to for a change. Someone who talks back.*

Karen tossed a glance over her shoulder. "Not a chance. I love to take care of my kids."

As soon as she'd said the words, Lyndie's face fell. Karen refocused her attention in front of her, new thoughts of Cassie whirling through her mind.

So far, this celebration of life felt anything but festive.

Lyndie followed Cassie's mom up the familiar staircase, surrounded by images of her best friend. Photos of years gone by lined the stairway—Cassie's smiling face at the center of most of them.

Funny how a photograph made time stand still.

If only life would allow Lyndie to do the same.

Lyndie slowed as Karen continued on upstairs, her eyes skimming the images as she reached the hallway. She landed on a framed photo of her and Cassie just after their senior year of high school, only a month before the accident. They faced the camera, both holding stuffed bears (the Belmont mascot)—gifts from their parents, who were so excited they were heading off to school together that fall.

Because they didn't live in the same town, Lyndie and Cassie had never attended school together, so since they both planned to study music, the choice seemed natural. Of course they'd go together. They would room together, watch out for each other, finish growing up together.

Instead, Lyndie had found herself in that tiny yet suddenly gigantic dorm room, empty and hollow and alone. She'd never felt so alone.

It took the university a full semester to send her a replacement roommate—a girl named Tabitha, whose first question to Lyndie was "You don't mind if my boyfriend sleeps over sometimes, do you?"

By second semester, Lyndie hadn't cared about much of anything, not after the previous six months. When she thought now of what she'd endured—all by herself—she wondered how she'd managed to graduate at all.

"You two," Karen said, now standing at her side and following her gaze to the photo Lyndie seemed unable to stop looking at. Karen touched it with a smile. "I miss her every day."

Lyndie looked away. "Did you put me in Cassie's old room?"

"Is that too weird?"

*Yes.*

"Of course not," Lyndie said.

"I put your suitcase in there for you," Karen said. "Elle can take the guest room downstairs or bunk up here with you, whatever you girls prefer. I figure you may both end up out on the sleeping porch anyway." She smiled, probably remembering all those mornings she'd found them all out there after a late night.

"I'll try not to wander around your house in the middle of the night," Lyndie said, smiling.

"Oh, it's just us and Tucker," she said. "Feel free to wander."

Right. Tucker. Probably not smart to wander anywhere near that one.

"Why don't you freshen up? We'll eat in about an hour."

Lyndie nodded a thank-you as Karen left her standing in the middle of the hallway. She watched the woman leave, still the picture of strength and grace. Who did a therapist confide in when her world shattered? Or maybe Karen didn't need confidantes, because she'd learned all the right things to say to herself to keep from falling apart.

Once Cassie's mom disappeared down the stairs, Lyndie caught a glimpse of the room across the hall.

*Tucker.*

When was the last time he'd been there? She should've asked. Not that it was any of her business. And not that she should care.

But she did care.

And there was the rub.

Gently, she pushed the door open. She wouldn't pretend she hadn't seen his room before. She had. More than once, when Cassie wasn't looking. She'd excuse herself to the bathroom and sneak a peek, hopeful for something—anything—that could connect her to her best friend's brother.

Looking at the room now, it was hard to believe even a day had passed. It looked exactly as she remembered it . . . gray walls, a quilt in varying shades of blue on the full-sized bed, plush rugs spread over wide-planked white hardwood floors. Tucker had decorated his walls with photographs of his favorite sports, action shots that likely inspired him to give in to his daredevilish desires.

Lyndie moved toward the built-in desk and bookshelves over in the corner. On each shelf was a collection of trophies and medals, and tacked to a bulletin board were photos, ticket stubs, and the usual paraphernalia—but all of it was at least ten years old.

It was like Tucker's room had been carefully preserved—frozen in time. When was the last time anyone had even stepped foot in it?

The sound of the front door opening sent a jolt of adrenaline through her veins, and Lyndie scooted out the door and into Cassie's room. Once she was safely behind the closed door, she shut her eyes and let out the breath she'd been holding. A few deep breaths later, she opened her eyes, unprepared for the effect of seeing her friend's bedroom, like Tucker's, preserved just as it had been when they were younger.

They'd painted the walls that happy yellow color the summer before high school. Cassie'd said she needed a change, and everyone thought the yellow suited her personality.

Everyone was right.

Lyndie closed her eyes and she was back there, standing barefoot in the empty room, rolling primer over the lavender walls that felt too "babyish" for a high schooler. She still couldn't believe Mama J. had let them paint the room on their own, but they'd done a pretty good job . . . except . . .

Lyndie walked over to the large window at the left of the room and pulled back the cushion on the window seat to reveal several drops of yellow paint they'd inadvertently splattered while trying to coat the six-inch space between the trim and the ceiling.

Cassie's mom had discovered it while hanging the cheery floral curtains, but she hadn't even gotten upset. "Guess I'm going to have to make a cushion for this window seat now." She'd smiled, like it was no big deal.

That's how Karen Jacobs had always been. Nothing really ruffled her feathers.

Under different circumstances, maybe Lyndie would've confided in her. Maybe Karen would've had just the piece of advice she needed. Maybe Lyndie wouldn't have had to make decisions—life-and-death ones—on her own.

But circumstances hadn't been different. Cassie was gone. Karen had been grieving. Lyndie had been broken. And the rest of it was in the past.

Where it belonged.

So far, though, her box wasn't holding up very well. The past was seeping into the present, and she was helpless to stop it.

She set the cushion back in its place and sat down on the window seat, admiring the white quilt with orange, pink and yellow flowers on the full-sized built-in bed. It was surrounded by bookshelves on either side, still housing Cassie's large collection. Canvases she'd painted with her favorite quotes, and even one with song lyrics Lyndie had written back in high school. Over Cassie's built-in desk, a bulletin board like Tucker's was full of photos and mementos, though there wasn't a single athletic trophy or ribbon anywhere to be seen. Cassie and Lyndie were the same that way. Far more into their music than any game involving a ball.

A photo on the bulletin board caught her eye—a picture of the two of them on what had turned out to be one of the best nights of Lyndie's life.

Lyndie didn't have the larger-than-life personality that Cassie had, so when her friend had gotten the brilliant idea that they should start a band the summer after freshman year of high school, Lyndie hadn't gone along with it at first. But Cassie could be so persuasive.

Lyndie smiled at the memory. All those years of forced piano lessons suddenly had a purpose. Cassie was such a leader—and once she had an idea, she didn't give up until she made it happen. Once Lyndie realized this, she knew it made no sense to protest.

Their first practice was in the Jacobs' garage. Lyndie showed up expecting Cassie but found Tucker and his friend Dewey instead.

"My mom made cookies," Tucker said with an eye roll. "Cassie ran inside to get them."

Lyndie stood awkwardly in the doorway. "She didn't mention you guys would be here."

"You can't have a band without a drummer and a bass player," Dewey said.

"What kind of dirt does she have on you to get you to agree to this?"

Tucker half smiled. "She told us with your songs, we could actually be famous."

"She didn't say that," Lyndie said, half-mortified, half-flattered.

"Yes, she did," Dewey said. "I figure the only chance I'll ever have at getting famous is if I hang around you three. So, I'm in."

Lyndie had no desire to be famous. She just had songs trapped inside her.

Yet as normal conversations went, Lyndie thought this one was going pretty well. She hadn't said anything stupid yet, so that was a plus.

She glanced at Tucker. "And you?"

He grinned. "Cassie doesn't know any of my dirt."

A scoff from Dewey. "Everyone knows your dirt, Tuck."

It was true. Tucker was a favorite topic of the Sweethaven rumor mill.

"Lyndie, you're here!" Cassie appeared in the doorway that led to the laundry room at the side of the cottage. She held a plate of cookies, which Dewey and Tucker promptly attacked. "Did you bring the song?"

Lyndie's face flushed. It didn't matter that neither of the guys was even paying attention. In that moment, she felt exposed.

"I'm not sure that's a good idea, Cass. Maybe we could start with a classic. Something everyone already knows."

"We're not going to be another lame cover band." Cassie handed Tucker the plate and walked over to her. "Original music. That's what we said."

"That's what *you* said," Lyndie told her. "I'm still not sure how I feel about that."

"It's fine, sis," Cassie said with her trademark grin. "This is a safe place."

Lyndie's eyes darted to Tucker, who'd shoved a whole cookie into his mouth. He took his seat behind a set of drums, still wonderfully oblivious that Lyndie had any kind of feelings for him. But this song Cassie wanted her to share—it revealed everything. What if he figured it out?

Worse, what if Cassie figured it out?

"Come on, Lyndie," Cassie said. "Get your guitar out. Lead sheets. Let's go."

Reluctantly, Lyndie handed over a sheet of paper with the printed lyrics, chords handwritten above the words, and strapped her guitar around her shoulder.

"It's called 'If Only,'" Cassie said. "It's amazing. You guys will pick it up in no time. Sing it, Lyndie."

Lyndie felt her eyes go wide. "You're the singer."

"You're *also* a singer," Cassie said. She could be so bossy. "Just remind me of the melody." She strummed the first chord of the song on her own guitar and waited for Lyndie to jump in.

After a long pause, Dewey said, "We can't play it if you don't teach it to us."

Lyndie turned away and finally strummed the A chord herself. She hummed a bit of the melody, then her fingers moved over the strings the way she'd practiced a thousand times. Instantly, she was transported— that was the magic of music. At least for her. It had a sort of power over her, the ability to take her outside of herself, if only for a moment.

That phrase was actually a lyric in the song.

She closed her eyes and started with the first verse. By the time she reached the chorus, there was a steady drumbeat underneath her melody. She opened her eyes and found Tucker watching her—trying to follow along, she assumed. Though a part of her let herself believe, just for a moment, that he watched her out of intrigue. That he was imagining, like she was, that there could ever be something more between them.

She moved on to the bridge, surprised that Tucker followed. Was her song predictable?

Cassie jumped in, singing some of her classic harmonies, which left only Dewey staring at the chord charts with confusion on his face.

Lyndie ended the song with a nod. The five seconds of silence that followed were excruciating. She turned away again, her heart pounding. Finally, after what felt like an eternity, Cassie let out a cheer (as only she could).

"That was awesome!" she shouted. "Didn't I tell you guys she's amazing?"

"You weren't wrong," Dewey said.

Lyndie faced them—cheeks flushed, she was sure, with the rush of adrenaline and embarrassment. She found Tucker's eyes, and realized it was his approval she was really after.

"I think the drums really made that song," he said, that lazy grin peeling across his face.

Cassie rolled her eyes, then turned to Lyndie. "It was awesome, Lyndie! We're gonna win Battle of the Bands for sure!"

And they did. They won! With her song!

And it was all because of Cassie. So many good things in Lyndie's life had been because of Cassie.

Now, staring at so many photos of her bright-eyed friend, Lyndie felt the defenses around her crumbling. But she'd grown strong as she'd gotten older—at least, much stronger than when she'd last been here. It would serve her well to remember that.

Never mind that she had a knack for dating guys with very few redeeming qualities (see: Foster Swinson). Despite that and a few other poor choices she'd made along the way, she was a competent, self-sufficient adult.

Lyndie grabbed Cassie's pillow, put it at the end of the bed and let her head fall back on it, filling her nostrils with the smell of the fabric softener that Mama J. used.

She stared at the white ceiling fan gently spinning in a soft circle, whirring back to simpler days when she lay in the same spot, Cassie on one side, Elle on the other, three sets of feet up on the wall.

What would Elle and Cassie say if they met Foster? Elle would likely tell her whatever she wanted to hear—because that's what Elle did. But Cassie?

Lyndie could only imagine . . .

She closed her eyes and it was like Cassie was there, next to her, feet up on the wall beside hers.

"I'm not a fan," Cassie would say. "This guy couldn't possibly be good enough for you. He's a distraction. You need to focus on your career now. Jalaire Grant is a huge deal."

"Foster is a decent guy," Lyndie said quietly.

"You can't tell me you love this guy."

"Who said anything about love?" Lyndie said. "I'm not looking for love."

"So, you only date guys you have no chance of falling in love with. Why do you think that is?"

"That's absurd."

"Is it? Tell me about the last five guys you dated."

Lyndie opened her eyes with a start and found the room empty. She sat up and looked at the spot next to her on the bed.

Even her own imagination was turning on her.

Ridiculous. What a stupid thing to think. Of course she wanted to fall in love. Was it her fault the last five guys she'd dated turned out to be all wrong?

Jared Kent—tall, lanky, bad personal hygiene.

Terrance Showalter—obsessed with video games.

Wes Charles—still lived with his mother.

Logan Sullivan—drunk 95 percent of the time.

And Foster Swinson—called her "baby."

"See?" Cassie was back. She stared at the ceiling, her dark hair cascading around her on the bed. "No chance of loving any of those guys. Why do you keep dating men who don't deserve you?"

Lyndie stilled. "What makes you think they don't deserve me?" she whispered.

"Because you're Lyndie St. James. Up-and-coming songwriter and all-around gorgeous girl. Smart. Funny. Kind. You've always made every good choice, Lyndie. Maybe if I made better choices, I'd still be here today."

Lyndie steeled herself against the imaginary words that pummeled her as an all-too-timely text came in from Foster.

I know you're missing me, baby. Here's a picture of me in your apartment.

Lyndie sighed as a photo appeared underneath the text. Foster, on her sofa with a bottle of beer in one hand and the remote on his chest.

"See? Not good enough for you." Cassie's voice rang through her mind.

Everyone thought Lyndie was one thing, but she was very much something else. If any of them knew that, what would they say?

She prayed they never found out.

# Chapter Ten

"Lyndie?"

Her eyes fluttered open, and it took her a moment to realize she'd dozed off. In Cassie's room.

Mama J. stood over her, a gentle smile on her otherwise weary face. "You fell asleep."

Lyndie sat upright in the bed. Somewhere in the midst of her imaginary conversation with Cassie, she'd actually pulled the covers over herself and fallen asleep that way, the same way she, Elle and Cassie used to. She hardly remembered doing that. "Sorry, I must've been really tired."

*And being here is killing me.*

"I thought you might be hungry," Karen said. "Come down for dinner?"

Lyndie swallowed, her throat dry. She nodded. "I'll be right down."

Karen stood still for several seconds, as if she had more to say. Lyndie's heart flip-flopped until she reminded herself of two things: *One, I'm strong now. And, two, she doesn't know what happened.*

Her cheeks flushed at the thought of it, and she was thankful that despite what their parents said, none of them really could read their minds.

"I'll see you down there." Karen finally walked out.

Lyndie closed her eyes and heaved a sigh. She could tell herself as much as she wanted that she was strong now, but if she still felt weak, the words were pointless.

She forced herself to sit up. Tucker would be here by now. She'd have to sit across from him at dinner and pretend, the same way she'd pretended when she was a foolish high school girl.

*I'm stronger now.*

The words still felt empty. With clammy hands and a pounding heart, she made her way to the kitchen, the sound of Cassie's laughter ringing through her mind like a distant melody. The memories haunted her. She hadn't realized how many were still there until she peeled back the surface and let a few of them out. Now, she felt paralyzed by their attentiveness to her.

The kitchen had been updated, but only slightly. It still had that same cottage charm Lyndie remembered. Air from open windows flowed through the room and into the dining room—a casual space surrounded on three sides by windows. The light of the sinking sun streamed in, making the house warm and cheerful and exactly the opposite of the way she felt.

Growing up, this kitchen had always been the hub of activity. The smell of cinnamon filled the room, just like it used to. Cassie's mom might have been a working mother, but during the summer, her full attention was on the kids, and that meant lots of time right here—in the heart of the home. Now, Lyndie could sense that the heart had been wounded.

A drab stillness hung in the air. A thick cloud of silence hovered overhead. The thought of it stung. This house had been their safe place. It had been full of laughter, of endless chatter, of so much love.

What had happened to the Jacobs family?

What had happened to all of them?

She passed through the kitchen and found Cassie's parents seated in the adjacent dining area. Four places had been set, but Lyndie breathed a sigh of relief when she discovered Tucker's seat was empty.

Her eyes found Karen, who appeared to stare at the empty spot across from her. Though the older woman wore a strong expression, there was unmistakable grief behind her eyes. Lyndie recognized that look.

Was she remembering the melody of Cassie's laughter too?

Lyndie cleared her throat as she approached, not wanting to make things uncomfortable, and the noise seemed to shake Karen back to the here and now.

"Lyndie, come in."

Mr. Jacobs stood and opened his arms to her. "Lyndie."

She stepped into his embrace, and a flood of memories rolled through her mind. Watching fireworks on the Fourth of July out on the family's boat. The time she backed out of their driveway and ended up in the ditch. The day Mr. Jacobs pushed her into the swimming pool—fully clothed, as if she were one of the family.

She missed feeling like one of the family.

"It's good to see you," Lyndie said.

He smiled—forced, she thought—and motioned for her to sit down next to his wife. "It's been too long."

Lyndie nodded. "It has." Her voice was quiet. Sad, though she hadn't intended it to be. She quickly recovered, eyes taking in the table—a feast by anyone's standards. "Everything looks wonderful."

Mama J.'s eyes moved to the folded hands in her lap. "I wanted to surprise Tucker with a dinner of his favorites. Of course, I have a few of your favorites in here too."

Lyndie glanced at the empty place next to Cassie's father. "Have you heard from him?"

Mama J. shook her head. "But we're all hungry now, so we should eat."

Lyndie's eyes lingered on the older woman, as if someone had shined a light on the depth of her sadness.

"Shall we say grace?" Mr. Jacobs asked, bowing his head.

Lyndie followed suit, but instead of listening to the prayer, she ran through a list of questions she really wanted to lay before the Almighty: *Why did You allow this to happen to these people—these very, very good people? They still believe in Your goodness, but they are clearly broken—anyone could feel the tension in this room. Where are You?*

She didn't want to think about that now. It was so much easier not to think of these things when she was back home in the quiet of her little apartment.

"So, Lyndie," Mama J. said after the prayer ended, "your mother told me about your exciting opportunity. Jalaire Grant is quite the celebrity."

Lyndie braced herself for the small talk that would carry them through this awkward dinner. As they ate, she caught them up on her family (absent most of the time). Her job (unpredictable but exciting—she left out the part about her emotionless lyrics). Her relationship status (in flux. Why overshare on a topic of so little interest?). Her apartment (sufficient). And every other minuscule detail they could scrape together to serve as conversation.

"Elle gets in tomorrow, I think." Karen set her iced tea down on the table. "Is that right?"

Lyndie took a sip of her own drink. "I actually don't know."

Karen's eyebrows pulled down in confusion. "You girls don't keep in touch?"

Lyndie didn't want to talk about Elle. She didn't really know how to explain why they'd lost touch. Not to Karen. Not even to herself.

"I suppose time marches on," Mr. Jacobs said. "We all lose touch even if we don't mean to."

A wave of exhaustion came over Lyndie, and she glanced down at her nearly full plate. She pushed a few loose kernels of corn around, tucking them under her mashed potatoes.

"Look at that," she said, drawing attention to her plate. "I must've dominated the conversation. I heard once that if you have a plate full of food at the end of a meal and everyone else is finished, you talked too much."

Mama J. laughed. "Not at all. You know we love having you."

Was that relief Lyndie saw skitter across the older woman's face? What was going on between Cassie's parents? Lyndie distinctly remembered the close-knit, playful banter that had always existed between the two of them. She'd envied Cassie for having parents whose *love* for each other was complemented by their *like* for each other.

There was no trace of that now.

"I have cookies, too, so save room. They're Tucker's favorite." Karen's voice hitched at the mention of her son.

Lyndie glanced at the clock. Where was he? It was almost eight, and he still hadn't bothered to show up. Had he even called? Texted? Told them he'd landed? He had to know his mom was waiting for him. Would they even know he was safe if Lyndie hadn't mentioned seeing him at the beach?

"I'm going to finish up in the yard before it gets dark," Mr. Jacobs said, pushing his chair away from the table. "Lyndie, we're so glad you're here."

He took his plate with him, rinsed it and filed it away in the dishwasher, then disappeared out the back door. Mama J. stared at Lyndie and her full plate of food.

"I'm sorry about Tucker," Lyndie said, wishing instantly that she could unsay it.

The other woman's face dropped, but she quickly recovered. "I'm sure he just got hung up. Probably ran into some old friends or something."

"Probably."

Awkward silence hung between them. "You know what, Lyndie? Would you mind terribly if I ran a quick errand before the store closes?

I realized I'm out of eggs, and I really want to make a big breakfast in the morning. I'm sure Tucker will be here by then."

It struck Lyndie at that moment how important this was to Karen—pleasing her son—as if she could draw him back to her with reminders of things he'd once loved.

"Of course. Please, go." She gave Mama J. an encouraging smile. "I'll finish eating and probably turn in early."

Cassie's mom, looking somehow frailer than Lyndie remembered, nodded and followed in her husband's footsteps, rinsing her dish and placing it immediately in the dishwasher. She returned to the table, took Tucker's empty plate and filled it with two pork chops, mashed potatoes, corn on the cob and some Jell-O salad Lyndie had passed over.

"I'm just going to leave this for Tucker," she said, covering the plate with plastic wrap. "Will you let him know it's here if you see him?"

Lyndie nodded despite her internal prayer begging the Lord not to let that happen.

"Thanks, hon." Mama J. grabbed her purse and car keys and headed out the front door.

Once she was alone, Lyndie let out a sigh—a deep, heavy, I've-been-holding-this-in-for-too-long kind of sigh. She took her plate to the garbage can and dumped the uneaten food into it, then covered that with potato skins and a discarded newspaper so no one would find it. She didn't want to be impolite, but this whole trip had stolen her appetite. She rinsed the plate, then put it in the dishwasher alongside the others.

When she turned around, she saw Tucker's plate staring at her. It should probably go in the fridge, though Lyndie wondered if Tucker would even be hungry when he got home. If he was out this late, chances were he'd probably already eaten. His rudeness surprised her. Tucker had put his parents through a lot growing up, as if he'd been born rebellious. Hadn't he changed at all?

Lyndie considered going out to find him and drag him home for his mother's sake, but she didn't know Tucker—not anymore. She didn't have any right to get in the middle of it.

Instead, she picked up the plate and opened the refrigerator, but when she did, her eyes landed on a full carton of farm-fresh eggs sitting on the middle shelf.

◆ ◆ ◆

Karen trudged out to the car, aware that Davis was watching her from the yard. He'd wonder where she was going. Good. Maybe if he wondered enough, he'd actually ask her. Or better yet, maybe he'd suspect she was going to meet a secret lover.

At least if she had a secret lover, he might pay attention.

Who was she kidding? Davis knew better. She knew better. Karen Jacobs was no cheat, no matter how far away her husband seemed.

She got in the car and took off down the hill, watching the cottage disappear in the rearview mirror. What was she doing? What were they doing?

Coming back to Sweethaven a few years ago had seemed like a good idea—it had been too long, and Cassie had started to feel almost as far away as Davis had. Almost.

After the accident, they'd gone home to Indiana—back to real life—but everything was so different. When Lyndie went off to Belmont that fall, they weren't there to help her move in. They didn't go for homecoming or Parents' Weekend. They didn't welcome Cassie home for fall break along with her bulging bag of dirty laundry.

Instead, they'd robotically gone through the motions, and Karen tried to do what she'd always done. She made Davis breakfast every morning— two eggs, scrambled with turkey sausage and two pieces of whole-wheat toast. They both went off to the same jobs they'd had before they became *the couple who'd lost their daughter in a terrible accident.*

She pulled up in front of the small cemetery outside Sweethaven Chapel and parked the car. She'd visited Cassie every day since they'd returned. Talking to her helped.

Or maybe she'd only convinced herself that it helped. After all, she didn't have anyone else to talk to.

The irony of it didn't escape her. Here she was, a celebrated therapist with a successful practice, but her marriage was falling apart, she rarely spoke to her son, and she spent more time communicating with the dead than with any living soul.

And communicating with the dead was alarmingly one-sided.

Karen got out of the car and walked toward the gravesite. The flowers she'd brought yesterday shone bright against the neutral background. She kept her eyes on them until she reached the headstone.

She'd never get used to seeing Cassie's name etched in stone. Karen studied it, as if it might've changed since yesterday.

What would Davis say if he saw her out here right now?

"You need to move on," he'd tell her. "It's been ten years, and we are still alive."

"Move on?" she'd holler back. "You want me to just forget her, is that it? Is that what you've done?"

A tear rolled down her cheek. "I could never forget you, my sweet girl." The words escaped, barely a whisper, and while she knew Cassie wasn't there—not her body and certainly not her soul—somehow Karen had to believe her daughter could hear.

Because while Davis and the rest of the world had gone right on living, Karen had vowed to keep her daughter close, to live like a woman who had two children, not one. To live as a mother would.

And if her husband couldn't understand that—well, then maybe there really was nothing more to say.

Tucker pulled his phone out of his pocket and slid his finger across it, tapping on the flashlight. He stumbled around his parents' front walk, searching for the little ceramic frog with the house key in its mouth.

When he found it, he tripped, knocking the frog over on its side. The key fell out into the dark soil of his mother's flower bed. Despite his intoxicated state, he was careful not to disturb the geraniums. The precious geraniums.

He picked up the key and tried—failed—to insert it into the key-hole. Finally, it slipped in, and he turned the knob, falling forward as he did. He righted himself, closing the door behind him and shoving the spare key in his pocket.

As he stood upright, his head spun, the remnant of his night on the beach taking its toll. He wasn't this person anymore. He was clean. He was sober. He ate kale. He met with his pastor. He sang in church.

He'd put this all behind him—hadn't he?

One step in this town and it all came rushing back.

*It should've been me on that boat—not Cassie.* He was the reckless one—everything about Cassie was good. So why had God taken her and left him? His dad wondered the same thing; Tucker could see it in his eyes every time he looked at him.

Being in the lake, knowing his sister's remains were somewhere at the bottom—that was all it had taken to send him straight back to intoxication. What would he tell Kyle?

He dropped onto the bench in the entryway, head in his hands.

*Get it together, man. You've come too far to fall apart now.*

Movement in the living room startled him upright again. He groaned. He didn't want to see anyone. Not now. Not like this.

A figure cut across the darkness—tall, slender, blond hair like an angel.

"Why don't you make a little noise?" she hissed.

Bossy.

She came closer, her face lit only by the streetlamp outside and the light of the moon streaming through the windows of the front door. *Not Lyndie. Not now.*

He forced himself to stand. "Sorry. It's so dark."

She flipped the light on, and he quickly flipped it off—though not before she could catch a glimpse of him.

She flipped the light back on. "What happened to your face?"

He covered the cut with his hand. "It's nothing."

"It's not nothing," she said. "Move your hand."

He did as he was told, trying not to admire the change in her. Lyndie had been so quiet when they were kids, always trailing behind—in Cassie's shadow, he supposed. But there was a sharp edge to her now, something that made her seem more confident. It suited her.

Still, he wondered if there was any trace of the shy girl he used to know.

"What does the other guy look like?" she asked lightly—her attempt at a joke, maybe, but in an annoyed tone. He must seem like such a child to her right now.

"Please turn the light off," he said, eyes on the floor.

"You need some ice," Lyndie said, flicking the light switch off and disappearing, taking with her all of the oxygen in the room.

He heard her rustling around in the freezer, and she returned a few minutes later with a plastic bag full of ice.

"Make a little noise, why don't ya?" His turn to try joking, but she didn't budge.

"Come into the living room." Judging by her tone, he didn't have a choice.

He'd always been oddly attracted to Lyndie's sweetness, probably because she wasn't like the girls who threw themselves at him. She wasn't like Cassie's friends at home, who were all so full of themselves. Lyndie had always been sort of a mystery to Tucker, though if he was honest, he'd never really known her at all, as much as he'd wanted to.

What difference did it make now, though? He'd screwed that up a long time ago, and from what he could tell, her sweetness was as far gone as any hope he'd ever had with her. Sometimes when he thought about the way he'd treated her . . .

"Do you need help?"

His head spun as he tried to stand, and she appeared at his side. She laced an arm underneath his, and even though she was a whole head shorter than he was, somehow her strength braced him and he could find his footing again.

She led him into the living room and sat him down on the sofa.

"You're being so nice to me." His words felt far away. He'd said them out loud, hadn't he?

She placed the ice on his stinging eye—and not carefully.

"Did you hear me?"

"Don't mistake this for kindness," she said, pressing the ice onto his swollen skin.

"I don't think there's any chance of that."

She radiated disapproval. Was she really that offended he'd been drinking? He put his hand on the ice pack, touching her cold fingers as he did.

She pulled her hand away, and he met her eyes for a brief, heated moment. She remembered. Of course she did. And so did he, no matter how many times he'd tried to forget.

She turned away. "I can't believe you."

"Not now, Lyndie, please." Was he slurring? He couldn't talk about this with her now.

Or ever.

For one glorious, word-free moment, he could pretend none of this was happening.

"Your mom left a plate for you," Lyndie said. "It's in the fridge."

She stood over him, the clock on the mantel ticking off the seconds like a metronome, the cover of darkness giving him a moment to study her. What was she like now? Was she still cautious? Did she still write the kind of music that would haunt his dreams?

"Lyndie . . ."

"You should rest," she said. "And keep that ice on your eye if you can." She turned away and started to leave. "And you should apologize to your mom."

Her words were quiet, but she'd made sure they were heard.

As he fell back against the couch, he watched her angelic figure slice through the darkness, disappearing without another word.

# Chapter Eleven

"You ready to go?" Travis stood behind Elle as she packed the last of her toiletries on Saturday morning.

"Almost."

He took a step forward and wrapped his arms around her from behind, creating a portrait-ready pose in her bathroom mirror.

"Are you ready to be Mrs. Travis Preston?"

She met his eyes in their reflection with a smile. "I've been ready for that for a while now."

He kissed her cheek, then her earlobe, then her neck, moving to her other side, hands on her hips. He drew her to him with a kiss that could've set her on fire.

"Elle?"

Nora's voice echoed from the hallway of Elle's apartment. That woman never knocked.

Elle pulled away, but Travis held on, a mischievous grin on his face.

"Stop it." Elle flashed him a smile, then called out, "We're in here, Nora."

Seconds later, his mother's reflection appeared in the glass. She'd entered Elle's attached bedroom and now stood in the bathroom doorway, gaping. "Travis, what are you doing back here?"

"Getting fresh with my bride."

Nora shooed him out. "Go load up the car. I have things to discuss with Elle."

Why did that scare Elle? She zipped up her makeup bag and joined Nora in her bedroom, hoping the freshly made bed met her standards.

"I bought you some new makeup for the wedding. And for afterward, I suppose."

Elle didn't wear much makeup, and she didn't want to look like a Barbie doll on her wedding day. If she had her way . . . well, there was no sense thinking like that. She didn't have her way. But she had Travis, so the rest of it shouldn't matter. Right?

"My makeup is fine," Elle said quietly.

"Well, sure, if you want to look 'fine.'" Nora laughed lightly. "It's a very special day, and I want you to feel special."

For some reason, Nora's words niggled at her. Nobody had ever cared to make Elle feel special. Surely this woman had some sort of ulterior motive? Surely this was more about Nora having control and not at all about how any of it made Elle feel.

"Did you get the outfit I sent over for the day-after-the-wedding brunch?" Nora asked.

The image of the knee-length, plain beige dress entered Elle's mind. "I did."

"Well?" Nora wanted her to tell her how much she loved it. But the truth was, Elle looked terrible in beige (did anyone look *good* in beige?), and the dress was boring and matronly.

"It's too much, Nora. I'm fine wearing the dress I bought." Truth be told, Elle didn't understand why she had to wear a fancy dress at all. The brunch was for the immediate family and a few of the Prestons' close friends—wouldn't a cute, casual outfit suffice?

"Oh, dear, don't be silly. If I can't spoil my daughter-in-law, who can I spoil?" Nora stood in the doorway, turning Elle's room into a prison.

Elle smiled. "Well, thank you for the gift. It's a beautiful dress."

Nora was helping Elle fit into her world. She should be grateful.

"Well, we don't want to keep Travis waiting, do we?" Nora's eyes widened and her perfectly mascaraed lashes fluttered as she put on that plastic smile.

Elle was still working on her perfect smile. It should come naturally, the kind of smile that said, *Everything in my life is perfect,* even on the days it wasn't.

That's what Nora had told her, anyway. "What we do is a lot about perception, Elle. You're going to be a pastor's wife. You can't have a bad day. If you do, nobody will feel comfortable talking to you about their own problems. After all, nobody wants to take advice from someone whose own life is falling apart."

It sounded daunting, but Elle had to try. She thought about the envelope that had arrived only a few days earlier. With a postmark that read "Sweethaven" and a familiar scrawl, the letter had been like a heavy dose of reality, even before she'd opened it.

It contained a newspaper clipping—her engagement announcement—and a note, written in red ink at the bottom:

*Does he know what you did?*

She should tell him. It was risky, yes, but he deserved to know the truth before he married her.

And yet, the thought of losing Travis, the best thing that had ever happened to her, kept her silent. How could she keep her mother silent too?

Travis was taking a risk in marrying her, and this was Elle's chance to finally make something of herself. She'd always dreamed of growing up and getting out of Sweethaven—away from her mother. She'd so wanted to make something of her life.

And now, she'd been taken under Nora Preston's wing. Nora would turn her into the woman Elle had always dreamed of becoming. One beige dress at a time.

They made their way out to the SUV—a brand-new Kia Sportage—where Travis was waiting alongside his father.

"All right, you two," Nora said. "Drive carefully, and we'll see you there. Elle, you've made arrangements for the week, yes?"

Travis took Elle's last suitcase and put it in the trunk. "I don't know why she can't just stay at our place. We have a million rooms."

Nora shot Travis a look. "Appearances are everything, dear."

He rolled his eyes.

"It's fine," Elle said. "I'll be staying with the Jacobs family."

"Won't your mother miss you?" Nora must've heard the stories about her mom. Elle had tried—hard—to keep that side of her life hidden, even as a child, but she knew how small towns worked. Was it too much to hope that somehow Nora had been too busy to pay attention to where Elle really came from?

"Mom, we've got it worked out," Travis said. "We'll see you there."

Nora's lips puckered, but she finally took a step away from the SUV. "Well, everything starts tomorrow with the mocktail party. Elle, come over early and we'll get you all ready. You'll be the belle of the ball."

Elle should feel like the belle of the ball, but mostly she felt like Nora didn't trust her to make herself presentable. After all, Nora hadn't even trusted Elle to pack everything she needed for the week. Why else would Nora show up at her apartment to see them off if not to check up on them? Thank goodness Travis had arrived first, so his mother couldn't corner Elle for too long.

They watched as Travis's parents got in their own car and drove away.

"I thought they'd never leave." He tugged on Elle's shirt, pulling her into his arms.

His kiss always filled her up. As if, somehow, it had a magical ability to give her exactly what she needed when she needed it. She hoped she could return the favor.

"Get in," he said, opening her door. "Let's get out of here."

Elle knew it was pointless to protest. Travis still believed in chivalry, no matter how old-fashioned it made him seem. He opened doors for her, held umbrellas for her, walked on the outside of the busy streets for her. Some days, he almost made her believe she was good enough to step into this role as the wife of Travis Preston.

Almost.

Travis joined Elle inside the compact SUV, which had been a gift from his parents.

"Do you miss your old pickup truck?" Elle asked as he pulled his seat belt around him.

Travis shrugged. "This is growing on me."

He'd picked her up for their second "first date" in that old truck. He'd kissed her goodbye in that old truck. He'd told her he'd never stopped loving her in that old truck.

"You miss it, don't you?" He must've read her mind.

"I always kind of loved it," Elle said. "Lots of memories in that beat-up truck. Reminded me of the boy I fell in love with."

He leaned over and kissed her cheek. "That boy is a man now, honey."

"A man in a Kia Sportage." Elle laughed.

"Are you saying my car isn't manly?" He revved the engine.

She rolled her eyes.

He waggled his eyebrows and shifted into drive. She resisted the urge to ask him—again—if he was sure about marrying her. He'd already answered that question about a hundred times, but she still needed reassurance. Something about it felt too good to be true. She was perpetually waiting for the other shoe to drop.

She pulled out her checklist to make sure she hadn't forgotten any-thing—she didn't want to be the girl who showed up to her own wedding without a dress. Nora would crawl out of her skin if that happened.

"Good?" Travis asked.

She did a quick survey of the back seat, then leaned over and kissed him—slowly, pulling away only far enough to meet his eyes.

"What was that for?"

Elle shrugged and sat back in her seat. "I just kind of like you, I guess."
*Thank you for rescuing me.*

"And that makes me the luckiest guy in the world." He connected his phone to the speakers in the car. After a few seconds of scrolling, he set the phone down, and a Sara Bareilles song filled the car. One of Elle's favorites—not his.

"But you hate listening to music when you're driving," she said.

"But you love it," he said. "I made you a mix. You can sing the whole way there."

Elle laughed. "You sure you want me to do that?" She could only sort of sing. Not like Cassie and Lyndie. She'd loved listening to those two harmonize out on the sleeping porch as she slowly drifted off to sleep. It had always made her feel safe somehow.

She glanced at Travis. Cassie had been so enamored with him for so many years.

But so had Elle. She'd just kept that to herself. It could've come between the two of them if Cassie had known about Elle's crush.

"Have you talked to Lyndie?" Travis asked as Sara belted out a high note like it was no big deal.

Elle stared out the window. "Just a little bit. I think she's already in Sweethaven, and she's staying with Mr. and Mrs. Jacobs, so we'll catch up then."

Travis took her hand. "Are you happy, Elle?"

She found his eyes, but he quickly looked back at the road. "Why would you ask me that?" Shouldn't she be asking *him* that question?

"Just checking." He could always see right through her. "Is it your mom?"

Elle's eyes returned to the passing cornfields as they drove north. She hadn't wanted to get married in Sweethaven. It was an escape for everyone else, but to her, it was like a chain around her ankle, a reminder of everything she used to be.

She had so much baggage, most of which she hadn't told Travis about. Did he even know who she really was? Had he seen the tiny trailer on the western edge of town, just barely inside the idyllic community that gave his family a deep sense of relaxation? Did he know that same town brought only a nervousness for her, a buzzing sensation that nagged her like a petulant child? Did he know about the ways she'd turned herself into a different person every summer, just hoping to fit in with the rest of them?

Did he know who she was when they weren't around?

*You're not good enough for him.*

She knew it was true, but oh, she wanted to be. She wanted to be elegant like Nora. She wanted to be helpful and wear that smile so people felt comfortable talking to her. She wanted a home that was clean and put together, the kind of place where a family could grow. Peaceful. Safe.

She wanted the exact opposite of the life she'd had.

But she didn't deserve it, and she knew it.

Nora knew it. How long would it be before Travis realized it too?

"Dad said there's a gift for us in the glove box."

"Another one?" Elle tried not to sound ungrateful. But the gifts were often too elaborate and required something of them, like giving up the pickup truck.

She was being ridiculous. Of course she was thankful. They had a brand-new car.

Never mind that it made her feel like someone she wasn't. But then, her whole life seemed to be doing that lately.

She opened the glove box and pulled out an envelope with their names on it. She peeked inside.

"What is it?" Travis asked.

"Two tickets to Hawaii." She practically whispered the words. She'd never even been on an airplane before.

"Whoa, really?"

"Really."

Elle didn't want to go to Hawaii. It was a dream trip, of course, but she was terrified to fly over the ocean, and she had her heart set on Disney World. Was it juvenile? Maybe. But she'd never been. While everyone else was off taking pictures with Mickey, Minnie and every princess Elle had dreamed of one day becoming, she had been home, trying to make sure nobody from social services grew suspicious of her living situation.

She'd figured out how to survive living with her mom. If Child Protective Services had taken her away, the alternatives could've been even worse. She could take care of herself. But life in the trailer park outside one of the state's most affluent tourist towns was less than ideal. And it certainly didn't provide her with any trips to Disney World. Or anywhere else.

Travis had promised to take her wherever she wanted to go, but Nora either wasn't listening or didn't care.

The phone rang, and Travis sent the call through the car speakers. "Hello?"

"Did you find our gift?" It was Nora.

Elle pulled the flight itinerary out of the envelope and stared at it. Hawaii was a dream. She should be grateful.

"It's too much," Elle said.

"We were planning to go on our honeymoon in a few months," Travis said, though Elle was certain he'd told his mother this already. "Disney World. Elle's never been."

It sounded so ridiculous when he said it aloud. Disney World over Hawaii? She'd have to be crazy to want such a thing. But . . . it was what she wanted—what she'd always wanted. And Travis had told her he was committed to making her dreams come true.

There was a long pause on the other end.

"Well, there's plenty of time for Disney World down the road," Pastor Preston finally said. "We wanted you to be able to get away now."

"This is so generous," Elle said. "Thank you both."

"We hope we didn't ruin your Disney plans, Elle," Nora said, making it sound even more ridiculous than when Travis had said it. "We just thought Hawaii would be so much more . . . appropriate."

Was Disney *not* appropriate?

"I mean for a honeymoon."

"We appreciate it, Mom," Travis said. "Thanks."

"So, you'll leave Sunday after the brunch and get back on Thursday. That way you'll be there for the college and career ministry on Friday night."

"Oh," Travis said, "Mo was actually going to cover for us Friday."

"I know you'd talked about that, but this will be better. Mo is fine, but he's not the kind of leader you are." Nora's tone signaled finality.

Travis stared at the road in front of them but said nothing. Sometimes Elle wondered how he *really* felt about working at his father's church.

It was a wonder they were getting the Friday before the wedding off.

Something like frustration niggled at her. She pushed it away. She didn't have the right to complain. She was lucky—no, *blessed* (Nora had corrected her on that word usage once before)—to be in the situation she was in.

Never mind that she wouldn't have a full week for her honeymoon. Lots of people didn't get to go anywhere. But though Travis had planned to take her to Disney World down the road, the week after the wedding they were planning to hide away, just the two of them. They were going to turn their phones off and be completely unreachable. Travis had a friend who wasn't using his cottage, a few towns away from Sweethaven—it was right on the lake. They'd had a plan.

Going to Hawaii felt big and difficult, and Elle was already overwhelmed getting ready for the wedding.

But, no. It was selfish of her to even think that way. Nora would help her get ready, and she'd be fine. She could do this.

"You're quiet," Elle said to Travis after they'd hung up with his parents.

He gave a soft shrug.

"Are you okay?"

He glanced at her, and his hazel eyes flickered. "I'm about to marry the most beautiful girl in the world. Of course I'm okay."

His smile faded as his eyes returned to the road. She wished he would tell her what he was really thinking. Sometimes she felt like he censored himself, even with her. Was he bothered that his parents had just unilaterally changed their honeymoon plans? Was he annoyed that he had to be back on Friday—that their weekend had been stolen from them? Was he feeling, like her, that they needed to walk very carefully to prove this union wasn't a mistake?

Would she ever feel like she belonged?

"Are you sure you won't stay at our cottage?" Travis asked. "I could sneak into your room late at night after everyone's gone to bed."

"And do what, Pastor?" She raised a brow in his direction.

He grinned. "Soon, whatever I want." He reached across the front seat and took her hand.

Their relationship was unlike her other ones had been. Every guy she'd dated from the time she was fifteen had expected certain things from a girl like her.

Travis had always been different, even when they were kids. But didn't he know what she was? Wasn't that usually why guys asked her out in the first place?

But he'd never treated her that way. Not once.

So why did she still feel like that's all she was? A disposable woman with nothing to offer except sex?

Tears stung her eyes, shielded by the protective covering of her sunglasses.

She watched the road as it brought her closer and closer to the place where she had become who she was.

*This will be the happiest week of my life.*

She said the words over and over in her mind, as if repeating them would make it so. In truth, she knew she just needed to get through this wedding and everything it entailed. And once she was married, then her life could begin.

# Chapter Twelve

Tucker squinted as the light of morning smacked him square in the face. He opened one eye, then the other, trying to remember how he'd gotten here—in his bed, in his room, in the Sweethaven cottage.

The memory of the previous night came rushing back in the form of a terrible headache and a very dry mouth.

*Lyndie.*

Her stern voice, filled with disappointment, echoed in his mind.

A sandwich bag half filled with water sat on the bed next to his pillow. His eye and lip stung, large and puffy despite the ice. He ran a hand through his hair and then over his unshaven chin.

He'd told Jade it was a bad idea to come back here. It was like a self-fulfilling prophecy, like he'd walked straight onto a page out of high school or college, his most rebellious years.

The fight had been so stupid. He didn't even know the guy, and he was pretty sure whatever he'd said to set Tucker off hadn't been that big of a deal. It was like Tucker had just needed to hit something, and the guy happened to be standing there.

Kyle would be so disappointed. Tucker had to do better. He couldn't help that he was here, but he could control his behavior while he was. Never mind that being in this house was suffocating, a reminder of every idiotic thing he'd done.

And Lyndie. Well, he hadn't counted on her. But then, he'd never counted on her.

He couldn't relive every wretched regret, one right after the other, like a slide show of his worst decisions. He couldn't come face-to-face with the people he'd hurt—his mom, his dad, Lyndie—and not suffer consequences.

Was this his punishment for walking away? Had he thought he could stay hidden forever? At some point, the past caught up to you— he knew that. He'd been lucky to escape his this long.

But, man, he didn't know if he was strong enough to be here.

It was different than when he'd given Kyle the CliffsNotes version of who he used to be. Tucker couldn't pretend with him, but he could leave certain things out. Here, with the people who knew everything he wished he could forget, he didn't have that luxury.

Would any of them accept the man he'd become? Or would they see him only through the lens of the boy he'd been?

He could hear the muffled sound of voices drifting up the stairs. He knew he couldn't put it off any longer. He sat up and tugged on a heather-blue T-shirt.

The sound of silverware clinking on plates, followed by glasses being set down on the counter, filtered in. He stood and opened his bedroom door, catching a glimpse of Cassie's room across the hall. The door to it was open, the bed made, and it was every bit as cheerful as he remembered. How many times had he tormented his sister only to hear her slam that door in anger? And how many times had he wandered in after a night out partying, only to find her ready and willing for a heart-to-heart in the dark?

He'd never been so open with anyone before or since.

His life was solitary by design. He was fine with that. He'd hurt enough people over the years—he couldn't risk hurting anyone else.

"You know part of this whole program is making amends, right?" Kyle had asked him one morning, after Tucker had finished telling him he thought he was in the clear with this alcohol thing. It was just a phase, and he'd grown out of it. He had no desire to drink anymore.

Tucker had shoveled a forkful of eggs into his mouth and shook his head at Kyle's question. "I don't believe in any of that."

Kyle frowned. "You don't believe in making amends?"

"I believe in moving on."

His friend watched him for enough silent seconds that it became unnerving.

"What?" Tucker finally asked, taking a swig of coffee.

"You know you can't really move on until you make amends."

Tucker shrugged. "I think I can. I'm doing a pretty good job of it so far."

Kyle had that look on his face, the one that said, *I have something to say, but I'm not going to say it because you'll react badly.* Tucker had seen that look before.

"Just say it." Tucker pushed his plate away from him.

"Some things have to be said out loud," Kyle said. "That's how they lose their power."

Tucker frowned. "What do you want me to say out loud? That I was an idiot? I was. I already told you that."

"But did you tell the people who actually need to hear it?"

The memory hung there, fresh in his mind as if Kyle had asked him that question yesterday. Tucker stared at the bright-yellow room, but he couldn't go in. Instead, he imagined what it would be like if Cassie were still alive.

*Give me strength, Lord.*

He felt like an idiot asking God for anything today, the day after throwing away years of sobriety. What had he been thinking? He was stronger than that.

Besides, he'd put this all behind him. All of it. Cassie. His parents. Lyndie.

It shouldn't have any effect on him at all. But still, when someone had stuck a beer in his hand last night, he'd cracked it open without a thought, as if it were the cure for everything that ailed him, when he knew it absolutely was not.

He had to do better.

His bare feet stuck to the wood floor, the June air thick with humidity. When he reached the stairs, he drew in a deep breath, as if another moment could give him the courage to face what was coming.

He hated the way this felt—walking into a room of people he'd let down more times than he could count. It had been months since he'd even spoken to his parents, years since he'd seen them. And Lyndie's presence made it all worse.

How could he face her after last night?

Who was he kidding? How could he face her after the night Cassie died?

He walked down the stairs and into the doorway of the living room, but stopped before going in. He could see into the kitchen, where his mom stood at the counter and, next to her, a woman who used to be just a girl his sister hung out with.

Last night's memories didn't do her justice. She wore a pair of gray shorts and a white V-neck T-shirt that hugged her in just the right places. Tucker's eyes lingered as he took her in. Her hair was pulled into a loose braid that fell over her right shoulder.

She glanced up and found him staring at her. He had no right to give her even a passing glance, and he knew it. *I have to do better.*

Lyndie watched him for several seconds. His mom stopped midsentence when she saw him standing there. Silent tension zipped back and forth between the three of them. Lyndie's eyes fell to the counter, but his mom's stayed fixed on him.

"Tucker," Karen whispered. Her shoulders dropped, as if a weight she'd been carrying had suddenly lifted. "You're home." She picked up a towel and dried her hands as she moved around the island and through the living room, arms stretched out in his direction. His height and breadth dwarfed her as she pulled him into a hug. He forced himself to wrap his arms around her, counted to three, then pulled away.

*Don't try to get close to me again.*

She kept her hands on his biceps, studying his face, eyes lingering on his and then falling to his split lip. "What happened?" She frowned up at him.

He waited for the disappointment to wash over her face, but it didn't. Instead, she simply watched him for an answer.

"It was stupid," he said. "I'll be fine."

She waited a few seconds, then appeared to convince herself not to push. "You must be hungry."

Back home, he would've been up hours ago. He would've had two cups of coffee, three eggs, two slices of bacon and a piece of whole wheat toast by now. His stomach growled as if to remind him of that schedule.

"I think I'll go for a walk," Tucker said, unsure where he'd left his rented SUV. "I need to go to the store and grab a few things."

"Lyndie was just heading out to the farmers' market," his mom said. "Go clean yourself up, and if you're lucky, she'll let you tag along."

His eyes darted to Lyndie, who refused his gaze.

"I don't want to intrude," he said.

"Oh, I'm sure it's no imposition," his mom said. "I'd join you both, but I have to head down to the park district office and finalize a few things for the party."

The *party*? That's what she was calling it?

Tucker wanted to groan. He wanted to get out in the surf and let the force of the waves pull him under. He wanted to somersault into a wave, unsure if gravity would right him before his breath ran out. He wanted to feel *alive*.

His mother had no idea what she'd just done.

Tucker watched as she gathered a few things, squeezed Lyndie's shoulder, then stopped in front of him on her way out the door. "I'm so glad you're home."

She smiled, walked out, and left him standing across the room from a woman he'd never thought he'd see again—a woman who probably hoped to never see him again.

"I'm really sorry about last night," he said, aware of how pathetic he sounded.

*I'm really sorry for everything else too.*

Their eyes met, and he forced himself not to look away—even though, for a few seconds, he felt like she was boring a hole straight into his soul.

"I'm not the one you should be apologizing to," Lyndie said. "I'll be waiting on the porch."

Ouch. He deserved that.

He just didn't expect it from her. Sweet, gentle, do-gooder Lyndie.

Time—and life—had a way of changing people. And up until last night, he would've worn that change like a medal he'd won for finally turning his life around.

Now, faced with the remnant of his missteps, he wasn't sure any of that change had actually been real in the first place.

And Kyle's words came back to haunt him yet again: *Some things have to be said out loud. That's how they lose their power.*

# Chapter Thirteen

Lyndie escaped into the quiet of the sleeping porch and tried to calm her racing pulse.

Strong or not, no one could be expected to face all of her demons in the same week. She hadn't even had time to acclimate to being back here, and throwing Tucker into the mix was really messing her up.

She'd said exactly what she thought, which she never did, and she could tell by the look on his face, it had surprised him.

But Tucker didn't know her anymore. She'd grown out of her shy, introverted ways. She'd found her voice and learned how to use it.

Or maybe she could pretend those things were true, and no one here would be any wiser. *None* of them really knew her anymore.

Although, maybe, in a way, they knew her better than anyone.

She let out a groan. No, Tucker, for one, had never really known her. That was just a fantasy she'd concocted in her head.

Humiliation rushed back at her, fast and fierce, like a tidal wave. How easily she could put herself back in that moment, the moment he'd broken her heart.

But how difficult to put herself back in the days that followed.

Lyndie dropped onto one of the three beds lining the screened-in porch. Each was covered with one of the old quilts Mama J. had picked up at a flea market "for a song." Lyndie had expected the porch sleepers to have been replaced by respectable furniture—a wicker sofa and matching chairs with a small coffee table and lamps for reading after dark.

But other than a few updates, everything about Cassie's house was the same as when they'd been kids. That should torment her, yet somehow, Lyndie found comfort in the white-painted floors. The old quilts. The walls of windows that made it possible for the light to fill every inch of the place. The house was vintage without feeling old, worn without feeling shabby. And in many ways, it was more of a cabin than a cottage, connected to nature on all sides.

She drew in a deep breath and let it out slowly. Why had she lied about where she was headed this morning?

"I think Elle is arriving later today, and then there's a cocktail party or something tonight?" Karen had said earlier as she slid a cup of coffee across the island.

Lyndie had picked up the mug and taken a sip. "I think that's tomorrow night, but they're calling it a mocktail party."

Karen frowned. "Mocktail?"

"Cocktails without the alcohol," Lyndie said with a shrug. "I suppose it wouldn't be right for a pastor to host a cocktail party."

"No, I suppose not," Karen said quietly.

There was a lull then, and in the soft silence, Lyndie reminded herself to look at all the emails Elle had sent. Other than tomorrow, she didn't know the week's schedule, and it was probably important that she familiarize herself with it.

"I'm going out to run some errands this morning," Karen said. "Do you want to come along?"

Her face was so earnest—Lyndie could practically feel Karen's desperation to connect. Lyndie must make her think of Cassie.

But Karen made Lyndie think of Cassie too. And so many other things.

"I was actually going to head down to the farmers' market for a little while, maybe visit a few shops." Lyndie wasn't a good liar. Her plan had been to go find some quiet corner one or two towns over and hide out for the day. She needed some distance from them—all of them, but especially from Tucker.

And now she'd been caught in her lie and forced to go to the farmers' market with the man, which was ten times worse than she could've imagined.

She told herself it was just that stupid first-crush awkwardness, but she knew there was so much more to it than that. Maybe she'd built him up to be something he wasn't, but that didn't change what had happened.

It didn't change anything. Nothing could—and not for lack of trying.

Tucker probably didn't even remember. He was a guy. The moments she replayed over and over had probably faded from his mind the second that summer ended. After all, she'd been just one in a string of many admirers. And every girl he'd looked at twice had hoped to be the one to change him, to make him the kind of guy that could commit.

Judging by the lack of a ring on his left hand, it seemed none of them had.

Not that she cared.

She forced herself to sit up. Enough wallowing. Enough freaking out. She was going to the farmers' market with Tucker Jacobs. And she was completely fine with that.

She pulled her phone out and checked for messages.

A text from Foster: Hey, baby. Miss me? You're out of shampoo.

Another one from Dylan: How's that new song coming along?

She groaned and stuck her phone back in her pocket. She should write today. That's what she should do. She should put herself in someone else's misery and go mining for emotion.

She stood. Where was Tucker? Was she obligated to wait for him? She walked back into the house and remembered she'd left her purse and sunglasses in Cassie's room.

Heading upstairs, she wondered how she would manage sharing space with Elle. And not just any space—Cassie's space. Maybe Elle would surprise Lyndie and take the guest room?

At the top of the steps, the bathroom door opened, steam from the shower wafting out like fog, and then *Tucker*.

Shirtless, towel-wrapped Tucker.

Lyndie stopped midstep and turned away. *Good lord.*

"Good timing." He probably thought this was hilarious. He was probably wearing that lazy grin that used to make her melt.

"Can you put some clothes on?" she asked, still turned away from him.

"Too tempting?"

She didn't appreciate him flirting with her. Not when he was hardly wearing anything and looking like he'd just stepped out of an Abercrombie & Fitch catalog.

But turning away like a scared little girl—that was the old Lyndie. The weak, mousy, anxious Lyndie.

She spun around and gave him a once-over followed by her most unimpressed expression before pushing her way past him, into Cassie's room.

She closed the door, let out a breath and dropped onto the bed face-first.

No way could she keep this up, not for a whole week.

Maybe she could make up a fake emergency, something that would force her back home.

But then she'd have to deal with Foster, and at the moment, that was equally unappealing.

*Get a grip, Lyndie.* Tucker had muscles—so what? He'd broken her heart before—who cared? She was a different person now.

Stronger. More capable. Protected.

Now she knew better. She had the benefit of past experience on her side. And that experience had informed most of her romantic life every day since.

*Keep them at an arm's length. Keep yourself safe.*

Words to live by.

Besides, going home now would crush Karen, and Lyndie couldn't stand being the one to do that.

The knock on the door came without warning, and Tucker didn't wait for her to respond before pushing it open.

She was still facedown on the bed when she heard him say, "Oh. Sorry."

"You have no manners," she said, righting herself.

But her reprimand was cut short when she saw the expression on his face. He'd walked into Cassie's room like it was no big deal, but now he looked taken aback. In a frame beside her bed was a photo of Cassie wearing a graduation gown, Tucker at her side, wearing his trademark smile.

Quietly, he walked over to it and picked it up, eyes studying the image intently.

*I miss her too.*

Several seconds passed, and finally, he set the picture down. "Let's get out of here." He walked out, leaving the door open as he passed through.

And leaving Lyndie with an unwanted sympathy for the man who'd broken her heart.

Tucker stood in the front yard, waiting for Lyndie.

He felt like he'd entered some sort of weird time warp being here. He shot off a text to Jade:

This was a bad idea. From now on, I'll handle my own travel arrangements.

If it weren't for her, he'd have the peacefulness of a hotel room. Actually, if it weren't for her, he wouldn't even be here yet. What did he care about his best-man duties?

He'd called the one hotel just outside of town to see if he could get his original reservation back, but naturally they were already booked, and staying at the local bed-and-breakfast would invite speculation.

And he knew it would hurt his mom. He needed to suck it up and deal with it. It was just one week.

Not surprisingly, Jade didn't respond to his text. He'd end up apologizing (again) later, but not now. Now, he was too busy trying to navigate the past as it plopped itself squarely in the center of the present.

The house was eerily preserved. Photos of Cassie, perpetually eighteen, brought out an unfamiliar ache—and with it, all of his regrets.

*I should've been there.*

*It should've been me.*

*I should've protected her.*

He pushed the thoughts away. He should skip the farmers' market and go call Kyle. If he didn't, he was likely to end up back in the same state he'd been in last night.

Lyndie walked out of the house, and when she turned to close the door behind her, he gave himself a second—just a quick one—to admire her.

By the time she turned back around, he was looking away.

He didn't want to call Kyle. He wanted to figure out a way to convince Lyndie to stop hating him.

*Leave it alone. You don't deserve her.*

Another unwanted thought he swatted away. Of course he didn't deserve her. He'd never deserved her, and he'd always known it. He wasn't a relationship guy—and Lyndie, well, marriage was invented for girls like her.

Which made what he'd done that much worse.

"Are we walking?" she asked as she approached.

He stood, hands on his hips, looking away. "I, uh, can't remember where I left my rental."

She crossed her arms over her chest and stared at him. "Seriously?"

"Don't start. It was a rough night."

"I have my car," she said, motioning to the very sensible-looking Toyota Camry in the driveway.

"Do you mind if we walk?"

She pressed her lips together, as if trying to decide if she wanted to be seen with him. "Fine." She dropped her hands to her sides. "After you."

Without thinking, he picked up her left hand, then glanced up at her. "No ring."

She pulled her hand away, tucking it into her pocket.

"Just an observation."

"Well, stop observing things about me." She started down the road in the direction of the boardwalk, where the farmers' market would undoubtedly be in full swing.

This was the cold shoulder she would've given him ages ago if the timing had been different. He would've deserved it.

Except that, if the timing had been different, maybe he would've called her. Maybe she could've saved him from himself.

But Lyndie had always been off-limits to Tucker. He'd promised Cassie.

Once, just a few weeks before the accident, he'd asked his sister about Lyndie. He'd noticed her before, though he pretended not to, but that year—something had changed.

"Hey, does Lyndie have a boyfriend?" They'd been sitting in the backyard while their parents tag teamed the dinner cleanup.

Cassie had glared at him from across the picnic table—the kind of glare that looked a lot like a warning. "Don't even think about it."

"Think about what?"

"About messing with Lyndie," Cassie said. "She is my best friend, Tucker, and you are not even close to good enough for her."

"I wasn't asking because I want to ask her out," he lied.

Cassie rolled her eyes. "Please. I saw the way you looked at her when she showed up at the beach."

Like he could've helped it. Somehow that summer, Lyndie had gone from being one of his sister's friends to someone he wanted to know. And he really *had* wanted to know her—what made her laugh, where she got those song ideas, where she'd learned to play the guitar, whether she dreamed of being famous, whether she was terrified to go off to college that fall—but when it came down to it, he'd messed it all up. Fell into his old patterns and treated her like he would've treated every other girl who'd looked his way, regardless of the fact that she was so, so different.

Cassie had been right—he was not even close to good enough for her. Something inside him ached for Lyndie's smile—anything to tell him they were okay, that she'd forgiven him.

"Are you always this warm and fuzzy?" he asked, jogging until he caught up with her.

She shot him a look that shut him right up. She had every right to treat him the way she was, and he knew it. Pretending he'd forgotten, making light of the situation—it wasn't working. Maybe he should just apologize and get it over with.

*I'm sorry I was such a jerk. You didn't deserve it. I pretended I didn't know how you felt about me, but I did. I screwed up. And the rest—words can't say how sorry . . .*

The words flittered into his mind and out just as quickly.

They walked in silence for several blocks, the tension between them thicker than the humid air.

"What do you do now?" he asked when his mind failed to find anything else to say.

She stared straight ahead. "I'm a songwriter."

He stilled, remembering the way she and Cassie would disappear for hours, writing, singing, harmonizing, playing. They'd even recruited him to play drums one summer. He'd never admitted it, but he'd loved being a part of their little garage band. Part of him had always believed they had what it took to make it big.

Lyndie did, anyway. Her music—her melodies—they were the kind that hung around, stuck in your head long after you tried to push them out.

"That's awesome. Would I know anything you've written?"

She stopped, eyes glistening like suncatchers. "Can we not do this?"

"Do what?"

"Catch up. Make small talk. Pretend that . . ." She looked away.

"That what?" He studied her, forcing himself not to make a joke, not to make light of her feelings. He deserved to feel her hurt, still so evident behind those glimmering blue eyes.

She balled her fists at her sides, her jaw tight. "Forget it."

If only he could.

She walked away.

The Sweethaven Farmers' Market, midmorning on a Saturday in June. Why had he agreed to this? Sure, the place held its own kind of charm—idyllic small town, local vendors with handcrafted goods, the smell of roasted jalapeño peppers filling the air, all set against the backdrop of the lake, the carousel, the boardwalk.

It didn't get much more cliché than that.

He'd always assumed his parents, like the rest of them, had stopped using the cottage. More than once, he'd told them to rent it out—people made decent money that way. How could they stand being here? Didn't they relive every moment of Cassie's life here?

But maybe that was the point? Maybe it made her feel close?

He followed Lyndie toward the crowd of people milling around the market. As he approached, Tucker felt a little like he was about to jump into the ocean, right in the center of a massive wave. Only, this dive would be far less exhilarating.

Before reaching the edge of the market, Lyndie stopped. He watched her for a few seconds, and for the first time, it seemed maybe he wasn't the only one struggling being back here.

"We don't have to go in," he said.

She lifted her chin like the stubborn woman she was and ignored him, walking straight into the heart of the crowd.

He followed her, but only because he didn't want to give her another reason to hate him. Though, it did occur to him that maybe leaving her alone would be a better tactic on that front.

"Jacobs!"

Tucker turned in the direction of the voice and found his old friend Dewey walking toward him.

"You left your car in my driveway, man," Dewey said.

Tucker, keenly aware of Lyndie's presence at his side, could feel her eyes on him. *What was it about this girl?*

"Sorry, man," Tucker said, extending a hand to his friend.

Dewey shrugged, gave Tucker a *what are you doing?* look and pulled him in for a hug.

Tucker wasn't really a hugger.

Dewey had always been built like a tank, but with the heart of a golden retriever, loyal, playful and uncomplicated. The man's friendship was unconditional. And boy, did he love to talk. Dewey pulled back at the sight of Lyndie, who quietly stood off to the side.

"Lyndie St. James?" He opened his arms to her, swallowing her up as he pulled her in for a bear hug.

"I didn't know if you'd remember me," Lyndie said.

"Are you kidding?" Dewey squeezed her tighter.

"Dude, you're going to crush her," Tucker said, sensing her discomfort.

Dewey let go and looked at her as he stepped back. Her face brightened. If only she'd been so happy to see Tucker.

"You look good, Lyndie Lou." Dewey glanced at Tucker. "Our little Lyndie grew up to be fine, didn't she, Tuck?"

Lyndie looked away.

"She's beautiful as ever," Tucker said.

Her eyes darted to his.

"Hey, you up for another adventure, man?" Dewey turned his attention back to Tucker. "Some of us are going out to Third Rock later." He stepped back and bowed like a servant in the presence of royalty, then, affecting a really terrible British accent, he said, "We would be honored by the presence of the King of Adventure himself."

Again, Tucker could feel Lyndie looking at him. She likely had no idea about him or his company and fortune. Better to keep it that way.

"I'm in," Tucker said, clapping his hand to Dewey's for a quick seal of the deal.

"What about you, Lyndie Lou?" Dewey asked. "You in?"

"Aren't we a little old to be jumping off cliffs in the middle of the lake?" There was a playfulness in her tone as she watched Dewey, awaiting his response.

Dewey put his hands up in mock surrender. "I get it. I get it. You're scared. It's understandable. You're a girl."

Her eyes narrowed, and while Tucker couldn't be sure, it almost looked like she was trying not to smile as she said, "I'm not scared."

"So many things could go wrong," Dewey said. "You could do a belly flop. You could get up to the top and chicken out. You could make the jump and your bikini top could fall off." He waggled his eyebrows. "Though let's be real—that last one wouldn't exactly be a bad thing."

Lyndie gave him a shove. He let out that hearty laugh that practically defined him, but he didn't budge. Lyndie St. James was no physical match for Tucker's old friend.

"Dewey, leave her alone," Tucker said. "If she doesn't want to go, she doesn't have to go."

And he could definitely use some time away from her. She embodied the sum of all his regret, right there in her tiny, slender frame. He glanced down and found her glaring up at him.

She turned to Dewey. "Thanks for the invite, Dewey. What time should I be there?"

"Yes!" Dewey gave a victory fist pump. "We're going around one. Travis will be here by then. Let's call it his final sail before he gets hitched."

"Pretty sure we'll be out on the lake again before next Saturday, but whatever," Tucker said.

"Yeah, whatever, man," Dewey said. "Meet us on the dock near the gazebo. We'll take my boat out there."

"How about I meet you out there?"

"Awesome. See you then. And Lyndie?" He turned to her. "Be sure to wear a bikini."

She smacked his shoulder as he walked away, but her face lit in amusement.

"Unbelievable," Tucker said.

"What is?"

"Five minutes with the guy and he's already got you smiling at his sexist remarks. Only Dewey."

The smile on her face faded, leaving him with her trademark icy glare. It was going to be a long afternoon.

# Chapter Fourteen

After about an hour, Lyndie and Tucker parted ways.

She wasn't being her best self. She was being embarrassingly awful. Holding on to this anger toward Tucker was exhausting. And unnecessary. Hadn't she moved on by now?

*Careful, your insecurity is showing.*

And now, to make matters so much worse, her stubbornness had caused her to agree to go out on a boat. In the lake. And jump off a cliff.

What was she thinking? Did she have something to prove to Dewey? To Tucker?

But then, what else did she have to do? Was she going to sit in Cassie's room all day? Hang around with Karen and pray she could find words to have a conversation with the woman? There was always her original plan to go hide out two towns over, but even that seemed a little ridiculous now.

She was here, and she wasn't about to let Tucker run her off. She was just fine, *thankyouverymuch*.

She pulled on her bathing suit (*not* a bikini), then covered it with a pair of jean shorts and a tank top, the whole time telling herself this was a stupid idea.

She drove to the beach and parked her car at the top of the dune. Grabbing her bag, a big towel and her water bottle, she made her way over the dune and down to the lake, once again struck by its vastness, but also by something else: the assortment of people that had assembled on the dock—her dock—which led out into the water where a gazebo stood. She stopped and stared at it. *That dock, that gazebo, that night . . .*

She'd purposely stood at the opposite end of the beach yesterday. Far enough away to pretend she didn't know the dock and gazebo were there. She didn't have that luxury now.

But those things were years in the past. She could handle this now. In fact, maybe she'd come out here to write later—it was the perfect spot. Quiet. Peaceful.

"Lyndie Lou!" Dewey waved from his boat, which was illegally tied to the dock. Lyndie waved back, scanning the others—*not* looking for Tucker. She knew he wasn't meeting them at the dock anyway.

So why did she still feel a twinge of disappointment that he wasn't there?

She trudged through the sand until she reached Dewey's boat, and Elle jumped off the dock and ran toward her.

"Lyndie!" Her auburn hair was pulled up in a loose bun, strands falling from the elastic meant to keep it all together. She wore a cute turquoise swim cover-up over her suit and a pair of big black sunglasses that made her look like a movie star.

Elle had always been beautiful, but also a little rough around the edges. Maybe the years (or Travis's mother) had smoothed those edges out?

Today, she simply looked stunning.

In a flash, they were twelve again, running down these very beaches, and the memory of it squeezed Lyndie's heart. She missed having friends like that—the kind who were as close as sisters.

"It's so good to see you again!" Elle pulled her into a hug and then stepped back and looked at her. Lyndie could see her own reflection in her friend's sunglasses. "You look amazing. It's like you haven't aged a day." She smiled.

"You too, Elle. You're going to be a beautiful bride."

Years of silence between them disintegrated, if only for a moment.

They turned back toward the water, where Travis stood on the dock next to a cooler and beach bag, and a clueless Dewey stood bare chested and big bellied in his father's speedboat.

"What up, Lyndie? Got that bikini on?" Dewey might have salivated as he said the words; she couldn't be sure.

"Good grief, Dewey." Elle rolled her eyes, then looked at Lyndie. "Some things never change."

Lyndie just ignored him. To be honest, it was refreshing that Dewey hadn't changed—one of the few who hadn't in the wake of Cassie's death. He was loyal, could always be counted on. Was that so bad?

"It's really been too long." Elle linked her arm through Lyndie's.

Ten years, really. Their communication after Cassie died had been sporadic at best. There was so much Lyndie had since wanted to tell Elle, who wouldn't have ordinarily judged her, but Elle had been so upset after the accident.

"If you'd been there, none of this would've happened, Lyndie," she'd said. "Why weren't you there?"

The accusation had melded with Lyndie's own feelings of remorse and put a wedge between them that time hadn't healed.

And now here they both were. Pretending.

"Where's Tucker?" Elle asked, pulling Lyndie back to the present.

"Meeting us out there later," Dewey said. "Come on, guys. Get in."

Lyndie obeyed, following Elle into the boat. Dewey stood behind the steering wheel while Travis untied the boat from the dock. Being there, on the lake, made Lyndie uneasy, but Cassie's accident had been after dark, and she was an inexperienced teenage driver. They were adults now, and it was the middle of the day.

They'd be fine. Lyndie said a silent prayer asking that they'd be fine.

"Lyndie, you got a boyfriend?" Dewey asked. "Or a husband or anything?"

In the corner of her eye, she saw Elle's face snap toward her. Once upon a time, Lyndie would've looked back, knowing they'd shared a kinship that enabled them to communicate without speaking. Now, however, Lyndie stared straight ahead, not willing to allow Elle in.

"I do, in fact," she said.

Dewey groaned. "Of course you do. Married? Engaged?"

"Just dating."

"Yes!" He pumped his fist. "There's still hope."

Lyndie fought off a giggle, which didn't match her mood, but for some reason, she'd always found Dewey amusing, despite his Dewey-ness. There was something so innocent about the way he saw life.

Once he'd detached from the dock, Dewey started the engine, and Lyndie took a seat near the front of the boat. Being under Dewey's watchful gaze was preferable to sitting beside Elle and Travis, who had cozied up near the back of the boat.

What would Cassie say if she were here now?

"You've got to get over this, Lyndie," she'd say. "It's holding you back."

"What is?" Lyndie would ask.

"Me. That night. My death. Those two. I'm happy for them—they seem really, genuinely happy—and Elle deserves that, doesn't she?"

"Does she?"

Cassie would shoot her a disapproving look then. She'd always been the gracious one. If she were still here, there was a good chance she would've even insisted on walking Elle down the aisle.

But she wasn't here, and maybe Elle was right. Maybe if Lyndie had been with them, the accident wouldn't have happened. Or maybe she'd be dead too—how would they ever know?

Lyndie shook the morbid thoughts aside.

They drove for about fifteen minutes in silence until the cliff known as Third Rock came into view. In the water, just below the jumping-off point, were two boats anchored near each other.

Lyndie squinted in the bright summer sun despite her shielded eyes—until she made out the familiar chiseled torso of the man she was desperately trying not to think about. Tucker stood behind the steering wheel of one of the boats, a tall woman with long legs and big boobs at his side. She wore a white string bikini and had her hair piled on top of her head in a loose bun. Two other women were tanning on the deck, but Lyndie's gaze was fixed squarely on Tucker.

Thank God for sunglasses.

Dewey slowed his boat to a stop, killing the engine a few feet from the others. He dropped the anchor, securing their location—right next to Tucker and his supermodel.

Lyndie forced herself to look away, but when she did, she caught Elle staring at her—what looked like a pitying expression on her face. Maybe her friend could still read her mind, even after all these years.

Elle had guessed Lyndie's feelings for Tucker a long time ago, and while Lyndie had denied it profusely, Elle hadn't bought her story that she saw him as an older brother. Still, Lyndie had never confessed her secret aloud. Instead, she carried it in her pocket like a lucky penny she'd picked up off the ground.

And yet, some secrets weren't so lucky at all.

Lyndie swallowed, despite her dry throat, and pulled her hair up into a ponytail.

"Didn't expect to see *her* out here." Dewey grabbed a beer from his cooler. "You want one?"

Lyndie shook her head. "No, thanks."

"You guys want a beer?" He turned toward Travis and Elle and held up the can.

"We don't drink, Dewey," Travis said.

"Right, *Pastor* Travis doesn't drink." Dewey cracked open his beer and took a swig. "More for me."

"Who is that?" Lyndie asked with a quick glance toward the woman at Tucker's side.

"You don't remember Tess Anderson?" Dewey raised his beer toward Tucker, as if giving a toast.

Tucker raised a bottle of water in reply.

"That's Tess Anderson?" Lyndie's heart sank. *Tess.*

Great, the whole gang was back together again. Lyndie wanted to go home. Back to Nashville, her little apartment and even uncomplicated Foster, whose presence never did anything to her heart.

A splash caught her attention. She turned in its direction and saw Tucker swimming toward their boat. Seconds later, he pulled himself up out of the lake, water dripping down each bulging muscle before falling to the floor.

"Still making waves, I see," Travis said, extending a hand to Tucker.

Tucker shook his old friend's hand, then waved in Elle's direction. "Hey, Elle."

Elle smiled in reply, but their reunion was short-lived as Dewey pushed himself between the two guys, one arm around each of them.

"Who's jumping?" Dewey asked.

Travis pulled away and tugged his shirt off. "I'm in."

"Travis," Elle said. "Is that really a good idea?"

"I think so." He grinned.

"Well, you know I'm in," Dewey said, yanking his shirt off to reveal one very large beer belly.

"Dude, you need to lay off the Michelob." Tucker laughed.

Dewey rubbed his ample stomach. "I worked hard on this one-pack."

Lyndie turned away to stifle a laugh.

"You in, Lyndie Lou?" Dewey asked.

"I'm fine right here." She ignored Tucker's gaze.

"You scared your boyfriend will get mad?" Dewey waggled his eyebrows. "Here, let's send him a picture of me and you—maybe he'll get jealous and dump you. Then I can have you all to myself." He pretended to take out his phone.

She waved him off, but not before she noticed Tucker staring at her. Their eyes met, and Lyndie quickly looked away.

"I can't believe it. Is that Lyndie St. James?" Tess had turned her full attention on them. The other two women also sat up and stared. Lyndie tried not to shrink under their prying eyes as she stood to face them.

"It *is* you," Tess said. "I never thought I'd see you again."

*I hoped I'd never see you again.*

Just like that, Lyndie was in middle school again, a late bloomer who still, at the age of twelve, looked more like a boy than a girl. At least when it came to her chest.

Tess was the girl who liked to point these things out. The kind of girl the boys wanted to date and the girls wanted to be. Or if they couldn't *be* her, they at least wanted to hang out with her. But not Lyndie. She'd never been swayed by Tess's magnetism—she was always turned off by her meanness. Cassie was, too, at first.

But when Tess started to pay attention to Cassie, they were fast friends.

Never mind that Tess was only using Cassie to get closer to Tucker. Never mind that Lyndie tried to tell Cassie that. Never mind that Tess was the cause of their first and only fight.

Never mind that the fight happened only a couple of hours before Cassie took off, without Lyndie, on a boat after dark. And never mind that Lyndie would never see her again.

If Lyndie were to write something for Jalaire Grant right this moment, it would be an angry song with a heavy bass line and severe drums.

It all seemed so juvenile now. What a dumb thing to fight over. Lyndie wouldn't have admitted it then, but she had been jealous. She couldn't stand the thought of losing her best friend to Tess Anderson.

If they hadn't fought, would Cassie have gone out on that boat? Or would they have done something else entirely—gone to a movie, gotten ice cream, hung out in Cassie's backyard?

"Where have you been all these years?" Tess still stared at Lyndie, flaunting her tan body, which somehow looked even better than it had in high school.

Lyndie searched her mind for an acceptable reply, hating that she still felt the need to choose her words carefully.

"Uh, earth to Lyndie . . ." Tess and her friends stared at her, waiting for an answer.

Lyndie shifted, then noticed Elle had joined her at the front of the boat and now stood directly beside her. Moral support. Lyndie recognized the move from when they were kids. Like a silent pact, she, Cassie and Elle had never let each other feel they were alone when Tess and her friends were around.

Maybe there was still something left of that friendship after all.

"I live in Nashville," Lyndie said, suddenly finding her voice.

"Lyndie's a songwriter," Tucker said.

She glanced at him. Was he impressed by her profession or mocking it? She couldn't tell.

"Nice," Tess said. "Are you married?"

Lyndie's left hand had never felt more naked.

"She's got a boyfriend," Dewey said. "Why, did you want to date her?"

Tess laughed the comment off but shot Dewey an irritated look.

"Are you married?" Lyndie asked. *Please say yes.*

"Divorced," Tess said. "But I got to keep the house." She smiled. "We should catch up. We're having a bonfire on the beach later on tonight. You should come."

Why was Tess being nice to her?

Tess stood on the front of the other boat and dove into the water. When her sleek head and shoulders emerged from the lake, she looked like a *Sports Illustrated* swimsuit model. Of course. She flashed a smile at Tucker. "Are we jumping?"

Lyndie looked away, not wanting to watch Tucker join Tess in the water, neither of them wearing nearly enough clothing. But that's exactly what he did.

"Who else is coming?" Dewey shouted, then did a cannonball into the lake. Travis kissed his fiancée on the cheek before diving in, which left Lyndie alone with Elle.

They watched as the others swam to the cliff and then navigated their way up the incline in swimsuits and bare feet. Tess's friends rolled over on the other boat deck, interested in nothing but getting tan.

"I didn't think it would be so weird being back here." Elle's words broke the tense silence between them.

"Feels like another world," Lyndie muttered.

"Feels like home," Elle said.

Lyndie glanced at her, knowing that word held dual meanings for Elle. In that moment, she couldn't tell how Elle felt about "home."

"How are things?" Elle was trying desperately to make conversation, but somehow Lyndie had lost the desire for small talk.

"Fine," Lyndie said. "You?"

"Good, yeah. Things are good." Elle stared out toward the cliff.

Lyndie followed her gaze and saw Tucker already at the top. He'd scaled the side of the rock like he'd done it a million times, stopping only to help the others when they got stuck.

"And Tucker?" Elle asked.

Lyndie watched as he reached a hand out to Tess, who scrambled up next to him, pressing her body against his. "What about him?"

"Is it weird seeing him again?"

Lyndie didn't move. "Why would it be?"

Elle stuck her sunglasses on top of her head and stared at Lyndie. "Are we still pretending I don't know how you feel about Tucker?"

"I don't feel anything about Tucker," Lyndie lied. "I feel like Tucker should grow up. I feel like he has some sort of death wish. I feel the same way about Tucker that Cassie would feel about him."

"False."

Lyndie turned her attention back to the cliff.

Tess still clung to Tucker, the way she had when they were younger. Several summers in a row, Lyndie had watched her drape herself all over him. Twice she'd accidentally walked in on them kissing, and once she'd spotted them on Tucker's front porch, arms wrapped around each other. She was embarrassed how long she'd watched them. They were older. More experienced.

And Tess had Tucker's attention—something Lyndie had never been able to obtain.

Tess was high above the boat now, standing at the top of the rock, squealing, feigning terror at having to jump, and begging Tucker to help bolster her courage.

"Like I said before, some things never change," Elle said.

"Aren't we grown-ups now?" Lyndie's words sounded harsher than she'd intended. "I mean, shouldn't we be more adult than this?"

"Than what, jumping off cliffs in the middle of the same lake where our friend died?"

The words stopped time. The world went silent. Lyndie imagined Cassie in the distance, unable to find the surface, unable to find oxygen. Was she terrified? Was she conscious long enough to call for help? Did she know she was going to die?

A look of horror swept across Elle's face. "I didn't mean to say that."

Had the past come racing back for her too? Was she devastated she couldn't save their friend? Did she still blame Lyndie?

The sun pulled light, almost-blond highlights from Elle's hair. Her eyes fixed on Travis as he reached the top of Third Rock.

Up there, Tess let out a flirtatious laugh, followed by another annoying squeal as she kept shimmying up against Tucker. Fearless, daredevil Tucker. His mother would have a heart attack if she saw him up on that cliff, though Lyndie was sure he'd jumped off much higher ones.

How did he do that? After everything they'd been through with Cassie? How did he still live as if his life didn't matter?

"I think you'll like Travis's one cousin," Elle said, thankfully switching subjects. "The other one isn't as nice. They're all so rich, I'm honestly not sure I'll ever fit in."

Lyndie studied her. "But it's what you've always wanted."

Elle started to say something, but her attention was drawn away when Travis hollered her name from the top of the cliff. He took a running start, then jumped, arms spinning in circles until he shot into the lake feetfirst. Lyndie held her breath until she saw his head pop up out of the water.

Dewey went next, causing quite a splash when he went in, and emerging from the water with a warrior shout. That left only Tess and Tucker up at the top. They were talking—probably Tucker giving her that boost of confidence she pretended to need.

As if confidence wasn't something Tess already possessed in spades.

"What do you think she's saying to him?" Elle asked.

"Who cares?" Lyndie plopped back down on the end of the boat. She wished she could lie in the sun like Tess's friends, oblivious to the world around them.

"Oh my gosh," Elle said. Lyndie followed her gaze to the top of the cliff. Tess had her arms draped around Tucker, her lips squarely on his.

"Get it, Jacobs!" Dewey hollered as he hoisted himself back up into the boat, Travis close behind.

Tess pulled herself away and ran straight for the edge, letting out a scream that followed her down until she hit the water.

Tucker stood at the top, staring across the lake as if working something out. Lyndie removed her sunglasses and squinted up at him, wishing she was beside him, wishing she had that peek into his soul. After several seconds and a bit of prodding from his spectators, Tucker ran toward the edge of the cliff and dove off headfirst.

Lyndie's breath caught in her throat as he entered the water, his form as perfect as an Olympic diver's. Clearly this wasn't the first time he'd dived off a cliff.

But none of them knew how shallow this water was. What was he thinking?

The seconds after he'd gone in ticked on as if life had shifted into some weird slow-motion movie with no soundtrack. Lyndie's mind went completely blank—no sound, no memories, only the sheer terror that Tucker, like Cassie, might not come up out of that water.

Even Dewey looked concerned after a while, leaning toward the edge of his boat and peering over the side.

"Where is he?" Travis asked, standing from where he and Elle had resumed their seats in back.

Lyndie jumped to her feet. "Go in."

"Give him a second," Dewey said. "He's always such a show-off. I mean, he's practically a fish."

But Lyndie's heart pounded in her chest. Her mind filled with the crippling fear that brought people to their knees.

"Go in, Dewey!" she yelled. "What if he hit the bottom?"

Dewey's eyes flashed with a dread that matched her own.

"I'm going," Travis said, moving across the length of the boat, but before he could jump in after his friend, Tucker shot up out of the water with a splash. He swam over to the boat, where he was met with cheers, as if he was a conquering hero, as if his stupidity deserved to be celebrated.

Dewey offered him a hand and helped him up. "I knew you were just showing off."

Tucker grabbed a towel and covered his face, wiping it dry with a deep exhale.

"Not cool, man," Travis said. "We thought you hit the bottom or something." He rejoined Elle at the back of the boat.

Dewey laughed. "Yeah, I thought Lyndie was gonna come out of her skin there for a second."

Tucker met her eyes, but she quickly looked away. "I do this for a living, remember?"

"What? Try to get yourself killed?" Lyndie crossed her arms over her chest.

Tucker stared at her. "Just having some fun."

"Well, it wasn't very fun for the rest of us." She shoved her sunglasses back onto her face, walked to the back of the boat and sat down. She just wanted to get back to the shore so she could find a way out of here.

Tess slithered up onto the boat and wound an arm around Tucker's shoulders. "I thought you had perfect form." He visibly stiffened at her touch, but Tess didn't seem to take the hint.

Lyndie rose to her feet.

"Dewey," she said. "I think I will have that beer after all."

# Chapter Fifteen

Tucker didn't know why he'd gone headfirst.

He really didn't know how deep that part of the lake was, but he hadn't cared. He'd wanted to dive. He'd wanted to feel the water whooshing over his face as he entered it from that height. And it had been pure adrenaline. He'd have done it a hundred more times if everyone hadn't gotten so bent out of shape.

If *Lyndie* hadn't gotten so bent out of shape.

He'd forgotten he wasn't back home with people who loved to watch him do the impossible.

Night had fallen, and a crowd had gathered around a bonfire on the beach. He made small talk with people he barely remembered, but kept one eye on Lyndie, who'd gone back to Dewey's cooler at least four times for beers Tucker knew she didn't want or like.

But then, he didn't know that, did he? He didn't know Lyndie anymore. All he knew was that she did not like him, and Kyle was right—Tucker needed to make amends. He couldn't apologize to every person he'd wronged over the years, but she was sitting only a few yards away. He could make it right with her.

Would she forgive him? Would she tell him it was stupid—they'd both been kids, and it was just a terrible coincidence that everything had happened the night Cassie died? Would she be able to convince him he wasn't to blame for his sister's death? Would Lyndie have the magic words to make the guilt of that night go away?

Or would she, as was her right, slap him across the face, tell him he was the reason she'd lost her best friend and confirm what he'd always suspected—that everything was his fault?

He'd hurt her, and he owed her an apology. But he wasn't sure where to begin. He'd been naïve enough to think time would make it all go away.

*Some things need to be said out loud.*

He watched as she pulled another beer from Dewey's cooler. She opened the can and took a drink, giving herself away with the grimace that followed. She wasn't a drinker—she never had been. Somehow that made Tucker feel protective of her.

But how hypocritical of him. Hadn't he done the exact same thing the night before? Stepping across the town line had been like stepping into his old skin.

Never mind that he wasn't that selfish kid anymore. Never mind the years he'd spent seeking out people to help, the business he'd built, the life he now lived.

He was not the same.

But last night, he'd believed he was. He'd proven he was. Was he a good person only when he was away from the people who'd known him when he wasn't? Had he been pretending the last several years, or was he pretending now? He didn't even know anymore.

Being back here must be difficult for Lyndie too. He should go to her, tell her all of this. Maybe he wasn't the only one feeling this way.

From off to his right, two guys he should probably recognize strummed guitars, filling the beach with music.

"That was quite a stunt you pulled," Travis said, joining him on the opposite side of the fire from where Lyndie sat. "Almost gave us a heart attack."

"Sorry, man. I forgot I was with a bunch of lightweights."

"You were under for a while," Travis said. "What did you do down there?"

Tucker didn't know how to answer that question. He couldn't put it into words, the way it had felt to be under that water. Beneath the surface, everything shut down. There was no noise. No reminder. No regret. No confusion. Only the freedom of floating.

"Nothing," Tucker said, ignoring his own thoughts. He could feel Travis's eyes on him, but he stared out over the fire.

"Are you ever going to let it go?"

Tucker paused at the question and took a passing look at his friend's face, dimly lit by a fire that needed stoking. "I don't know what you're talking about."

Travis crossed his arms over his chest. "You might have everyone else fooled, man, but I can see right through you."

"What's that supposed to mean?" Tucker bristled. The last thing he wanted was to be seen through, not when everything was still so confusing.

"It wasn't your fault, man," Travis said. "You're still punishing yourself for something you had no control over."

The words hung there, heavy in the darkness. Tucker didn't want to talk about this. He'd confess what a jerk he was. He'd apologize to the people he'd mistreated or taken advantage of. But he would not talk about this. Not this.

"I'm fine, man," Tucker said.

"But you're not—"

"I said I'm fine."

Elle appeared at Travis's side and smiled at Tucker. Maybe she'd sensed the tension between them.

"Tucker, Travis told me about your business," she said. "About all the charity work you do."

Tucker wished she'd keep her voice down.

"It's nothing," he said.

*It's the least I can do.*

"It's not nothing," Elle said. "It's really cool. You should be really proud. It sounds like you've made a pretty incredible life for yourself."

Proud? He should be proud? Elle didn't know what she was talking about.

"Yeah, Tuck, when are you gonna take me out on one of your big adventures?" Dewey stuck a stick with three marshmallows on its end into the fire while he held a can of beer in his other hand.

With the exception of last night, it had been a long time since Tucker had been out with friends whose idea of a good time was getting loaded on the beach. He had no desire to relive the old days, and somehow he suddenly felt like a cranky old man.

"You come out anytime, Dewey," Tucker said.

"He might be too much of a liability." Travis laughed as Dewey shoved one of the roasted marshmallows in his mouth.

On the other side of the fire, one of Travis's friends sat down beside Lyndie, who looked like the stereotypical lonely girl at the party—and she'd managed to choke down enough beer to dull her senses, Tucker was sure.

The guy inched closer to Lyndie and triggered something inside Tucker. He knew guys like this one. He'd been a guy like this one.

He looked away and found Elle staring at him. She raised one eyebrow so slightly he almost missed it, then she glanced at Lyndie as if she were trying to communicate with Tucker telepathically. What did she want him to do? Lyndie was a grown woman.

Besides, he was the last person in the world to judge anyone for the things they did when they were drunk.

The rest of them chattered on around him. From the conversation, he learned that the guy sitting too close to Lyndie was Travis's rich cousin Jackson, who was a financial advisor and first-class jerk.

Lyndie laughed—too loudly—and draped an arm around his shoulder.

Was anyone else seeing this?

Seconds ticked by, and Tucker watched as Jackson's hands grew more and more familiar with her shoulders, her neck, the small of her back. Tucker had no claim to her, and yet . . .

Their eyes met, and she lifted her chin—defiant, like a toddler breaking a rule. He might've imagined it, but he could swear she moved closer to Jackson.

Tess appeared at Tucker's side as if out of thin air, and Lyndie looked away.

"There you are," Tess said. "Brought you a beer. You looked like you could use one."

He held up a hand to refuse her offering. "I actually don't drink anymore."

Tess laughed. "I heard about last night, Tucker." She set the beer down on the ground next to him.

"That shouldn't have happened." Tucker faced her. "I don't drink."

Tess's eyes filled with a look he would've recognized anywhere. *That look.* "What else don't you do anymore?" Her hands found their way to his arms and worked their way up. She clasped them around his neck.

He pushed himself away, stopping her with both of his hands. "Tess, please."

Her face drew down in a pout—a face she tended to use to get what she wanted—but it wasn't working on him. He remembered her all too well.

Kyle had said this would happen. Familiar things from his past would remind him of the person he was and try to get him to believe he was still that person. He'd given in last night, but he wasn't going to do it again.

*I'm not that guy anymore.*

"I should go check on . . ." He turned toward the fire, but Lyndie was gone. He scanned the rest of the group, but there was no sign of her or Jackson.

"Come on, Tucker," Tess said. "We're two consenting adults." She laughed. "And it's not like we haven't done it before."

Tucker groaned at the reminder of a life he'd left behind as Tess's hands slipped inside his T-shirt. He shifted away, but she wasn't taking the hint.

"You can't resist me forever," she said with a laugh.

His eyes searched the distance for any sign of Lyndie and Jackson, but he saw only darkness. He started off toward the beach. What if he couldn't find her? What if he couldn't protect her?

"Where are you going?" Tess's laugh rang out on the wind. "Tucker, come back."

He walked toward the dock, the one with the gazebo, the one where he and Lyndie had met on a night not unlike this one. Dark. Quiet. Filled with possibility.

He'd give anything to go back to that night. He would've done so many things differently.

Dewey's boat was anchored near the dock, and as Tucker moved closer, he could hear voices.

"Did you bring more beer?" Lyndie spoke in a loud tone, slurring her words together like she'd just woken from a deep slumber.

"You've had plenty of beer," a man's voice said.

"Oh, then what are we going to do out here all alone?" Lyndie laughed flirtatiously.

What was she thinking? This wasn't who she was. The girl who'd worn the purity ring. The girl who'd been saving herself. And hadn't Dewey said she had a boyfriend?

Surely she hadn't abandoned her values over one mistake? But then, Tucker had no idea how their night together had impacted Lyndie, because he'd practically run the other way in the light of morning.

"I think you know," he heard the man say.

Rage whipped through Tucker as he approached the boat and found Jackson's linebacker body covering Lyndie's. He reached into the boat and pulled Jackson onto the dock, then squared off with him.

"What's the deal, man?" Jackson shoved Tucker—hard—in the chest, and Tucker shoved him back. Jackson fell onto the dock.

"What are you doing? She's obviously drunk." Tucker took a step toward him.

"I didn't think she was with anyone, dude. Relax." Jackson stood, brushing off his clothes.

"I'm *not* with *him*," Lyndie said. "Jackson, don't go."

Jackson dabbed his lip with the back of his hand. "It's fine. I'll catch up with you tomorrow."

"Probably not a good idea." Tucker followed Jackson to the end of the dock, back to shore, and watched as he walked away.

"You're nuts, man," Jackson hollered when he was far enough away that it wasn't worth Tucker going after him.

Slowly, Tucker turned toward the boat, toward Lyndie, toward the mess he'd made. He walked the length of the dock, still breathing heavily from the energy of fending off Jackson, stepped down into the boat and stood a few feet away from her. She sat on the floor with arms wrapped around her legs, head buried in her knees.

"Lyndie?"

"Go away!" She practically spat the words at him without looking up.

"I'm sorry," Tucker said as he knelt in front of her.

Finally, she met his eyes. Her face was stained with tears, and his thoughts turned to yesterday, the way she'd taken care of him after his string of stupid decisions. He owed it to her to do the same. He owed her so much more than that.

"Why are you here?" she slurred.

"I wanted to make sure you were okay," Tucker said, not daring to touch her.

She laughed. "That's funny. *You* want to make sure I'm okay."

Tucker stood over her, wondering if this was the fallout of what he'd done. Is this who she'd become?

"Just go away, Tucker. Go find Tess. I'm sure she'll give you what you want."

Ouch.

No question about it now. Lyndie hated him, and he could never make up for the way he'd treated her.

But he'd no sooner admitted defeat when she said, "I didn't mean that." She used the end of her shirt to pat her cheeks dry. "I never drink."

It was too much to hope anything more than alcohol was warming her to him just now. But Tucker would take any chance he could get to make things right with her.

"Everyone else drinks," she went on. "You drink. You get to forget about everything. I wanted to forget about everything, too—just for one night." She looked away. "Instead, I made everything worse."

Tucker sat down next to her. "It happens to the best of us."

They sat in silence, backs against the side of the boat, staring up at the stars. Tucker wished he had the right to put an arm around her, to comfort her, to prove to her he wasn't the same guy he'd been back then.

"The trouble is, and I learned this the hard way," he said, "everything is still there in the morning."

"You protected me," Lyndie whispered as her head tipped down, resting on his shoulder. He wanted to pretend she'd done it on purpose, and not that she'd simply lost the will to hold her head upright—but how could he? He knew better. By morning, her hatred for him would return.

"Of course I did."

She sat up and looked at him. "Why?"

Her eyes dared him to tell a truth that she couldn't possibly know. The way she looked at him set something inside him off-kilter. He brushed a strand of her hair behind her ear, fingers shaking as his skin grazed her cheek. She looked up at him—eyes wide, expectant—and in a heartbeat, he was back in that same spot ten years earlier.

Lyndie had been more innocent then, before anyone had broken her heart. Before *he* had broken her heart.

He'd been around long enough to know when a girl liked him, and he'd caught Lyndie staring at him more than once. And though Tucker had pretended not to notice when she'd grown out of her little-kid body, he couldn't help it. He'd noticed. On the beach. At his house. At band practice. She was also smarter than every girl he'd ever dated, and she scared the heck out of him.

But she was Cassie's best friend. He was supposed to think of her like a little sister. And he'd promised he'd steer clear. But then, Tucker had never been very good at doing what he was supposed to, had he?

He'd tried his best, though, by dating just about every other girl in Sweethaven—all the while pushing Lyndie further and further away. He'd told himself that's what was best for her—though when she saw him out with someone else, the longing in her eyes told a different story.

And then one summer, things changed. She didn't feel as off-limits as she had before. Something was happening between the two of them, but neither had the courage to say it out loud. Keeping it secret was easier, but so much more complicated.

That night a decade ago, he'd worked late at the pizza parlor, and by the time he'd gotten off work, his friends were all out. Dewey and Travis were supposed to be at the beach, so he'd headed down to the dock. When he got there, he found Lyndie sitting in the gazebo alone, legs pulled up underneath her, just as they were now.

He strolled up the dock, still smelling like tomato sauce and baked mozzarella. "Hey."

She turned toward him, then dropped her feet to the ground in front of her. She wore white Converse tennis shoes with no socks, a pair of shorts and a green T-shirt from some Bible camp she'd attended one year.

"Aren't you supposed to be out with my sister?"

She shrugged.

When he sat down next to her, he could've sworn every muscle in her body tensed. He could put her at ease with a single touch, and he knew it. He'd done it before, so many times with so many other girls.

The thought shamed him. It's not who he wanted to be, but resisting temptation wasn't his strength—and why should he? He was having the time of his life.

It didn't matter that he had a deep emptiness inside. Maybe Lyndie would be the one to fill it.

"What are you doing here by yourself?"

Lyndie sniffed, then looked away. Was she crying?

Tucker angled himself toward her, inching closer. "Are you okay?"

Her eyes flicked upward, lashes fluttering as if trying to hold back tears. "Cassie and I just had a fight. A really bad one."

Tucker frowned. In all the years she and his sister had been friends, he couldn't remember those two ever fighting. "I'm sure it's nothing. It'll blow over."

"No, Tucker." Lyndie's voice hitched in her throat. "I said some really awful things. It was so stupid. I was so stupid."

He watched her shift under his gaze. "I'm sure it feels like that now, but you guys have been friends forever. Just tell her you're sorry, and everything will be fine."

She shook her head. "You don't understand." She pulled her feet back up onto the bench and hugged her legs to her chest, head tipped down onto her knees.

He sat still for a few seconds. Then, as if in slow motion, he reached out and put a hand on her back. Her breathing seemed to stop, but she didn't move away from his touch. He slid closer, wrapping his arm around her shoulder, pulling her body closer to his. At first, she stiffened, but he let his hand drift down the side of her arm, as if he could brush away the sorrow. After a few brief moments, she began to sink into him.

He'd planned to comfort her. That was all. He wanted to do anything he could to make her feel better. But it took only one quick glance to turn everything sideways.

She stayed still for what felt like a long time—and just for a minute, he let himself enjoy the warmth of her. He inhaled the clean scent of her hair, rested in the way her body felt against his. He hadn't been this close to Lyndie his entire life, but something about it felt perfect, like he'd been waiting for this moment for a long time and hadn't even known it.

She turned and faced him, her eyes shaded in the darkness of the night. "I feel like such a baby."

His gaze fell to her lips, soft and full and begging to be kissed.

He'd been here before. He had a choice. He could do the right thing and walk away—after all, she was vulnerable, emotional. Or he could . . .

His hand found its way to her face. He wound his fingers behind her neck and up into her hair as his thumb brushed her cheekbone. Time stopped. The world stood still, and every thought slipped out of his mind. In that moment, there was only Lyndie.

As if by some unseen force, she sat up straighter and brought her eyes level with his. He squared off in front of her and drank her in, for the first time seeing her the way he'd been forcing himself not to for years.

"Lyndie," he whispered. "I see you now."

Her eyes fell, but he lifted her chin, forced her to hold his gaze. He took her face in his hands and kissed her—carefully, gently, intentionally—the way she deserved to be kissed.

She was tender, special, pure.

She was pure. But he didn't want to think about that now. All he wanted was to get lost for a little while, to give in to the feelings he'd kept at bay for too long.

Their kissing turned into something else—something more—and he let it. He was older, wiser and more experienced, and he knew the second she turned toward him that she was his for the taking. His suspicions of her feelings were confirmed, and he liked the way it felt to be wanted. He let his ego drive the night, knowing Lyndie would do anything for him. That's exactly why he should've walked away.

Why didn't he walk away?

Afterward, he could see the shame on her face. She gathered her clothes from the floor of the gazebo, then sat a few feet away from him, turning that purity ring around on her finger, staring out at the water.

Tucker dropped his head in his hands. He was supposed to protect her, like an older brother would've, and it turned out the only thing she needed protecting from was him.

They walked back to his cottage in silence, though how he resisted the urge to run away, he'd never know. When they turned the corner onto their block, they saw the lights of a squad car at the corner house. His house.

They walked inside and found two police officers standing in the living room and his parents sitting on the couch. His dad had an arm around his mom, who was crying softly.

"What's the matter?" Tucker asked. "Where's Cassie?"

"Where were you?" His mom stood. "Where've you been?"

Tucker glanced at Lyndie, whose cheeks were flushed, her eyes full of guilt.

His parents did nothing to fill the awkward silence in the room.

"I had to work late," Tucker finally said. "I ran into Lyndie at the dock."

"Why weren't you with Cassie?" His mom's voice cracked.

"Mom, what happened?"

"She's gone, Tucker. Your sister is gone."

The words knocked the wind out of him. He didn't remember anything that happened after that. Just that he'd run out into the street and kept running until he'd reached the beach.

While his sister was dying, he'd been out robbing her best friend of her purity. He would never forgive himself for that.

Now, here they were, back on the same dock, surrounded by the sounds of night, and Lyndie waited for his response to her question with an expectancy that set his pulse racing. Why had he protected her tonight?

*Because I should have all along.*

His eyes slid to her lips—soft and full and, once again, begging to be kissed.

He'd convinced himself Lyndie was just one in a string of countless girls, but he'd never felt about anyone else the way he did about her, not before or since. After that night, his relationships had grown even more shallow and meaningless. He didn't deserve anything more than that, and Lyndie certainly deserved better.

He'd never even called her. His family had gone back home to Indiana, Lyndie had gone off to school, and Tucker had pretended the whole thing had never happened.

He'd cleaned himself up since then, sure. He went to church and read his Bible. He gave to charities and took care of the less fortunate. But no amount of penance would ever make up for what he'd taken from Lyndie.

Kyle was right. It was time to make amends. Tucker owed her an apology, but not like this. Not when she likely wouldn't remember it in the morning. Not sitting down here by that gazebo, with the regret deeper and fresher than it had been in years.

"Why did you come down here, Tucker?" She blinked twice, slowly, eyelids looking heavy as the night wore on.

He turned toward her and clapped a protective hand on her knee. "Come on, Lyndie, you know you're like a little sister to me."

The tension in the air shifted. She sat up straight and pulled her gaze from his, a remarkable hurt settling in her eyes. "Right. A little sister."

"We should get you home."

"I'm fine." Her voice caught in her throat. "Just leave me alone."

Tucker drew in a deep breath. He didn't want to leave her alone. He wanted to stay there and take care of her. He wanted to walk her home and make sure she was safe. He wanted to make up for the way he'd treated her once upon a time, to prove to her that, despite the way he'd acted, she wasn't like all the other girls.

But as he walked away from the dock, the memory of a night so long ago still fresh in his mind, he told himself that leaving her alone was the best thing for her.

# Chapter Sixteen

Karen watched the clock as if doing so would calm her weary nerves. When midnight rolled around, she flopped onto her back and stared at the ceiling, the streetlight outside illuminating her husband's sleeping face.

How did he do it? How did he find peace in spite of everything that could go wrong? Did he notice that the air between Tucker and Lyndie was tense? Did he wonder where they'd gone off to or if they were still together or why they weren't home?

"They're adults, Karen," he'd tell her.

And he would be right. Of course they were adults, but that didn't stop her from worrying. That didn't stop her from imagining disaster every time she closed her eyes. No wonder she was still wide awake.

She threw the covers off, tossed one more irritated look at a sleeping Davis and trod out of the room, down the stairs and into the kitchen, where she turned in a circle like a rat in a cage.

Was she losing her mind? Was being here a huge mistake? Was planning a celebration of life—for a daughter whose life had been cut far too short—sending her into an anxiety spiral?

She walked over to the window and looked outside. What had she thought—that she'd find Tucker and Lyndie and Elle magically arriving at that exact moment?

"You're losing it, Karen," she said aloud as she snapped the curtains shut.

Her mind raced through all the places the kids could be: At the beach. At the bars. At someone's house. They couldn't get into much trouble here in Sweethaven.

But then, if that were true, her daughter would still be alive.

She opened the refrigerator and stared inside. She wasn't hungry, and she wouldn't eat, she just didn't know what else to do with herself.

"Karen?"

She closed the door and turned toward her husband's voice. Davis stood in the doorway of the living room, sleep still in his eyes.

"Is everything okay?"

She felt caught. What would she tell a patient suffering from worry-induced insomnia? Once upon a time, she might've told them to read their Bible, to rest in the promises of a God who never leaves us or forsakes us—but it had been a long time since she'd relied on scripture to get her through anything.

What would Davis say if he learned she'd lost her faith?

"I couldn't sleep," she said.

He watched her from across the room, as if deciding whether to stay. She could still remember the nights when Davis would've known exactly how to calm her worry. He always seemed to have the right words. He would've sat her down at the kitchen counter and made her a cup of mint tea. She'd make sure it was decaffeinated, and he'd toss her that look that said, *What do you take me for—an amateur?*

He might even smile at her and tell her this wasn't his first rodeo with sleeplessness.

The kettle would whistle and he'd pour her a cup, adding just a touch of milk and a little bit of sugar, and then he'd sit down across from her, and his gentle voice would calm her down.

It's the way it had gone when the kids were little, before the accident, before their world was turned upside down.

She met his tired eyes. Was he remembering it too?

He pressed his lips together, then gave one solid nod. "Don't stay up too late, okay?"

She nodded as her gaze fell to the living room floor.

Davis left the room, and Karen's eyes wandered over to the stove, to the empty teakettle, where she did her best to banish the memories that seemed to bring only more sorrow.

When Travis had told her the whole gang was going out to Third Rock, Elle had initially been excited, a part of her craving the way things had been when they'd all spent their carefree days down at the beach. But being back there, all of them together without Cassie, had only reminded Elle that her carefree days were over.

Not that her days had ever been fully carefree to begin with.

Travis had said going out on the boat would be good for her—a way to put the past behind her, to help her finally come to terms with Cassie's death. But Travis didn't know the details of that night, and Elle wasn't about to tell him. Her only recourse was to pretend she was fine. She'd gotten pretty good at pretending.

After all, she'd been doing it most of her life. She was still playing a part. Still trying to fit into the lives of the people she called friends, still trying to be good enough for Travis.

She'd hoped the tension between her and Lyndie would've dissipated by now, but Elle still felt like an outsider, trying to scale the wall her old friend had built up around herself.

What had she expected? Elle had practically blamed Lyndie for the accident, even though she knew who was really at fault. She should apologize—maybe then everything between them would go back to normal.

But bringing it all back up felt like so much work.

They'd docked Dewey's boat just before dark—Elle's only condition on going out, as if darkness had caused the accident. Then someone had started a bonfire on the beach, and Elle's mind tumbled back. How many summer nights had they spent out here, under these very same stars? There'd been days when Elle thought she'd never get out of Sweethaven. Days when she thought she would jump straight into the same cycle as her mom—deadbeat boyfriend, too much alcohol, unwanted pregnancy.

But look at her now. She'd done it. She was out—and about to marry one of the kindest men she'd ever met.

"Is that Elle Porter?" A guy's voice pulled Elle's attention. He was tall, thin and looked a lot like someone her mom would've brought home after a shift at the bar. "It *is* you. I'd recognize those luscious lips anywhere."

Finally, she made eye contact with him. His hair was long, straggly, and he flicked the ashes from his cigarette onto the beach.

She saw Travis across the circle of people, but he was talking with one of his cousins—Jackson, the smarmy one, who seemed upset.

Elle tried to ignore the guy, but he took a few steps closer to her—too close. "Don't pretend you don't remember me."

"I'm sorry," Elle said, "but I don't."

"It's me, babe." A slow, calculating grin spread across his face. "Dave Messer."

She kept her eyes fixed on Travis, suddenly praying he wouldn't turn around. Dave Messer. Sophomore year. She hadn't loved him—she'd just wanted to get away from her mom, and Dave had a place of his own. Of course, staying there had come with a price.

Was it worth it?

"You look real good, Elle," he said.

She didn't respond.

"Wanna get out of here? You know, for old times' sake?" He licked his lips, eyeing her like she was a plate of food and he hadn't eaten in a month. "I know you didn't forget all the good times we had."

"No, thanks," she said. "My fiancé will wonder where I've gone."

"Fiancé? You're engaged?"

Elle nodded.

"Who's the lucky guy?"

She looked at Dave, images of what her life could've been if she'd never met Cassie and Lyndie flashing before her.

"Come on, I want to meet him."

She nodded across the way at Travis. "He's over there."

Dave laughed. "One of those guys? No wonder you look like you do."

She steeled her jaw.

"You get engaged to some rich tool, and you forget where you came from?"

*If only I could forget.*

She started to walk away, but the guy grabbed her arm, stopping her.

He leaned in closer, face right next to hers. He inhaled a deep breath, as if drawing in her scent. "You can show up here looking like you do, but you still smell like a whore."

Elle stared across the fire, not sure if she should pray that Travis didn't turn around or pray that he did.

"Get your hand off me." She kept her voice low.

He narrowed his eyes, but he didn't move. "You haven't changed at all, have you? You're still a tease."

She faced him and pulled her arm away. "If you need me to spell it out for you, I will. Don't you ever touch me again. Is that clear enough for you?"

He held his hands up in mock surrender as a few people nearby turned toward them.

She brushed past him, and he turned around. "Does he know what you really are?"

Dave's voice was loud enough to get the attention of everyone else around the bonfire, including Travis, who met her eyes and asked, "Elle?"

She blinked back tears as Travis came to her side.

"What's going on?" he asked.

"It's nothing," she said.

Dave gave her a once-over. "Got that right." He walked off down the beach.

Travis pulled her away from the rest of them. "What was that about?"

She didn't know how to explain. How much did he know about her past? She'd told him almost nothing, but he rarely asked—did that mean someone else had filled him in on the sordid details of life with Lily Porter?

Elle couldn't assume that, but it was easier than telling him everything herself. She'd been drowning before he'd come back into her life, certain she was about to fall apart. Travis had made her think she was worthy of his love.

Telling him about any of this now would ruin that.

"It's nothing," she repeated. "Just a guy I used to know. Kind of a jerk."

"Did he hurt you?" Travis looked off in the direction Dave had gone, but there was only darkness to see—thankfully. Elle loved Travis, but he wasn't a fighter. Besides, she had a feeling Dave didn't fight fair.

"Can we just forget about it?"

"Did he hurt you, Elle?"

She shook her head. "I promise I'm fine."

He took her face in his hands. "Are you sure?"

She forced a smile. "I'm sure."

Travis's phone buzzed in his pocket. He pulled it out, looked at the screen and frowned.

"What is it?"

"It's Tucker. He says we need to go get Lyndie out of Dewey's boat. That we need to get her home safe."

Elle frowned. "Is she okay?"

164

Travis shrugged. "That's all it says."

He started off toward the dock where they'd left Dewey's boat, Elle following close behind. And while her attention had turned to finding Lyndie and making sure her friend was okay, the angst of having her past thrown back in her face still lingered.

How long could she go on pretending to be something she wasn't?

How long until Travis realized what she was?

And how many happy, cheerful, phony faces did she have to put on in the meantime?

# Chapter Seventeen

"Rise and shine."

*Elle.* Far too chipper for a morning like today. Lyndie rolled over and stuffed her head under the pillow.

"What happened to you last night?" Elle asked. "You just kind of disappeared."

Last night . . . last night . . . Lyndie tried to latch on to the scenes that played out in front of her. Her head throbbed. She'd gotten drunk. But she never drank—why had she done that?

*Oh, no.* She'd gotten drunk with Travis's cousin.

And then . . . Tucker.

"Do you even know how you got home?" Elle sounded like a nagging mother.

Lyndie groaned. "I walked." (She thought she'd walked.)

"No. Travis practically carried you up the dune to his car." Lyndie felt Elle plop down on the end of the bed. "What's going on with you, Lyndie?"

Lyndie didn't want to talk about it. She'd had a lapse in judgment, that was all. But she knew it was more than that. She didn't like being back here, and she'd stupidly thought she could make it all go away— the hurt, the insecurity, the shame—especially the shame. She'd been searching for a way to be rid of that for years, and always came up empty.

Turns out alcohol wasn't the answer either.

Elle pulled the pillow off Lyndie's face and studied her. "Are you okay?"

"Of course," Lyndie said. "Everyone else was drinking—what's the big deal?"

Elle shrugged. "Everyone else seemed to know when they'd had enough."

Lyndie stuffed the pillow under her head. She wished she could go back to sleep. When she was sleeping, she didn't think about what had happened with Tucker on the same night her best friend had died, or the anguish that followed. She needed to talk to him about it, but how could she?

"I just don't want my maid of honor to spend the whole week plastered out of her mind," Elle said.

"I wasn't plastered, Elle." Lyndie slid her legs out from under the covers.

"You forget who I grew up with," Elle said. "I know what plastered looks like."

Lyndie stopped and looked at her. Elle wore a cute yellow sundress, and her long hair was loosely curled. "I'm sorry, Elle. It was stupid. I guess being back here is harder than I thought it would be."

Elle reached over and covered Lyndie's hand with her own. Lyndie stood and drew her hand away. The act of comfort would make her cry, and Lyndie could not cry today. She pulled her hair up into a ponytail. "I won't be drinking anymore."

There was a moment of silence that Lyndie couldn't fill. She pretended to busy herself with something in her suitcase.

"We've got big plans today," Elle said. "You didn't forget, did you?"

*Thank you for changing the subject.* "Remind me what's on the schedule?"

"Lyndie, you have to keep track of these things." Elle stood. "Tonight is the mocktail party. Dinner at the Preston cottage. From the sounds of it, Nora has a few other surprises in store."

The image of the Preston cottage floated through Lyndie's mind. Travis came from old money, and their fortune had only increased when his father's little Chicago church became one of the largest in the country. The lower level of the house—with its pool table, theater room, kitchenette, Ping-Pong table and video-game setup—had been outfitted for Travis and his friends. Lyndie could remember all the years they'd shown up for Travis's get-togethers, Cassie whispering prayers the whole night long that he would finally notice her.

"Hurry up, slowpoke." Elle started for the door. "Church is in an hour."

Lyndie glanced at her. "Church?"

"Travis's dad is the special guest this weekend, and if I don't make an appearance, his mom will never let me hear the end of it."

"Why do I have to go?"

Elle shrugged. "Moral support?"

Lyndie tried not to groan as she sat back down on the edge of the bed.

"You *are* my maid of honor."

Guilt nagged her. She should've insisted Elle find someone who was better at these sorts of things to be her maid of honor.

Elle stood in the doorway, surveying the room. "It's weird being back here."

Lyndie couldn't disagree.

"I miss her."

When Lyndie said nothing, Elle finally turned and walked away.

*I miss her too.*

◆ ◆ ◆

After nearly an hour tiptoeing around the house in an effort not to wake—and face—Tucker, Lyndie met Elle on the front porch.

"Finally," Elle said, starting down the walk.

Lyndie ran to catch up to her. "You could've gone without me."

"Just hurry."

Lyndie's phone dinged.

"Who's texting you on a Sunday morning?" Elle asked, clomping up the hill.

Lyndie glanced down and saw Dylan's name on the screen. She clicked on the message.

How's our song coming along? I know it's only been a few days, but you're working on it, right? Clock's ticking.

Seconds later, another text came in.

Chance of a lifetime.

She groaned and shoved her phone in her bag. She didn't have time to think about Dylan or Jalaire or how in the world she was going to fake her way through an "emotionally charged" song. Maybe she'd just yell uncle. Maybe she wasn't cut out for this artistic life after all. She could get a job teaching music or working at Starbucks.

She could be happy with that, right?

They walked the familiar path to the old church on the hill. The chapel was a big screened-in space with several large ceiling fans that did nothing to ward off the brutal heat of a Michigan summer. How many times had they made that same Sunday-morning walk after a weekend of laughter or tears? The rule was always that the girls could spend Saturday night together only if they made it to church on time.

For the most part, they'd obeyed.

When they reached the end of their second block in silence, Elle cleared her throat. "I know about you and Tucker."

Lyndie stopped and stared at her friend. "What are you talking about?"

"Travis told me years ago." Elle grabbed Lyndie's hand. "Are you okay?"

Lyndie yanked her hand away. "What did he tell you?"

Elle held her gaze. "About what happened. The night Cassie died."

Lyndie's heart dropped to her ankles, which left her feeling as naked and exposed as if it had been all her clothing.

"Tucker told Travis he kissed you," Elle said. "He was trying to figure out what to do about it. Did he ever do anything?"

"He told Travis we kissed?" Lyndie's pulse started to steady.

"Yeah," Elle said with a shrug. "He seemed kind of upset about it, I guess. I mean, maybe he thought he broke some kind of code or something. Why do you think I kept asking you about him? And why didn't you tell me? You swore you didn't like Tucker like that."

*I loved Tucker.*

"I didn't. I don't. It just sort of happened." Lyndie started walking again.

"Is that why things were so tense between you two last night?" Elle's question hung in the air. "It must've been some kiss." She laughed. "I'm sure it was hard to see Tess wrapped all over him like that."

"Elle, please," Lyndie said, realizing she didn't want to think about any of this, let alone talk about it. It all felt too ridiculous to say out loud.

She'd been eighteen. She'd lost her virginity to her best friend's brother, who'd turned into the man who was now sleeping down the hallway. People lost their virginity every day. What was the big deal?

It was ten years ago. *Time to grow up, Lyndie.*

Of course, she knew what the big deal was.

"Sorry," Elle said. "I'm here if you want to talk. It's been a long time since we've had one of our heart-to-hearts."

"I know." Lyndie's mind fluttered back to those nights on the sleeping porch when everything inside her had poured out so easily. But talking was not the way to handle these feelings. Ignoring them and pushing them aside suited her much better.

"Travis is meeting me here," Elle said as the little church came into view. "He and Tucker were out kayaking early this morning."

"They were?" Having seen Tucker's closed bedroom door, Lyndie had assumed he'd slept in.

"Yeah, apparently it's all part of Tucker's 'clean living.'" She made air quotes with her fingers.

"What 'clean living'?"

Elle pulled open the chapel's screen door and led them inside. Rows of chairs had been set up facing the small stage where Lyndie and Cassie had sung so many times over the years. Near the front, Lyndie spotted the Preston family, including Travis, who wore a tan suit with a crisp white shirt and a green tie that matched his eyes.

"Clean living," Elle said, gaze focused on Travis. "You know, no alcohol, no processed foods, daily exercise."

"I don't think that's how Tucker is living." Lyndie's thoughts turned to his drunken stupor the other night—not that she had any room to judge.

Elle nudged her arm. "I think he's a lot different than he used to be. I'll be back."

Lyndie lingered by the door as Elle made her way to her future in-laws, and scanned the room as nonchalantly as she could. Elle was wrong, of course. People didn't change. Lyndie imagined Tucker probably had a whole list of women he could call for casual, shallow nonrelationships. Why else would he still be single?

Maybe it was all an act. Maybe Tucker had everyone else fooled.

But she knew what he was really like.

Her eyes found Karen Jacobs sitting quietly beside her husband. Lyndie knew they would welcome her in their row, but she didn't want to sit up front or with anyone she knew. She didn't belong in church, and she couldn't pretend she did.

Not after last night.

Not after ten years ago . . .

Instead, she tucked her head down and slipped into the back row, hopeful the service would hurry up and start so she could make a quick exit as soon as the final hymn was sung.

A bearded man wearing a pair of too-tight khakis took the stage, and the crowd stilled.

"Welcome, everyone, to the Sweethaven Chapel. We've got a wonderful service planned for you today."

Lyndie half listened while the man announced Elle and Travis's wedding. She wished they would also announce the many events leading up to the big day. Lyndie never had gotten around to reading the itinerary, and she realized now that was a mistake. She would've felt better if she'd mentally prepared to spend every single day and night of the week celebrating when she felt like doing anything but.

That wasn't fair. She was happy for her friend. Elle deserved a better life after the childhood she'd had. Maybe Lyndie could try focusing on that instead of her own misery for a change.

When Cassie's photo appeared on a screen behind the man onstage, Lyndie's breath caught in her throat.

"And of course, on Thursday we will join with Karen and Davis Jacobs in the celebration of life for their beautiful daughter, Cassie, who passed away ten years ago to the day. You're all welcome to attend. The celebration will be held in the park, behind the chapel."

The photo faded away, the same way Cassie had.

"Now, if you'd all stand with me to sing, we have a guest worship leader this morning. Let's give a warm welcome to Tucker Jacobs."

Tucker walked out from the right wing of the stage, wearing a guitar crossways around his torso. He'd traded his board shorts and T-shirt for a pair of black pants and a pinstripe button-down, sleeves rolled to the elbow. Lyndie stared at him, questions racing through her mind. When on earth Tucker Jacobs had learned to play the guitar? And what gave him the right to stand on a church stage after all he'd done?

*Grace gives him the right.*

She scoffed at the unwelcome thought, forcing herself to stand with the rest of the congregation.

Tucker started with something folksy—a song she didn't recognize. Of course, she hadn't been to church for a while. As he sang, it was almost like he didn't even know he was on stage, like he'd been transported to a far-off place where no one else mattered.

How did he do that? She thought about her own guitar, packed away in the trunk of her car. If Dylan knew she hadn't touched it since her meeting with Jalaire, he'd be furious.

"Don't mess this up," he'd told her before she left Nashville. "You're going to have to find some time to get a new song written, or you can kiss this opportunity goodbye."

Lyndie hated that everything seemed to ride on this one song—and she hated even more that she couldn't write it unless she figured out a way to let herself feel every one of the emotions she'd been trying to forget.

She read the words projected onto the screen, words about grace, forgiveness, the goodness of God. She'd rejected those ideas a long time ago, and hearing Tucker sing them didn't change that, though she had to admit, something about him seemed very different when he was up there.

His voice had a rich fullness about it, the kind of voice that should be heard, and he strummed the strings of his guitar with the ease and precision of a man who'd played his whole life. He closed his eyes and sang, leading a room full of people to the throne room of God.

Tucker Jacobs.

Surely the rest of the congregation knew about Tucker. His reputation had been legendary in Sweethaven. How could he stand up there and pretend he had the right to lead worship?

Tucker's hands left the guitar strings and stretched upward to heaven as he continued the chorus a cappella. The voices of the people around her joined him, and for a brief moment, the church became a true holy place, hushed by the presence of the angels.

Around her were the bowed heads of sinners who found it so easy to reach up to heaven and pull down grace—to go on with their lives despite their sin. Why couldn't Lyndie?

The song ended, but the hush remained. Pastor Preston slowly took the stage, clapping a hand on Tucker's shoulder. "Let's pray."

She knew it was appropriate to bow her head with everyone else, but she found it impossible to look away from Tucker as he closed his eyes in prayer. Images of him in his drunken state raced through her mind, along with memories of the guy who'd taken her virginity without a word.

People didn't change, so why was he up there pretending to be someone he wasn't?

As Travis's dad finished the prayer, Tucker's eyes opened and locked onto hers. For a moment, they seemed like the only two people in the room, but with the pastor's languid "Amen," their connection was severed, leaving Lyndie with her humiliation once again.

She tore her eyes from Tucker's and scooted out of the row as the folks around her followed the pastor's directive to "turn and shake hands with those around you."

She shouldn't be here. She had no right.

She pushed her way out of the chapel, the screen door clapping shut behind her. The thick June air did nothing to aid her pursuit of a deep breath as her heart raced. Could they all see through her? Could they see her brokenness through her façade of strength?

"Lyndie?" Tucker strode toward her, guitar still strapped around his shoulder. He'd exited out the side and stepped straight in her path, with a concerned look on his face.

She reminded herself it was the look of an older brother—not of a boy who loved a girl. No matter how much she'd wanted that once, it was not meant to be.

*I have so many things to tell him, but how to say the words?*

"I'm going for a walk." She veered off in the other direction.

"Wait." He jogged closer.

She spun around. "What were you doing up there?" That was not what she'd meant to say. She was wrong to judge him, but she didn't understand. How had he moved past the person he was to stand onstage with his arms up in surrender?

That's what worship was, right? An act of surrender? How did a person ever get that free?

He took a step back. "What do you mean?"

*You never even said you were sorry. I had to deal with the fallout of your callous decision while you got to walk away like nothing ever happened.*

That he felt perfectly fine standing up there on that stage, when she didn't feel worthy of even sitting in a pew, seemed tragically unfair.

"Forget it," she said.

He moved in front of her. "Lyndie, stop."

*I'm overreacting. This is not who I am. I'm strong. I'm independent. I'm . . . broken.*

"I don't understand," she said, "but it's none of my business, so just let me go."

"They asked me to sing," Tucker said.

"In a church?"

"I sing in my church at home," he said. "Someone got wind of it, and here I am. I think maybe Travis told them, and maybe—"

Her humorless laugh cut in. "Tucker Jacobs, worship leader."

She watched as her words injured him, and in a flash, she saw something familiar behind his eyes.

Shame.

How he dealt with his was of no consequence to her, so why was she acting like it was?

"I'm sorry," she said. "That was uncalled for. I think it's great that you're still into music. Really."

Tucker stared past her toward the cottages across the street. "I know I don't have any right to be up there," he said. "But I'm trying, Lyndie. I'm trying to be a better man. I've tried everything else. Nothing's worked."

"Church."

He shook his head. "No. God."

"Same thing."

"No, they aren't. I'm screwed up. I've screwed up. And I have to live with that. But this"—he motioned back toward the church with a shrug—"it helps."

Lyndie hadn't found anything that worked. So far, all that had even come close was pretending none of it had ever happened in the first place.

"Do the people at your church know all the things you've done?" She hated the crack in her voice as she nearly whispered the words to him.

He didn't say anything else. Instead, he searched her eyes for some kind of connection. But she wouldn't give that to him again. She lifted her chin, steeled her jaw and waited, until finally he turned and walked away.

# Chapter Eighteen

Tucker slipped back into the church, but he was too distracted to listen to the pastor's message. Something about celebrations or details or forgiveness? He couldn't say.

What he could say was that he felt like a complete fraud. Lyndie was right, and it was likely everyone else in the congregation felt the same way about him being up on that stage. Who did he think he was?

If Kyle were here, he'd slap Tucker upside the head for that train of thought. Tucker knew who he was—a sinner, saved by grace.

But grace felt so far away when he was sitting in the wake of his screwups.

Travis found him after the service. "We've got this lunch thing with my parents, but the welcome party is tonight. You should wear something nice."

"Fine," Tucker said. "I'll wear my good wet suit."

Travis laughed, then met Elle and his parents by the chapel door. Tucker put his guitar in its case, and when he stood back up, his parents were standing next to him—staring. His mom's eyes were glassy.

"Hey." He set the guitar on the floor next to him. "Sorry I didn't see you guys this morning. I went—"

"Kayaking with Travis. We know." His mom smiled. "Will you be home for lunch?"

Sunday lunch at the family cottage. How long had it been? Even though he'd cleaned up his act, he still found it difficult to be around his parents. Why?

"Please say you'll come, Tucker," she said. "It would mean the world to me."

His eyes darted to his father, then back again. "Sure."

"Oh, good. I'm making a big feast. Feel free to invite whoever you want." She reached over and touched his face. "I'm so proud of you, Tucker."

His heart dropped. What a phony. He'd let his mom believe he was a man with answers, a man who lived a righteous life—but he was still so flawed.

She wandered away, and he stood face-to-face with a father whose approval he'd never won. Sadly, he knew it wasn't his dad's fault—Tucker hadn't given his parents much reason to be proud.

"I wouldn't mind taking the kayaks out with you," his dad said. "If you're up for it."

Tucker doubted a kayak trip could smooth over the bumps in their relationship. In minutes, they'd be arguing. Just like old times.

Yet he said, "Sure, Dad. If you think you can keep up."

His dad's face lit with a genuine smile. "You'll pull me along if I fall behind, right?"

"If you're lucky."

"Well, let's make a plan for tomorrow morning. I have to go help your mom with lunch. You're really coming, right?"

"Do I have a choice?"

His dad's mouth twisted into a smirk. "If I don't, you don't."

"So that's a no, then?"

"That's a no, son." He gave a stern nod, then walked away, leaving Tucker standing at the center of a nearly empty church, the burden of his flaws weighing him down. He'd forgiven himself for so many missteps—chalked them up to the stupidity of youth—but there were a few he'd yet to make peace with, and it seemed the ghosts all resided here in Sweethaven.

*Some things need to be said aloud. That's how they lose their power.*

Kyle's advice seemed ever-present, but Tucker had begun to doubt it. How would he ever say what needed to be said?

◆  ◆  ◆

Karen shouldn't fuss over her son—her *grown* son—but how could she not? Look how far he'd come.

All the things she'd prayed for Tucker seemed to have happened. Well, except for the wife and the kids, but there was still time for that.

Karen and Davis had decided to walk to church that morning, but now, with the walk home in front of them, she wished they hadn't. A silent car ride was one thing, but a silent walk was something else entirely.

They left the chapel through the back door, and Karen caught a glimpse of the small cemetery out back. Her eyes lingered, and her pace slowed. Should she tell Davis to go on without her?

"You coming?"

Karen turned and faced her husband, who seemed unaffected by the cemetery's presence.

"If you're going to make the big feast you promised, we should probably get going." Davis's smile looked forced, and she would know after all this time. She knew when he was genuinely smiling (with his golf buddies, mostly) and when he was pretending (with her, mostly).

But what could she say? She couldn't disrupt the week—not this week.

She followed him around to the other side of the chapel, trying to focus on how it would feel to have a full house for Sunday lunch again and not on how it felt to leave their daughter's memory buried underground.

"You're really going kayaking?" Karen tried not to sound skeptical of the father-son conversation she'd overheard.

Davis's raised eyebrows told her she'd failed. "You don't think I can keep up?"

She waved at the Clausens, who were getting in their car. "With Tucker?"

"I'm not so old." Davis looked at her. "We aren't so old."

She met his eyes, but only for a second. It didn't matter how old they were—it mattered how they'd lived, and their life had been brutal. Why didn't he understand that?

"Anyway, it'll be good to get out there with Tuck," Davis said as they crossed the street. "Maybe we can have a heart-to-heart, and I can find out how he's really doing."

"He seems to be doing well."

Davis nodded. "He really does."

Davis would try to make up for lost time with their son, and they would bond. The two of them used to speak a language all their own, but in those days, Karen had Cassie, so she never minded. Now, somehow, she felt as though she were being left behind.

Life was leaving her behind.

Everyone else had figured out how to go on living, and she'd barely figured out how to keep her brave face neatly in place.

"I'll run to the store if you make me a list," Davis said when they reached the bottom of their driveway. He strolled off into the garage and busied himself—anything to keep from having to talk to her for another second.

Or at least, that's how it seemed.

And despite the cliché, silence wasn't always golden. Sometimes silence was the hardest thing of all.

Elle told Travis she had a quick errand to run after church. He didn't question her. She'd never lied to him about something like this before— why would he suspect her of lying now? She'd done a great job hiding how she'd felt after her run-in with Dave Messer.

Last night, after he and Elle had gotten Lyndie safely home, Travis had pulled her into his arms and kissed her out on the Jacobs' porch. "Are you sure you're okay? You're so quiet."

She nodded. "I'm fine."

"I don't know what that guy said to you, but I know it doesn't matter. Not to me, and not to anyone else."

But it mattered to Elle. She wished it didn't, but it did.

"Have your relatives responded to the wedding invitation?" He paused. "Your mother at least?"

The question was innocent. If only the answer could be.

"I don't think she's coming," Elle said absentmindedly. Sliding her arms down from his shoulders, she stepped away, but Travis reached over and took her hand.

"What's going on, Elle?"

She'd always been closemouthed about her childhood, but she assumed he knew all about the trailer park. Yet for someone like Travis, that place was so far removed from his life, he could never understand. Not unless he saw it for himself—and no matter what, that could not happen.

But it was so much more than where she'd grown up. The men, the alcohol, Cassie's accident. Elle had too many secrets to keep track of, and any one of them could send Travis running the other way.

The only times her life had had some semblance of normalcy had been during the summers when she'd spent day after day living with Cassie's family. Karen had never seemed to mind the extra mouth to feed.

Meeting Cassie and Lyndie had been Elle's saving grace—like someone had thrown her a life jacket the day those two walked into her life.

Elle remembered how, that day, she'd gone to the market for milk, something she hadn't had in weeks. Her mom was working nights at a bar on the outskirts of town, which meant she would sleep all day and then go to work just after Elle got home from school. Elle didn't often venture outside the trailer park, but she was hungry, and the only thing in the cupboard was a box of stale Frosted Flakes.

She wandered down the aisles of the market until she found the cooler with milk in it. She didn't have enough money for a whole gallon, so she reached inside and pulled out half a gallon. As she started toward the front of the store, she saw two girls, one dark-haired and one blonde, standing in the candy aisle talking about bubblegum.

Elle hadn't had bubblegum in a long time. She liked the fruity kind.

"Hey, what's your favorite gum?" the dark-haired girl asked when she walked by.

Elle's eyes went wide. "Me?"

"Yeah. Lyndie likes mint gum, but I like strawberry. Be our tie-breaker and we'll give you a piece." The girl's smile was big and toothy.

The milk carton was cold in Elle's hands as condensation formed on the outside of it.

"Well?" The girl held up two packs of gum and gave each a little shake. "Which one?"

Elle pointed at the strawberry bubblegum, and the girl held it up like a trophy.

"Awesome." She picked up two packs of strawberry gum and one pack of mint, then started toward the front of the store with her friend.

"I thought you had to pick one?" Elle followed close behind them.

"No, I just wanted to know which kind you liked." The girl didn't turn around. "I'm Cassie, and this is Lyndie. Who are you?"

Elle had never met anyone like this girl. Usually the summer kids stayed far away from her side of town. "I'm Elle."

"We're going to the beach later. Wanna come?"

Elle's eyes widened again. "The beach?"

"Yeah, we're riding bikes. Do you have one?"

Elle shook her head as Cassie set the three packs of gum on the checkout counter.

"I have an extra. It used to be my brother's, so it's a dirt bike, but it's yours if you want it." Cassie dug in her pocket for two dollars, which she handed the girl behind the counter.

The teenage clerk, whose name tag said "Tiffany," gave her change, and Cassie swiped the packages of gum off the counter. She stuck one in her pocket, handed one to the blond girl and then handed one to Elle.

"Take it," she said. "I got it for you."

Elle set the milk on the counter and did as she was told.

Tiffany gave her a once-over, then rang up the milk. "Two dollars, thirty-four cents."

Elle reached into her pocket and pulled out a handful of change, which she handed over to Tiffany, who looked irritated she had to count it out. "You're short fifteen cents."

Elle stuck her hands in both pockets, knowing full well she would come up empty. Cassie and Lyndie watched for a split second, and then Lyndie reached in her pocket and pulled out a quarter.

"No, it's okay," Elle said.

"Take it," Lyndie said.

"Thanks." Elle could feel her cheeks flush with embarrassment. Usually, she could pretend everything was fine. She could act like the things that bothered her—not having a mom in the audience at the school play or being the only one whose field-trip permission slip was never signed—didn't bother her.

But even back then, it was like Lyndie and Cassie had known better than that. Elle had never been able to hide who she was from them, because they'd known from the beginning.

And it had never mattered to them.

But Travis was different. And Nora was different. And while they knew Elle had been poor, they didn't know how poor. They didn't know how unwanted. And they definitely didn't know the things she'd done trying to make up for that.

Now, parked outside the trailer, she could almost smell the musty odor of cigarettes and liquor. She could almost hear the door creak open in the middle of the night and the sound of her mom in bed with whatever guy she'd brought home from the bar. She could sense the utter loneliness of another dark night in that tiny trailer by herself. There had never been anyone to comfort her when the darkness scared her.

When her summer "family" would go back home, Elle would be left alone again, as if the fairy tale was over and the magic spell had ended. That's when guys like Dave Messer started to seem like a good idea, like her only way out.

She'd been so naïve to think any of them could be the solution, but nobody had taught her otherwise. It wasn't until she was first dating Travis that she'd even considered there might be more out there for her.

She should've insisted they get married at their church in Chicago. Or at city hall. Or on top of a mountain in Antarctica. She should not be getting married here, in Sweethaven.

Had her mother heard she'd made it back to town? Did the locals still talk about Elle like she was the poor, unwanted outcast she'd always felt she was?

Her eyes fell to the envelope on her lap. She'd kept it tucked inside her purse since the day it had arrived in her mailbox. She didn't get many handwritten letters, but when she'd seen the postmark, her stomach had dropped. For a split second, she'd thought maybe someone had written to tell her that Lily Porter had died. Truth be told, Elle couldn't believe her mom had lasted this long, not with the way she lived.

But the contents of that envelope were so much worse.

A knock on the car window startled Elle, and she glanced up to find an old lady standing beside the small SUV.

The woman's face was deeply wrinkled, her thin lips the same color as her skin. She motioned for Elle to roll down the window. Against her better judgment, Elle did.

"Can I help you with something?" the lady said. "You've been sitting here almost a half hour."

"No, I'm sorry, I'll go." Elle started to roll up the window, but the woman put her hand on it.

"You looking for Lily?"

Elle shook her head. "No."

"She's probably in there, you know. The bar gives her Sundays off. Well, most Sundays. Do you know Lily?"

Elle looked back at the dingy trailer. Ten years, and her mother hadn't moved forward even an inch. She was still stuck right there at the edge of town, probably still working at Smitty's, serving drinks to men who grabbed her from behind and looked at her like she wasn't even a person at all.

"She'd probably like the company," the old woman said. "Doesn't get many visitors."

"Oh, I can't stay," Elle said. "But thanks." She started the engine of her car, but the woman didn't back away.

"What'd you say your name was? I'll tell her you stopped by."

"No, don't."

The woman frowned, her brow pinched.

"I don't know her very well, is all." Elle shifted into drive. "Sorry to bother you."

Finally, the old woman took her hand off the SUV, and Elle drove away, her heart pounding.

What had she thought? That she'd show up outside the trailer and suddenly have the courage to confront her mother? To make her promise she wouldn't tell anyone what had really happened the night Cassie died? Did Elle really think she could reason with Lily—make her understand how important Travis was to her?

She should've known better.

She passed through the park's gate, feeling no more confident than when she'd first pulled into town. After all, if her mother knew the truth, it was just a matter of time before Elle's chance at a fresh new life went up in flames.

# Chapter Nineteen

After Sunday lunch with his parents and a sullen Lyndie, Tucker took the boat out for the afternoon—anything to get out of the house and out of Lyndie's crosshairs.

The way she looked at him—or didn't look at him—was a constant reminder of the pain he'd caused. And while some women dealt with that the way Tess did, he'd always known Lyndie was different.

Lyndie had been the girl who hardly wore makeup, who didn't show off her body, who didn't apologize for being a prude. Whenever it was her turn to pick the outdoor movie, she'd bring DVDs like *The Parent Trap*, *Pollyanna* and what she called "a little-known gem"—*Summer Magic*.

The outdoor movies were a tradition, and Tucker had known there was no sense complaining. Lyndie was like part of the family, and everyone got a turn picking the movie. Still, her choices were so *Lyndie*.

Once, moments after she'd unveiled *Pollyanna*, she caught him rolling his eyes. Instead of shrinking under his irritation, she put on that pointed glare and said, "Next you're going to tell me you don't like Holly Golightly either."

"Holly go-who?"

She gasped. "You've never seen *Breakfast at Tiffany's*? Audrey Hepburn. It's a classic. My favorite movie ever."

He stared blankly.

She did nothing to hide her disappointment. "You don't know what you're missing, Tucker Jacobs."

He hadn't then, but he did now.

He'd tried not to let everything turn so upside down. He'd tried to make himself call her at Belmont, but he couldn't do it. He was so embarrassed by what had happened between them, and devastated that he'd been so foolish on the very night his sister died.

The same thought kept tumbling around in his head—*If I'd been with Cassie, maybe she would still be here.*

He'd mostly banished that blame in the last few years, finally making peace with the fact it had been an accident he couldn't have prevented even if he'd been there. But now, being back here, surrounded by all these haunting memories, he felt like a failure. His business, his charity work, his clean lifestyle—none of it mattered if he failed at the things that were really important.

Now, as Tucker washed the remnants of a day alone on the lake from his skin, he prayed for wisdom, because he knew he didn't have words to heal Lyndie's still-wounded heart.

She was strong and successful and beautiful, but something was still broken inside her. He'd broken it, and he had to figure out a way to put it back together. That's the conclusion he'd come to out on the lake. He owed it to her to have the hard conversation, the one that would make him feel vulnerable and humiliated and exposed. Wasn't she worth it?

But how? When? Was he going to apologize for taking her virginity and never calling her again, on the way to tonight's mocktail party?

He showered and dressed—nice clothes, as Travis had suggested—then went downstairs, his heart still racing at the thought of confronting Lyndie, of making it right. But before he walked into the living room, he caught a glimpse of her standing at the counter.

Her hair was long and loose, wavy and falling over her shoulders, and she wore a white sundress that showed off her tan. He watched her for a few seconds before she finally looked up, caught him staring. He turned away.

How was he going to survive a whole week with her?

"Well, don't you two look nice?" His mom's voice took on a particularly cheerful tone, making Tucker shift where he stood. "They're going to keep you busy this week, from the sounds of it." She sat at the counter, looking at something on her laptop.

Tucker ran a hand over his stubbled chin. "I should go." He started for the door.

His mother stood. "You're going together, aren't you?"

Lyndie shot him a look, and he could see she didn't like the idea any more than he did. After all, she'd made her feelings about him known that morning.

Suddenly, his plan to apologize felt really, really stupid. He'd be better off avoiding her for a while. He had the whole week to figure out a way to bring it all up.

"It would just be silly for Lyndie to drive when you're already going," his mom said, "and, besides, you should be a gentleman and see that she gets home safely."

*A gentleman. Right.*

"Fine with me," Tucker said. "You ready?"

Lyndie picked up a small purse from the counter and nodded as his mom beamed. "You both look very nice tonight—even better standing side by side."

"Mom," he warned.

"You do," she said. "I can't help it if you're both gorgeous. Let me take a picture." She held her phone up and away, peering at it as if she couldn't quite make out which button to push. "Ah, here we go." She pointed it at the two of them. "Get closer."

"It's not the senior prom, Ma."

"Well, I didn't get to take photos of that, did I, Tucker?" She eyed him. Point taken. He'd crashed his senior prom—drunk—with some of his buddies. He'd almost gotten expelled for that little stunt.

He stepped closer to Lyndie, who appeared to barely tolerate the whole scene, and waited until his mom snapped not one but five photos.

"You finished?" he asked when she paused for a second to look through the images.

"I'm not sure . . ."

"You're finished," he said. "We gotta go."

"Oh, okay." His mom smiled up at them, then pulled Lyndie into a quick hug. "Now, try to have fun, okay?"

*Fun. Right.*

Outside, Lyndie tromped off down the stairs and into the driveway. "I can drive myself."

"Don't you think that'll make good old Karen a little suspicious?" Tucker asked, squaring off with her. "You know she's watching from the window."

The tension raced back and forth between them like an electrical current until, finally, Lyndie relented. "Fine." She marched over to his car and stood by the passenger door until he unlocked it and let her in.

Before he opened his own door, he heaved a sigh, wishing he could put this entire week behind him.

The drive to the Preston cottage was chilly at best.

"You look nice." Maybe flattery would chip away at her icy exterior.

She stared out the window.

Maybe not.

He turned onto Jonquil Street, parked the car down the road from the Preston cottage and turned off the engine. Surrounded by quiet, he dared a quick glance at her. She stared straight ahead, as if engrossed by something in the road in front of them.

"You ready for this?" he asked. "Lyndie?"

"Let's just get it over with," she said, and exited the car without another word.

◆　◆　◆

Lyndie didn't wait for Tucker to follow her to the Preston cottage. Instead, she kept at least three yards between them all the way to the door. She didn't trust herself around Tucker, especially not when he was wearing that black suit with a blue shirt that made his eyes look like they'd been plugged into an electrical socket.

Every time her mind wandered back to the boat the night before, her stomach rolled over and she thought she might be sick. Hadn't she learned anything? This was not who she was, and it was especially not who she wanted Tucker to think she was.

She'd pulled herself up so many times, and she'd turned herself into a competent woman. She was doing well for herself. She'd just had a meeting with Jalaire Grant, for Pete's sake.

Why, then, did she turn into a hopeless teenager all over again whenever Tucker was around?

She chastised herself the whole way to the front door, wishing she could rewind the past two days. If only she'd waited until today to arrive, she could make a grand entrance at the party, pretending that neither Tucker nor anyone else made her feel anything but a casual nostalgia.

But instead, she'd been blindsided by an outpouring of *feelings*. And she hated feelings.

She walked up the driveway toward the white cottage, a wide building with a connected three-car garage off to the left and the rest of the house stretching out to the right. From the front, it almost resembled a ranch home, but from the sloping lake view out back, three distinct stories were visible—and each floor had its own unique amenities. Calling this place a "cottage" seemed a bit off base.

Lyndie rang the doorbell, thankful when the door opened before Tucker joined her on the porch. He entered behind her and found Travis immediately. As they walked off, Lyndie searched for somewhere safe to hide.

Elle was in the front room, being gushed over by Travis's relatives, and as Lyndie looked around, she realized there weren't many people she knew. She wandered into the dining room with its wall of windows that faced the lake. Watching the boats pass by, she wished for a polite way to escape the evening.

She'd gotten lost in her thoughts when someone came up behind her, standing a little too close.

"Brought you a drink."

Lyndie turned and found Jackson, who wore a smile suggesting he had high hopes for the two of them—and in a flash, her humiliation returned.

"Oh, thanks, I'm fine," she said.

"Come on, you aren't going to make it through this stuffy evening if you don't drink something." He thrust the glass toward her.

"It's a mocktail party." She stared at the yellowish beverage.

"I added a little something to it." He grinned.

She took it—not because she wanted to drink the fruity concoction, but because she didn't feel like arguing with him. "About last night—"

His upheld hand cut her off. "It's not your fault Tucker showed up acting crazy. We can pick up where we left off later." He smiled again, and when he did, Lyndie realized he wasn't attractive. Another man with whom a relationship would amount to nothing. But she already had one of those.

"Actually, Jackson . . ." Lyndie thought of Foster and all the guys before him. All the words she'd held on to but should've said to them. For a songwriter, how was it she could never find the words?

"Oh, Lyn, I'll be right back. Looks like they just brought in the nachos."

*Lyn?* Again with the Lyn.

Lyndie cringed as she turned and watched him go, but as she did, she caught Tucker staring at her from the other room. She gave herself a quick three seconds to hold his gaze, then looked away.

Was he checking up on her?

After the appetizers, Travis's parents ushered everyone out back, where tables had been set up underneath a large white canvas tent. White lights were strung from one end to the other, and candles decorated the center of each table. Lyndie attempted to sit at a table near the back, but Elle quickly found her and led her up to the very front, where Travis and Tucker were waiting.

"We wanted our best man and maid of honor with us tonight," Elle said, beaming. She leaned in closer to Lyndie and whispered, "I hope it's not too awkward."

Lyndie forced a smile, mad at herself for being such a terrible friend. It shouldn't matter that she and Elle had drifted apart. Lyndie was her maid of honor. She should set aside her own issues and act like it.

Somehow.

Elle sat down next to Travis, and Lyndie stared at the empty chair next to Tucker. He stood and pulled it out, motioning for her to sit.

She looked down to conceal the heat that had rushed to her cheeks. "Thank you," she said quietly as she took her seat.

They were joined at their table by Travis's cousins Russell, Violet and Sarabeth . . . and Jackson.

Jackson sat as far away from Tucker as he could—probably wise.

Pastor Preston and Nora made their way to the front of the tent and waited until the murmur of quiet conversation died down.

"We're so happy you could all join us for this very special week celebrating two very special people," the pastor said, not unlike he probably would on the stage at his church. "Travis and Elle met right here in Sweethaven, so it's only fitting they start their life together right here."

Lyndie glanced at Elle, who studied her hands in her lap.

"Before we eat, we'd like to return thanks," Nora said. "If you'd all join hands around your table."

Lyndie's heart dropped. Sarabeth reached over and took her left hand, and Lyndie froze, staring at Tucker's empty hand on her right.

She paused for several seconds, then found him watching her. He glanced down as he turned his hand upward, inviting her to slip hers inside, like a letter in an envelope. Slowly, she reached over and placed her hand in his, noting the tingle that shot up her spine as he wrapped his fingers around hers. His thumb traced a line from her wrist to the top of her thumb, making it impossible for her to concentrate on the pastor's prayer.

When "Amen" rang out, Sarabeth dropped Lyndie's hand, but Tucker held on for too many unfair seconds. Unfair because she didn't want him to let go. And she sensed that he knew it.

She slid her hand from his, hopelessly aware of the coolness she felt from the absence of his touch.

"So, you all grew up together?" Sarabeth asked, turning her attention to the four friends sitting on one side of the table.

"We did," Travis said. "Tucker, Lyndie and I spent our summers here—our parents all had cottages."

"And what about you, Elle?"

Lyndie glanced at her friend, picturing the trailer where Elle had grown up. During the summers, Elle had almost never gone back home. She'd practically lived with Lyndie and Cassie, and neither of their families seemed to mind. Sometimes, Lyndie had thought that if the Jacobs family could've adopted Elle, they would've.

One summer in middle school, Lyndie and Cassie had arrived in Sweethaven a day early. Anxious to see their friend, they'd ridden their bikes over to the trailer park on the outskirts of town, quickly realizing that even Sweethaven had a wrong side of the tracks.

"Is this the right one?" Cassie asked when they pulled up in front of a dingy white trailer with a crooked front porch.

Lyndie glanced at the house number she'd written on her hand after Mama J. had looked up the address in the phone book. "Three Fifty-Two Magnolia. This is it."

They parked their bikes in the dirt out front and made their way to the door. The little trailer seemed even smaller with garbage bags full of stuff piled high on one side.

"This is where Elle lives?" Cassie whispered.

They'd been friends for two years by that point, but Elle had always met them in town. Now Lyndie understood why.

She knocked on the door and waited, listening to the sound of movement inside the house.

"Elle! The door!" they heard a woman shout.

Seconds later, the door opened. Elle's eyes widened, then quickly fell in obvious embarrassment. "What are you doing here?"

Maybe they shouldn't have come.

"We got in a day early," Cassie said. "We wanted to see if you could come over for a bonfire tonight. We're making s'mores."

"Who is it?" the woman yelled.

"It's for me, Ma," Elle said, turning away. She turned back to face Lyndie and Cassie. "I don't know if I can."

Lyndie couldn't see much through the partially opened door, but from what she could tell, the trailer's interior resembled the porch. Piles and piles of garbage bags and boxes filled the room just beyond where her friend stood. Empty bottles littered the floor, and shabby curtains hung closed over the windows.

The image of Mama J. coming home with "an extra shirt I found on sale" skittered through Lyndie's mind. Cassie's mom must've seen what the girls couldn't—that Elle didn't have anyone taking care of her.

"Well, we'll be at my house," Cassie said. "You're more than welcome. My mom bought extra marshmallows just for you."

Elle smiled. The summer before, she'd rejected the graham crackers and chocolate in favor of toasted marshmallows, and they'd teased her about how many she'd eaten. In that moment, Lyndie realized she probably didn't get treats very often.

"Thanks, guys," Elle said. "It's really good to see you. I'll be over as soon as I can."

Lyndie now made eye contact with Elle from across the table, wondering what had ever happened to her mom. She certainly wasn't at this ritzy welcome party.

"I grew up here," Elle said in answer to Sarabeth's question.

"That must've been amazing," Sarabeth said. "And you all were so lucky to leave real life for a whole summer."

"I don't think any of us realized it," Travis said. "We were just kids."

The small talk continued throughout dinner, and by the time dessert was served, Lyndie'd had enough of memory lane. How much longer did she have to stay?

Travis rose and moved to where his parents had stood, then waited, as they had, for the silence of the crowd. Once he had everyone's attention, he smiled warmly. He'd gotten more handsome over the years, and Lyndie wondered if Cassie would've been over him by now—or if she'd be the one standing next to him on his wedding day.

"I'd like to thank you all for coming," Travis said. "It means the world to Elle and me to have you here, in Sweethaven, where we first fell in love. It seems like only yesterday I stole my first kiss behind the present table at her graduation party."

Travis went on, but Lyndie's heart stopped.

She stared at Elle, who wore an unmistakable look of panic.

"To Elle," Travis said, raising his glass.

"To Elle," the crowd repeated, raising their glasses in the direction of the bride.

Tucker set his glass down and glanced at Lyndie. "You okay?"

"I need some air."

She threw her napkin on the table and stood, still glaring at Elle, who didn't meet her eyes. Lyndie rushed from the tent and onto the back patio of the Preston cottage.

"Lyndie, wait."

She spun around at the sound of Elle's voice. "Our graduation party?"

"I can explain."

"You and Travis hooked up at our graduation party," Lyndie said, letting the idea of Elle's betrayal sink in. "You told me it happened after Cassie died."

"I can explain," Elle repeated.

"You told me it was weeks later, and that was bad enough, but you did this to her while she was still alive?"

The question hung in the air as Tucker and Travis appeared at the tent's entrance.

Lyndie faced them. "Did you know how much she loved you?" she said to Travis.

He looked away.

"If she had known about this, it would've broken her heart."

"It wasn't like that, Lyndie," Elle said. "It was a silly kiss and it never amounted to anything until later."

"How could you do this to her, Elle?" Lyndie's voice cracked, despite her whisper. Suddenly all of those *feelings* were right at the surface, bubbling over and spilling out onto everyone else.

*Why am I falling apart?*

She wiped a tear from her cheek, waited too long for a response that didn't come, then finally turned and walked away.

# Chapter Twenty

Tucker drove up and down the quiet streets of Sweethaven, searching for Lyndie for an hour. He checked the beach, the gazebo, even Dewey's boat docked in the marina, but there was no sign of her anywhere.

Around midnight, he finally went back home, struck by the quiet of the cottage at night. The moonlight streamed in from the windows, illuminating the sleeping porch, where he found Lyndie fast asleep on one of the beds. She was still wearing her sundress and sandals, as though she'd just collapsed there and couldn't be bothered with appropriate sleepwear.

He pushed open the screen door and walked onto the porch, watching her for a moment and wondering what kind of havoc this trip was wreaking on her. Lyndie had a chip on her shoulder, but that didn't mean she was as resilient as she wanted everyone to believe. She seemed to be unraveling, and he couldn't help but wonder if that was all his fault.

She'd fallen asleep on top of the covers, and in her rest, she looked peaceful. As if all her cares had fallen away.

Tucker knelt beside the bed and gently removed her sandals, holding each foot delicately so as not to wake her. Then, he picked up a thin afghan from the end of another bed and spread it across her sleeping body.

She didn't even stir.

He reached over and brushed a stray hair from her cheek, tucking it gently behind her ear. "I'm so sorry, Lyndie." The words escaped, barely a whisper, and as they did, the door to the porch creaked.

Tucker spun around and found his dad standing there, face shadowed in the moonlight.

"Everything okay?" his dad whispered.

Tucker stood. "She had a rough night." He moved into the kitchen, wanting to disappear. He didn't want his dad to see the regret on his face, but somehow, it seemed too late for that.

"Would you like some tea?" His dad flipped on the light over the sink and filled the kettle.

"Tea?" Since when did his dad drink tea?

"It's decaf. I drink it when I can't sleep."

"Which is . . . often?"

His dad set the kettle on the stove and turned the knob until the burner clicked on and the flame appeared. "More often than I'd like." He watched Tucker. "What happened with Lyndie?"

Tucker exhaled a deep breath at the myriad of answers to that question. "I think she's just having a hard time being back here, is all."

"I meant what happened with you two ten years ago?"

Tucker's eyes shot to his father's as his nerves carved a hollow spot in his chest. "What do you mean?"

"Fathers are sometimes in the dark where their kids are concerned, but somehow I think I went on hyperalert when it came to you."

"And you think something was wrong between me and Lyndie?" How did he know? And more importantly—how much did he know?

"If I had to guess—yes."

Tucker considered coming clean right there. His dad was no dummy—and he knew Tucker was no saint. But how could Tucker ever admit what he'd stolen from Lyndie, a girl who'd been like a daughter to Davis?

"Nothing happened," Tucker said.

His dad eyed him. "I think she cares about you. And I think you care about her too."

Tucker looked away.

"Have you told her?"

Tucker shook his head. "I think you're confused, Dad. There's nothing to tell. You and Mom need to stop playing matchmaker and maybe spend a little more time communicating with each other."

His dad stilled. Had Tucker gone too far? Was it off-limits to bring up the tension in the air between his parents? Could he call them out on all the things they weren't saying, or would that make him a hypocrite?

The water in the teakettle boiled, threatening to blow its whistle. "We just want what's best for you, son."

"I have a good life now, Dad."

"I know you do. And we're very proud."

The words didn't ring true.

"There was a time we thought we'd lost you too." His dad pulled the kettle from the flame and turned the stove off. "Just feels like there's something that's got a hold on you, like you need to get something off your chest. Maybe making things right with Lyndie would be a good start."

The whispers that had filled his head only moments ago danced in his mind. "I'm fine, Dad. Just tired."

His father nodded and poured the hot water over a tea bag inside a ceramic mug.

"I'm going to bed." Tucker started for the door.

"Kayaking in the morning?"

Tucker turned. "You were serious about that?"

"Of course." His dad smiled. "Gotta spend as much time with you as I can before you head back to that good life of yours."

Tucker nodded. "Okay, then. I'll see you first thing."

His dad held up his mug as if to offer a toast. "See you then."

◆ ◆ ◆

Lyndie awoke Monday morning to the sound of voices filtering through the window over her head.

"Is she okay?"

"I don't know, Ma. Why don't you ask her?"

"I don't want to be nosy."

"Obviously you do."

"She seems fragile to me. Like she's putting on a brave face, but something inside her is crumbling."

"You know she's a grown woman, right?"

"It has to be hard, being here. Especially without Cassie. Was she upset last night? Is that why she slept on the porch?"

Lyndie opened her eyes, realizing she was, in fact, on the sleeping porch, still wearing last night's clothes. Someone had removed her sandals and covered her—probably Mama J.—but she'd slept soundly from the moment she'd closed her eyes until now. She sensed it was early and that Tucker and his mom were trying to be quiet, but they weren't doing a very good job of it.

"I think she had a rough night, Ma," Tucker said. "And I'm sure you're right, it's not easy being back here—for lots of reasons."

"What does that mean?"

Before Tucker could answer, Lyndie opened the screen door, probably looking like a complete disaster.

"Lyndie," Mama J. said, turning toward her. "You're awake."

"You two probably woke her," Davis said. "The window is open."

"Oh, goodness, you're right," Karen said. "I'm so sorry about that. Do you want some coffee? Breakfast? The boys are going kayaking, so I'm making bacon and eggs. Gotta get their energy up."

"Some coffee would be good," Lyndie said.

"No eggs?"

"I don't eat in the morning."

"It's the most important meal of the day," Davis said, winking at her from over the top of his newspaper.

"Don't mock, Davis. It *is* the most important meal." Karen shot him a look, then returned to the stove. "Tucker, pour Lyndie a cup of coffee."

Lyndie wanted to protest, but Tucker was already finding a mug in the cupboard. He pulled one down, poured a cup, added creamer and a little bit of sweetener, then set it in front of her on the island at the center of the kitchen.

"Thanks," she said.

Gosh, she'd treated him badly. She'd treated Elle badly. And had she really yelled at Travis? This trip was beginning to feel like one exercise in humiliation after another. What had happened was in the past. She needed to leave it there.

Tucker sat down on the stool next to her, and Lyndie's mind floated back many years. The morning after almost every sleepover at the Jacobs' house ended with a big breakfast standing around this very island.

Travis, Tucker and oftentimes Dewey would push the girls out of the way to stuff themselves with the many options Mama J. put in front of them. They'd had no idea Karen always saved plenty for the girls— she would reveal it only after the boys had left the kitchen. And while the room felt much too quiet now, that same joy was still in Karen's eyes as she provided for her people.

She handed out plates, then set trays of bacon, eggs and pancakes at the center of the island. "Dig in."

Tucker and his dad followed her orders, but Lyndie sipped her coffee, marveling at how she could feel so out of sorts and yet so at home at the same time. If only the comfort of being here could win out over the regret.

Elle breezed into the room, freshly showered, hair done and makeup neatly applied, looking like a carbon copy of Nora Preston.

"Good morning, Elle," Karen said, pulling out another plate. "Come, join us."

Elle glanced at Lyndie, who quickly looked away. "Maybe just coffee."

"You girls," Mama J. said. "I wish you'd eat something."

"I have my final fitting this morning," Elle said, taking the steaming mug Cassie's mom offered. "Are you coming, Lyndie?"

Tucker's eyes dashed to Lyndie as she set her mug down on the counter. "Of course."

"Good," Elle said, smiling. Probably relieved Lyndie hadn't tattled on her for being a terrible friend.

"I should go get ready," Lyndie said. "Thanks for the coffee." She took her mug and hurried up the stairs, waiting until she was safe behind the door of Cassie's room before letting out a deep breath.

Seconds later, there was a knock on the door. She opened it and found herself standing face-to-face with Tucker. She said nothing.

"I just wanted to check on you," he said, leaning against the doorjamb. "I looked for you last night, but I couldn't find you." His jaw twitched as he waited for her to reply.

She didn't know what to say. Finally—and only because he wasn't going away—she said, "I'm fine."

He pressed his lips together, and Lyndie wished he wasn't so good-looking. "You don't seem like it."

She studied the floor. She didn't need his concern, not when these feelings were following her around like they had a right to.

"Do you think we could call a truce?" he asked.

Her eyes shot back to his. "A truce?"

"Yeah."

"Do you really think that's necessary?"

"Yeah."

*I don't trust myself enough to be nice to you.*

She chewed the inside of her cheek. "Sure, Tucker."

"Really?"

She stuck her hand out. "Truce."

He stared at her for too many seconds, then took her hand and shook it. "So, we're friends, then?"

She nodded. It was all they'd ever be.

"So, will you tell me how you're really doing?"

Her eyes filled with tears she could not let herself cry. She couldn't stand it if he was nice to her. How could she continue to hate him? It was hard enough after hearing his speech yesterday in the churchyard.

Had Tucker really changed?

And if he had, what did that mean? Nothing, really. Good for him. She hoped he had a great life in California.

But that wasn't honest either, was it? Thinking that Tucker had changed meant thinking about the way he used to be—about what he'd done to her. It meant thinking about that night, the accident, feeling like she'd let her best friend down.

"Lyndie." Her name, whispered on his lips, tugged at the knot inside her. She wanted to forgive him—wanted to forgive herself—but how?

He reached up and touched her cheek, wiping a stray tear away with his thumb.

"Don't be nice to me, Tucker," she said.

"Lyndie, I—"

"Tucker?" His father's voice called up the stairs.

"Go," she said. "I'm fine."

He just stared at her again for a long, heavy beat, then pulled his hand from her face. She gently closed the door, sinking into a heap on the floor and allowing gentle sobs to overtake her body.

If Cassie were there, she would've come to her side, wrapped an arm around her and let her cry. She would've insisted that crying was therapeutic, as much as Lyndie hated it, and she would've told Lyndie to feel all those feelings.

"It's good for you," she would've said.

"I hate it," Lyndie would've replied. "I don't even like crying at sad movies."

"I know, Lyndie Lou, but when you feel something, you've gotta feel it all the way—otherwise it'll just eat you up inside."

Feeling any of this "all the way" was not an option. Lyndie needed to pull herself together, shove it all back in its box where it belonged and power her way through the next week.

If she didn't, all these feelings would destroy her.

# Chapter Twenty-One

"You really going to try and tell me there's nothing going on there?" Tucker's dad tossed a look back toward the house as they walked to Tucker's SUV.

"Give it a rest, old man."

"I daresay I can still keep up with you, even if you are a big adventure-seeker these days."

They drove down to the lake, the same spot where Tucker and Travis had gone kayaking yesterday. The waves were tame, the water manageable. Perfect for a beginner like his dad. Unloading their kayaks and gear, they started off into the water.

Davis paddled straight into the surf and kept on going. As much as Tucker hated to admit it, he had to rush to catch up.

Okay, so, not a beginner.

"You were holding out on me," Tucker said, coming up alongside him.

His dad grinned. "You're not the only one who loves the great outdoors."

Usually the best part about being out there was that it didn't lend itself to conversation, and right now, that was just fine with Tucker. But his dad seemed intent on talking despite the physical exertion.

"Sounds like things are going well for you out there," he said. "You know, your business and everything."

Tucker nodded. "Yeah. Things are good."

"I'm glad, son."

"Are you?" His sideways glance landed on his father as Tucker added a bit of extra strength to his paddling.

"Course I am," he replied. "We wish we saw you a little more, but we're happy you're doing well."

Tucker stared ahead, trying to drink in the open air, the way the sunlight danced on the water. He should let it go and take his father at his word. He didn't need to go picking a fight, not today. Never mind that he'd always thought his dad blamed him for the accident. Never mind that he assumed both his parents thought it should've been him out there and not Cassie. Never mind that he believed those things too.

He didn't have to get into any of that right now.

And yet, there was still so much unsaid.

"I know you guys were against my business from the start." Tucker knew because, when he'd called his dad for business advice, the first thing Davis said was *I'm not sure this is a great idea for you, Tuck.*

"That's not true," his dad said, glancing at him. He slowed his paddling, just slightly. "That's not true at all."

"Mom always thought it was too risky," Tucker reminded him. "And you didn't think I had a head for business."

His dad shook his head. "I just wanted you to be responsible. I was worried about you. Your mother worries about you."

"Mom worries about everything," Tucker said.

"That's true."

"Are you two okay?"

His dad pressed his lips together. As the years passed, Davis Jacobs had become a lot mellower than Tucker remembered. Almost like his light had gone out. Or maybe he'd just stopped caring.

"We're fine," he said.

"But really?"

His dad sighed. "Your mom hasn't found a way to move on. She's lost without Cassie, without you. She doesn't know who she is if she's not taking care of everyone."

"She's got her practice," Tucker said.

He shrugged. "She does. But it's not the same. You know how she is, Tuck. She always said she was born to be a mother—she's not happy unless she's mothering."

Tucker drew in a deep breath, and a pause fell between them. He hadn't thought about it that way. His mom missed him—not because she was overbearing, but because he was part of her identity. He made her who she was, who she most loved to be—a mother.

"Without you and Cassie here, she ends up mothering me," his father said. "I think she's upset because I don't need that. Because I've found a way to go on. I mean, of course it's not the same—it never will be—but I'm still here. And unlike her, I don't think laughing is a sin."

Tucker didn't respond. Instead, he paddled onward, wishing he'd been a better son to his parents, not just since Cassie's death but even before.

They carried on in silence, eventually turning around to head back to shore. When they reached it, Tucker got out and pulled his kayak onto the beach.

"Mom thinks you're trying to punish yourself for Cassie's death," his dad finally said.

Tucker stopped moving. "Punish myself? Why would I do that? I wasn't even there."

Davis eyed him. "Maybe you think it was your fault?"

Tucker shrank under his father's gaze. Parents had a way of reading your mind. "That's ridiculous."

"I agree." His dad dropped his kayak onto the sand. "But do you?"

"Of course. I didn't know she was going to go out in the boat that night."

"Right."

"And I couldn't be with her all the time."

His dad shook his head. "No, you couldn't."

Tucker looked away. He didn't believe a word of it.

"It wasn't your fault, Tucker." Davis clapped a hand on his shoulder. "It wasn't your fault. And all this stuff you're doing, trying to cheat death—you can stop that now."

Tucker met his father's eyes. "Is that what you think I'm doing?"

"Isn't it? Because it seems like you don't care at all if you die."

"No, Dad, I care that I *live*."

His dad held his gaze but didn't respond.

"If there's one thing Cassie's death taught me," Tucker continued, "it's that life is too short. It's too short not to do the things that make you feel alive."

"Fine, but do you really have to do so many dangerous things in order to feel alive?" Davis had raised his voice now—and Tucker saw a little spark of who his father used to be.

"Cassie didn't do anything dangerous, Dad, and look what happened to her."

"Exactly." Davis squared off with him. "She never did anything dangerous, and look what happened to her."

Tucker went quiet. "Is that what this is about, Dad? Why don't you just come out and say it? She was the good one. I was the reckless one. It should've been me—not Cassie. You've always thought so."

"That's not true." His father looked away. "That is absolutely not true. But you and your mother—you're all I have left, and I can't imagine what I would do if anything happened to either one of you. You've always gone looking for trouble. Always. I just wish you were a little more settled."

"I am settled," Tucker said. "I'm settled in a life that I really love."

"But you're completely alone."

Lyndie's face popped into Tucker's mind.

"I don't want you to be alone." His dad's shoulders slumped. "You're my son, Tuck, and I love you."

Tucker could count on one hand the number of times Davis had said "I love you." Yet, looking at him now, Tucker believed him.

His dad met his gaze. "I've never once thought it should've been you out there."

Tucker pressed his lips together, but he couldn't respond. He didn't have words or resolve. It went against everything he'd always believed, but what if his parents *didn't* blame him? Could he stop blaming himself?

"It was an accident, and I'm not going to let you carry the weight of that. If anyone should've been protecting Cassie, it was me." His dad bent over to pick up his kayak, then started dragging it up toward the SUV. "Now, what are we going to do about Lyndie?"

Tucker picked up his own kayak and followed, wishing his father had changed the subject to something like baseball or the validity of pig latin as a foreign language.

"We're not going to do anything about Lyndie."

Davis leaned the kayak against the SUV and stared at Tucker. "Do you know what you have here?"

Tucker unlocked the doors. "A kayak and a nosy father?"

"You have a unique opportunity—a second chance."

Tucker groaned. "It's not happening, Pops. You might as well let it go."

"Are you really telling me you can get on that plane back to San Diego next Monday without at least exploring the possibility?"

Tucker heaved his kayak up on top of the SUV and strapped it down. "I think the best I can hope for is that Lyndie St. James finds a way to look at me without cringing. And in this case, I'm gonna call that a win."

◆ ◆ ◆

Elle stood at the center of the makeshift staging area Nora had created in the master bedroom of the Preston cottage. Celia pulled the train of her dress out and laid it gently on the ground at her side.

"It's just beautiful."

"Thank you, Celia," Elle said, admiring herself for a brief moment—and pushing aside the fact that Lyndie was twenty minutes late.

"And I didn't take it out even a smidge," Celia whispered.

Elle gasped, then let out a quiet giggle. "Nora will be able to tell."

"Trust me," Celia said. "She'll have no idea. It was perfect the way it was, and it's perfect now."

Sarabeth and Violet appeared from behind the changing screens, wearing their deep-teal bridesmaids' dresses. The gowns were classic and traditional, yet still playful and fun—at least that's what Nora said. But after one look at Violet, Elle couldn't help but think they'd made a mistake going with a strapless dress.

"I'm falling out of this thing," Violet said.

At least there was a belt around the waist.

"I love it," Sarabeth said, spinning as she took in her own reflection. "I think this is the one time I'm not jealous of your boobs."

Nora whisked into the room but took a step back when she saw the girls. "Oh, dear, Violet, are you sure the measurements you gave us were correct?"

Violet's cheeks turned a bright shade of pink.

"It's not so bad," Elle said. "Maybe we can add a strap?" She tossed Celia a pleading look. The woman—saint that she was—sprang into action.

"Of course we can." She turned Violet around and faced her toward the mirror. Then she yanked at the dress, pulling it tighter around the torso and explaining how she was going to swoop in and save the day.

After a few minutes, Violet's face returned to its normal shade of pale, and the attention in the room shifted.

"Where's Lyndie?" Nora frowned.

"I think she's on her way," Elle said in her best *no big deal* voice.

"You think?"

"She'll be here. Besides, Lyndie won't be hard to fit—she can wear anything."

"She should still be here," Nora said. "She's your maid of honor. Do you have her phone number?"

"I'll text her, Nora," Elle said. "She told me this morning she was coming—she's just a few minutes late. I'm sure she has an explanation."

Sadly, she was also sure she knew what it was. Lyndie was still mad at her. But Elle had a feeling Lyndie had been looking for a reason to explode since the moment she'd arrived in Sweethaven. Elle could relate.

Elle should've told Lyndie about kissing Travis at the graduation party, but after the accident, an innocent kiss seemed like nothing in comparison. She was angry with Lyndie that night because Lyndie hadn't been there, and Lyndie was angry with Elle because she had been.

Had they really carried all of that with them all this time? How could they get past it? And once they did, would Elle ever be able to tell Lyndie the whole truth?

"We're going to be late for our lunch if we aren't out of here on time," Nora said. "Text her now and make that clear, please."

Elle stepped off the staging block and moved into the hallway, where she suddenly felt like she couldn't breathe. She fished her phone from her purse, but before she could click it on, Lyndie walked up the stairs and into the hallway.

Elle turned and faced her. "You're here."

Lyndie's eyes found the floor. "Sorry I'm late."

"No, it's fine. Your dress is waiting for you. I hope you like it."

"It looks good in the pictures. And that teal is one of my favorite colors."

"It'll look good on you," Elle said. "With your eyes and everything."

Lyndie nodded.

"I'm sorry," Elle said. "That I didn't tell you about Travis. I should have—"

"Don't, Elle." Lyndie held up a hand that silenced her. "I just need to try my dress on. We don't need to talk about it." She walked past Elle and into the bedroom where the others were, sucking the oxygen straight from Elle's lungs. Was it too much to hope that Lyndie would forgive and forget?

No, Lyndie would never trust her again. And the worst part was, she didn't even know the worst part.

Lyndie stood still while a short, plump woman wearing her hair in a bun poked at her and told her how beautiful she was.

She said nothing as the others pranced around, acting a little too giddy. Nora entered the room and gave Lyndie a once-over.

"Oh, you made it," she said. "We thought perhaps you overslept."

Lyndie stared at her but said nothing. She'd never much cared for Nora Preston. The woman had a condescending air about her and a grand sense of entitlement. Would that attitude rub off on Elle?

"Celia, let's shorten this a little," Nora said, waving a hand somewhere around Lyndie's ankle, where the dress hit.

"Actually," Lyndie said, shocked that she'd found her own voice, "I'd like to keep it where it is."

Elle and the others did a slow turn. It wasn't often anyone disagreed with Nora, but Lyndie was the one who had to wear this dress. And if she couldn't speak her mind to anyone else, she could speak it now. Because she didn't care one little bit what the woman thought of her.

"Dear, it's unflattering at its current length. These dresses are meant to be tailored." Nora held her gaze.

"I prefer it this way," Lyndie said, though it wouldn't have bothered her one bit to shorten it. Mostly, she felt the need to prove a point—perhaps to remind herself she had a voice at all.

"I see," Nora said. Her eyes left Lyndie and landed on the seamstress. She gave a quick nod, as if issuing a directive.

"You can change, dear," Celia said. "And just bring the dress back to me so I can press it for you."

"I'll take it home," Lyndie said. "I can press it myself." She didn't miss the nonverbal exchange between Celia and Travis's mother. She didn't miss Nora's tightened jaw or the deep breath she drew in either. It felt exhilarating, speaking her mind. Why couldn't Lyndie do that with the people who really mattered?

She caught Elle's gaze and saw her friend's wide eyes, begging her to behave. Lyndie had always been the kind one. The meek one. The one who'd gone along with the rest of them and never said a word.

But that's not who she was anymore. She needed to be strong now. And strong women spoke their minds. Strong women didn't cry.

Nora Preston wasn't the one she was mad at, though.

Lyndie vowed to do better—for Elle. Lyndie was the maid of honor, after all. So, she made sure to be pleasant during lunch, engaging in conversation even though the small talk made her weary.

As they finished their meals, Nora held up a hand to get their attention, and the idle chatter faded away.

"We just want to thank each of you for being here for Elle," Nora said. "We know she doesn't have a large family, and we want to do all we can to make this a very special week for her."

Lyndie glanced at Elle, whose cheeks turned rosy. How much did Nora really know about Elle's family?

"Just a reminder that the fun continues this evening at the cottage. We have a very exciting night planned for all of you." Nora smiled. "Now, if you'll excuse me, I'm needed at the flower shop downtown."

Lyndie watched as Nora scooted her chair away from the table and walked out of the restaurant.

"Elle, if you're okay with it, we're going to head down to the beach," Sarabeth said. "I mean, you can totally come. We just want to work on our tans before the wedding."

"I think I'll pass," Elle said. "I don't want to freckle."

"Okay, we'll see you tonight!" Violet and Sarabeth disappeared, leaving Lyndie and Elle at the table alone.

For the first time since Elle had asked her to be maid of honor, Lyndie wondered how Elle was feeling about this wedding.

"We're going to Hawaii for our honeymoon," Elle said.

Lyndie frowned. "What happened to Disney World?"

When they'd finally spoken on the phone after Elle's texts about the wedding, Lyndie had felt like maybe Elle had been working overtime to fill the silence, but she remembered hearing that excitement in her voice when she'd talked about their honeymoon: "It won't happen right after the wedding, but we've blocked off a week later on this year. I can't believe I'm going to Disney World, Lyndie!" she'd said.

For a fleeting moment, Lyndie had felt ashamed, because she'd been to Disney World several times and never treated it like anything more than something she was entitled to. Elle had never been given those opportunities.

Now, Elle gave a soft shrug, staring at something on the wall behind Lyndie. "It's not really a grown-up honeymoon."

Was that what Nora had told her? "Elle, are you sure this is what you really want?"

"What do you mean?" Elle looked at her.

"Marrying into Travis's family. We both know what they're like."

"They're not that bad."

Lyndie shot her friend a look.

"They aren't as bad as we thought."

"How much of this wedding have you gotten to plan?" Lyndie asked. "Nora's running off to the flower shop—why aren't you going with her? Did you pick the dresses? The cake? Anything?"

Elle ran a hand through her long red hair. "I picked the groom." She paused. "And I picked you."

Lyndie studied her for a few seconds. "But why?"

Elle's perfectly plucked eyebrows drew downward into a V. "What do you mean, *why*?"

"We've hardly spoken in years."

"I know." Elle's eyes found her lap. "But there is no one else, Lyndie."

Lyndie glanced at Elle, and for the first time, she recognized something in her eyes—loneliness. Lyndie should've tried to make things right sooner. When they should've been leaning on each other, time and unspoken words had pushed them apart instead.

"I'm sorry, Elle."

"You all got to leave here after that summer, and I had to stay. And then the next summer, you didn't come back. I kept waiting, but you didn't come back."

"I couldn't." Lyndie felt vulnerable saying it out loud.

"It was the worst time of my life."

Lyndie looked away. *Mine too.*

"I didn't have anyone else to ask," Elle said. "I don't have a lot of friends. I have Travis. And Nora may not be perfect, but at least she cares. At least she's here."

"I know. I'm sorry, Elle. I'm happy to be a part of your wedding. Really." Lyndie grew quiet. "Have you told your mom you're in town?"

"Do you really think I want my mother showing up at our wedding?"

"The announcement will be in the newspaper. And people all over town are talking about it. She's going to find out."

"I'm sure she already knows," Elle said. "You know, I didn't want to come back here."

"You didn't?"

"I wanted to elope. Or have a small wedding in Chicago."

Lyndie frowned. "Then why are you going along with all of this?"

Tears filled Elle's eyes. "Because I've never been the center of anyone's attention. And if they want to make my wedding into a huge event all about me, well, I'm going to let them. And maybe if I'm good enough, then I'll finally feel like I belong."

Lyndie watched as Elle folded her napkin and set it on top of her plate. "You're not the only one who doesn't have anyone else."

Elle stilled.

Lyndie reached across the table and put a hand on Elle's. "And you're not the only one who feels like an outsider."

Elle's eyebrows twitched ever so slightly. She wouldn't understand, not without further explanation, but she'd have to take Lyndie at her word for now.

Lyndie didn't say anything else, but something passed between them in the silence. Two old friends who could sometimes communicate without words, and for the first time in many years, Lyndie felt like maybe what had been lost could be restored.

At least, she hoped so.

# Chapter Twenty-Two

The Preston cottage buzzed with chatter.

The entire wedding party, including ushers, a personal attendant, the wedding planner and various family members, milled around.

Lyndie caught fragments of conversation as she slowly moved from one room to the next.

Sarabeth and Violet were talking to an older woman about the best place to go for a prewedding waxing.

"Zax Wax over on Lilac Lane." The older woman spoke with a lazy southern drawl. "They are absolute magic with the hot wax."

Lyndie shuddered.

A small circle of guys were discussing a years-old golf game that had apparently ended in a fistfight, and two old men stood by the punch bowl, rambling about a fishing trip they planned to take "once all this wedding nonsense" had died down.

Tucker sauntered in wearing cargo shorts, a T-shirt and a pair of flip-flops and looking like he belonged on a billboard in Times Square. Lyndie watched him move through the room for a smidge longer than she should've, then forced her eyes away.

He made his way over to Travis, clapped a hand on his friend's shoulder and shook hands with Travis's cousin Russell.

Lyndie watched—then didn't watch—then watched him for several seconds, wishing his magnetic pull on her wasn't so strong. Every hair on her body seemed to stand to attention when he was in the room.

*Just get through this week, then you can go back home where it's safe.*

Emotional safety. That's what she needed most. And she wasn't going to get that here.

Nora stood in front of them all, holding a stack of envelopes. "Now, if I could have everyone's attention. We are going to have a wonderful fish fry on the beach this evening, but first, let's have some fun."

The small crowd murmured, and Lyndie wondered if anyone would notice if she slipped out the back door and hid for a few hours. She doubted she shared Nora's idea of fun.

"Because Sweethaven is so special to our family and to our bride and groom, we've developed a Scavenger Hunt of Romance—a fun way for you all to get to know the love story of our dear Travis and Elle. In my hand, I have a variety of clues leading you to various places around town that are special to everyone's favorite couple. You and your partner will locate these places, take your photo when you reach them, and text us your picture at each location. The first to text all of their photos will win a very special prize."

Lyndie would rather die.

"Lyndie, we should team up," Dewey said. "We'd kick some serious tourist butt."

"We've taken the liberty of dividing you all into pairs," Nora continued. "So, gentlemen, come on up and get your envelopes, then find your assigned partners and meet in the driveway out front."

A flash of middle school anxiety shot through Lyndie as she watched the guys walk to the front of the room and take a lavender envelope from Nora. When Dewey made a beeline for Violet, Lyndie's heart sank. Dewey, she could handle. Jackson or, worse, Tucker—she couldn't.

Jackson met her eyes as he read the name on his envelope, but he sauntered toward Sarabeth, which left Lyndie hopelessly aware that she was most likely paired with the best man.

"Looks like it's you and me," Tucker said. "Travis said his mom put together a pretty good prize, and I think we have the home-court advantage."

*You called a truce,* she reminded herself. They were friends now. Friends weren't mean to each other. So, she bit back the sarcastic comment that had entered her mind and forced a smile. "I think you're right."

They made their way outside, where the others had gathered.

"There's just one more rule," Nora said after quieting them all down. "No cars."

A collective groan wound its way through the crowd.

"We've made sure that everything is within walking distance. You can come back here when you're all finished, and we'll have the fish fry down on our beach."

"Isn't it funny that she actually thinks they own the beach?" Tucker whispered so only Lyndie could hear. She couldn't help it—she laughed.

Nora raised a pointy brow in her direction and then turned her attention back to the group.

"Okay, everyone ready?" Nora's voice took on a high pitch. "On your mark! Get set! GO!"

Lyndie, suddenly struck with a competitive spirit, glanced at Tucker, whose attitude about this whole thing was decidedly nonchalant.

"What's the first clue?" she asked as the other teams started off down the hill toward town.

"We could skip this whole thing and go parasailing," he said. "I'm dying to do something other than paddle a kayak."

She followed him down the driveway, aware of the waning daylight and the fact they were the last to leave. "We're going to lose if you don't hurry up."

"Is that a no to the parasailing?" He grinned. He was obviously kidding, but he still seemed to expect a reply.

"I don't like heights."

"You don't like anything risky."

She stared off, avoiding his eyes. If only that were true.

He pulled out the first card and read the clue out loud: "'Love has never been as sweet as it was on Travis and Elle's first date. Table for two, anyone?'" Tucker looked like he was trying not to roll his eyes.

"The Sweet Shoppe," Lyndie said. "Where Cassie always said she and Travis would go on their first date."

Tucker stuffed the card back inside the envelope. "You really didn't know about Travis and Elle?"

She shot him a look. "You did?"

"He told me," Tucker said. "Almost got in a fight with some local guys who were talking trash about her. He always had a thing for Elle."

"I had no idea."

They strolled down the street without another word until they reached Wildflower Lane, then turned right and headed to Main Street.

"Travis always thought of Cassie like a little sister." Tucker's words renewed the sting of those he'd said only days before. "I don't think that was ever going to change."

"I thought Elle was a better friend than that," Lyndie said. "Maybe it's a girl thing."

"No, it's not." Tucker stepped to the opposite side of Lyndie, putting himself between her and the road now that there was no sidewalk.

"Probably stupid to even care about it now," Lyndie said. "I overreacted last night. It's just . . ." How did she explain her outburst? It made no logical sense.

"I get it," he said, letting her off the hook. And for some reason, she thought he actually did.

They walked in silence, and she searched her mind for small talk. Under other circumstances, walking down the road with Tucker Jacobs would've been exciting and fun. Under the weight of what she was trying to keep buried, however, it simply felt overwhelming. He deserved to know what it was that she couldn't say.

"Your mom said you run some sort of adventure business?" Lyndie asked, doing her best to pretend she hadn't googled him only that morning. She'd pretend she didn't know about his charity work or about the big spread that named him one of San Diego's most eligible bachelors. He was a catch—even the media thought so.

She wished she could disagree.

"Figured I'd turn my fearlessness into a profit," he said with a shrug.

"Is that what you're calling it?" Lyndie laughed.

"Mostly I help people conquer their fears," he said, slowing to a stop at the corner of Wildflower and Main.

"Really?"

"It's part of my brand." He said it as if quoting someone who'd convinced him of such a thing.

"So, who's helping you conquer yours?"

"Who says I'm afraid of anything?" He looked away.

"Aren't you?"

Another shrug, then he met her eyes. "There's really only one thing that keeps me up at night."

She stared at him for a moment, trying to hear what he wasn't saying, but he didn't let her hang on to the idea for too long before he pulled open the door to the Sweet Shoppe. "Here we are."

Lyndie reminded herself they were nothing more than two truce-forced friends as she strolled past him into the store. She inhaled the sweet aroma of homemade waffle cones, a hint of vanilla and cinnamon, with a touch of something Lyndie couldn't place. Black and white tiles covered the floor, and while it was a small space, the owners had made good use of it. A variety of two-top tables were situated around the shop, and behind the front counter—a large wooden structure—was a thickly framed chalkboard boasting a handwritten menu of their various treats.

"So, what do we do? Take a picture here?" Lyndie asked, pulling out her phone.

"I think the first thing we need to do is get some ice cream."

She frowned. "I'm pretty sure that's not on the list."

"It's on my list," Tucker said, planting his feet on the opposite side of the counter. "Peppermint stick, right?"

"How did you know that?" She turned toward him.

"I remember," Tucker said. "My mom always had a gallon in the freezer for you."

Lyndie laughed. "She did. You're right." *But it's weird that you'd remember.*

He shrugged, then ordered and paid for two waffle cones. When the girl behind the counter handed them over, he gave Lyndie hers and sauntered to a table by the window.

"Isn't the point of this thing to go as fast as we can?" Lyndie ate a bite of her ice cream. Homemade right there in Sweethaven, the ice cream at Sweet's had made it onto the Food Network more than once. She could see why. How long had it been since she'd indulged in something so decadent?

She moved the cone away from her mouth and watched Tucker, who had no problem enjoying his.

"I'm not in the business of hurrying," he said. "Unless I'm trying to catch a wave."

She laughed. "Why doesn't that surprise me?"

"Here." He moved across the table so that he stood shoulder to shoulder with her. He took out his phone and held it up selfie-style. "Let's get our ice cream in the shot."

Lyndie held her cone up and smiled as he took a series of photos.

"My mom was right—we're darn good-looking." He grinned at her, then bit into his cookies 'n' cream. "Ready to go?"

Lyndie followed him out to the sidewalk, where they strolled down Main Street, taking in the typical Sweethaven charm of its boutiques, art galleries and coffee shops.

"This place has hardly changed," she said absently.

"Some things never do," Tucker said.

Lyndie said nothing because, in the last few days, she'd realized that while things had stayed the same on the surface, so very much had changed underneath. And no part of her knew how to feel about that.

◆  ◆  ◆

Karen stood at the kitchen sink, washing the pots and pans she'd used to make dinner and wishing Nora Preston hadn't planned wedding events for every single day Tucker was home.

If Karen had her way, she would've made a feast three times a day just to keep him and Lyndie close. It almost made life feel normal again. It almost gave her a purpose.

But that wasn't fair. She had her patients, many of whom relied on her. Never mind that doling out therapeutic wisdom made her feel like a fraud.

The light in the garage went off, which meant Davis was on his way in, which meant the knot in her stomach would tighten. She'd counseled couples like her and Davis. She knew all the right things to say, but now, living it—well, none of her tactics seemed right. She'd tried to connect to her husband, but the space between them was more like a fortress than a wall, and she wasn't good at navigating it.

The door swung open and he appeared in the kitchen, holding his golf cleats, one in each hand. "Need to clean these out."

He set them on the counter Karen had just wiped down, walked over to the cupboard, pulled out a glass and filled it with water and ice from the fridge.

Karen stared at the dirty shoes on her clean counter and forced herself to breathe in slowly, then let out a long, deep exhale.

"You okay?" he asked.

She shut off the water, picked up the shoes and set them out on the sleeping porch.

"What are you doing?"

"I just cleaned the counters."

"I can wipe it down again." He opened the door to the porch and retrieved his dirty shoes.

"But you won't." Karen wiped her hands dry on a kitchen towel and then walked into the living room.

"What's gotten into you?" He dropped his shoes by the door and followed her, stopping on the other side of the couch.

"Oh, nothing, Davis, everything is just fine." Sarcasm didn't become her. She was faced with a decision—to jump into an actual argument headfirst or to quietly walk away, pretending everything was, as she said, fine.

She wanted to jump.

He frowned. "Karen, what is it?"

"I spent half the evening cooking, then the other half I spent cleaning, so forgive me if I don't want your dirty shoes on my freshly cleaned kitchen counter."

He looked at her—that look—the one that told her he thought she was cracking up, the one that silently screamed, *You're overreacting.*

Maybe she *was* overreacting, but she didn't care.

"I'm sorry?"

It was the question in his voice that set her off. "Are you or aren't you?" she hissed.

"What?"

"You said it like it was a question. Are you sorry or not?"

"Karen, are you okay?"

"Am I okay?" she scoffed. "Am I okay?"

He only stared.

"Well, if you have to ask, then I'm not even going to get into it with you."

She knew this wasn't the proper way to have an argument. She was supposed to be good at communicating her feelings, but something inside her had snapped, and "supposed to" didn't seem to matter. Maybe she was simply too tired—too fed up—to care.

"Don't do that," he said. "You always do that."

"Do what?"

"Turn it around on me. If you have something to say, then say it."

"Say what?"

Davis's eyes searched the air as if the right words were hanging in front of him somewhere. "Say anything! Are you mad? Do you want to throw something? Do you want to punish me because I put my shoes on the counter?"

"It's not about the shoes!" Karen's voice had turned shrill, stopping time for a split second.

Davis stilled. "Then what is it about?"

Tears clouded her view of him. No. No. No. She couldn't get into this—not now, not when Tucker was finally home and they were set to celebrate Cassie's life in just days.

"Forget it." She sat down in her reading chair and picked up her book.

Davis walked around the couch and stood directly in front of her. When she didn't look up, he grabbed her book and snapped it shut. "I'm not going to forget it, Karen. What is this about?"

"What are you doing?" She glanced up at him as a tear slid down her cheek.

"Say it. Get it out. At least then we know what we're dealing with. At least then we can work on making it right."

"It will never be right!" She leaned forward. "Our daughter is gone. Our daughter is dead, Davis, and you hardly seem to notice."

His eyes turned glassy, and he took a step back. "Is that what you think?"

"You've got your golf games, your friends. You tell jokes and carry on like nothing ever happened, like there's no hole in the middle of your chest that keeps you from breathing. Don't you even care that she's gone?"

"Of course I care." Davis's calm voice brought the adrenaline down. "How can you even ask me that?"

"You never even cried, Davis. You never got mad or questioned any of it. You just accepted it and moved on, like it was a blip on your radar. And I'm over here dying inside—literally dying. I can't breathe. I can't sleep. I don't know who I am anymore if I'm not her mother." The tears came quickly now, and a sob escaped. "I don't know who *we* are if we aren't her parents."

A stunned silence filled the room. Davis stood stock-still in front of her. Years had passed, and the truth had never been spoken aloud, but Karen had spoken it now. And it was up to him what happened next.

"Finally."

She looked up at him, wiping her cheeks dry with her hands. "What?"

"Finally, I know what you're thinking." He knelt down in front of her. "I've been wondering for years."

She met his eyes and found kindness in them, softening her toward him. He was still the man she'd always known, the man she loved, but they were not the couple they'd been. "We've grown apart."

He took her hands in his. "I'm not sure how to find my way back to you. You want me to suffer by your side, but I've chosen to find a way to go on living. Not because I don't miss her or I'm not grieving, Karen, because I am. Every single day."

"But you never talk about her."

"Because it hurts you when I bring her up."

Karen's mind raced. What was he talking about?

"I tried." Davis let go of her hands and sat on the edge of the couch a few feet away, kitty-corner from where she sat. "For months after we got back home, I tried to talk about her. I tried to relive some of our best moments, but it only made you sadder. And little by little, you slipped away, until it became easier not to talk about it at all."

"So it's my fault." Karen's mouth went dry. "You're saying the fact that we are practically strangers is my fault."

"That's not what I'm saying."

The clock on the wall ticked so loudly, it was distracting. The light over the kitchen sink hummed a steady tune. Even in the silence, the world wasn't silent. Her mind wasn't quiet.

She found Davis watching her. "Are we too far gone?"

He leaned forward and took her hands again. "I hope not, but I can't live my whole life in misery."

"I know."

"But you don't. You want me to grieve the way you grieve, and I can't do it. I have to work, and I have to get out of the house. I still believe that my life can mean something, maybe even more now, because of what I've lost. And yours can too."

"But it feels like I'm betraying her," Karen said. "Every time I laugh or have a moment where she's not the most important thing on my mind."

"She wouldn't want this for us," Davis said. "She was full of joy, full of life—you remember, don't you?"

Quietly, Karen nodded.

"Do you really think she wants you to spend the rest of your days living in the dark with this chain around your ankle? Tucker said something to me about why he's always after the next adrenaline rush—"

"To make me cry?" She half laughed through her tears.

"To feel alive." Davis's eyes found the ceiling. "When he said it, I realized I haven't really felt alive in a very long time."

A tear fell from her cheek and onto Davis's hand, still closed around hers. He didn't move to wipe it dry. Instead, he picked her hands up and brought them to his lips. "Come back to me, Karen."

He gave her hands a soft tug, then pulled her onto the couch next to him, enveloping her in his strong arms.

She had no more words, nothing more to say to heal their wounds or repair what was broken between them. And as the clock ticked and the light hummed, she accepted that for tonight, what had been said was enough.

And she prayed that tomorrow she'd find the courage to speak again.

# Chapter Twenty-Three

The scavenger hunt was like a trip down memory lane.

After they left Sweet's, Tucker and Lyndie snapped selfies at the local coffee shop, the restored wooden carousel down on the boardwalk, the pizza parlor where Tucker and Travis had both worked, and city hall, where Travis and Elle would get their marriage license.

"This is too easy," Tucker said.

"They probably want to make sure everyone gets back in time to eat the fish." Lyndie laughed—a laugh that could've sustained him for a week.

She must've noticed him looking at her, because she suddenly turned self-conscious, and her smile faded.

They walked in silence down the boardwalk toward familiar stretches of beach. He knew this place inside and out, though the memory of the boy he'd been felt distant. He wanted it to be distant. He wanted it gone.

His past was not something he was proud of, and he had things to say to Lyndie about it. Things he should've said years ago but had been too stupid or too embarrassed to.

But now wasn't the time. Not when they were laughing and getting along. Not when he seemed to have chipped away (at least a little bit) at her coldness toward him. Not when there was some hope for the two of them to actually be friends.

Or maybe that made this the best time to unburden himself?

Before he could find the courage to broach the subject, the dock with the gazebo came into view.

Tucker could feel the shift in the air between them.

*Everything keeps leading us right back to where we started.*

Lyndie hugged her arms around herself, as if she needed protection from what lay in front of them.

"I think the clue is talking about the gazebo," Tucker said, rereading the riddle on the card. "'Glass houses aren't for living in, but when it comes to proposals, this one is perfect.'" He tucked the card in his pocket and looked away. "Even though the gazebo isn't made of glass."

"Yeah," Lyndie said quietly. "Travis brought Elle here to propose."

"I saw the photos. Seems strange they'd photograph such a private moment."

"Probably Nora's idea. Good PR."

"I guess nothing is private anymore."

And yet, some things were.

They stood at the start of the dock, waiting to take their first steps back to the exact spot that still haunted Tucker. Lyndie stared out at the water, probably trying—like Tucker often did—not to think about the mistake they'd made.

What would've happened if Cassie hadn't died that night? Would he have gone to Lyndie the next morning to see how she was? Would he have asked her out on a proper date? Would he have found her the next day and held her, knowing the guilt she felt, too, over what had happened between them?

He'd never know.

The warm summer wind pulled her hair from the elastic that held it in a low ponytail, and Tucker resisted the urge to brush it out of her face.

"So, what, we take a picture in the gazebo?" She looked at it like it was a trap, like the pathway to reach it was a plank over shark-infested waters.

Or maybe that's just how it seemed to him.

"Yep," he said. "We can just take a quick picture." Did his nonchalance sound as phony as it felt?

She looked at him with those violently blue eyes, and he had to look away. He couldn't let on how often he still, ten years later, thought about that night—not just because of Cassie's death, but because of Lyndie. Unlike how he'd felt about most girls he'd known at the time, he'd actually cared about her. Shouldn't that have translated into treating her differently?

"Great," she said. "Let's get this over with."

Why did he get the feeling she was getting so many things "over with" this week?

They stepped out onto the dock and started toward the gazebo, as if they were walking in slow motion. In a way, he felt like Lyndie was a ticking time bomb. She'd nearly come unglued when she'd found out Travis had kissed Elle. How much longer did Tucker have before Lyndie focused her anger on him again?

"When did you learn to play the guitar?" she asked.

The question took him off guard. Friendly conversation didn't seem to be her thing. At least not with him.

He stuffed his hands in the pockets of his cargo shorts. Lyndie had practically been born writing and playing music—it almost felt silly for him to talk about it with her, like a first-year piano student talking to a maestro.

"I started taking lessons a couple of years after the accident," he said. "Cassie always said she was going to teach me, as long as I taught her how to play the drums." He laughed at the memory, which drew a smile from his quiet companion.

"I can see her behind that drum set," Lyndie said, and then paused. "She would've been happy to see you up there on Sunday."

He slowed his pace. Sunday. "Yeah, I think she would've."

"When did you start playing in your church? Or maybe what I'm really wondering is, why?"

"Because I don't belong up there, right?" He kept his tone light, so as not to incite her.

"I'm sorry I said that," Lyndie said. "It was thoughtless."

"It's fine." They'd reached the gazebo, but they both stopped before they walked in. "You're right—I don't belong up there, but I felt like it was what I was supposed to do." He shrugged.

She squinted up at him, the fading light of the sun shining in her eyes. "You didn't feel . . . out of place?"

"Oh, no, I definitely feel out of place."

"Yeah, me too." Lyndie stilled.

"I surf every morning," Tucker said, turning toward the water. He leaned against the rail on the dock and stared across the lake. "I met a guy down there one day, and he kind of helped me turn my life around." He could feel her eyes on him, as if she was deciding for herself whether what he said was true.

"Really?"

"Yeah, he helped me understand a lot about myself. About the past. He thinks it's important that I own up to it all." Tucker could feel shame, that familiar bedfellow, start to creep in.

"Own up to what all?"

"The way I was," he said. "I hurt a lot of people."

He glanced at her, but she was now focused on a sailboat in the distance.

"I hurt you."

"Tucker, don't—"

"No, I need to say this."

"But I don't need to hear it." She faced him.

236

He met her gaze. "Yes, you do."

Her eyes were glassy, and she looked back out toward the water.

"I didn't handle things well that night," Tucker said. "And I've made a lot of mistakes, but that is the one I regret most. That's the one that keeps me up at night."

A tear slipped down her cheek. It *did* matter. It all mattered. And the words, however painful they were to say, were important for her to hear.

"I messed it up. I actually cared about you, and I messed it up." Tucker tripped on the words. "I should've done better."

"It's in the past, Tucker," Lyndie said. "Let's just leave it there."

"I've tried that, but seeing you here, it's made me realize that pretending it never happened isn't working. I still feel responsible." He ran a hand through his hair. "I feel awful. And someone told me the only way to feel better is to tell the truth. Out loud, so it will lose its power." He drew in a deep breath. "I'm sorry, Lyndie."

Her jaw twitched, and she stayed silent for seconds that felt like minutes.

"Say something."

"I'm fine, Tucker, really. You don't need to apologize."

"I know that's not true."

"It is," she said. "I promise. I'm fine."

"Is that why you were so kind to me when we first got back?" He was prodding her now, and he didn't have much leeway. He risked ticking her off all over again, and he knew it.

Still, somehow, it seemed worth the risk.

"I don't want to talk about it," she said.

He didn't either, if he was honest. He didn't enjoy feeling like he was walking a tightrope to get to her. He wanted it to be easy.

But it wasn't.

"You should try surfing," he said.

She looked at him like the comment was as out of the blue as it was.

"When I'm out there, it's like everything else goes away. It's the only time I feel sure of anything, and I know it sounds stupid, but it's like God talks to me."

She shifted. "It doesn't sound stupid. It sounds nice." She pressed her lips together and tucked a loose piece of hair behind her ear, seeming to debate whether or not to indulge him with conversation. He said a silent prayer that she would—if not about the past, then even about something ordinary.

He'd love it if their friendship felt normal again.

"I had a meeting with Jalaire Grant last week," she finally said.

He felt his eyes widen. "Jalaire Grant?"

"It's not a huge deal." It almost looked like she was trying not to smile, like she wanted to downplay the whole thing. "You surf. I write."

"Are you writing for her?" Tucker asked.

"It was sort of a pitch meeting. But she said there wasn't enough emotion in the songs."

"Ouch."

"Yeah, apparently I'm emotionally unavailable." She threw him a pointed look.

"You disagree?"

"No," she laughed. "I actually am a little unavailable. I don't like *feelings*."

Now he laughed. "Feelings can be messy."

"She gave me another shot. Asked for one more song." Lyndie sighed. "But being back here, it just makes everything harder. I haven't touched my guitar in days."

"Because of the feelings?" Tucker nudged her shoulder with his own.

She glanced up at him. "I do forgive you, Tucker."

He held her gaze. "You do?"

She nodded. "I do. Or I want to, anyway."

"I'll take it." He smiled at her, and the knot loosened in his stomach. "Now, what about that song?"

She shrugged.

"Do you ever play just for fun?"

She thought about it awhile, then shook her head. "Not really. I spend a lot of time playing for work."

"Sounds boring," Tucker said.

She laughed. "I'm doing something I love. How many people get to say that?"

He regarded her for a moment. "What are you doing the rest of the night?"

She narrowed her eyes. "Don't get any ideas."

He grinned. "Too late."

"I don't know what you're up to, but I'm sure I want no part of it."

"Let's take this gazebo picture and go. We've got better things to do." He pulled his phone out and snapped a shot of the two of them with the gazebo in the background before Lyndie even had a chance to look at the camera.

"Wait!" she hollered. "I wasn't ready." She tried to grab his phone away, but he held it out of her reach, focusing on the buttons and finally hitting "Send."

"There. Scavenger-hunt success."

"I can't believe you did that," Lyndie said. "I looked awful in that picture."

Tucker's eyes studied the planks of the dock beneath his feet. "Not possible."

She didn't move as the air between them thickened. When he met her eyes, she looked away.

"You know Nora will have a fit if we don't get back there," Lyndie said, eyes focused on the shore. "We're on the clock the rest of the night."

He shrugged. "I've never been one to play by the rules." He grabbed her hand and pulled her down the dock toward the beach. As she fell into step beside him, he realized he hadn't let her hand go. One glance at her told him she'd realized it too.

As nonchalantly as he could, he loosened his grip, forcing himself to focus on the walk in front of him, but wishing he had the right to hold on to her.

◆ ◆ ◆

Lyndie stuck her hand in her pocket, trying not to think about how it had felt for him to grab it, as if that were the most normal thing in the world.

His touch shouldn't excite her the way it did, especially not an accidental hand-holding.

But he'd apologized. He'd gotten everything off his chest that he needed to, and she was sure he thought it was enough. Did he feel relieved, not carrying that with him anymore?

It didn't matter. She'd grown accustomed to lugging her secrets around with her. Telling anyone the truth at this point was . . . pointless.

And yet, Tucker hadn't thought so.

"Where are we going?" She followed him to the top of the dune.

"You'll see." He grinned at her.

How she'd survived being back on that dock—their gazebo only a few feet away—she couldn't say. All the years between them and that night, and she could still conjure exactly how she'd felt when he'd sat down beside her.

And exactly how she'd felt when she realized she would likely never hear from him again.

She shouldn't be cordial to him at all—but here she was, following him like a disoriented toddler, telling him she forgave him for the way he'd treated her when she absolutely didn't. Not yet. How could she?

Still, the silence between them now wasn't tense and awkward like it had been. A mending had begun.

They walked in the opposite direction of the Preston cottage, where they were due back any moment. What would Elle say if the two of them didn't return in time for the fish fry?

"Are we just pretending we have nowhere else to be?" Lyndie asked.

"We'll get there. We've just got something else to do first." Tucker looked down at her and smiled.

His smile always could stop her heart.

She looked away. "This is insane. We're in the bridal party."

He laughed. "You don't break the rules very often, do you?"

Never. She never broke the rules. Except when she had—and look what had happened.

Tucker grabbed her hand and gave her a tug. "You walk so slow."

She jogged a few steps and caught up to him as the churchyard and Sweethaven Chapel came into view. "The church?" Lyndie could hear music coming from inside. "What are we doing here?"

Tucker didn't respond. Instead, he walked to the screen door and pulled it open, leading her inside. Music sounded through the church speakers, and Lyndie felt like an intruder. Why would he bring her here—wasn't it obvious how much she didn't like being in this place?

"I left my guitar here," he said, starting through the lobby.

Lyndie hung back. "I'll wait here."

Tucker frowned. "Come with me?"

She stood, unmoving. She didn't like churches. Yet some part of her was curious—if Tucker could find a place in his life for God, maybe she could too?

He extended a hand in her direction. "Come on."

She slipped her hand in his and felt only a little bit stronger. Being in a holy place with this man felt almost blasphemous, but his past wasn't keeping him a prisoner. Maybe he could teach her how to let go of hers. Years of shoving it away had protected her heart, but the stitches around it seemed to pull now.

Tucker had apologized to her, and things between them had shifted. Should she tell him the rest of the story? Would that be the key to setting her free?

No. He'd apologized to her, and maybe that had made him feel better. But they were different people.

She forced the thoughts aside as they walked through the lobby toward the back of the sanctuary, which had none of the traditional stuffiness of a normal church. She hadn't appreciated it yesterday, but the chapel was a wonderful kind of informal. Even the cross on the wall had been made with driftwood. Lyndie liked that driftwood cross. It hung there with its imperfections, not the sleek, shiny wood most churches used for the symbol of their faith. It seemed to suggest that, like it, she also didn't have to pretend to be something she wasn't.

But pretending seemed a requirement for religion. She'd watched for years as her own parents and all their friends "put on their Sunday faces," and it exhausted her. She couldn't be that person—she didn't know how. After that night with Tucker, after Cassie had died, she'd longed for anything but a Sunday face.

She didn't want platitudes and empty words. She wanted to understand why God had allowed her best friend to die. She wanted to know why she'd been so weak that she'd given in to Tucker so easily. She wanted to know why, in the months that followed, everything fell apart.

The loneliness of those days had nearly killed her, but how could she have told anyone in the church what she was thinking or feeling? She doubted women like Nora Preston or even her own mother would understand how it felt to be so angry at God, she almost thought she hated Him. What would've happened to the Sunday face if she'd ever said that out loud?

She hadn't belonged here then. She didn't belong here now.

But something drew her to the doorway at the back of the sanctuary. She stopped moving and tugged her hand away from Tucker as the only woman in the entire room captured her attention.

Sylvia Honeycutt had been a staple in Sweethaven for as long as Lyndie could remember. She was at the front of the church right near the stage, with her back to them, moving around in a way that couldn't quite be described as dancing. Both of her arms stretched up toward the ceiling, and she swayed in time with the music while moving back and forth and singing along softly.

Lyndie (and everyone else in town) had always thought Sylvia Honeycutt was eccentric. More than eccentric, really—most people thought she was nuts.

But standing there now, Lyndie was mesmerized by the way Sylvia moved, how she seemed to worship with complete freedom.

The voice that came through the speakers sang, *Your love covers my guilt and shame.*

Lyndie's eyes clouded over.

Sylvia now began to pace back and forth, her eyes closed, her face earnest, her hands folded in front of her. She seemed to be praying—but a prayer so different from the ones Lyndie remembered in church. There was nothing perfect or put together about Sylvia or the way she moved, only a deep passion as the woman called out for something she desperately needed.

Could someone like Sylvia understand the broken parts Lyndie tried so hard to keep hidden? Would she pull Lyndie into her arms and convince her that His love covered even her guilt and shame?

Lyndie continued watching as the song came to an end. Sylvia stopped moving, her face and arms stretched up toward heaven.

Would Lyndie ever feel that free? Free enough to come before a God whose heart she had broken—to surrender herself, faults and all?

In the silence, a hush fell on the chapel. Lyndie thought they should leave, but Tucker just stood in the doorway beside her, watching the woman too. Wouldn't Sylvia be embarrassed to learn they'd observed her in what seemed such a personal moment?

But the old woman turned around, as if she sensed their presence, and smiled. Her hair was gray and wild, her clothes long and loose, hanging on her tall, thin frame.

"Good evening, kids." If Sylvia was embarrassed, she certainly hid it well.

"We're sorry to intrude."

Lyndie was thankful Tucker had spoken up, because she'd yet to find her voice. Why was she so overcome with emotion watching a crazy lady sort-of dance to a worship song?

"No intrusion at all. I come over here every evening to pray. That's the good part about the chapel doors being open all the time. I think it's like heaven that way." Sylvia walked over to the small sound booth near the back of the room and pulled her CD out of the player, then pointed a bony finger in Tucker's direction. "You sang on Sunday morning."

Tucker walked farther into the room, leaving Lyndie still standing in the doorway, wondering how a simple song on a CD could change the atmosphere of the little chapel. Wondering what she was doing here. She didn't belong here.

Not here.

And yet, she wouldn't have been able to move if she wanted to.

"I did," Tucker said.

"I liked it," Sylvia said matter-of-factly. "I don't have time for all that performance nonsense. Cut straight through the flash and sizzle and give me Jesus, that's what I say." When she smiled, the wrinkles around her eyes became more pronounced. Her skin was nearly translucent, she was so pale and so thin, and while she spoke with a gruff voice, there was kindness behind her eyes.

"I agree," Tucker said. "I like to keep things simple. Trying to get my friend Lyndie to sing with me next week."

Sylvia leaned over, peeking around Tucker to Lyndie, who felt naked.

"That right?" Sylvia's eyes narrowed. "You sing?"

"I write, mostly," Lyndie said.

"But she sings too," Tucker said.

Lyndie looked away.

"Would you sing something for me now?"

Lyndie knew very little about Sylvia Honeycutt, but one thing she did know is that the woman lived alone and had lived alone ever since Lyndie was a kid. She'd always pitied Sylvia, but standing here now, she could see a strength in her that Lyndie did not have.

For all her complaining about the church and its pretending, its Sunday faces and facades, Lyndie had been doing the exact same thing.

Something told her Sylvia Honeycutt didn't know how to pretend.

"I'm out of practice," Lyndie said.

"Oh, bollocks." Sylvia waved a skinny arm in the air.

"I don't know this kind of music."

"Who said it had to be this kind of music?" Sylvia asked. "Sing me something of yours."

The melody for "Cassie's Song" danced through Lyndie's head.

"There!" Sylvia came out from behind the sound booth. "You just thought of a song, I could see it on your face. Sing that." She motioned to the stage, where Tucker's guitar still sat.

"It's not finished."

Sylvia shrugged. "Maybe you'll be inspired."

Lyndie hadn't been inspired in ten years.

She glanced at Tucker, who watched her with raised eyebrows and a lazy smirk. Had he planned this?

Hesitantly, she walked toward the stage and took the guitar out of its case, trying to understand why she didn't simply run the other way. She didn't owe Sylvia a peek into her most private thoughts, even if the woman had inadvertently given Lyndie a peek into hers.

Yet here Lyndie was, slipping the guitar over her shoulder. Tucker leaned against the half wall surrounding the sound booth, but Sylvia trekked to the front of the sanctuary and sat down in the front row, as if settling in for her own personal concert.

*All the things I never said . . .*

The phrase popped into Lyndie's mind as she strummed the first chord of what she thought would be "Cassie's Song" but quickly became something else, like her fingers had connected to a place inside her that her head hadn't found yet.

She strummed for a bit, then started humming an unexpected melody. The words filtered into her mind as she closed her eyes and saw a picture of Sylvia, arms upward, heart so free in this very same space.

Lyndie wanted to feel that free. She wanted to connect to the words she was writing, the music that filled her soul, and not for Jalaire, not for Nashville or for her career, just for herself. She had something to say—and this was the only way she knew how to say it.

The song welled up within her, words and chords spilling out as she struggled to keep up with it. She didn't stop to question or correct; she simply let it flow out of her, one measure at a time, as if the creativity had a will of its own.

Then Lyndie's fingers stalled on the strings, and she sat in the quiet, eyes still closed, struggling to hear the next line, the next chord, struggling to hear what it was her heart needed to say.

For a moment, she forgot where she was and who was there, but the memory rolled in like high tide, and she opened her eyes. There was Tucker in the back of the sanctuary, eyes fixed on her, and Sylvia sat as still as a statue in the front row, tears streaming down her face.

"Oh, Lyndie." Sylvia stood and stepped toward her, putting her hands on Lyndie's knees. "There is a great gift inside you, and you haven't begun to use it, my dear."

Lyndie's eyes locked onto the old woman's, as if looking away might break their connection.

"There's more," Sylvia said.

"More?"

"You have more to say. You've only scratched the surface of what's inside you, and if you let yourself be vulnerable, if you use your music to speak truth, to bring light—it will mend broken hearts." She pointed at Lyndie. "Starting with your own."

Lyndie's eyes clouded again, and she struggled for a deep breath. The world was closing in on her, and she needed out.

*Out.*

She set the guitar down and stood, meeting Tucker's eyes when she did. He stared at her, and she wondered if he could see right through her, like he knew.

But he didn't know. He couldn't. And she wasn't going to tell him.

"I have to go."

"Lyndie, wait."

But as she ran out of the chapel, she heard Sylvia Honeycutt—the woman who was supposed to be crazy—say the smartest thing anyone had said in a long time.

"Let her go, Tucker. Right now, she needs to be alone."

# Chapter Twenty-Four

Elle forgave Lyndie and Tucker for showing up late after the scavenger hunt. She might not have, except she hadn't really wanted to go to a fish fry either. She didn't like fish, and she didn't understand why Nora had insisted on such a thing, considering the fish weren't even freshly caught from Lake Michigan—they were halibut, flown in from Alaska that afternoon.

Lyndie had rushed in two hours after the prizes were awarded. She and Tucker had won, but when they didn't show, Nora gave their prize—a big basket filled with Sweethaven favorites—to Violet and Dewey. Dewey had gone straight for the bags of locally-made potato chips and told Violet she could have everything else.

Elle had fallen asleep that night on the sleeping porch, the distant sound of Lyndie's guitar carrying on the breeze from out back where she played.

Now, Elle was hurrying out to meet Travis and his parents for breakfast, and she could already tell she would be late.

She hopped in the car and raced downtown, eyeing a parking place on Main Street just outside of a locally owned restaurant called Sleep. She was surprised Nora had suggested it—Elle had read that it catered to a younger crowd, often feeding those who stayed out all night partying. But it was the talk of the town this summer, having just opened in April, and supposedly Nora liked to stay current.

Apparently, their pancakes were to die for—not that Elle would be eating pancakes this close to the wedding.

She squeezed the Sportage into the empty spot and turned off the engine. She could see Travis waiting outside the restaurant for her, and took the briefest moment to admire him, still smitten by how handsome he was.

Handsome and kind and *good*. The *good* always tripped her up. Travis had always been a genuinely good guy. It's why Cassie had loved him then. It's why Elle loved him now. But it was also what made him feel so foreign and unreachable to her, as if, even when he was in her arms, he was still a world away.

Did he sense that she didn't belong? Had he taken one look at Dave Messer and decided *that* was the kind of guy Elle was suited for?

He rushed over to her side of the car and opened the door.

"Sorry I'm late." She got out and stepped into his arms.

"No big deal," he said. "We just got here." He held her for several seconds, her head fitting nicely under his chin. Travis once told her they fit together perfectly, as if they were two pieces of a puzzle that had been put back together, but Elle had never quite believed it.

The envelope in her purse kept her from believing it. *Does he know what you did?*

Travis pulled away and took her hand. "Did you sleep okay?" They started for the door.

"I did," Elle said. "Mostly."

She'd been dreaming a lot lately. And while she wished she were dreaming of walking down the aisle and becoming Travis's wife, mostly she was dreaming of the night Cassie died. Of a night dark as pitch and the sound of water as it stole her friend away.

"Mostly?" Travis opened the door for her, and she walked into the restaurant.

"I'm fine," she said. "I just don't like being in Cassie's house as much as I used to."

His eyes filled with understanding. "I'm sorry."

She smiled, knowing that if he could've single-handedly reprogrammed her dreams, he would've.

As they walked toward their table, Elle marveled at the way the light filtered in *just so*, illuminating the exposed brick on both sides of the small restaurant. Thick planks of roughed-up hardwood flooring and a long glass countertop stretched out across the rectangular space. Behind the counter, a large menu board showcased locally inspired favorites. Small, mismatched tables and chairs were positioned opposite the counter, and for being brand-new, Sleep was quite busy.

Elle had to admit, the place didn't suit Nora at all. While most of the people chattering around two- and four-top tables were dressed in shorts and T-shirts with disheveled hair and five o'clock shadows, Nora and Pastor Preston were perfectly coiffed, wearing clothes that looked more suited for a business meeting than a casual breakfast.

Elle wore a white eyelet sundress and a pair of tan sandals. Today the bridal party would go on their picnic at the beach. While Elle had initially been enamored with the idea of a week of wedding events, she had a feeling that by Friday night, she would be completely exhausted.

And she wanted to just be married already. Once they were married, it wouldn't matter if Travis found out what she'd done. She would be his wife, and vows meant something to people like him.

And to people like her, who'd been the recipient of only broken ones.

"You're looking lovely this morning, Elle," Pastor Preston said.

Travis pulled out the chair across from Nora, whose back faced the front door. Elle sat down and took a look around the restaurant. A young, muscular man behind the coffee counter flirted with two older women (tourists), who seemed to eat up everything he said. Over to the left were tables of college-aged kids who'd clearly not been home last night, and toward the front of the restaurant, sitting at the long counter stretched beneath the front window, was a wiry woman with a familiar profile. The woman sat on a stool meant to face out the window overlooking Main Street, but instead, she was facing the restaurant, and now, more specifically, Elle.

*Mom?* Elle's heart raced as she fumbled placing a napkin on her lap, and a wave of nausea rolled through her stomach. *Not here. Not now.* Her mother wouldn't hesitate to make a scene.

*Does he know what you did?*

The words hung there, taunting Elle, as they had since she'd received the newspaper clipping in the mail. They were always there, at the back of her mind, threatening to destroy the life she'd been building for months.

Maybe her mother wouldn't tell. Maybe she didn't want to ruin Elle's chances at happiness.

And yet, Lily Porter had never wanted Elle to be happy. She'd been the kind of mother who thought that if she had to endure a certain hardship, Elle did too. Things would never be okay between them, and Elle knew it.

"I've checked on the flowers and the cake," Nora said. "The photographer is all set and will be joining us for the picnic this afternoon, so maybe we should put you two in coordinating colors."

Elle stared at her menu intently, her heart still pounding.

"Elle? Did you hear what I said?"

Travis glanced at Elle, whose face had probably turned pasty white. Even her freckles lost their color when she panicked. "Elle?" He put a hand on her knee.

"Sorry, yes, I heard you, Nora," Elle said.

"Maybe let's talk about something other than the wedding," Pastor Preston said.

Nora frowned. "It's kind of important that we talk about the last-minute details, don't you think?"

Travis took Elle's hand underneath the table. "I think the details will work themselves out."

Elle's eye caught movement near the front of the restaurant. Her mother stood and now moved toward the back of the space, eyes locked on Elle.

*No. No. No.*

Elle half stared at her menu as the woman approached their table. The sounds of the restaurant faded, and Elle's ears rang. Should she cut her mother off before she reached them? Was there any way to save face with Lily Porter for a mother?

Seconds that felt like minutes ticked by, slowly, methodically, and Elle braced herself for the fallout of what was to come. She drew in a deep breath, pressed her lips together and glanced up as her mother slowed her pace, stopping right beside their table.

Elle instinctively squeezed Travis's hand. He looked at her, then at Lily. Elle stared straight ahead, latching on to the memory of how things were in that exact moment, because she could sense they would never be the same again. Her mother was about to speak aloud the very words that could damn Elle forever.

She was about to lose everything, to be reminded once again that someone like her did not belong—not here, not with these people.

Nora glanced over at Lily, and as she did, Lily bent down and picked up the cloth napkin that must've fallen from Elle's lap. "You dropped this."

Elle reached for the napkin, but her mother held on to it for a second until, finally, she let it go and walked away.

"That was strange," Nora said. "Do you know her, Elle?"

Elle watched as Lily walked to the front of the restaurant and out the front door, not turning around again.

"Elle?"

She turned her attention back to the three of them, all watching her with earnest expressions, awaiting an explanation.

"No," she said. "I don't know her."

# Chapter Twenty-Five

After Elle left for breakfast in town, Lyndie found herself standing in the kitchen alone. With Tucker. They hadn't spoken since she'd run out of the church the day before, and while it was quite possible she owed him an explanation, she couldn't seem to find the words.

Lyndie poured herself more coffee. "Look, I'm—"

"Hey, I wondered—" Tucker started at the same time.

"Go ahead," she said.

"No, you." Tucker sat at the other end of the counter, but he still felt near. It was getting more and more difficult to concentrate on anything but the way his eyes intensified when he looked at her.

It gave her too much hope, and she knew she needed to stop romanticizing whatever this was. He'd apologized. She'd said she forgave him. But building it into something it wasn't would be a terrible idea.

Lyndie turned the mug in her hands, the warmth of it heating her fingers. "I just wanted to apologize. You know, for yesterday."

Tucker watched her with such curiosity that Lyndie looked away.

"You don't have to apologize."

"I don't know what my problem was," she lied. She knew exactly what it was. For the first time in as long as she could remember, a song had risen up out of her. It wasn't something she'd put together in her head because the notes were pleasing or should work well together in theory—it had taken over as soon as she'd started playing, like it had a life of its own.

It had surprised her.

"Sylvia Honeycutt is your new biggest fan," Tucker said with a grin.

Lyndie laughed, thankful for the levity. "I might be her new biggest fan too."

"The song was . . ." He seemed to search for the right word. "It was pretty incredible."

She could feel her cheeks flush. "Thanks."

"I recorded it." He pulled out his phone and started scrolling. "It seemed like maybe you hadn't sung it before, and I didn't know if you'd forget it."

She watched him as he earnestly opened the video and slid the phone across the counter toward her. Clicking play, she listened as it transported her back to yesterday, and she felt full all over again.

Tucker didn't know she didn't forget music once she'd written it. Songs had a way of sticking with her, but he'd wanted to be sure she didn't lose this one. That was thoughtful, something a friend would do.

Maybe they *were* friends now.

When the clip finished playing, she watched the screen go to black and pushed it back toward him.

"You've got a gift, Lyndie."

She took a sip of her coffee, suddenly uncomfortable with his undivided attention. Where were Karen and Davis when she needed them?

Her phone buzzed on the counter, and Foster's picture popped up. She quickly turned it facedown. He had the worst timing.

"You need to get that?"

Lyndie shook her head.

"Good," Tucker said.

"Good?"

He laughed. "I mean, not great for him, but good for me."

She frowned.

"I wondered if I could take you out tomorrow?" he asked.

Lyndie found his eyes—intent on her. "You want to go out? With me?"

Tucker laughed again. "Don't sound so surprised."

She shook her head. "Like . . . a date?"

He nodded. "Like I wish I would've taken you on ten years ago."

"But I'm like a kid sister, remember? I wouldn't want to get the wrong idea."

"You won't." He still held her gaze. He hadn't looked away for even a moment.

She should tell him everything now. That would change his mind in a hurry. He still believed she was pure and innocent, but she was neither.

He moved around the counter toward her and took her hand. "You deserve to have someone fall all over himself for you. I'm volunteering to be that guy."

She laughed. "Tucker, I—"

"It'll be fun." The way he looked at her—it turned her insides in a circle.

"Fine." She failed to hide her smile.

"Fine?" He raised his eyebrows.

"I'll go with you."

"Yes!" Tucker leaned in and kissed her on the cheek, and she swore her heart stopped. "I'll pick you up tomorrow at eight."

He started out the door.

"You'll pick me up from where? The living room?" she called out after him.

"Just be ready at eight!"

After he'd gone, she stood in the kitchen alone, the memory of his nearness lingering.

◆ ◆ ◆

The wedding party met for a picnic on the beach that afternoon, but Lyndie found it nearly impossible to concentrate on anything but her forthcoming date with Tucker.

It occurred to her that she owed Foster a phone call, though the thought of explaining this to him was nearly unbearable. She didn't want to get into any of it over the phone.

But Lyndie followed the rules. And she couldn't go on an official date with Tucker unless she made it clear to Foster where they stood, which was, of course, nowhere.

She took out her phone and sent him a quick text: Hey, we need to talk.

He wrote back immediately: Uh-oh. That's what girls say when they want to break up with you.

. . .

She didn't know how to respond. She didn't want to hurt him, but there was nothing between them. Surely he sensed that.

You're breaking up with me, aren't you? he wrote.

I wanted to have an actual conversation with you about this. Lyndie couldn't lie, she would be relieved to do this over text message, even though she knew it was tacky.

I don't want to have a conversation about it. If you're breaking up with me, let's just call it over.

I'm sorry, Foster.

"You should put your phone down and enjoy the weather." Nora stood beside Lyndie, peering down at her, the way she always seemed to.

"Sorry, work." She tucked her phone away.

"Have you spoken with Elle this afternoon?" Nora's eyes fixed on Elle, who was sitting in a chair next to Travis with a dazed look on her face.

"Actually, no," Lyndie said. "Is everything okay?"

"I don't know. I was hoping you could tell me."

Nora looked at Lyndie, and for the first time, Lyndie looked back. Usually, she only half looked at Nora Preston, afraid to make actual eye contact—she'd always found the woman intimidating.

But seeing her now, Lyndie saw something unexpected in Nora's eyes—actual, legitimate concern.

"Do you think she'd ever call off the wedding?" Nora asked.

"Why would she do that?" Lyndie said. "She loves Travis."

"I don't know, just something that occurred to me. She hasn't been very interested in the planning, and she's been acting strange since breakfast this morning. Can you talk to her?"

Lyndie followed Nora's gaze to her old friend, who admittedly didn't seem like herself today.

"Lyndie, please. She adores you."

Lyndie wasn't so sure about that. "I'll see what I can do."

"Thank you." Something at the top of the dune caught Nora's eye. "Oh, the food is here. I'll be back."

She whisked away, calling out to a caterer wearing khaki shorts and a white button-down.

Lyndie made her way over to where Elle was sitting.

"Let's go for a walk," she said.

Elle squinted up at her, then shielded her eyes from the bright afternoon sun. "Now?"

Lyndie nodded.

"The food just got here."

"Are you actually hungry?"

Elle shrugged. "No."

Lyndie held a hand out to her, and when Elle took it, Lyndie gave her a playful tug out of her chair. Sometimes the distance between them still felt so great, and other times it felt like no years had passed at all.

Which would this be?

Lyndie linked an arm through Elle's, the way she used to when they were younger. They walked along the shoreline in silence for several moments, drinking in the day, the sunshine, the memories that haunted them both. Elle had never said so, but Lyndie knew being with Cassie the night she'd died had taken a toll on her.

How could it not? As many reasons as Lyndie had to not return to Sweethaven, Elle had a thousand more.

"Are you okay?" Lyndie asked.

Elle slowed her pace. "I saw my mother today."

Lyndie stopped. She waited for Elle to face her, and when she did, Lyndie saw the anguish in her eyes. "Did you talk to her?"

Elle shook her head. "But she saw me."

They started walking again, but this time, Elle wrapped her arms around herself, as if that could shield her from what Lyndie had been too blind—too selfish—to see up until now. It embarrassed Lyndie, how self-absorbed she'd been since she'd arrived, as if her issues were all that mattered.

She had to do better. Not just for Elle, but for all of them. They were all hurting—they all had reason to. Yet she'd convinced herself that her pain was worst of all.

"Maybe you should go talk to her," Lyndie said. "Maybe it would help? Give you closure."

Elle scoffed. "I don't know if there will ever be closure for the things I've done."

Lyndie frowned. "What do you mean?"

"Oh, Lyndie, someone like you would never understand."

In the silent seconds that ticked by, the words taunted her. *Someone like you.* Elle thought she knew so much about her. She thought that just because Lyndie had grown up privileged and in church, she'd never faced anything real or life-changing the way Elle had. Sure, life hadn't been particularly kind to Elle, but that didn't mean Lyndie hadn't also suffered.

That didn't mean Lyndie was blameless.

"What do you mean, 'someone like me'?"

Elle glanced at her, then hugged herself a little tighter. "Someone who's never made a single mistake."

"Is that what you think?" Lyndie stopped walking.

"Believe me, it's not a bad thing," Elle said. "You won't find anyone thinking that about me."

Lyndie looked out across the water. "You had a lot of boyfriends, but that doesn't make you a bad person."

That was her polite way of saying Elle had slept around. They'd all heard the talk about her the summer after sophomore year—their friend had already gotten a reputation, and while she'd tried to hide it from Cassie and Lyndie, neither of them was stupid. Cassie's mom had said Elle was searching for love and approval, but she wouldn't find it with any of the sex-crazed boys she was spending time with.

Karen always did have her finger on the pulse of her girls.

At least she did before Cassie died. After that, it seemed like everything slipped past her, including Lyndie's transgressions. It shamed Lyndie to think of it now, that Cassie's death had made it easy for Lyndie to keep her own secrets. It had stolen everyone's attention long enough to allow her to work through it all on her own. And when she cried for no apparent reason, the adults in her life always assumed she was crying over Cassie.

And sometimes she was. But sometimes, she cried for what else she'd lost because of that night.

"Just forget it," Elle said. "I shouldn't have said anything."

"I don't want to forget it. You're getting married on Saturday. You deserve to be happy, Elle. You deserve to be loved for real—it doesn't seem like you know that."

Elle looked at her with glassy eyes. "I don't deserve anything good, Lyndie, and if my mom has her way, she'll make sure everyone else knows it."

She turned and started back toward the rest of the group, her long red hair blowing in the wind, leaving Lyndie standing alone in the hot sand, wondering if she and Elle had more in common than she'd originally thought.

# Chapter Twenty-Six

It wasn't that Lyndie didn't like pedicures. She simply didn't like people touching her.

And when you spent the whole day at the spa, you were touched. A lot. The bridesmaids had met early on Wednesday for coffee, then spent the next several hours getting massages, facials, manicures and pedicures. The day was meant to replace a bachelorette party, but nobody seemed in the mood. Sarabeth and Violet were both terribly sunburned, Lyndie was preoccupied, and Elle still seemed to walk around in a daze.

Nora had hired a photographer to capture the day, and Lyndie could only imagine the shots she'd gotten with the sour mood hanging overhead at the spa.

Now, as Lyndie drove back to the Jacobs' house, nerves danced in her belly. She had a date. With Tucker. Tonight.

She'd dreamed of this so many times, but with the history between them, she wasn't sure how to feel. She wasn't excited like she would've been ten years ago, but maybe she was cautiously hopeful?

Hope was dangerous, and she knew it.

She'd go on this one date and thank him for the lovely evening, and that would be it. He'd leave feeling like she'd forgiven him, and she'd get back to her real life, where things made sense.

She still had a few hours before Tucker picked her up, though, and the song she'd started in the church the other day had been stuck in her head ever since. Twice, she'd stopped her masseuse—a man named Les, who hadn't said a word the entire hour, God bless him—to write down lyrics, chords, ideas. The song was nearly finished, but she wanted to play through the whole thing, work out a few rough parts.

Deciding to take a detour on her way to the cottage, she parked in the lot next to the chapel and got out of the car, then pulled her guitar out of the back seat.

The building was never locked, and the people of Sweethaven never messed with it. It was sacred somehow, and that was exactly what she needed to finish this song.

A sense of reverence.

Something she'd taken for granted in the past.

Lyndie pulled open the screen door, letting it snap shut behind her. The sanctuary was quiet, the ceiling fans whirling silently overhead. She walked in and looked around.

A quiet peacefulness filled the space, and Lyndie drank it in. How long had it been since her soul had been at peace?

*You don't deserve peace.*

The familiar voice was louder than usual, but she pretended not to hear it. She didn't need reminding of her unworthiness; she carried it with her as a part of who she was.

Just yesterday, she'd told Elle that her past didn't make her unworthy of love—why couldn't Lyndie believe that for herself?

She did another quick scan of the chapel, just to make sure she was alone, then pulled a notebook from her bag and made her way to the front. She took her guitar from the case and sat on the stool at the center of the stage. Setting the notebook on the music stand in front of her, she closed her eyes and began to play the first chords of her song.

She played through the first verse, then stopped. Something was different. While the song had practically spilled out of her initially, today the creativity slowed.

In her mind, Lyndie returned to two nights ago, trying to reset the scene, re-create that moment. She started again, this time keeping her mind fully engaged on the words, letting the music flow out on its own.

Again, something stopped her from moving forward.

She let out a hot stream of air. The roadblocks were back—the flood of creative freedom must've been a fluke.

She stood and put the guitar back in its case.

"Giving up so quickly?"

The rough, graveled voice called out from the back of the room, and when Lyndie turned, she found Sylvia Honeycutt standing in the doorway.

"I'm not feeling it today," Lyndie said.

The old woman's gray eyebrows shot upward. "That so?"

"I'll get out of your way."

"Maybe you just need to set the atmosphere."

Lyndie stared at her blankly.

"Monday, you came into a room already filled with a certain kind of presence," Sylvia said. "Today you're just waltzing in here, expecting the same thing."

Maybe everyone was right. Maybe Sylvia was crazy.

"I suppose it depends on who you're writing this song for," Sylvia continued.

Lyndie felt exposed standing on the small stage as Sylvia Honeycutt gave her a once-over. "I'm writing it for myself," she said.

Sylvia grimaced. "Well, then I can't help you." She turned and started for the door.

"Wait."

Sylvia turned back around.

"Who should I be writing for?"

One of the old woman's eyebrows quirked. "Who do *you* think you should be writing for?"

Lyndie was going to fail whatever test this woman was issuing. "I'm not sure."

"Anyone but yourself, I think," Sylvia said. "You've been given a gift, but a gift is worthless unless you give it away."

"I'm not sure I follow."

"The reason that song rose up out of you the way it did is because you had a chance to give away a piece of yourself, to let it bless someone else."

"I don't think anyone wants pieces of me."

Sylvia walked toward the stage, eyes focused on her. "Why, because you're broken?"

Lyndie couldn't hold the old woman's eyes.

"We're all broken, young lady."

Nobody else seemed broken. Sylvia certainly didn't. Would a broken person be able to worship with such abandon?

"You have to find a way to give in spite of that brokenness," Sylvia said.

"I don't have anything to give, Mrs. Honeycutt," Lyndie said, her voice wavering.

"We all have something to give, dear. You give away the very thing you need. If you need hope, find a way to give others hope. If you need a friend, find a way to be a friend. If you need forgiveness . . ." She paused. "Give forgiveness."

The words of Lyndie's song must've tattled on her.

"So you give and give and give, and it always comes back to you."

"What makes you think I need anything?" Lyndie steeled her jaw, but she had a feeling Sylvia could see right through her façade.

"We all need something, my dear." Sylvia turned and walked back toward the sound booth. "So, what is it? What is it you really need?" She flipped on the same song that had played two days before.

Lyndie didn't know how to answer that question. What did she need? Hope? Friendship? Forgiveness? All of the above?

Couldn't someone swoop in and tell her what she needed? Why did she have to figure it out for herself?

"Whatever it is," Sylvia called out over the music, "all you have to do is ask for it."

Lyndie didn't know how to do that. She didn't know how to ask for something she didn't deserve.

Sylvia turned and walked out, and Lyndie stood on the stage of the small chapel, alone.

She saw the woman through the window, trudging down the hill. Whatever Sylvia had come there for, she'd either gotten it or decided it wasn't as important as leaving Lyndie with her words of wisdom and a song that spoke of grace and shame.

Had the writer of those words understood grace and shame? Shame like Lyndie's—deep, powerful, threatening. Had it really held her captive all this time? Had locking it away done her no good? Lyndie wanted to know the kind of grace the song talked about—amazing and real, given freely for someone who didn't deserve it.

Someone like her.

She closed her eyes and let the music wash over her as tears slipped down her cheeks. The box she'd buried so deeply inside her hadn't simply disappeared as she'd wished so many times before—it was still there, its contents still threatening.

She had to let it go, but she didn't know how. How did she unburden herself of something that no one else could carry for her?

A key change sent the song soaring, and Lyndie came down off the stage so she could face the driftwood cross hanging on the wall.

She didn't know what she was doing, not anymore, and yet, something about this all felt exactly right. She knelt down on the floor in front of the stage, eyes still fixed upward, and she imagined herself taking her well-buried box out and setting it down at the foot of the cross.

She might not be as free as Sylvia, and she might not understand what she had to do in order to win God's grace, but she wanted to try. She wanted to surrender.

And as the music faded and another one of Sylvia's songs began to play, Lyndie took a deep breath and raised one timid hand toward heaven.

"I can't carry it anymore," she whispered.

And in the quiet of the chapel, she had the feeling she wouldn't have to.

# Chapter Twenty-Seven

The best thing about Wednesday was the massage. Elle lay on the table while a woman named Roberta rubbed tension from every muscle in her body.

Roberta didn't talk to her. She didn't ask questions or tell her what would happen next. She didn't comment about the weather or try to make small talk.

She didn't ask about Elle's past or whether Travis knew the truth about it.

Roberta left Elle alone with her thoughts. And when Elle started crying, Roberta quipped that the massage must be just that good.

When Elle left the spa, she didn't tell anyone where she was going. She drove over to the beach, parked the car and got out. She stood at the top of the dune, above the water, peering down at it as kids chased the surf and young mothers chatted the day away, as if the day should be chatted away.

Elle took off her flip-flops and made her way down the dune. Nora would scold her if she saw her now, newly pedicured and walking through hot sand, but Elle didn't care. In that moment, she didn't care about anything.

She simply wanted to disappear.

It had been foolish to think she could keep it hidden, what she'd done. "The truth always finds you out," her mother used to say. Elle had assumed that was a scare tactic, but maybe Lily was right. After all, Lily was the one who could make sure of it.

Seeing her at breakfast the day before had set something off inside Elle.

*Tick-tick-tick.*

How many seconds did she have before Lily Porter ignited the fire that sent Elle's whole life up in flames?

It might seem implausible that a parent would purposely ruin her daughter's life, but some women weren't cut out to be mothers, and Lily was one of them. The woman's philosophy didn't include wanting more and better for her only daughter. She would be angry that Elle was marrying someone wealthy and kind and good when Lily herself had never been with a man who was any of those things.

So how long would it be before she dropped that bomb?

Elle couldn't wait around to find out. She had to tell Travis the truth. She would pray that he could forgive her. Still, knowing that her confession could be the end of them kept the words locked somewhere at the back of her throat.

How did she say it out loud—that *she* was the reason Cassie was dead?

Travis would never understand. And if Lyndie found out, their friendship—what was left of it—would be over.

Tears pricked at the corners of Elle's eyes as she stared out across the lake. She'd found an empty bench to sit on away from the families, the happiness.

The sunlight shimmered on the water, dancing like twinkling lights as the waves scurried toward the shore. Not too far in the distance, a little girl in a red bathing suit with white polka dots ran toward the waves, screaming with glee when the water met her chubby feet. Her dad raced in and scooped her up, threw her in the air, then dipped her feet back in the water with a shout. The girl's giggles danced like music on the wind.

A tear streamed down Elle's cheek, and she quickly wiped it away. The bitterness of imagining a life she didn't deserve welled up like bile at the back of her throat.

"Elle?"

She turned and found Travis standing behind her. He'd rolled his golf pants up at the bottom and carried leather flip-flops in one hand.

"You okay?" In a second, he was sitting at her side, holding her face and wiping her tears with his thumbs.

"I'm okay." As soon as the words escaped, she wished she could take them back.

*I'm not okay. I haven't been okay my whole life, and not even you can change that.*

She'd reinvented herself, left all of this behind, and yet it was still there, underneath the surface—the memory of who she'd been, the choices she'd made. How did she make them go away? How did she keep them from pulling her under, filling her lungs with water, drowning her?

She had to tell him. She had to get it out, and if he hated her, if it ruined everything, then she'd have to deal with that. But she couldn't keep it in any longer.

"My mother said you left the spa in a hurry." Travis's forehead wrinkled in a deep frown.

"I just needed a few minutes alone."

His shoulders deflated. "Do you want me to go?"

She took his hands in hers. "No, of course not."

"Is it my mother? I know she's overbearing. I can talk to her."

"No, Travis, it's not your mother," Elle said. "Though it would be great if you could talk to her."

He smiled, his hazel eyes searching hers with genuine concern. "What is it, Elle? Are you unhappy? Are you getting cold feet . . . about the wedding?"

She shook her head. "There's nothing I want more than to be your wife."

His brow knit into a tight line. "Then, what?"

"I'm afraid you won't want that"—Elle's eyes found her feet—"once you know the truth."

"What do you mean?"

She looked out over the water, drawing in the moment just before everything would change. "Can we go somewhere?"

"We are somewhere, Elle," Travis said. "You're scaring me—just tell me what's going on."

"I need to show you something." She stood and reached a hand toward him. He stared at it for a moment, then finally took it and stood as well.

They walked in silence back to where Elle had parked their SUV, and she assumed the driver's seat again. Then they drove to the outskirts of town, familiar to Elle but unknown to Travis. Kids like Travis weren't allowed to venture over there.

When they reached the trailer park, she pulled in and stopped the car a few yards away from her mom's trailer.

"What are we doing here?" he asked.

"We can't get married."

"Elle—"

"Until you know who I really am."

Travis frowned. "I know who you really are. I know you better than anyone."

"But you don't know everything."

"I don't care." He faced her. "I don't care about any of this, Elle. I love you."

Her eyes clouded over. He didn't know what he was saying. "I grew up here. Right there, in that white trailer with the pink curtains showing through the windows." She pointed. The curtains were more of a dusty pink tinged with brown from years of going unwashed. "My mother"—she nearly choked on the words—"she still lives there."

She dared a glance at the man she loved. He was still looking at her intently.

"Do you remember the woman at the restaurant yesterday—the one who picked up my napkin?"

He nodded.

"That was her." Elle's voice broke. "My mother."

"You said you didn't know that woman."

"I know what I said."

He stilled. "Is this supposed to make me love you less? Knowing this is where you grew up? I already figured that out a long time ago, and I don't care. I only care about you." He took her hand.

A soft sob escaped. If only what he said was true.

The door to the trailer opened, and her mom walked out. She squinted in their direction, eyeing the car suspiciously.

"Maybe you should go talk to her?" Travis traced his thumb softly up and down the side of her hand.

Elle stared at her mom, who was obviously out of the trailer because she'd discovered them watching it. As if she was challenging Elle to come forward and speak.

And all over again, Elle felt like that timid little girl, too ashamed and embarrassed to speak up, convinced she had nothing important to say.

But she wasn't that girl anymore, was she? She'd escaped all of it, and whether or not Travis would still want to marry her, she would never come back to this place again. And that's what she wanted her mom to know.

She got out of the car and glared at Lily. Travis followed.

"Well, look who's here," her mom called out. "Did you come to invite me to the wedding?" She laughed that same wry cackle she'd always laughed when being mean.

Elle walked toward her, and for the first time, the veil covering her eyes fell. This woman had no power over her—not anymore. This woman was miserable and unhappy and bitter. And the last thing Elle wanted was to turn out like her mother.

For a long time, Elle had excused Lily's behavior because she knew her mother had been raised by a man ten times meaner than Lily. Elle could only imagine the life Lily had known.

And who knew? Maybe without the influence of Cassie's and Lyndie's families, Elle would've become a carbon copy of her mother.

"Did you come here to flaunt it in my face?" Lily spat. "Your fancy car, your prissy clothes"—she looked at Travis—"him?"

Elle shook her head. "I don't know why I came. Maybe to say goodbye to a life I've put behind me?"

"A life I worked and sacrificed to give you."

The tears were stuck in Elle's eyes, pooling there, and the second she blinked, they would stream down her cheeks. She held her eyes open as long as possible.

"You've always been ungrateful," her mother said.

"And you've always been mean."

Lily laughed again, louder this time. Elle turned and started for the car.

"And you've always been spineless!" Lily called out.

Elle spun around. "No, spineless is bullying a child. Spineless is telling your daughter nothing she says matters, so it's better not to say anything. Spineless is leaving your child alone for hours at a time and bringing home a different guy every night." She'd been walking like a shot straight back to her mother as she spoke and now stood only inches from her. "Spineless is what you are, Lily Porter. And you should be ashamed of yourself."

Lily laughed. "I should be ashamed? *I* should be ashamed?"

Elle could feel it coming, the secret she'd struggled for years to keep. Lily was going to let it explode like a rocket. And while the truth needed to come out, it didn't need to come from Lily.

"Travis." Elle turned back to him and made herself look him in the eyes. "It's my fault that Cassie died."

*Tick-tick-tick.*

Her mind whirled in circles, begging him to respond, praying that somehow he could find it in his heart not to hate her for what she was about to tell him.

"What do you mean?"

Tears came quickly now. She didn't like to think about that night. She didn't like remembering how, in her own juvenile jealousy, she'd led Cassie to her death. But if she continued to carry it with her, she'd die bitter and angry and alone, just like her mother.

"I thought I could keep it from you," she said. "I thought it would be easier, but I don't want to start our marriage until everything is out in the open between us."

Travis took her hand and pulled her back toward the car, away from her mother. "What is going on?"

Elle's mind wandered back, and there she was ten years ago, just a kid, really. A stupid kid who'd made stupid choices.

"Cassie and Lyndie had a fight," Elle said. "They never fought, and I guess I sort of felt"—saying it out loud would sound terrible—"happy?"

"Happy?"

"I was always the third wheel," she said. "They took pity on me and let me hang out with them, but they were friends first. They had their music and were going off to school together in the fall, and I was staying"—she looked around the trailer park—"here. I knew where I really stood. I was the charity case."

"Elle, I don't think that's how they saw you at all," Travis said.

She held up a hand. "I love you for trying to make me feel better, but let me get through this."

He pressed his lips together and watched her, and in his silence, Elle let her mind wander back to that night.

The three of them had made plans to hang out, but earlier that day, Cassie had been with Tess and some of the other girls. Girls who'd made it clear exactly what they thought of Elle. Lyndie had been so mad that Cassie would waste her time on Tess, but even madder because Tess was likely just using Cassie to get to Tucker.

It was drama, stupid high school drama, but they were all caught up in it, and when Lyndie and Cassie got into an actual argument, Elle found herself hopelessly in the middle. How could she navigate a fight between the only two people in the world who actually seemed to care about her? That must have been how normal kids felt when their parents split up.

"Lyndie took off," Elle said. "We didn't know where she went, but Cassie was fired up. She was mad at Lyndie, but it was more than that."

Travis frowned.

"She was upset about you."

"About me?"

Elle looked away. "She really loved you, Travis. Or at least, she thought she did."

They'd all been sitting on the sleeping porch when Lyndie stormed out and Cassie broke down in a puddle of tears seconds after. She'd been trying to get Travis's attention that day, but her efforts had been fruitless.

"I need to pretend he doesn't exist," she'd said. "I need to forget all about him."

Elle watched her for a minute, happy that for once she had Cassie all to herself, yet almost wishing Lyndie was still there, wishing they hadn't argued. Lyndie would've known what to say—she always knew what to say.

Cassie sniffed, wiping her cheeks with the back of her hand. "This is pathetic."

"You're right," Elle said. "It is. We need to make this all go away—at least for tonight."

Cassie's mascara ran in black streaks underneath her eyes. "How?"

Elle sprang up, holding a hand out to her friend. "Come with me." She gave Cassie a tug up and off the bed, then led her out to her car. "Keys?"

"I'll drive," Cassie said. "Just tell me where to go."

They got in Cassie's Honda Civic, and Elle directed her friend which way to go until, finally, they reached the trailer park.

"What are we doing here?" Cassie asked when Elle told her to pull in and turn off the lights.

"There's one surefire way to forget all your troubles, and it's in that dingy little trailer." Elle grinned. "Come on."

It was only the second time Cassie had seen the trailer, and usually, Elle wouldn't have allowed it, but these were desperate times. If Lyndie had been there, they might've circled around the fire pit in Cassie's backyard and roasted marshmallows and watched movies on the side of the garage. Or maybe walked arm in arm to the ice cream parlor, where they would've consumed a zillion calories and not cared one little bit.

But Lyndie wasn't there. Only Elle. And this was the only thing Elle could think of to cheer her friend up.

The trailer was dark inside, lit only by the lamppost just behind it. The light streamed through the dirty pinkish-brown curtains, shining just bright enough for Elle to see her mother's liquor.

Even when the fridge was empty, there was always—always—liquor.

"What are we doing here?" Cassie asked.

Elle held up a bottle of rum in one hand and tequila in the other. "Medicine to help you forget all your troubles." She grinned, then sang in her best Jamaican accent for Cassie not to worry about anything, to the tune of Bob Marley's "Three Little Birds."

Cassie laughed. "If you say so." She grabbed one of the bottles and took a swig, grimacing as she forced herself to swallow. "Whoa. That's strong."

"The stronger, the better," Elle said. "Let's go."

Cassie walked out, but before Elle got out the door, something on the opposite side of the trailer caught her eye. Her mother, sitting in the tattered avocado-green chair she'd found on the side of the road. Elle held her gaze for a long moment, waiting for the unpredictable Lily Porter to react—not to Elle's disobedience, but to the fact that Lily was now short two bottles of liquor.

But Lily said nothing, letting Elle slip out silently in the darkness of the night.

# Chapter Twenty-Eight

Lyndie stood at the mirror in Cassie's room, all those years of longing for Tucker's attention swimming through her mind. How many times had she wished for this exact night? And now here she was, ten years later, finally getting ready for her first date with Tucker Jacobs.

Her stomach somersaulted at the thought.

She'd called Foster twice, but he hadn't answered, not that she could blame him. Later, he'd texted her, I'm out of your place. No fight from me. If you don't know what you're missing out on, then I'm out of here.

She did know what she was missing out on, and she wasn't all that sad about it.

Her mom had tried telling her that dating these guys was dangerous, but Lyndie always rejected the idea.

"You're not thinking about their feelings at all, Lyndie," Susan had said the day after her daughter broke up with a guy named Joe, who'd had a particularly embarrassing meltdown in a restaurant upon receiving the news. (So much for having the hard conversations in public places to avoid that kind of humiliation.)

"Mother, this guy has an unusual amount of feelings," Lyndie had said.

"Many guys have a lot of feelings. And you're not accounting for the fact that while you're not serious about them, they very well could be falling in love with you."

The comment had made Lyndie laugh out loud, but her mother's stern face sobered her right up. "Nobody is falling in love with me, Mom. Trust me." And Lyndie had believed that, but she was starting to see Susan's point (not that she would ever admit it). What if Foster had actual feelings for her? How had she never considered them before?

What if protecting herself had wounded others? What if she'd been the cause of their heartache, the same way Tucker had caused hers?

Her realization of her selfishness once again reached up and smacked her across the face.

She didn't want to think about it. She couldn't think about it.

But she could do better. She picked up her phone and sent Foster a quick text: I'm really sorry, Foster. I should've been honest with you from the start. I know you're going to find someone who will make you very happy.

She tucked the phone in her purse and gave herself a once-over in the mirror.

She'd put messy, loose waves in her blond hair, and just a dab of lip gloss on her lips. She kept her look simple, with a deep-pink blouson dress and a pair of wedge sandals that gave her two inches of height.

Who could fall in love with someone so plain? So broken? Certainly not Tucker Jacobs. She needed to remind herself that Tucker lived in San Diego. She lived in Nashville. There were many miles—and a load of baggage—between them.

But oh, she couldn't deny the hopefulness inside her as she walked out of Cassie's room and downstairs.

In the living room, she found Karen and Davis on opposite sides of the sofa. Karen had a book in her lap, and Davis had his eyes glued to the television. Golf.

For a fleeting moment, Lyndie wondered if Cassie's parents ever talked anymore.

Karen glanced up when Lyndie walked in the room. Her eyes smiled before her mouth did, and she snapped the book closed and set it on her lap.

"Look at you." Karen stood up. She was going to fuss over her. Lyndie prepared herself for it. "Look at her, Davis." She walked over and put both hands on Lyndie's shoulders. "Isn't she gorgeous?"

Davis glanced at Lyndie. "She certainly is."

"You two," Lyndie said. "You better stop or I'll get a big head."

"Sylvia Honeycutt told me she got to hear you sing the other night," Karen said, eyeing Lyndie.

Lyndie'd had no idea Karen spoke to Sylvia Honeycutt.

"And I said, 'That cannot be. Lyndie hasn't sung a single note for me since she's been back.'" Karen winked at her.

"It wasn't planned," Lyndie said.

"She said it was quite remarkable. Maybe you'd be willing to sing at Cassie's party?" Karen asked. "I was thinking of playing a recording of her favorite hymn, but maybe you'd sing it instead?"

Lyndie's breath caught in her throat. "Oh, wow. I don't know."

Karen's eyes were so hopeful. "'Amazing Grace' might seem old, but Cassie did have a spot in her heart for tradition."

"I'll think about it, Mama J.," Lyndie said. "I'm really not a singer. I just write music."

Karen frowned. "That's not what I heard."

"Where are you off to tonight, Lyndie?" Davis asked, muting the television. "Do Travis and Elle have you booked?"

Tucker hadn't told them? She glanced at the clock in the kitchen. It was a few minutes after eight. What if he didn't show? She couldn't tell them he was taking her out if he wasn't going to show—how embarrassing would that be?

"No, we had a day at the spa, and they gave us the night off. I think they've got something planned for their family."

"Oh," Davis said.

The pause told her they expected her to tell them her plans. What was the big deal? She and Tucker were just two friends getting together; surely Karen and Davis wouldn't read anything into that.

Before the break in conversation got too awkward, the front door opened, and a frazzled-looking Tucker walked in. "Sorry I'm late." He glanced at Davis and smiled. Karen visibly noticed the look between the two men, then turned her attention to Lyndie.

"Oh, look, it's Tucker." Karen smiled that maternal smile.

They were all acting weird.

Tucker stood in the doorway for a few seconds, then met Lyndie's eyes. "Wow," he said. "You look beautiful."

Did he just say that out loud? In front of his parents?

Karen's smile widened, her face beaming. "Finally."

Lyndie imagined a sheepish expression on her own face. She reminded herself that Karen didn't know about her history with Tucker.

"Yeah, our son finally wised up," Davis said.

"Okay, guys, enough." Tucker held a hand out to call them off. "You ready to go?" he asked Lyndie.

She nodded, but before she could move, Karen pulled her into a tight hug. "You both have a wonderful time."

"Thanks." Lyndie wished she deserved Karen's praise. She wished she could be the kind of woman a mother would want for her son. She could never be that now, but she wanted to try.

*I laid it all down.*

Tucker opened the front door for her and let her pass through. Once outside, he led her right past the car and onto the sidewalk.

"We aren't driving?"

"Not where we're going," Tucker said.

He took her hand, and they walked away from the house toward the lake, toward Silver Beach.

"We're not doing something crazy, are we? Like a hot-air-balloon ride or parasailing?"

He smiled.

"Or rock climbing or cliff diving? I'm not really dressed for that kind of activity." Not that she'd have the courage to do any of those things anyway.

"You're impatient."

"You're not the first person who's told me that." She kept her eyes forward, but she couldn't keep the smile from her lips.

When they reached the dune, Lyndie expected to head down toward the water; after all, a beach date would be appropriate, though maybe a little predictable. At this point, she didn't really care what they did, though it seemed to matter to Tucker, who acted a little bit nervous.

She'd never seen Tucker Jacobs nervous in her whole life.

Instead of walking to the water, they hung a left at the dune and continued for a block before taking another left at the corner of Lavender Lane. And when they got to the end of the lane, Tucker turned left yet again, back toward his parents' house.

"Okay, now I'm really confused," she said.

He led her back to the front walk and up the driveway, but instead of going inside, he moved around the house and into the backyard.

"Tucker, what is going on?"

His only response was to motion toward the gate that led to the yard behind the garage.

Lyndie followed his gaze and saw a table and chairs set up underneath the giant oak tree, which had been strung with white bulb lights and lanterns ages ago. Karen used to host parties in their backyard, cooking for a neighborhood of people. In those days, it had been filled with chatter and excitement and *life*.

Now, there was a distinct *quiet* in the space, and Lyndie found it peaceful.

The light of the sun had started to wane, and the twinkling lights spilled a golden hue across the table.

"We're eating here?"

"Don't worry, I didn't cook." Tucker gave her hand a tug toward the table, then stopped to pull out her chair. "I didn't think cooking for you would be the smartest idea."

"You set this all up?"

"I had a little help." He glanced at the house, and Lyndie saw Tucker's parents peeking out one of the windows. They quickly shut the curtain and disappeared.

"They knew?"

"Yeah, they knew." Tucker's grin was lazy, lopsided. "But the idea was all mine," he added quickly. "They just helped with the setup."

"That was nice of them."

"I think it was good for them. They needed a project."

Lyndie smiled. "Well, everything looks wonderful."

"I'll be right back." Tucker went inside through the back door, and Lyndie sat at the table under the glow of the lights. The evening was warm, but a breeze kept it from being too hot, and her hair was thankful the humidity wasn't too bad tonight.

She glanced over at the house just as Tucker emerged, carrying two plates.

"I hope you like Italian," he said. "It's from Capri."

The sweet little Italian bistro was a town favorite, and Lyndie couldn't imagine anyone not wanting to devour every last bite. The smell of marinara sauce wafted her way, and she drew in a deep breath of it, her mouth watering with anticipation.

"I'm starving," Lyndie said. She hadn't eaten much that day, and her stomach let her know it didn't approve.

"There's more inside," Tucker said.

They ate in silence for a minute or two, but then their conversation found a nice pace, a steady volley between two people genuinely interested in what the other one had to say.

He asked about college, about Nashville, about writing music.

She asked about owning a business, about surfing, about living in San Diego.

They talked like two old friends with much to catch up on. They talked like two people who enjoyed each other, two people without a past, without history, without regrets.

And then there was a lull.

"Did you ever think this would be the life you'd be living?" Tucker asked.

She knew he meant the question lightheartedly, just polite conversation. Though maybe not as polite as when he'd described the way it felt to jump out of an airplane or when she'd told him about her meeting with Jalaire Grant. That had felt safer, less intrusive, whereas the weight of this question somehow landed squarely on Lyndie's shoulders.

This was certainly not the life she'd intended to live. Somewhere along the way, she'd gotten stuck in neutral, and she'd just been going through the motions ever since. She'd never seen it before, but sitting across from Tucker, her first love, finally the recipient of his attention, she saw it clear as day. Or maybe it had been in the church earlier, when she realized she'd been carrying her burden all along instead of burying it.

And while normally at this point in the conversation she shut down, turned off her emotions, put up her wall—she thought she might try a different approach for once. She thought she might wade into the waters of honesty and see where they led.

"I don't know what kind of life I thought I'd live," she finally said. "A fuller one, maybe?"

He was midsip on his glass of water. He swallowed and set it down. "What do you mean?"

She twirled a strand of spaghetti around her fork. "I'm not sure. What makes a life full?" Because at that moment, hers felt decidedly empty. Maybe he would have the answers?

Tucker broke off a hunk of bread and dragged it through the olive oil and salt he'd poured onto a small plate. "I'd have to say probably the people who are in it."

She dabbed the corner of her mouth with her napkin and set it back on her lap. "Maybe that's my problem, then. I need to get more people."

Tucker fixed his gaze on her. "Or maybe just the right ones?"

She dropped her eyes to her plate and cut her meatball in half. "This is amazing, by the way."

"Dewey said you have a boyfriend."

She looked up and saw he wasn't looking at her anymore. "And you still asked me out?"

"I figured if it were true, you would've said no."

"You figured wrong."

Now he met her eyes. "You do have a boyfriend?"

She let the pause hang between them as the seconds passed. "I did," she finally said. "Until yesterday."

His smile was nearly undetectable, but she spotted it.

"I should've broken things off weeks ago, really," Lyndie said. "It was never going to be anything real."

"Why not?"

"Because I don't want anything real," she said without thinking. "I mean, not with him."

"So, why were you dating him?"

*Keep the wall up.*

Lyndie took another bite, though her appetite had nearly disappeared. "What about you? Are you dating anyone?"

Tucker shook his head. "No."

She chewed her food. Swallowed. Prayed for a reprieve.

"You changed the subject," he said.

"You noticed that, huh?"

A breeze kicked up, and she leaned into it, taking an especially long breath. What if she told him the truth? Would he get up and walk away? Pull her into his arms and hold her until the tears subsided? Would he speak aloud the words that attacked her mind—that she was disgusting, that some sins could never be forgiven?

"I seem to only date a certain kind of guy." She set her fork down.

"What kind of guy?"

"The kind I could never actually fall for."

He reached across the table and took her hand. "I know a little something about that."

"You date guys you know you won't fall for?"

He smiled. She liked making him smile.

"You're funny," he said.

"I try."

He squeezed her hand. "I don't let anyone in either. I don't want to hurt anyone else."

"I don't want anyone to hurt me."

His eyes scanned hers as they clouded with fresh tears. Did he understand what she wasn't saying?

"I don't want to hurt you again, Lyndie."

*You won't. I won't let you.*

But then, she wanted to believe him. For the first time in her entire adult life, she wanted to believe the words a man said. But he wasn't just any man, he was Tucker, and he'd hurt her before. How could she ever put that behind her?

*Give away the thing you need.*

The memory of Sylvia's advice startled her, and in a flash, Lyndie was kneeling in front of that cross, laying down every sin, every regret. She'd asked to understand forgiveness, and maybe this was her answer.

Maybe she had to forgive Tucker first. And maybe she needed to follow his example, because no matter how much she'd wanted him to be the villain, he hadn't been alone that night. She'd been a willing participant.

"Are you okay?"

She nodded. It wasn't true, but what could she say?

And yet, if she said nothing, she'd never truly be free. Her secret would always have control over her. Tucker had mentioned that idea earlier, but only now did the realization settle inside her. She had to tell Tucker the truth.

"I got dessert too," he said.

She widened her eyes. "I ate so much."

"Maybe we can save it," he said. "We can eat it during the movie."

"Movie?"

Tucker cleared the plates and disappeared back into the house. When he returned, he carried two small plates of tiramisu, but he didn't set them down on the table. Instead, he motioned for her to follow him over to the side of the yard, where she now saw a small seating area had been set up facing the side of the garage.

"An outdoor movie?" Her mind whirled back to those glorious evenings under the stars. They'd sprawl out on blankets, all of them, surrounded by snacks and pillows. They'd rest up against each other with the familiarity that came from being truly *known*.

Lyndie had forgotten how much she missed that. The simple, sweet things they'd all done together, yes, but more importantly, the way it felt to be so loved and accepted.

She'd lost that the night Cassie died.

Tucker had spread out two quilts from the sleeping porch and assembled several oversized pillows on the ground. Now, he set their dessert plates down on a tree stump they'd always used as a makeshift coffee table, and he motioned for her to take a seat. She did, then watched as he started messing with the projector.

When the picture finally showed up on the side of the garage, Lyndie gasped. A 1960s taxi drove toward the camera and came to a stop. Audrey Hepburn stepped out of the cab dressed in that perfect black evening gown, hair pulled back in an impeccable bun.

"*Breakfast at Tiffany's?*" Lyndie practically whispered.

"It's your favorite, right?" Tucker sat down beside her.

"How did you remember that?"

He laughed. "You gave me a pretty stern lecture about this movie. How could I forget?"

She watched as the movie title appeared on the screen. "I didn't think you were paying attention."

Tucker leaned forward, eyes fixed on hers. "I always paid attention, Lyndie. You were so different than everyone else, and I treated you like you weren't."

"I thought we put that behind us."

"I know." He reached over and placed his hand on the side of her face.

She should tell him. She owed it to him.

But if she did, it would change everything. It would change the way he was looking at her right now—like she was something beautiful to be desired, special and worthy, even if she wasn't.

She had to be honest, no matter how much it hurt.

"Tucker, I . . ."

But before she could say anything, his lips were on hers. He cupped her face with his hands, and she let herself get lost in the sweetness of his kiss. His lips were soft and full, and she drank him in.

He pulled away for a brief second and searched her eyes.

And while everything about it should remind her of the night she'd made the biggest mistake of her life, it seemed entirely different and new. As if the second chance she'd given him had been a true starting over for them.

And it gave her hope that maybe she'd get a chance to start over too.

◆ ◆ ◆

"They're going to catch you," Davis said, snapping the curtain closed.

Karen had been watching Tucker and Lyndie from their second-story bedroom window overlooking the backyard. "I just want to make sure he's not messing it up." She peeked outside again.

Seeing Tucker and Lyndie together was therapeutic, but when Tucker had asked her and Davis to help him prepare for the dream date he'd created in his mind, Karen had nearly jumped for joy.

How long had it been since she'd felt so excited about something? Even planning for the celebration of life, with all of its details, hadn't filled her up the way tonight had.

She and Davis had listened as Tucker outlined his plan, and when he'd mentioned *Breakfast at Tiffany's*, a lump formed at the base of Karen's throat. She remembered watching it with the girls so many moons ago. Cassie hadn't shared her friend's appreciation for classic movies, but Lyndie would sit in awe of Audrey Hepburn the entire time.

"How did you know she loved that movie?" Karen asked.

"She told me once." Tucker blew it off, like it was a normal thing for him to have paid attention to. Karen shared a conspiratorial look with Davis, who was obviously as surprised as she was.

Karen would've helped her son plan anything, just to spend time with him, but she realized he had most of it figured out. Dinner from Capri—don't forget the dessert. He wanted the white lights on, the big pillows out and the projector working.

Karen and Davis listened intently, and after Tucker left, they got to work.

Did their son purposely give them a task that forced them to spend the day working together?

"Where do we start?" Davis had asked her.

"Let's go out back and get a plan."

He followed her through the garage and into the yard. She hadn't spent any time out there this summer, but she was grateful Davis hadn't let it go. He'd kept the yard perfectly manicured, the fire pit well cared for, the trees trimmed.

"It's going to be the perfect place for their first date."

Together, Karen and Davis worked to make Tucker's wishes a reality. They discovered the string of white lights had died, so off they went to the hardware store to get new ones. They restrung them and positioned the table underneath the big tree.

"Do you remember the summer we all piled out here and introduced the kids to *The Goonies*?" Karen started filling a large glass vase with flowers she'd trimmed earlier from the garden.

When Davis didn't respond, she glanced up at him, found him watching her.

"I remember," he said.

Karen smiled. "Tucker would never admit it, but he was actually scared of those Fratelli brothers. But Cassie loved it—remember how it made her want to be a pirate?"

"She walked around the house for weeks wearing a pirate hat, quoting that stupid movie." Davis laughed.

"She did, I'd forgotten that." Karen stilled. "So many good memories out here."

He'd nodded, then went back to setting up the projector.

Now, standing in their dimly lit room, she moved away from the window and sat on the bed. "I had fun today."

He scooted back toward the pillows and glanced over at her with a smile. "Yeah, I did too."

Davis flipped the television on and pulled the covers over both of them. The memories of so many nights spent with her on one side of the bed and him on the other flittered through her mind.

She inched over, nestling into him as he reached his arm up and around her, making it easy for her to rest her head on his shoulder.

For a few minutes, they stayed like that and watched the local news, two broken people who very much wanted to find a way to put each other back together.

And for the first time in years, Karen thought they might actually succeed.

# Chapter Twenty-Nine

Elle paused for a moment, trying to deduce what Travis was thinking, but his face registered no emotion.

Somehow, she found the courage to go on.

"We went down to the marina," Elle said.

The night had been dark—really dark. There must've been a new moon, because if it hadn't been for the lamps, they wouldn't have been able to see anything. They'd sat on the dock for a while, but Elle lost track of time.

"We should take my dad's boat out," Cassie said.

"Um, that's a terrible idea." Elle nodded toward the bottle in Cassie's hand.

"You've hardly had any," Cassie said. "You can drive."

Cassie was right. Elle had barely drunk anything—she didn't even like alcohol.

"Come on!" Cassie grabbed the other bottle and raced toward her dad's boat, anchored in the marina.

"I don't even know how to drive a boat," Elle said.

"It's easier than driving a car," Cassie said with a laugh. "You *do* know how to drive a car, don't you?"

Elle had learned, but she hadn't had much practice—and she didn't have her license. It wasn't as if her mother would drive her to the nearest

Michigan Secretary of State office, birth certificate in hand, and take care of all the paperwork required to get her learner's permit.

Cassie jumped into the boat. "You were right, Elle, I'm forgetting all the bad stuff. Come on!"

Elle followed her. "Where are the life jackets?"

Cassie laughed. "Nobody actually wears those things."

"I do," Elle said, her footing unsteady as the water rocked the boat ever so slightly. "I'm not a good swimmer."

"I am," Cassie said. "If you go overboard, I'll save you."

Elle watched as Cassie started the engine. "I'll get us out of the marina," Cassie said, "but you have to take it from there."

"This is a bad idea, Cass."

Cassie groaned. "You sound like Lyndie." She revved the engine, then moved the boat slowly out of the marina. Good thing they were parked near the end—otherwise, they would've likely damaged other boats docked there.

Once they'd successfully (for the most part) maneuvered out onto the lake, Cassie motioned for Elle to come take the wheel.

"Come on," Cassie said. She put her hand on a lever. "Move it up. Boat goes. You steer."

Elle took a step forward and put her hands on the wheel while Cassie continued to work the throttle. "Go slow."

Cassie had been driving the boat since she was fourteen, but what was second nature to her was definitely not familiar to Elle. She took her time to get used to the feel of the boat in the water, moving her way slowly around the levers and buttons on the panel in front of her.

After a few minutes, Cassie walked to the back of the boat and picked up the bottle of rum. "Good thing my dad keeps soda in here." She opened a built-in cooler and found a can of Coke. "Want one?"

Elle didn't look away from the lake in front of her. "No, thanks."

"You said we were drinking," Cassie said with a giggle. "So far, I am drinking and you are being a stick in the mud."

"I can't drink if I'm driving the boat," Elle said. It dawned on her that she couldn't let Cassie get too drunk either; otherwise, who would dock the boat when they got back to the marina? They'd end up leaving it on some other dock somewhere, and then Cassie's parents would know they'd taken it out.

Elle kept her eyes focused on what she thought was the horizon, though the sun was long gone. Mostly, she felt like she was driving them straight into nothing.

After about fifteen minutes and a full can of rum and Coke, Cassie appeared at Elle's side. "We cannot keep driving like a pair of boating grandmas."

Elle widened her eyes. "Are you kidding me? I'm still learning how to do this!"

"Well, you're a slow learner." Cassie tossed her head back and laughed. "Get out of the way."

Elle white-knuckled the steering wheel.

"Come on, move. I'll show you how to actually drive it."

Slowly, Elle slid out of the way as Cassie took the wheel. Cassie steadied the boat for a few seconds, then pushed the throttle forward, sending Elle forward with a jolt. "Cassie!"

"Oops." Cassie laughed again. "Sorry about that. You might want to hold on."

Elle found a life jacket and stuck it over her head.

"You are such a baby," Cassie said.

"Don't be stupid. You need to put one of these on too."

Cassie's only response was to kick up the speed another notch.

For the most part, she held the boat steady. But she continued to pick up speed, and before Elle knew what was happening, Cassie let out a cheerful holler, taking the boat around a sharp turn to go back the way they'd come.

At that speed, the turn was too sharp, and Cassie lost control.

In the chaos, the boat flipped over, tossing both girls into the water. The cold shot up Elle's spine, and in the blackness, her hands searched for something—anything—to grab on to. The headlight of the boat shone into the water, illuminating various items as they floated out of the boat and down to the bottom of the lake. Elle's life jacket hadn't been securely tightened around her neck, but it stayed on, and she used it to buoy herself to the surface. She gasped for air, her heart pounding as if she'd sprinted a mile.

"Cassie!" Elle called out. Where was Cassie? Elle searched, turning in circles, heart still racing, her breathing labored. "Cassie!" She swam over to the overturned boat as it filled with water and began to sink. She went under and looked around, but she could see only wherever the boat's headlight glowed.

Rising back to the surface, she began to sob. What was she going to do? How would she get back to land? Where was Cassie?

Elle turned in more circles, scanning the water for anything that would indicate Cassie's location, but there was nothing.

Now, standing outside her mother's trailer, Elle couldn't look at Travis. She didn't feel better knowing her secret was out—she felt worse. She felt caught, exposed, ashamed.

So ashamed.

She wrapped her arms around her midsection and turned away, crying softly.

"You must've been so scared out there alone," Travis said quietly.

Her mind raced back to the moment the boat had disappeared into the depths and she'd realized Cassie was gone. She covered her face with her hands and cried, waiting for Travis to get in the car and drive away, to leave her here with Lily where she belonged.

When his hands found her shoulders, Elle stiffened at his touch.

He turned her around and pulled her to him in a tight hug that allowed her to bury her face in his chest. She'd just confessed her role in Cassie's death, and he was worried about her? She didn't deserve his kindness, but she soaked it up, letting it fill her the way water filled a sponge.

"It was my fault, Travis," she said through her tears.

He brushed her hair away from her face and kissed the top of her head. "It was an accident."

She shook her head and pulled from his embrace. "She was drunk because of me."

Travis held her eyes for a beat, then glanced over at the trailer. Only in that moment did Elle realize her mother had gone back inside. "Not because of you," he said. "Because of her."

Elle searched his eyes.

"You were a kid, Elle. Who was taking care of you? If my parents saw me sneaking out of the house with two bottles of alcohol when I was eighteen, do you think they would've let me go?"

She shook her head.

"Yeah, it was a stupid choice to get it, and it was Cassie's stupid choice to drink it, but the way I see it, the adult in the picture is the one who should've known better."

Elle thought about all the lonely days and nights she'd spent in that trailer. She'd learned to make cinnamon toast and mac and cheese when she was eight. She'd started saving coins to buy milk and bread when she was nine. And she'd started getting herself up and ready for school that same year, after three tardies in a row.

Her mother should've been there.

"Are you saying it was her fault?" Elle sniffed.

Travis drew in a deep breath. "I'm saying you can't shoulder all the blame for an accident."

"It was my idea. It was my fault she was driving, because I didn't know how to go any faster." Her voice broke again. "I searched for her, Travis. For almost an hour, I kept searching. I was so afraid to go under, but so afraid to swim away from that spot—I knew I'd never find it again. It was so dark."

In the end, a fisherman had happened upon her, and in nearly running her over, discovered she was out there alone. He'd rescued her, called the Coast Guard and took her back to the shore.

Everything that happened after that was a blur—a mess of memories tangled with guilt and shame. The police officers had questioned her as she'd sat in a hospital bed for observation.

She'd answered them as best she could:

*I don't know if Cassie hit her head. After the boat rolled over, I never saw her again.*

*Cassie was driving.*

*Yes, I searched for an hour straight, but I'm not a strong swimmer, and I was scared.*

*No, I don't want to speak to Cassie's parents right now.*

And finally, *No*, there was no one to call to come sit with her at the hospital.

She pulled away from Travis, but he wouldn't let her get far.

"You've been carrying this around with you for a long time," he said.

She nodded. "A very long time."

"Why didn't you say something sooner?"

She found his eyes. "I was afraid of what you'd think of me."

"I think you're amazing."

She shook her head. "I'm a mess."

"A beautiful mess." He took her hand and turned her around to face the trailer. "All of this is a part of your past, Elle. But it's not a part of your future."

A tear slid down her cheek.

"Your future is with me, and I don't care where you came from or who you used to be or what you did or didn't do. I know you." He crossed around in front of her and forced her to meet his gaze. "And I love you. Maybe more now than I ever have before."

"Really?" she whispered.

"Really." The corner of his mouth lifted in a slight smile. "It's time to forgive yourself."

"I don't know how to do that."

"One day at a time," he said. "And I'll help you."

She sank into his arms.

"I love you, Elle."

"I love you too."

"Let's go home." He took the keys from her, opened her car door and ushered her inside.

*Home.* She'd never truly known how *home* felt, just a taste of it at Cassie's house, but she knew she wouldn't find it here. It was time to put this place—with all of its bitter, painful memories—in the past.

As Travis turned the car around, she caught a glimpse in the side mirror—her mother, standing outside the trailer, watching as Elle drove away.

Putting it all behind her once and for all.

# Chapter Thirty

The memory of Tucker's sweet kisses stayed with Lyndie long after they said good night. Lying in bed, she'd replayed each moment of what had to be the best first date she'd ever been on.

Tucker had been so attentive to her, the date tailor-made to her likes and dislikes. He knew her, even after all this time, which meant he'd been paying attention all those years she'd thought he hadn't.

And she'd rediscovered the cozy feeling of being known. How she'd missed that.

Now, as the morning sunlight seeped through the curtains, rousing her from a sweet dream, Lyndie drew in a deep breath. She tried to sort out the mix of emotions the week had already brought her. She tried to understand how, in spite of all her regret, a small piece of hope was peeking through, like grass pushing up in the cracks of a sidewalk.

She'd buried her feelings for Tucker so long ago, but here they were again, reappearing so easily, as if they'd never gone.

Was it just nostalgia that made it all feel so real?

The door opened and Elle walked in, still wearing her clothes from the day before. She'd vanished after the spa, and Lyndie hadn't seen her again until that very moment.

"Did I wake you?" Elle said, slipping her flip-flops off.

Lyndie shook her head. "I was just lying here."

"Daydreaming?"

"Something like that." Lyndie rolled onto her side and faced Elle. "Are you just getting in?"

Elle smiled.

Lyndie's eyes widened. "Were you and Travis . . ."

"We went down to the dock," Elle said. "The one with the gazebo."

Lyndie knew it well. She looked away.

"We just talked," Elle said. "Have you ever felt like something was keeping you from knowing someone—like, really knowing them?"

Lyndie found Elle's eyes.

"And then, when it's all in the open between you, everything changes." Elle practically beamed.

"Are you talking about you and Travis?"

She nodded, then ran a hand through her long auburn waves. "He loves me, Lyndie."

"Well, yeah, you're getting married."

Elle's eyes filled with tears. "But he *really* loves me."

Had she not known this before?

"In spite of everything, he still loves me." Elle plopped down on the bed beside her. "If I'd never opened up, I wouldn't know that now." She fell back onto the pillow, pulled the covers over her and looked up at the ceiling. "I'm so glad I know it now."

Elle's face looked more relaxed than it had since the day she'd returned to Sweethaven, and Lyndie wondered what had burdened her before.

"I hope you let someone love you like that someday," Elle said.

"I just haven't found the right person." But Lyndie thought of Tucker, the way his eyes had searched hers the night before as he'd said good night on the porch. Never mind that there'd been only a hallway of distance between them all night long—he'd still walked her to the front door like a gentleman and kissed her good night under the light of a moon so full, surely it had been lassoed closer to the Earth just for them.

"Then why are you smiling?" Elle sat up and studied her.

Lyndie changed her expression. "I'm not."

Elle's eyebrow twitched upward. "What aren't you telling me?"

The knock on the door saved Lyndie from answering, but sent a wave of panic through her—what if it was Tucker? Would he feel the same today as he seemed to feel last night?

"Come in," Elle called out before Lyndie could protest.

Lyndie tugged the blanket up a little closer to her chin as the door opened and Karen's face appeared. The older woman smiled at the two of them, as if the memories were playing on repeat in the corners of her mind.

"I just love having you girls back here," she said.

"We love being back, Mama J.," Elle said.

And it was true. Lyndie did love things about it. She loved the bittersweet memories of how things used to be. She loved Mama J. and the way she took care of them all.

What if Elle was right? What if this thing Lyndie carried was the one thing that kept her from really knowing anyone? What if she exposed it herself—got it out in the open on her own terms—so it couldn't torture her anymore?

"I came to let you know I have a few errands to run this morning," Karen said. "I'm having the party catered, but there was a last-minute change, so I have to go make a few decisions."

Lyndie nodded.

"But I made cinnamon rolls for you girls." Karen grinned.

"Homemade?" Elle asked, eyes wide.

"Is there any other kind?"

"I'm not going to fit into my dress." Elle threw the blanket off her, gave Karen a quick hug and ran out the door.

"I love it when you girls still act like you did when you were kids." Karen sat on the edge of the bed.

"I don't think Elle had many people baking homemade anything for her growing up."

"No, sadly, I think you're right."

"This is amazing!" Elle yelled out from downstairs.

Lyndie followed Karen's gaze to a photo on the bulletin board—Cassie and Tucker on Cassie's graduation day. "She had her whole life to look forward to," Karen said.

Lyndie sat up, leaned against the headboard and pulled her knees to her chest, wrapping her arms around them. "Today must be hard for you."

Karen shook her head slightly, as if waking from a dream. "And for you."

A knot formed at the base of Lyndie's throat. She reached over and put a hand on Karen's. "For both of us."

There was a quick pause.

"Did you and Tucker have a good time last night?" Karen asked. Her purposeful subject change was a welcome one, even if Lyndie wasn't sure she wanted to wade into her feelings for Tucker with his mother.

But Lyndie couldn't help but smile. "It was perfect."

"I used to hope Tucker would become a man worthy of you, Lyndie."

"You did?"

Karen nodded. "I saw the way you looked at him."

Heat rose to Lyndie's cheeks.

"But he wasn't ready for someone like you." Karen squeezed her hand. "In fact, I think it's a good thing you two never went out back then—who knows where that could've led?" She laughed.

Lyndie's shame returned.

"Sometimes I think relationships are all about the timing, don't you?"

Lyndie forced a smile and nodded.

"Well, come down and eat a cinnamon roll," Karen said. "It's a big day."

When she walked out, she left the door slightly ajar, and Lyndie could see Tucker's bedroom door from where she sat. It was open—he'd probably been up since dawn.

Her eyes found the ceiling as she replayed Karen's words, feeling like a fraud and wishing she had the courage to run after her and tell her everything.

*But what would she think of me?*

"You look lost in thought." Tucker's voice pulled her back.

She glanced back at the door and found him standing outside its threshold, looking in.

"The door was open," he said.

She thought about what Elle had said about getting everything out in the open, about letting someone love her. Where had Elle found the courage to do either of those things?

"Wanna go parasailing?" Tucker asked.

Lyndie shot him a dubious look. "You're kidding, right?"

"I'm half kidding."

"I think we're going to that vineyard this morning," Lyndie said, "before the celebration of life."

Tucker stared at her blankly.

"Elle and Travis. The wedding party. The whole reason we're here."

He gave her a half shrug, then grinned. "Joking. I know what's on the agenda. But I'd rather spend the day alone with you."

She smiled as he disappeared, leaving her with nagging thoughts spinning through her mind.

◆ ◆ ◆

"You and Lyndie?" Travis and Tucker trailed the rest of the group as they strolled through the Rolling Hills Vineyard on a tour nobody but Nora seemed to care about.

Tucker shrugged.

"'Bout time," Travis said. "Been a while since your first kiss." He laughed.

Tucker had been so racked with guilt over what had happened between him and Lyndie back then, he'd needed to tell someone—but all that had come out was a half-truth: *I kissed Lyndie.* Still, Tucker was surprised Travis had never guessed things had gone further than that.

"Don't tell me you feel guilty again," Travis said.

Tucker shook his head and caught a glimpse of Lyndie up ahead, next to Elle. "No, I don't feel guilty at all."

"Good." Travis followed his gaze. "She'd be good for you."

And Tucker hoped he'd be good for her too.

Earlier, he'd texted Pastor Kyle about this new development: I did it. I mean, I know I can't apologize to everyone I was a jerk to, but I made things right with Lyndie—and you were right. I feel a million times lighter.

Awesome to hear, buddy, Kyle had replied. Push it out into the light and it can't mess with you anymore. That's what I always say.

I believe you now. And besides . . . she's worth it.

Whoa. Is it possible San Diego's most eligible bachelor is thinking about settling down?

Too soon to tell—she's way too good for me.

Can't wait to hear all about it. Proud of you, man.

Tucker now walked with the group through the vineyard, listening as the guide explained what they were seeing, but Tucker wasn't interested. He inched his way forward in the line and fell into step next to Lyndie.

She looked up at him with those bright-blue eyes and smiled, and for a moment, the world seemed to stop.

And if he could've stopped it, he would've. The depth of his feelings for her had surprised even him, but the moment she'd forgiven him had been like a gift he was determined not to squander. He'd made so many missteps, but apologizing to Lyndie wasn't one of them.

He slipped his hand around hers and gave her a little tug. They fell to the back of the group and then turned off the path and down one of the rows, vines on either side. He pulled her along, away from the group, then stopped and faced her.

"What are we doing? We're going to get lost."

Tucker didn't care. He hadn't stopped thinking about Lyndie since he'd kissed her good night. He couldn't wait to do it again. He took her face in his hands and searched her eyes.

"I don't even drink wine," he said.

"I don't think we're here for the wine," Lyndie said. "I overheard Nora say something about the beauty of the landscape."

"Well, you are the only beautiful landscape I care about," Tucker said.

She laughed, and he closed the gap between them. His lips found hers—soft and sweet—and he drew her even closer, inhaling her. He kissed her the way he'd dreamed of kissing her, full and free—no regrets between them, no secrets weighing them down.

Being forgiven made him feel like a bird that had just escaped its cage. She'd given him a second chance, and he'd never take it for granted.

"Lyndie!" Elle called out, and Tucker pulled away, but not in time.

Elle stood at the end of the row, eyes wide. "You two?"

Lyndie turned away, her cheeks rosy the way they always were when she was embarrassed.

"Sorry," Elle said. "Carry on."

She disappeared back into the fray, leaving Tucker and Lyndie standing face-to-face. He stared at her for a few seconds, and then they both burst out laughing.

"She has the worst timing," Lyndie said.

He took her hand and led her back through the vineyard and toward the winery, pretending for a moment they weren't part of a wedding party or there on someone else's schedule. And he liked the way it felt to imagine she was his.

◆ ◆ ◆

Being at the vineyard with Tucker made Lyndie feel almost normal, as if they were just two people at the start of a relationship.

With Elle and Travis's blessing, they left early and drove to the lake, where Tucker took her kayaking, something she'd never done before.

"We'll find that adventurous bone in your body if it kills us," he told her.

She was a hopeless paddler, but she gave it a solid try. Thankfully, Tucker was used to guiding people, even those not accustomed to adventure.

Their conversations were lighthearted and fun, the kind she'd never really had with anyone she'd dated—because, while the tone stayed upbeat, she was actually talking about herself, something she made a point to never do.

But she wanted Tucker to know her. He'd let her in—told her about the pastor back in California and apologized for the way he'd treated her.

She had to at least try to be open with him.

They pulled the kayaks from the water, and Tucker secured them to the top of his rented SUV while Lyndie carried the paddles.

"Not bad for your first time out," he said.

"I'm not the most outdoorsy person."

He laughed. "I remember."

She frowned. "Remember what?"

"The time my dad took us all camping."

Lyndie handed him the paddles. "I'd forgotten all about that."

"You woke everyone up in the middle of the night because you were sure you saw the shadow of a bear walking by your tent."

"Don't remind me," Lyndie groaned.

"You could've had a career in horror movies with a scream like that."

"It looked a lot bigger than it was." She jutted her chin out in her own defense.

"It was a raccoon, Lyndie."

"Still totally gross!"

He laughed and shook his head. "You're so beautiful, you know that?" He tugged on her shirt and pulled her body toward his as he leaned against the back of the SUV. He wrapped his arms around her, holding her tightly.

"I must've at least made up some points with my perfectly roasted marshmallows," she said. "Or my mad campfire singing skills."

He tucked a piece of hair behind her ear. "True. Nobody could sing a campfire song like you and Cassie."

*Cassie.* Lyndie had never been anything but honest with Cassie . . . except when it came to Tucker. "How do you think she'd feel if she knew this was happening?"

"*This* meaning us?"

She nodded.

"I think she'd love it." Tucker kissed her. They'd stolen kisses all morning at the vineyard, and she prayed he didn't sense her hesitation, and that if he did, he didn't misinterpret it.

She loved kissing him. It could become her favorite pastime, but how could she let herself get too close?

This thing between them, it was fun. Yet it was Tucker, after all, and no matter how much he'd changed, she doubted he was the settling-down type. And besides, it would break all her rules.

She needed to remember they weren't headed somewhere serious. Even if they both wanted it to be more, how could she ever get to the place where she let someone love her fully? It would require the kind of emotional sacrifice Lyndie didn't know how to make.

But she had to try. Didn't she owe it to herself to try?

"You know," she said, "I don't know if I'd be writing music at all if it wasn't for Cassie."

Tucker's eyebrows popped up. "You don't think?"

"The first song she made me play for you guys—do you remember?"

His eyes searched the sky, and he started humming until he landed on it—the song Cassie had sworn was gold-record worthy.

"That's the one," Lyndie said. *Here goes nothing.* "I wrote that song about you."

Tucker held on to her gaze, refusing to let her look away as a slow smile crept across his lips. "You did?"

She nodded. "I was so horrified you might figure it out when Cassie made me play it in front of you guys." Lyndie pulled herself from his arms, though she wished she could wrap herself in them for the rest of the day. She looked out at the lake. "She only discovered I wrote music because she overheard me through the door one day when she came to pick me up."

"Well, then I'm glad she was so nosy."

"And bossy," Lyndie laughed. "She was so bossy . . ." Her voice trailed off as she remembered. Tucker took a step forward and stood next to her, also staring across the lake that had become Cassie's grave.

"I hate knowing she's still out there," he said.

"I do too. I wish they'd found her." She slipped her hand inside his. "For everyone's sake."

"She was something, wasn't she?" Tucker's smile turned sad.

"She was the best." Lyndie watched the still, serene water.

Tucker drew in a breath. "I should've been there for her."

She could see the guilt on his face and realized that even forgiveness couldn't erase all the pain of a past mistake. And maybe that was okay. Maybe it wasn't meant to make it go away. Maybe it simply took the sting out.

"Tucker, I . . ."

"Sorry," he said. "I didn't mean to get all heavy."

*I have something to tell you.*

"We should probably get back. The party is starting soon." He leaned in and kissed her one more time, stealing her resolve.

Maybe forgiveness was overrated and secrets were meant to be kept.

# Chapter Thirty-One

Lyndie sat on a white wooden chair at the front of the park outside Sweethaven Chapel. She wiped her hands on her skirt, then folded them on her lap.

She was nervous.

This was why she was the songwriter and not the singer. This was why Cassie had always been the lead and Lyndie the backup. Something about standing in front of a crowd unnerved her, exposed her, like all her faults were on display.

Cassie had never much cared what anyone thought of her. Lyndie envied her that.

How did it feel to be that free?

The word struck her again, like a mallet on a bass drum, reverberating in the depths of her soul. *Free.*

She thought of the way Sylvia Honeycutt worshiped. The way Elle's smile had left Lyndie feeling breathless. The way that song she had played in the chapel Monday night had poured out of her like a tidal wave that couldn't be quelled.

She wanted to live with that freedom—what was stopping her? She was tired of asking the same questions and finding no answers.

Davis walked over to Karen, who was sitting in the front row, and whispered something in her ear. She stood and walked behind the music stand in the front that would serve as the podium for the service. The rows of wooden chairs were filled with friends and family, some faces familiar, others not. Tucker sat on one side of Lyndie and Elle the other.

Lyndie tried to focus. This was important, not just to Karen, but to her. Maybe her mother had been right: a little closure would go a long way.

She half listened as Karen gave a poignant and beautifully bittersweet speech about her only daughter. When it got hard, Lyndie clung to Tucker's hand, wishing she had the assurance that he would love her no matter what.

But life wasn't about assurances, and freedom didn't come without sacrifice.

She stopped daydreaming just in time to hear Karen say her name.

Lyndie's eyes widened, and Tucker gave her a nudge. "You're up."

She nodded and stood, walking to the front of the space on wobbly legs. She reached Karen, who pulled her into a tight hug, then sent her off to do her thing.

But Lyndie was unsteady. How would she do this without Cassie there to steady her?

She looked up to find all eyes focused on her. She slung the guitar over her shoulder, the strap crossing her diagonally. The microphone was almost a hindrance, amplifying her voice just enough to distort it, so she set it aside. "You don't mind if I don't use that, do you?"

A few mutterings came from the crowd, but Lyndie had already begun to tune them out.

"Cassie and I grew up together," Lyndie said. "She was one of my very best friends. We were supposed to go off to school together, but the accident was the summer before college, so I went on my own." She found Karen's eyes, warm and caring.

How had Cassie's mom found the strength to move forward after everything she'd been through? After she'd lost Cassie, and Tucker moved away? Who had sustained her?

"The night she died"—Lyndie glanced at Tucker, whose eyes fell— "she and I had our first-ever fight. It was dumb, especially for two girls who said they hated drama." Lyndie's throat went dry. "Sometimes I wonder what would've happened if we hadn't been so stubborn that night—if we'd just realized how silly it was, how much we loved each other, and moved on." Another glance at Tucker. "Things would've been so different."

Her fingers hit the strings of the guitar, reminding her why she was actually up there.

"But we can't know how things might've been," Lyndie said. "We can only know how things are. And we were all forced to move on in a world that was much bleaker, having lost Cassie Jacobs."

Beside her, a small screen had been set up, and an image of Cassie's face appeared. Lyndie strummed the first chord of a song she'd known since she was a little girl, but whose words had never meant anything to her.

Hymns weren't her kind of music, but Cassie'd always had such appreciation for them. It contradicted who she was, in a way—always trendy and popular—but she was still rooted in something greater than her.

Lyndie wanted that—to be rooted—and maybe she had been, once. She wanted to know how it felt to be free, no matter the cost. She wanted to understand the power of *grace*, the depth of *forgiveness*.

*I don't deserve these things.*

She strummed the first chord of Cassie's favorite hymn, reminding herself of words that felt foreign and forced.

*Amazing grace, how sweet the sound*
*That saved a wretch like me.*
*I once was lost, but now I'm—*
She stopped. *Found.*

Her heart latched on to the word, as if it held more weight than any five letters should. She wanted so desperately to be found.

Being found meant being known—and wasn't that what she'd been craving all along?

She caught Tucker's gaze from where he sat in the front row. His eyes were wide, expectant. The slide show had stopped scrolling.

Her fingers slipped on the strings, and her voice disappeared.

Inside her, unspoken words spun and tumbled, like a wheel rolling down a hill. She would never be found—never be free—until she spoke the words out loud; then they would lose their grip on her, just like Tucker had said.

Just like Tucker had done.

That grace, it was there for her to reach up and take, a gift freely given. She'd already known this, hadn't she? And yet she'd forgotten. She'd convinced herself her sins were too great, her shame too deep.

In a flash, Lyndie realized she was still standing in front of the crowd. Davis glanced at Tucker, who'd knit his eyebrows in concern.

"I'm sorry," Lyndie said. "I can't . . ." She set down the guitar and ran down the aisle and toward the chapel.

Grace was only amazing if it was yours. And Lyndie had never found a way to make it so.

She rushed through the churchyard and over the hill, then kept walking toward the beach.

When the gazebo came into sight, a sob that had been building like a hurricane inside her broke loose. She'd messed up so badly, and it had all started on that night. She'd forgiven Tucker, but she could never, ever forgive herself.

She took off her shoes and stumbled down the side of the sand dune. She reached the bottom and ran out toward the gazebo. "Why did You let this happen?" The words came without her permission. "Why didn't You keep me safe?"

She yelled out at the water, wishing someone was out there to hear her, but no answer came, only the sound of waves pushing their way onto the shore.

She was mad at God. And that shamed her almost as much as her past.

"I made one mistake," she yelled out at the water. "One unforgivable sin. Were You punishing me? Are You still punishing me?"

Still no answer. Only silence from the One who was supposed to never leave.

But where had God been that night? Where had He been the next day, and the days after that? He'd taken Cassie and then given even more pain.

"Lyndie?"

She spun around and saw Tucker standing at the other end of the dock. The weather had turned as the clouds rolled in, spitting rain down from the heavens.

"What's the matter?"

He'd found her.

*I once was lost, but now I'm found . . .*

She spun back around and faced the gray water. In a dark place inside of her, where the light wasn't allowed to shine, she felt the rumble of a storm.

The words rolled around. They wouldn't stay locked away anymore. They had a will of their own, and they'd been hidden away inside an imaginary box for too many years.

She sensed Tucker start to walk toward her, and she faced him. "Don't."

He froze in place. "Don't what?"

"Don't come closer." The rain turned to mist, creating a dreary backdrop that perfectly complemented her mood.

His whole face fell. "Why? What's wrong?"

Her breath caught in her throat, and her heart raced. She raked a hand through her hair and met his eyes. "I have to tell you something."

"Whatever it is, Lyndie, it can't be that bad."

If only that were true. She rubbed her temples with both hands, willing the words away, but they got only louder and stronger in her mind.

*Tell him the truth.*

"What is it about?" Panic washed over his face, and she *wished* she could sugarcoat this for him. Wished there was an easy way to say it, but there wasn't.

This was her sacrifice.

This was the requirement for her freedom.

And in spite of all her pretending, she didn't know if she was strong enough. Her eyes fell to the dock underneath her feet. *God, if You're there now, I need You.*

She pressed her lips together and steeled her jaw, bringing her chin up so she could face him.

"After Cassie died," she began, "my parents didn't think I should go to school. They said I seemed sad and withdrawn. I got a free pass on having to talk about it, because everyone just assumed I was still grieving over Cassie—and I was. But I had to get out of there. I couldn't be around my parents, knowing what I'd done—what we'd done. Every time I looked at them, I felt like a liar, like I'd let them down. If they found out, I knew it would break their hearts. So, I insisted they let me go to school—alone.

"But I hated it there. Cassie was supposed to be there with me—we were going to take the music world by storm. Find ways to play all over Nashville together, like real musicians. I needed her confidence, because I didn't have any, especially not after that summer."

His eyes found the dock. "I'm so sorry, Lyndie."

"You've already apologized." Her eyes clouded over. "This isn't about you or what you did or didn't do. This is about me and what I did."

Confusion swept across his face.

"I got pregnant."

Tucker didn't move.

The words hung between them, a cord of electricity connecting them. She'd never said it out loud. Not a single person on earth knew this about her except the doctor in the health center on campus at Belmont.

"What?"

Lyndie looked away. She knew better. She'd known better. Her mother had warned her this could happen, in that awkward conversation they'd had when they picked out her purity ring. Lyndie had known the dangers and pitfalls of having sex, but she'd wanted Tucker to like her. She'd wanted to be the one he adored.

When he didn't call, she realized how misguided she'd been, but by then it was too late. She'd given away a piece of herself, and she could never take it back.

They'd all gone through the motions in the days that followed Cassie's death. It wasn't the time to show herself pity, not when her sorrow couldn't compare to that of Cassie's family. As the days went by and Cassie's body wasn't recovered, Lyndie struggled to find her place. She wasn't family. She couldn't soothe their broken hearts, but still, she longed for Tucker—to know he was okay.

Without a body to bury, the funeral became a memorial service, with Lyndie and her parents on one side of the church and Elle sitting alone on the other. Lyndie had needed someone to blame, not only for what had happened to Cassie, but for what had happened to her—what she'd allowed to happen—and Elle had been on that boat.

It was her fault, wasn't it?

But after the service, when Tess appeared out of thin air and stuck by Tucker's side the entire afternoon, Elle seemed to know it broke Lyndie's heart. She linked an arm through Lyndie's, took her out onto the bench in the little cemetery behind the chapel where a headstone would be placed in honor of their friend, and didn't say a word.

Sometimes, in grief, there were no words to be said.

And sometimes that was okay.

But now was not one of those times. Standing in front of Tucker, having blurted out the secret she'd gripped tightly with both hands, Lyndie struggled for the courage to continue.

He walked toward her.

She held up a hand. "Don't, Tucker."

He stopped. "Lyndie . . ."

"Let me say this." Her voice wavered as she struggled for air. "Let me finally say this."

He was only a couple of feet away now, too close for her to think. She spun around and drew in a deep breath.

"About a month after I got to school, I started to feel sick, so I went to the clinic on campus, and the doctor asked if I could be pregnant. I hadn't thought of it before, but it made sense. Sure enough, the test came back positive."

"Lyndie . . ."

"I never felt so alone in my life."

"Do your parents know?"

She shook her head. "You're the first person I've ever told."

"All this time?"

She nodded. Turning from the water, she took a step toward him, wishing she was already on the other side of what was about to come.

He met her gaze. "What did you do?"

Tucker's eyes shone in spite of the rainy weather. He looked unsteady, as if he could collapse without warning. She told herself she would have to be the strong one.

*This is going to hurt.*

"I was so young and ashamed. I grew up in the church. I knew better."

"So did I, Lyndie. You weren't the only one there that night—this was both our faults."

"But I'm the one who had the abortion." A sob got stuck at the back of her throat as her eyes filled and tears spilled onto her cheeks. She covered her mouth with her hand. What had she done?

How many nights had she dreamed about that cold, sterile clinic? They'd rushed her in, told her there were people waiting and they needed to get started.

She'd hurried onto the table, then waited, alone, for the doctor to show up.

Lyndie's eyes unfocused as she stared past Tucker toward a pair of Jet Skis zooming across the lake in the direction of the marina. "The doctor came in. He was a small man with bushy eyebrows. He didn't look at me once, not the whole time I was there."

She started to turn away, but Tucker reached for her. She shrugged from his grasp—she didn't deserve his kindness.

"Lyndie, please," he said, moving toward her.

She tried to push him away, but he wouldn't let her. Instead, he grabbed her by the arms and pulled her toward him. She tried to push again, but he held on to her, too strong for her to move. He wrapped his arms around her and pulled her to his chest.

She didn't deserve his compassion.

*Was lost . . . but now I'm found.*

Was this how it felt to be forgiven?

She stopped resisting and sank into his embrace, drawing on his strength, praying it would make up for her own weakness. The tears came freely now, ten years' worth, cried only in the dark of night until she'd finally banished them, forcing herself to move on.

But she'd never really moved on, had she? Instead, she'd packed up her sorrow and carried it with her. It was so, so heavy.

"I'm so sorry, Tucker." She buried her face in his chest, willing the hurt away. But it didn't magically disappear like she'd hoped it would. Instead, it wrapped itself around her heart and squeezed as the memories of the worst months of her life rushed back.

The loneliness she'd felt in those days had been crippling, and it left her with an inability to trust herself or anyone else. It was why her relationships were always so purposely short-lived. She couldn't risk her heart like that again.

He held her for so long, letting her cry an ocean of tears. But what must he be thinking? She couldn't mistake his embrace for forgiveness.

She regained her composure and pulled herself from his arms. "I'm sorry."

"No, don't be."

She dared a glance and found his eyes glassy and red. He ran both of his hands over his face—his beautiful face—and turned away.

*He thinks I'm disgusting.*

"I can't imagine what you must think of me," she said quietly. Her mascara had to be gone by now, her face puffy and red. What she wouldn't give for some tissues.

He stood with his back to her, unmoving, still facing the water.

"I'm sorry, Tucker." She watched him for a few seconds. His muscles seemed tense.

"Why didn't you tell me?"

"I hadn't talked to you since that night."

"I could've helped you, Lyndie." He turned and faced her, eyes full of sorrow.

She saw it then, the bitter regret. "Don't make this your fault, Tucker," she said. "This was my choice."

His eyes searched hers. "You were pregnant." His voice broke as he said it, and he quickly turned away again, swallowing the last word as he did.

She dared a step toward him.

"This *is* my fault." He moved to the edge of the dock and leaned on the railing of the gazebo, facing the water. "This is all my fault."

She followed him, then forced his gaze. "This was our fault. We were both there, you said it yourself."

Tucker pressed his fists into his face, clearly wanting his emotion not to show. "You shouldn't have had to go through that alone."

She wished she hadn't. She wished things had been different. But she couldn't change the past, and neither could he. The only thing they could do now was put it behind them.

"Do you hate me?" Her question sounded like something a third grader would ask, but she needed to know the answer.

He turned toward her and took her face in his hands, using his thumbs to wipe away a trail of tears that ran down her cheeks. "I could never hate you, Lyndie St. James."

The words dangled in the air, and for a moment she kept them from penetrating the wall of her heart.

"I could never hate you," he said again, as if he knew she needed to hear it over and over to believe it was true.

She looked up into his eyes, which looked more gray than blue, matching her mood. "Do you forgive me?"

He brushed her rain-dampened hair away from her eyes, still holding her face in his hands. "I forgave you the second you told me."

The knot in her throat returned. How did he so easily offer her something she so obviously didn't deserve?

She steadied her breathing. "Will God forgive me?"

"Oh, Lyndie," Tucker said, as if seeing her pain for the first time. "He will always forgive you."

"But what I did . . ."

"That's what grace is for." He pulled her close, holding her tightly, the way she'd longed to be held for all those years she'd kept everyone at arm's length. "We all screw up. Do you know how long it's taken me to forgive myself for the stupid things I've done?"

His question filled the space between them, unanswered.

"I don't know how to forgive myself for this," she said.

"Well, you don't have to figure it out alone."

"But I am alone."

"You're not anymore."

# Chapter Thirty-Two

The morning after the celebration of life, Karen awoke early, intent on a big breakfast for anyone and everyone who would eat it.

She stood at the stove, whipping eggs, milk and vanilla, then coating both sides of day-old bakery bread to make the most wonderful French toast.

How would she survive when Tucker went back to San Diego, Lyndie back to Nashville and Elle back to Chicago?

She'd waited up as late as she could last night, hoping to catch Lyndie before she went to bed and make sure she was okay, but Karen had been so worn out after the party. So many people had come out to help them celebrate and remember Cassie. So many stories—so much joy. Only weeks ago, she wouldn't have been able to hear any of it without breaking down, but she'd turned a corner. She and Davis had laughed as their friends and family recounted their favorite things about their bright-eyed, happy little girl.

She didn't have it all figured out, but it was a start.

Davis strolled in from outside and drew a deep breath. "Smells amazing in here."

"I hope it rouses our sleepyheads from slumber," Karen said, cracking another egg into her bowl.

"If not, more for me." He smiled, kissed her on the cheek and poured a cup of coffee. "You're beautiful, you know that?"

She waved him off. "And you're in my way."

He wrapped an arm around her waist, hugging her from behind. "Am I in your way now?"

She turned her face to his and responded to his kiss. How long had it been since they'd had this kind of playful flirtation? She missed it. She missed him.

From behind them, Tucker cleared his throat, and instinctively Karen pushed Davis away, spilling a drop of his coffee on the floor.

"I'll get it." Davis set his mug down and cleaned up the spill while Karen tossed French toast onto a plate and shoved it toward Tucker.

"Breakfast," she said.

"I'm not all that hungry."

That wasn't like her son. "Is everything okay? Is it Lyndie? I was hoping to talk with you both after the party last night, but we just crashed."

Davis handed Tucker a hot mug of coffee.

"Thanks."

"You didn't answer me, Tuck."

His eyes darted back and forth between them. "It's fine. She feels bad she ran out. I think she just got nervous. Maybe don't mention it to her? She's embarrassed enough as it is—feels like she let you down."

"I have to ask her if she's okay," Karen said.

"She's fine. Can you just trust me that she's fine?"

Karen frowned. "I suppose I can."

"Good. I really think it would be best," Tucker said. "Gonna go shower. I told Travis I'd meet him at the lake."

He disappeared, and Karen's gaze lingered on the space where he'd been sitting.

"Don't read into it," Davis said. "If he needs us, he'll let us know."

Karen nodded. She couldn't promise she'd stop worrying about her kids, but she could try not to let that worry consume her. It's what she would've told herself if she were her therapist.

"Let's go for a walk," Davis said. "Get some fresh air and exercise so we can eat as much French toast as we want."

Karen smiled, flicked the stove off and followed her husband outside.

◆ ◆ ◆

Saturday morning, Elle's entire bridal party was due at the Preston cottage at an ungodly hour.

When Elle arrived, she walked into a flurry of activity. Various workers bustled through the entryway, racing from room to room with tasks no doubt assigned by Nora.

Elle walked up the stairs to the room where she and the rest of the girls would be getting ready. A young woman worked on Sarabeth's hair while Violet sat next to her, scrolling on her phone.

"Elle!" Sarabeth's reflection met Elle's eyes.

Elle smiled.

"It's your big day." Violet practically swooned.

"Have you seen Travis?" Elle set her purse down on the sofa near the door.

"No, and you can't see him either." Sarabeth's eyebrows knit into a stern line.

"I can't see him once I'm dressed," Elle said.

"You can't see him at all," Violet said. "Aunt Nora will kill you both."

The woman working on Sarabeth's hair glanced at Elle, and the look on her face said she knew from personal experience that Nora was not to be crossed. But Elle didn't care. She wanted to see Travis—just for a minute.

Ever since she'd told him about the night Cassie died, Elle felt closer to him, as if now he really—finally—knew her. All of her. And he loved her in spite of it. She'd never known a love without condition.

Growing up, her mother had paid attention to her only if Elle was in trouble, or if Lily needed Elle to do something for her. And while Elle would always regret her part in Cassie's death, she understood now that forgiveness didn't come with conditions. Not the kind of forgiveness Travis had offered her, anyway.

Still, a part of her worried he might change his mind. Maybe in carrying her secret around with him for a full two days, he'd realized what she'd always known—that she didn't belong here. That she wasn't worthy of this family, this life or his love.

She crept down the hall toward Travis's room, where she could see a line of light from the cracked door on the hallway floor. Just before she reached the room, the door opened and Nora walked out.

Nora's raised eyebrow instantly made Elle feel like a child getting in trouble. "Good morning, Elle."

"Morning, Nora."

Nora eyed her. "Looking for someone?"

"I'm looking for Travis."

Nora put a hand on Elle's shoulder and turned her around. "You know the rules."

From behind, Elle heard the door reopen, and she turned to find Travis standing there, watching her.

"Travis," Nora said. "Get back in that room."

His face warmed into a wide smile. "We're getting married today."

Elle smiled back. "We are."

He rushed out of the room, took Elle in his arms and kissed her—right there in front of his mother. Happiness welled within her. He still loved her.

Travis pulled away. "I can't wait."

"You two are breaking every rule." Nora sounded exasperated, but Elle didn't care. She inhaled Travis, feeling that with his love to steady her, she could handle just about anything life (or Nora) threw her way.

"Oh, there you are," Nora said to someone behind Elle. "Would you tell these two to knock it off? This is bad luck."

Elle turned and saw Pastor Preston looking at them. "Ah, but my dear, we are people of faith—we don't believe in luck."

Nora groaned. "I can't get anyone to cooperate with me around here. It's a wonder I've managed to pull off this wedding at all."

Travis found Elle's eyes and said with one raised eyebrow what he couldn't say out loud. She had a feeling they'd share silent jokes about his mother for years to come. The battles that weren't worth fighting they'd weather in silence, and those that needed to be dealt with they'd tackle together.

As a team. As a family.

This was going to be her *family*.

"Elle, Marcie is waiting to do your hair and makeup," Nora said. "She's the better of the two girls. She'll do our hair and Lyndie's while the other girl will handle my nieces and the flower girl. Where is that little Ainsley?" Nora trailed off as she wandered down the hall. When she was several yards away, she turned back. "Are you coming?"

Pastor Preston put a hand on Elle's shoulder. "You sure you want to join this crazy family?"

Elle glanced at Travis, who squeezed her hand. "I can't think of anything in the world I want more."

Travis's dad gave her a paternal hug, then sent her on her way.

She reached Nora at the end of the hall just as Lyndie came up the stairs. Her friend looked exhausted, pale. She carried her dress, covered in clear plastic.

"Oh, my goodness," Nora said. "What happened to you?"

"I haven't been sleeping very well," Lyndie said.

Nora's brow quirked. "You're not hungover, are you?"

Lyndie glanced at Elle, as if deciding how polite she wanted to be to Nora. Elle shot her a look that said, *Please don't make a thing of this.*

"I am not hungover. Just tired." Lyndie must've gotten the telepathic message. "I'll be fine after I get some coffee." She looked at Elle. "I hope today is perfect for you." She reached over and squeezed Elle's arm. "You deserve it."

Only three days ago, Elle would've mentally protested that statement. She still struggled to believe she deserved anything good, but she prayed that one day she would truly accept it.

Lyndie strolled off down the hall, leaving Elle standing face-to-face with Nora, who watched as Elle's friend disappeared behind the door of the ready room.

"She's right, you know," Nora said.

"About what?"

"You deserve to be happy." Nora smoothed her hands on her black dress pants as if they were wrinkled. "You make Travis so happy."

Elle smiled. "I try."

"I know you might think I'm hard on you, Elle," Nora said. "And I don't mean to be. I know I can come off as kind of . . ." She seemed to search for an appropriate word. "Abrasive."

Elle didn't argue.

"I guess I want to protect you from certain aspects of this life we live."

"How so?"

Nora had never in her life touched Elle, except for the occasional forced hug that seemed more of a societal expectation than anything else. But in that moment, she reached over and put a hand on her shoulder. "People expect certain things from us."

Elle didn't move. She knew all about their life in the public eye of ministry. They were held to a higher standard. Their sins carried more weight than other people's. They were practically supposed to be superheroes.

Elle knew she could never live up to that kind of pressure, and she didn't want to try. She wanted to be real, down-to-earth and honest. Maybe that's what people were really craving?

"When I married Travis's dad, I wasn't ready for any of that. I thought we'd be pastors of a little church one day. When his ministry took off, I quickly realized everyone had an opinion about the way we did things. This was before social media, so it was a good old-fashioned rumor mill, and the hurtful things people said—about my shoes, my clothes, the way I responded to someone's question, the way I raised my child—it all got back to me. People love to share all the mean things other people are saying behind your back."

For the first time, Nora seemed like a real person.

"I suppose I developed a public face and a private face," she said. "And sometimes the two collide."

"I don't think I can handle having two faces, Nora."

Nora smiled sadly. "And I would never want you to."

"Are you sure?"

"I haven't been trying to change you. I've been trying to prepare you. I don't want you to feel like you aren't good enough, the way those women made me feel for so many years, and I certainly never intended to make you feel that way myself."

Elle could feel the pinprick of tears in her eyes.

"I only want the best for you and Travis," Nora said. "Why else would I make myself crazy planning this wedding?"

Elle let out an involuntary laugh.

"I wanted to welcome you to the family in the best possible way," Nora said. "And maybe have an excuse to taste test all kinds of cakes."

Another laugh. Was Elle bonding with Nora? What a strange turn this morning had taken.

"I've never really had a family," Elle said.

"Well, now you do. And you even have an overbearing and bossy mother who is about to tell you to hurry on down to the ready room and get your hair done." Nora pulled her hand back and looked at Elle. "You're the daughter we prayed for."

A tear hurried down Elle's face, and she quickly brushed it away. "Thank you, Nora. For everything."

Nora smiled. "Now, go."

Elle did as she was told, her heart full with knowing that while Nora wasn't perfect—she was controlling and, yes, abrasive—she was about to become Elle's family. And that meant loving Nora for who she was.

And Elle couldn't wait to extend that courtesy.

With her hair and makeup done, Elle stood in the doorway, admiring the little chapel that might just barely hold the number of guests Nora had invited.

The church had been decorated with sprays of wild, eclectic-looking flowers, not the kind that Elle had ever seen at a wedding. The aisle was marked by a beautiful white fabric that led from one end to the altar, and the stage had been lined with beautiful barnwood lanterns. Nora had taken good care of those details, and in the end, Elle was thankful she'd gotten out of her mother-in-law's way.

"She outdid herself."

Elle turned and found Lyndie standing behind her. "She really did."

"I'm sorry if I was rude to her before. I've just been processing some things."

"I know the feeling," Elle said.

Lyndie glanced at her, and for a split second, something silent passed between them—an understanding, a forgiveness, a moving on.

"The day after Cassie died . . ." Elle didn't know if she could find words. They were so much better at pretending everything was fine.

"It was a crazy day," Lyndie said.

"I said some things." Elle tossed her long, curled locks behind her shoulder and faced her friend. "I said if you'd been there, things would've been different, that maybe Cassie would still be alive."

Lyndie's face twitched.

"The truth is, I was trying to blame you for something that wasn't your fault," Elle said. "To make myself feel better."

"I think we all wanted someone to blame."

"Cassie loved you, Lyndie," Elle said. "Even in the middle of your fight. You know that, right?"

Lyndie nodded. "What happened out there, Elle?"

Elle's eyes clouded over with tears she refused to cry. It would ruin her makeup. It would make her nose red. She blinked quickly and looked up at the ceiling. "She lost control of the boat, and it flipped over."

"Just like you always said."

Elle pressed her lips together. "But she'd been drinking."

Lyndie frowned. "She had?"

One tear streamed down her cheek, and Elle quickly wiped it away. "She was so upset. About Travis and about you." Her voice broke. "I'm so sorry, Lyndie."

She expected Lyndie to turn and walk away, and Elle wouldn't blame her if she did. After all, they both knew there was only one place they could've gotten the alcohol. But that's not what Lyndie did. She reached over and pulled Elle into a hug.

"I'm sorry I wasn't there for you," Lyndie said. "I'm sorry I let so much distance get between us."

"I'm sorry I couldn't save her." Elle hugged Lyndie back, and in a flash of forgiveness, the years and distance between them disappeared.

"I know how it feels to carry a heavy burden," Lyndie said. "You don't have to do that alone anymore."

Elle nodded. And she knew her friend was right. She'd begun to see the answers to her prayers—in Travis, in Lyndie and even in Nora.

She had a life full of people who loved her and wanted what was best for her. It was all she'd ever wanted in the world.

"We should go," Lyndie said. "You've got to have that Sasha lady fix your makeup."

"Her name is Marcie."

Lyndie frowned. "I've been calling her Sasha all morning."

Elle laughed as they turned to walk downstairs to where the make-shift bridal room was, but when she looked up, she found they weren't alone. A familiar worn face glared at her.

Lyndie balked. "Elle?" she said quietly.

Elle glared back at her mother. "It's okay, Lyndie."

Lyndie didn't move.

"It's okay," Elle said again, hoping to reassure her.

"I'll be just out there if you need me." Lyndie glanced at Elle's mother before walking out of the small church lobby.

"What are you doing here?" Elle asked.

"Came to find out where my invitation is," her mother said.

"I didn't think it would be a good idea to invite you," Elle said. "You can imagine all the reasons why."

Lily's eyes narrowed on her. "This is quite the fancy shindig you've got in here. How much did it cost?"

"What do you want, Mother?"

Her mom took a step toward her. She wore black jeans and a black Metallica shirt. Her messy hair had been pulled back into a ponytail. "You think you're so much better than me now?"

"I don't think I'm better than anyone," Elle said.

"I still see the real you, and if you think marrying this rich kid is going to change any of that, you're mistaken, little girl."

*Little girl.* Lily had been calling her that for years. The words dripped with condescension.

"You should've protected me." The words escaped without permission. Elle didn't want to get into any of this with her mother—not here and especially not now.

The door behind Lily swung open, and Nora appeared.

Elle was struck by the stark contrast between the two women. Nora, already dressed for the wedding in a formal peach-colored gown, and Lily, dressed like she'd just pulled an all-nighter at the bar.

Nora glanced at Elle and then at Lily. "Elle, you're not dressed yet?"

"I was just going," Elle said.

"What are you, her boss?" Lily practically spat the words.

"Don't talk to her like that," Elle said. Lily had no right to be jealous over a daughter she'd never loved.

Her mother scoffed. "You've become one of them. It's disgusting."

"I'm sorry," Nora said, "who are you?"

Elle's heart raced. "It's fine, Nora. I'll take care of this."

"I'm her mother." Lily faced Nora like a gunslinger lining up for a shootout. She was a good six inches shorter than Travis's mother, but she was feisty, and Elle started to worry about what Lily might do or say. She was hell-bent on ruining this day for Elle.

"Her *mother*?" Nora angled her gaze down at Lily.

"That's right," Lily said. "She tries to pretend she's one of your kind, but truth is, she's one of mine."

Nora's eyes darted to Elle, then back to Lily. "A mother—a good mother—loves without condition. She's there when her child is hurting and when her child is overjoyed. She celebrates little victories and huge accomplishments. She would never leave her child to fend for herself, not even as an adult, but especially not as a child."

What was Nora saying? She couldn't possibly know about Elle's childhood, could she?

"Your daughter used to walk around town barefoot, in clothes that hadn't been washed in weeks," Nora said. "Were you her mother then?"

"You're so self-righteous," Lily said. "Who do you think you are?"

"I'm one of the mothers who came together to make sure your daughter had everything she needed."

The image of Cassie's mom bringing Elle a brand-new backpack stocked with brand-new school supplies raced through Elle's mind. Shoes Mama J. had "picked up on a buy-one, get-one deal." Clothes she'd "found for a song" on one of her many shopping trips. The table had always been set for Elle. Her school lunches always paid for.

*Nora?*

"But as much as we tried to protect and take care of your daughter, you still found your ways to hurt her."

Lily would surely relent. She'd break down and apologize in light of everything Nora had said. Wouldn't she?

Elle's mother glared at Nora instead. "You think I owe you something? I never asked you to take care of what was mine."

Nora took a step toward her. "We didn't do it for you. We did it for her."

Lily's glare moved from Nora to Elle and back again. "And you really thought she was worth all that trouble?" Her wry laugh set something off inside of Elle.

"Get out," Elle said.

Lily faced her. "What did you just say?"

"I said get out." Elle stared at her. "I don't want you here. Not today and not ever."

"Those are big words for a little girl." Lily eyed her.

"I'm not a little girl," Elle said. "And you don't get to hurt me anymore. Someone taught me about forgiveness, and even though you don't deserve it, I do forgive you. And I forgive your father for turning you into the person you are. But just because you're forgiven doesn't mean you get to be a part of my life."

Elle waited for her mother to retaliate, but after several seconds of silence, she only scoffed, gave Nora a once-over and walked out of the chapel.

Elle let out the breath she'd been holding, and Nora rushed to her side. "Are you okay?"

"You knew? This whole time, you knew where I came from?"

Nora's eyes softened. "Of course I did."

"And you're still letting your son marry me?"

She smiled. "Oh, sweetheart, there isn't a person alive who could keep that son of mine from marrying you."

"Thank you, Nora." Elle flung her arms around her future mother-in-law. "For everything."

"Don't ever mention it again," Nora said. "You were never supposed to know."

"Well, I'm glad I do. And one day, I hope I can do the same thing for someone else."

Nora pulled away. "You will. But not if you don't hurry up and get dressed. You're going to stall the wedding."

Elle laughed. Despite everything, she still laughed. Because this was going to be the happiest day of her life. The day she finally found a place to belong.

# Chapter Thirty-Three

Elle walked down the aisle to a beaming Travis. They said their heartfelt vows earnestly. Their ring bearer, a distant cousin, ran down the aisle in the opposite direction the moment Pastor Preston called for the rings.

All in all, the ceremony was perfect, exactly what Elle would've dreamed of if she'd ever let herself dream of a wedding.

Once she and Travis had been pronounced man and wife, he slowly removed the thin veil covering her face and kissed her, tenderly, gently, then whispered, "Till death do us part."

Elle still didn't feel she deserved such a precious moment or such a wonderful family, but as they turned to face their guests, her eyes met Nora's, and Elle felt thankful. Nora wasn't a perfect mother, but Elle could hardly fault her for caring too much, not after growing up with a mother who hadn't cared at all. She saw that now.

They walked out of the church as wedding guests showered them with rose petals (Nora's idea) and ushered them straight into a limo that would take them from the chapel to the cottage. Elle turned the pair of rings around on her finger.

"You are the most beautiful bride." Travis leaned in and kissed her on the cheek. "I got you something."

He pulled a small gift bag from beside his seat and set it on her lap.

"Were we supposed to do gifts?" Elle could hear the panic in her own voice.

"No." He smiled. "This is kind of for both of us."

She searched his eyes for a hint, but he had a great poker face.

"Open it," he said with a nudge.

She pulled the tissue paper out of the bag, then reached inside and felt some kind of soft fabric, which she pulled out next. She frowned as she studied the lacy white Minnie Mouse ear hat. It had a small tiara of jewels between the ears and a veil attached to the back.

"I don't understand."

She glanced at Travis, who was now wearing a black Mickey Mouse ear hat with a top-hat-and-tuxedo motif.

"Travis . . ."

"We're not going to Hawaii."

"I don't understand."

"I knew you would never say anything, and I also knew you had your heart set on a Disney honeymoon—so, I had the tickets changed."

"You what?"

He grinned.

"What about your parents?"

"They're cool with it," he said. "I promise."

"You mean, we're actually going to Disney World?" She felt like a little kid, a giddy little kid with parents who'd just surprised her with everything she'd ever wanted.

"Of course we're going to Disney World," Travis said. "And I hope it's just the first of many dreams I can make come true for you."

She wrapped her arms around her husband and drew in a deep breath. "You are my favorite dream come true, Travis."

He kissed her—unhurried and full, with the kind of attentiveness she'd only ever dreamed of. She was his wife—in spite of where she'd come from. In spite of being unwanted by a mother who had only ever brought her misery, she'd found the purest of loves in a man she vowed to love, too, for the rest of her life.

As he laid her back on the limo seat, he deepened the kiss. His hands rushed over her body with the longing he usually pushed away, and she knew those vows she'd said only moments before would be her pure joy to fulfill.

◆ ◆ ◆

After he toasted Travis and Elle, Tucker went looking for Lyndie. They hadn't had any time alone together, only a few passing glances, as every moment of the day had been planned, scheduled and accounted for.

Now, with the photos done, the toast over and Travis and Elle happily dancing their first dance, Tucker hoped he and Lyndie could get a moment to themselves.

He'd been trying to process her confession since Thursday night. Friday, they'd endured countless wedding activities, ending with a rehearsal dinner and moonlight cruise on the lake. Their time had been largely spoken for, and Lyndie had been standoffish. He could only imagine how she felt. He'd promised her she wasn't alone anymore, but how did he show her?

It all made sense now, the way she'd treated him when they first arrived. He'd taken so much more from her than he'd originally thought, and he had no idea how to make it up to her.

He knew only that he wanted to try.

He'd prayed earnestly as he'd gone to sleep the past two nights, knowing that just down the hall was a woman who'd once been pregnant with his child. He wanted to believe things might have turned out differently if he'd known, but he had been in such a different place back then, he couldn't say that for sure. Truth was, he likely would've disappointed Lyndie even more if she'd told him.

He'd been watching Lyndie the entire day today, but she'd slipped out of the big white tent unnoticed sometime between the first dance and the tossing of the bouquet. He walked outside and circled the perimeter of the tent until he saw her silhouette on a bench down by the water. Music from inside the tent drowned out the sound of the guitar he could see she was playing.

He should probably leave her alone, especially if she was writing, but as he watched her, he realized he couldn't. He had to make sure she was okay.

Quietly, he walked down the long walkway toward the private dock behind the Preston cottage. As he approached, her song grew louder, and he recognized it immediately from that day in the church.

Her eyes were closed, her voice—beautiful and steady—singing lyrics he hadn't yet heard. It felt like a private, peaceful moment, and while a part of him thought he shouldn't intrude, another part couldn't walk away.

Lyndie was still something of a mystery to him. Hard to know, with an exterior that would be difficult to crack, but he wouldn't stop trying until she let him in. Something told him she would be worth the extra effort—did she see that about herself? Would she ever?

She stopped and wrote something in a notebook sitting on the bench beside her. He took a step toward her, and she spun around.

"Sorry," he said. "I didn't mean to scare you."

Panic washed across her face, then skittered away. "Hey."

"I think Jackson was looking for you," he said, trying to lighten the mood.

She rolled her eyes. "Tell him I flew back to Nashville."

He stood next to the bench. "Do you want to be left alone?"

"No." She moved over, making a place for him. "Sit."

He did, feeling the warmth of her body next to him in an instant. "Sounds like your song is really coming along."

She'd kicked her shoes off and now sat cross-legged on the bench, the skirt of her teal dress covering her legs and feet. "It is."

"Jalaire Grant is going to love it."

Lyndie smiled. "I hope so."

A silence fell between them.

"You're going back to San Diego," she said, as if she'd only just remembered.

"And you're going back to Nashville."

"I actually might stay here for a little while."

"Here?" He frowned.

She drew in a deep breath. "My head feels clearer here. I can write. I'll send Jalaire demos of the songs I write for her—I don't have to be there in person. I cleared it with my manager."

"Lyndie, I think that's a great idea."

She reached up and touched his face, running her hand along the line of his chin. "But it won't be the same once you've gone."

In that moment, he wished he could stay on that bench forever.

"Well, I haven't gone yet," Tucker said. "And maybe after you get your fill of this place, you can come to San Diego. There's nothing quite like the ocean."

"Really?"

He nodded.

She turned to face him, uncrossing her legs and scooting closer as she leaned her guitar up against the bench. "You still forgive me, right?"

"Of course I do." Years of heartache raced between them, and a knot formed in the base of his throat. He'd forgiven her instantly, because he knew how it felt to require forgiveness, to need grace that wasn't deserved. Of course he would offer it to Lyndie. And while he hadn't quite figured out a way to process what she'd told him, he knew she wasn't the only one to blame.

He'd forgiven himself for so many sins, but it had taken years— could he forgive himself for this one too?

She inched forward, meeting his eyes, then took his face in her hands and kissed him, the kind of kiss that made him wish for so much more. After so many years with women who'd meant nothing to him, he now recognized the real thing.

Lyndie was it. For him, she was all he needed.

So much pain still hung like low fruit on the tree of their life. It needed to be pruned, and while they'd made those first important steps, there was more to clear away.

They needed closure.

His arms moved up her back as he pulled her closer, years of unspoken memories melting away between them.

When she finally pulled away, they were both breathless in the wake of a kiss made urgent by the dwindling time before distance would split them apart.

"Will you play your song for me?" Even in the darkness, he could see her cheeks flush. "You can pretend I'm not here."

She smiled. "You know that's not possible."

He knew. Every cell of his body was certainly aware of *her* nearness.

She picked her guitar back up and tossed him a look over her shoulder.

"This is unheard of, you know." Her smile could've lit up the night sky.

"What is?" He leaned back on the bench.

"Playing an unfinished song in front of another person. Even my manager has never heard an unfinished song, and this is twice now for you."

"I feel honored," he teased.

"You should."

"You're stalling."

She laughed.

But what came next could've stopped his heart. She strummed the chords, humming softly before the words began, and then she started singing.

And while he may've been clueless about the first song he'd ever heard her play, there was no doubt in his mind now that this song was about them.

And about forgiveness and grace, but mostly them. Their story set to music.

When she strummed the final chord, she didn't look at him, and he could see in that moment how difficult it was for her to share anything real about herself with anyone.

But she'd shared it with him. He'd never take that for granted again.

"You're amazing. You know that, right?"

"You like it?"

"No," he said. "I love it."

*I love you.*

The words jumped into his mind, but it would be ridiculous to say them aloud. People didn't fall in love in a matter of days.

But it hadn't been days, had it? He'd always known Lyndie, and while so much about them had changed, so much had stayed the same. He'd never felt this way about anyone else before.

He didn't want to say goodbye to her on Monday morning. He didn't want to go back to his life as if everything was the same. How would he function in a world without Lyndie now that he'd had a taste of what his world could be with her in it?

"Will you meet me tomorrow after church?" he asked. "I'm sure my parents will have a big send-off lunch, but before that—can we do something?"

Lyndie stilled. "Of course."

"Wait for me at the chapel, then," he said. "After the service."

She nodded.

He tried not to let the promise of goodbye seep in as he leaned down and kissed her again and again and again.

# Chapter Thirty-Four

Lyndie stood at the back of the chapel before the service started, feeling awkward and out of place.

Admitting her regrets out loud had released something inside of her, though, like a giant exhale after years of holding her breath. The burden that had weighed her down was still there, but now she felt like she wasn't carrying it alone.

In all, she felt relieved. She'd come clean, and Tucker had forgiven her. What else was left?

"You look different." It was Sylvia Honeycutt, standing right next to Lyndie and eyeing her like a detective would eye a suspect.

"I feel different."

"Lighter," the old woman said.

"Freer." Lyndie smiled.

Sylvia sized her up for several seconds, then abruptly walked away, leaving Lyndie standing in the aisle of the church when the music began. She glanced up at the stage and saw Tucker standing behind the microphone. He'd be going back to California the next morning.

She'd think about that later.

She slipped into one of the seats on the end of the aisle and listened as Tucker began to sing. Her feeling of unworthiness was still there (would it ever not be?), but this time, instead of letting it paralyze her, she imagined herself picking it up and setting it down right underneath the driftwood cross on the wall behind Tucker, right next to the box of regrets she'd placed there only days before.

When the song ended and the moment turned quiet, she opened her eyes and found him looking at her from where he stood on the platform.

He played a familiar chord.

It was soon, maybe too soon, to relive that moment at Cassie's memorial, but when Tucker sang the first line of "Amazing Grace," Lyndie was back there in an instant.

*Amazing grace, how sweet the sound.*

Was he doing it on purpose? Was he trying to make her cry?

She looked at him—his eyes closed, face earnest—and she saw that this wasn't about her at all. Tucker had stepped into a moment of holiness. The rest of them were free to join him if they wanted to.

She closed her eyes too.

*That saved a wretch like me.*

Tears plucked the edges of her eyes.

*I once was lost, but now I'm* . . . Tucker paused, as if he, too, understood the depth of that word—*found*.

Memories scrolled through her mind—the way Sylvia worshiped, the way Lyndie herself wished to be free. Here was her chance to truly surrender.

But what would people think? *Do they know how broken I am?*

Her mind corrected itself: *Do they know how broken I was?*

Slowly, she raised her hands right in front of her, trying not to think about the other people in the chapel or what they would say if they knew the truth of her past—none of those thoughts had the power to torment her anymore. She'd shined a light on her deepest regret, brought it out into the open and exposed it for what it was—a mistake, one that she mourned, but not one that controlled her.

Not anymore.

She wanted whatever God was offering, so she reached up to heaven and asked Him to give it to her.

Warmth filled her from the inside, and for the first time in ten years, Lyndie thought maybe one day she'd be ready to love—and let herself be loved—again.

◆　◆　◆

People bustled around the churchyard, making afternoon plans. Lyndie overheard lunch invitations, beach invitations and even one man who seemed to be asking Sweethaven's librarian Tilly Waterson out on a date. She watched while Tilly fumbled with an excuse, eventually mumbling something about her family and walking away with a shell-shocked expression on her face.

Lyndie made her way back inside the chapel and nearly ran into Karen on her way out.

"Oh, there you are," Karen said. "You're coming back for lunch, right?"

Lyndie smiled. "I wouldn't miss it for the world."

"Good." Karen took both her hands and squeezed. "Will you see Tucker?"

Lyndie scanned the dwindling crowd. "I hope so?"

"Remind him that we're expecting him too. We're grilling out, and we've got a feast. If he doesn't show up, he's in big trouble."

Lyndie smiled. "I'll tell him."

"We'll be so sad when you both go back home." She released Lyndie's hands.

"I actually might stick around for a little while," Lyndie said. "I made a few calls, and it looks like the little red cottage might be available for a few weeks."

"Really?" Karen gasped as she said it.

"I forgot how much I like it here."

The older woman pulled her into a tight hug. "You could certainly stay with us. We'd love it."

"Really?" Lyndie had thought of asking, but she didn't want to impose.

"Of course," Karen said, pulling back to look at her. "Our cottage is feeling big for the two of us, and I'd love someone else to cook for."

Lyndie smiled. "I'll think about it."

"There's nothing to think about," Karen said. "I'll be personally offended if you waste your money on a cottage when you are more than welcome to stay with us." Her eyebrows turned down in a slight frown. "Unless you want your space—I don't mean to force myself on you."

Lyndie laughed. "Of course not. I appreciate the invitation."

How differently she felt about it now compared to only a week before. She had to admit, being able to stay and not pay rent on a cottage was certainly appealing. Besides, now that she'd found the Jacobs family again, she hardly wanted to let them go.

"Are you okay, Lyndie? Tucker told me not to ask you that, and I resisted as long as possible, but I'm worried about you. *Are* you all right?" Karen studied her, probably thinking of the way Lyndie had run out of Cassie's memorial. And while maybe there would come a day when she would explain everything to Karen, a day when she'd had more time to accept her regrets and sit with God's grace—today wasn't that day. Today, Lyndie was simply trying to move forward, one moment at a time.

"I am now," she said. "I'm sorry I ruined the song."

"Oh, don't be silly," Karen said. "We all miss her so much."

Lyndie nodded.

"What about Tucker? About you and Tucker?" Karen waved her hand in the air. "Never mind. That's none of my business. I'm just so happy you're thinking about staying for a little while."

Lyndie smiled. It was nice to be loved.

"I have to go make the deviled eggs," Karen said. "I'll see you in a little bit."

Lyndie watched as she walked away, and the words of the old hymn floated through her mind.

*But now I'm found.*

She'd been so very lost. Could she hold on to this feeling of being found?

She realized she should've asked Tucker exactly where they were meeting when she surveyed the back of the chapel and didn't see him. She wandered back toward the small park where Cassie's memorial had been held. Behind it was the cemetery that held Cassie's headstone.

Lyndie had visited it only once, the morning she'd left Sweethaven for good.

There was such a finality in seeing Cassie's name etched in black on that large gray stone. Even on Thursday, she'd avoided looking at it.

But maybe she needed to accept it once and for all.

Cassie was gone.

Lyndie's emotions about Cassie's death were tangled with everything else that happened that summer and the following fall. It had been too painful to sort through any of it.

She approached the cemetery, the voices from the churchyard growing more and more distant. As she came up over the hill, she spotted it, the marker that stated Cassie had lived—and died—right here in Sweethaven.

Lyndie wondered if she'd have the courage to tell Cassie how sorry she was, for everything, and how much she missed her. But as she walked around the front gate of the small cemetery, she saw she wasn't alone.

Tucker knelt beside his sister's grave on the edge of the cemetery. He brushed a leaf from the top of Cassie's headstone.

Lyndie thought about leaving—the moment felt intimate—but he turned and saw her before she could. "Sorry," she said. "I didn't mean to . . ."

He stood. "I'm glad you found me. I was just going to come look for you."

"It took me a minute." She moved to his side. "Your mom wants me to make sure you know you're expected for lunch."

His smile hung lazily at the corners of his mouth. "She told me three times this morning."

Lyndie looked at Cassie's name on the headstone in front of her. *Cassandra Joy Jacobs.*

"Remember how your dad used to call Cassie 'Joy'?" Lyndie had forgotten until now.

"He said it suited her."

"It did." Lyndie had never met anyone so full of life. She wanted to be more like that. To let herself feel things again.

Tucker bent behind the headstone and pulled out a small plant, a bag of soil and a couple of garden trowels.

"What's all this?" Lyndie asked.

"I've been thinking a lot about what you told me."

The sting of his words tried to pull her attention, but she wouldn't let it. She'd been forgiven. She'd accepted grace. When it hurt, she'd remind herself of those things.

"And I thought maybe you and I needed our own memorial." His eyes met hers, and she saw a familiar vulnerability there. "I don't think we need to make a public display or anything," he said. "But I thought maybe we could plant this rosebush here, next to Cassie's grave, in memory of the life we created."

*The life I took.*

She wouldn't go there. Not now. *I'm forgiven.*

"My mom talks a lot about closure," Tucker said. "I guess I thought maybe it was a good idea?"

Last week, Lyndie would've wanted to take that rosebush and bury the whole thing underground. But it seemed appropriate now to create a memorial, not only for the life that had once lived inside of her, but in honor of the life now in front of her.

"I think so too." Lyndie reached over and picked up one of the trowels. Tucker handed her a pair of gloves, then knelt and started digging.

Together, they cleared away the dirt, digging a hole big enough for the rosebush, and together, they pulled the plant from its plastic container and set it in the earth.

Tucker patted the root ball gently into place as Lyndie filled the small opening with soil. They packed the dirt around the freshly planted bush, and then Tucker covered Lyndie's hand with his own.

They sat in silence for several moments, looking at the rosebush neatly tucked beside Cassie's grave in a cemetery too small to have rules about such things. And Lyndie stilled as an undeniable peace filled her up from the inside.

This was how it felt to be forgiven, to be found.

"Tucker," she said.

He looked at her, his eyes wet with emotion.

"Thank you."

And as he wrapped an arm around her and pulled her body to his, Lyndie felt the bricks of the wall she'd spent so many years building crumble to the ground.

# ACKNOWLEDGMENTS

Every book is a journey, and I wouldn't have wanted to go on this one without the following people, who encouraged me along the way.

My kids, Sophia, Ethan and Sam. Thank you for being wholly unimpressed that I have books in the bookstore and for reminding me what's really important.

My Studio kids. Thank you for giving me purpose outside the four walls of my writing cave and for making my life so very unpredictable.

My parents. Thank you for giving me a good start, for believing in me and for thinking everyone should read my books. I'm so thankful to have you in my corner.

Natasha Kern. Thank you for your wisdom and for your invaluable advice.

Katie Ganshert and Becky Wade. I mean . . . seriously? What would I do without you? Thank you for brainstorming with me, for talking me off the ledge, for helping unravel the knots in my stories and for being my friends. I am so grateful for both of you.

Sheryl Zajechowski and Colleen Wagner. Thank you for making my story stronger and for helping me bring these characters to life on the page. I am forever grateful.

And lastly, Adam. The husband who has to put up with my random questions, my self-doubt, my talking to myself—you are my very best friend, and I am so thankful I have you cheering me on.

# ABOUT THE AUTHOR

 Courtney Walsh is a *New York Times* and *USA Today* bestselling novelist as well as an artist, theater director and playwright. She is the author of the Sweethaven series—including *A Sweethaven Summer*, which was a Carol Award finalist in the debut author category—as well as the small-town romances *Paper Hearts, Change of Heart, Just Look Up, Hometown Girl* and the forthcoming *Just Let Go. Things Left Unsaid* is her ninth novel. She lives in Illinois, where she and her husband own a performing-arts studio and youth theater. They have three children. Visit Courtney online at www.courtneywalshwrites.com.